TONGUES ON FIRE

CARIBBEAN LESBIAN LIVES AND STORIES

EDITED BY

ROSAMUND ELWIN

Canadian Cataloguing in Publication Data

Main entry under title:
Tongues on fire : Caribbean lesbian lives and stories

ISBN 0-88961-226-9

1. Short stories, Caribbean (English) — Women authors.
2. Lesbianism — Fiction. 3. Lesbian — Caribbean Area —
Biography. I. Elwin, Rosamund, 1955-

PR9205.8.T65 1997   823'.0108353   C97-931553-0

Copyright © 1997 Rosamund Elwin

Credits:
"Out on Main Street" by Shani Mootoo is reprinted from the collection *Out on Main Street* (Press Gang Publishers) with permission of the author. "Baby" by Makeda Silvera is reprinted from the collection *Her Head A Village* (Press Gang Publishers) with permission of the author. "Screen Memory" from *Bodies of Water* by Michelle Cliff. Copyright 1990 by Michelle Cliff. Used by permission of Dutton Signet, a division of Penguin Books USA Inc. "Man-Royals and Sodomites: Some Thoughts on the Invisibility of Afro-Caribbean Lesbians" has previously been published in *Piece of My Heart* (Sister Vision Press). "A Rejuvenation of Sorts" by Vashti Persad was previously published as "Untitled Journal Entry" in *Piece of My Heart* (Sister Vision Press).

Editing: Rosamund Elwin, Ann Decter
Copy Editor: Sapna Patel
Cover Illustration: BANSHII
Cover Design: Denise Maxwell

All rights reserved. No part of this book may be used or reproduced in any manner whatsoever without written permission except in the case of brief quotations embodied in critical articles and reviews. For information address Women's Press.

This book was produced by the collective effort of Women's Press.
Women's Press gratefully acknowledges the support of the Ontario Arts Council and the Canada Council for the Arts for our publishing program.

The Canada Council | Le Conseil des Arts
    for the arts | du Canada
      since 1957 | depuis 1957

Published by Women's Press, Suite 302, 517 College Street, Toronto, Ontario, Canada M6G 4A2.
Printed and bound in Canada.
1 2 3 4 5 2000 2001 1999 1998 1997

CONTENTS

Introduction: Tongues on Fire, Speakin' Zami Desire — 7

LIVES

Darling, Are You Gay?	*Avanel*	13
When I Have A Girl	*Rhonda Sue*	19
Two Happy People in the World	*Carol Thames*	27
Man-Royals & Sodomites	*Makeda Silvera*	41
Catchin' My Tail	*Tinkerbell*	49
Free to Touch	*Daphne*	57
They Called Lesbians Anti-Woman	*Mae*	67
I Was Born the Day I Came Out	*Pamela Richards*	73
Growing Up a Lesbian in St. Lucia	*Pulcheria Theresa Willie*	81
The Real Erotica	*Gerri*	89
My Entire Being	*Camile*	99
Looking for Equality	*Alex*	105
My Own Blackness	*Aakilah Ashanti Ade*	111
All My Friends Were Gay	*Clarise*	121
A Legitimate Choice	*Debbie Douglas*	125
The Mountain All Around & Your Carib in Your Hand	*Verlia Stephens*	135

Stories

Horace's Marriage Proposal	*Lesley Chin Douglass*	145
Momentary Lapses	*Jannett Bailey*	157
Out on Main Street	*Shani Mootoo*	169
Coquibacoa	*Maria de los Rios*	179
As American As...	*Tonia Grant*	183
Hablas Espanol?	*Mary Vazquez*	191
Best Friends	*Ayiah Jahan*	197
On The Road With Marcel Proust	*Desoto Wong*	213
Sister	*Desoto Wong*	217
A Rejuvenation of Sorts	*Vashti Persad*	225
Baby	*Makeda Silvera*	231
Screen Memory	*Michelle Cliff*	239
Contributors		253

Acknowledgements

Bringing this anthology from an idea to a complete book took the help and support of many people. The order in which I extend thanks does not in any way suggest a rank of importance to the development of this book.

I want to say thank you to Ann Decter for the hard work she put into editing and transcribing and overseeing the completion of *Tongues on Fire*. Thank you to Women's Press for encouraging my dreams and making them realities. Anthony Chong spoke to several women in Trinidad and convinced them to tell their stories for inclusion here.

Tongues on Fire is an important book, a hot book, because all the women whose stories are published here spoke their truth, confident that their stories were worth repeating. Thank you to all of them, and to the many other women whose stories were not published here. And to BANSHII, who did the beautiful cover art, illustrating her vision of the hidden lives of Caribbean lesbians. To all the people mentioned here and those not here who gave me encouragement and praise — my deepest gratitude.

TONGUES ON FIRE
SPEAKIN' ZAMI DESIRE

I read somewhere that Christopher Isherwood once said our sexual orientation lies in our romantic feelings and in our ability to fall in love with someone of our gender, rather than to simply enjoy sex. We are women living in the Caribbean and women of Caribbean heritage living outside the Caribbean and we love each other romantically, just like women anywhere else in the world. To paraphrase Carol Thames, a lot of Black women are dykes, a lot of Black women identify as dykes. Some Black women came out of heterosexual relationships and realized men are not what they need. Some Black women practise bisexuality before they realize they are lesbians. Women who make up the dominant lesbian movement cannot take away our lesbian voices, cannot deny us as "true dykes." Despite the lack of lesbian organizing in the Caribbean, there have always been lesbian lives, hidden but present.

While grappling with the issue of lesbianism in the Caribbean, I thought of putting together an anthology of lesbian stories from the point of view of women living in, or culturally connected to, the Caribbean. I wanted to create a space where Caribbean lesbian voices could be heard loud and clear, apart from the realms of Black women's voices and women of colour voices. Such an anthology would focus on Caribbean lesbian lives. And I saw a need to document the hidden lives of Caribbean lesbians.

Among the dominant lesbian group in North America, there is an assumption that because women from the Caribbean have intimate relationships with men, they are not real lesbians. This anthology clearly displaces that prejudice. The lives, and therefore the stories, of Caribbean lesbians are unique in themselves.

Though it can be argued that lesbian experiences have similarities across the globe, the circumstances of our lives, the ways of telling, the language used to tell, the words chosen and the rhythm of those words make our individual stories different and interesting. For me, there could not be a collection of Caribbean lesbian stories without the stories of women who are not writers. In transcribing and editing the interviews into stories, I tried to capture those things that Caribbean lesbians said which show the uniqueness of their lesbian lives.

This anthology would be diminished and its authenticity watered down without the stories of women who are mothers, poor, or illiterate. The women who are represented in this book come from the middle class and the poor of the Caribbean. They are rural lesbians as well as lesbians who dwell in cities. Some women tell us what it is like to grow up poor and hard-working in the Caribbean. Others tell what it is like to be from an aspiring middle-class family whose members are disappointed in their life choices. Many of the women in this anthology have lived their lives in both the Caribbean and North America. Their sexual awakening is as different and unique as their backgrounds.

Through these women we know that for Caribbean women, the family — especially children — is everything. The yard, a communal space, is where Caribbean women get their first sense of self and community. We learn about attitudes to and intolerance of homosexuality, and the role television has played in forming attitudes. Talking about her life before coming to Canada, Angela Richards shares what it was like to grow up in a family with an absent mother. And she brings us her sense of belonging to a strong community and culture, her strong feelings of self-esteem and the pain of having that change with emigration.

I recognised and accepted the responsibility of getting those stories and presenting them in the ways they were told. Editing the interviews for this anthology was challenging. Contrary to popular belief, the peoples of the Caribbean do not all speak alike or sound alike. It was very difficult to retain the various dialectic references which give each story its punch, and at the same time clearly communicate what is being said to a broader audience.

In the course of the interviews, I attempted to get information about local women whom the interviewees may have known, heard about or observed in their childhood. Makeda Silvera's *Man-Royals and Sodomites* is an excellent story, revealing to us the lives of such women. Through her mother, grandmother and the women who hang out around her house when she is a child, she learns the gossip of lesbianism in her community. What is overheard through childish ears, allows her — much later in her life — to find her Caribbean lesbian history.

In this anthology, women recall what may have been but was never acknowledged. I am seeking to present a sense of lesbian history and continuity in the Caribbean. I want to tell you, the reader, about older women, who by many people's definition would not be considered lesbians because their intimate sexual liaisons with women were hidden and not spoken about. And there was nothing else to tell us they were lesbians. In some parts of the Caribbean, it is still not regarded as proper for women to wear pants. The strict North American definition of lesbianism has codes of behaviour, rules around dress and personal appearance. Women who strictly wear pants, wear their hair short and natural, and no make-up, fit into the stereotype of the North American lesbian. In the absence of that, how do we know who is? Yet in the Caribbean, women find each other. Sometimes it is hard to hide behind your clothes. Although it is a challenge finding a Caribbean lesbian, we are there, we are here. And, like lesbians everywhere, we do find each other. This is one thing lesbians all over the globe have in common. But, it is the difference between us that creates the uniqueness of this anthology.

As human beings, we are capable of having sex with males or females. Denying our sexual desire for one sex or the other is made on a personal, as well as a political, basis. Heterosexuality is as political a definition of human sexuality as lesbianism. Heterosexuals enjoy the ideological privileges and protection of the state for their choice to sleep with the opposite sex. Heterosexuality has nothing to do with people's sexual desires; it exists to curtail and control. There are a lot of ramifications — most negative — for going outside the norm of heterosexuality. Most women in the Caribbean are vulnerable to the negative ramifications of breaking society's norms, as are women in the north. However, lesbians in North America and Western Europe have a lot more opportunity, and in some instances even legal protection, if they choose to live exclusively as lesbians. None of this exists in the Caribbean. Listen to the Trinidadian women in this book speak about how homosexuality is a crime in Trinidad. Despite the difficulties of living as a lesbian, whether in the Caribbean or in the north, we continue to make our presence known.

We are fortunate to have lesbian writers from the Caribbean who bring our stories to an international audience. The characters in all the stories in this anthology explore the varied experiences of Caribbean lesbians. In *Out On Main Street*, Shani Mootoo gives us a peek into the lives of an Indo-Caribbean lesbian in a sweet shop. Lesbianism is sweet, we don't always know its name. Sexuality is a complex rite to be negotiated. But for many of us, there are more important and pressing issues — racism, alienation from self, culture and identity — to confront on a daily basis. Shani Mootoo raises the question of what is more important: fighting for lesbian rights, cultural identity, or the right to take up space?

Twenty years ago, when I left the Caribbean for Canada, I did not know the word lesbian. I knew the word zami. Women made zami or your zami was your closest friend. Whether the word was used as a noun or a verb, it was understood that a zami was intimate with other women or with another woman. When I returned to the Caribbean many years later, male politicians were using the word lesbian as an insult against their female opponents. In the Caribbean, the word lesbian is gaining political strength. It has many connotations. As one woman said in her interview, the word is loaded; it tells women what they are. As more women get to know the word and its political meaning, life will change for us wherever we are.

The life stories in this anthology were constructed out of interviews conducted over three years ago. They reflect realities and perceptions of the individuals at that time. I hope they will be read with this in mind. It is my hope that at the end of reading this anthology, lesbians in the north will have a better understanding of lesbianism in the Caribbean and a greater respect for the unique experiences of lesbians everywhere. And lesbians of the Caribbean will recognize their own lives somewhere in the breadth of these pages. Read and enjoy this book in sisterhood.

Rosamund Elwin
Toronto, June 1997

LIVES

DARLING, ARE YOU GAY?
Avanel

I was born in 1972, in Port of Spain, Trinidad. I have one brother and two sisters. I am the eldest. My brother is thirteen years younger than I am. I wasn't close with my sisters, only my brother, because my mom and dad separated when I was young. My sisters are really my step-sisters, and my brother is my step-brother.

FROM THE TIME I COULD THINK

I had basically everything I wanted from an early age. I was spoilt rotten. It was only me and my mom for a long time. There were guys in and out of her life, but she never really made them the centre of her life. I knew from a young age that I could get away with murder with my mom, 'cause I was everything to her. She used to tell me that every night.

I knew I was different from the time I could think. I remember my fifth birthday. There were girls and boys at my party, but I didn't like the boys. They were showing off what they could physically do, and I was only interested in playing with the girls. In hide-and-seek, I always went for the girls. Girls were more interesting. They looked better. They sounded better. I was always more interested in the girls than the boys, but I didn't really think anything was different until I started going to primary school. There, physical aspects of girls used to intrigue me more than anything else.

I was tomboyish, very much a loner, except when girls asked me to do something for them. Then, I wanted to be the centre of attention. If I could please that one individual, it make me very happy, but other than that I just stayed on my own.

I didn't really pay attention to much of anything, except going to school, pleasing, and trying to figure out where the hell I fit in. From a young age, I thought I was adopted. I looked different from my mother. So, anything she liked to do I like to, though I would rather climb trees with my cousins, or sit down playing doctor with the girls. But I was just so different. My aunts, my uncles, everybody showered me with love.

Growing up, I didn't have an idea what a lesbian was. I just admired my mother's friends because they were very funky. They were two Africans — one was a Nigerian, and the other was from Nairobi — both teachers. They had two other friends who, I later found out, were lesbians. All of them were. As far as I was concerned they were my aunts, they were Mother's best friends, and that was it. They didn't seem different to me, except that they were women.

We Come Down From Heaven

From the age of ten, I was aware of my attraction for women. I think the awareness happened because of an incident concerning a guy my mother was really interested in. He used to take me on long trips to his mom's, and one of his friends seemed really, really interested in me. At ten. I didn't know what the hell he was thinkin'. I just knew from that age that anything to do with men was gross to me. It was abnormal to me, for a man and woman to be together. It just seemed really strange.

My best friend and I were best friends from the time we could crawl. She was the one who was playing hide-and-seek with me when I was five. Later, I was going through some trouble at school. Girls were teasing me for being different. And it just came to a head. I just knew she was the one person I could turn to. And I would find security and love, and everything would be right. It felt so natural.

It went on for almost a year. I was really scared the first time I did anything with her. I knew that if my mother ever found out, I'd be dead, or thrown out of house. That was always my phobia. I didn't really stop to think that she had always loved me and will always love me. My real great fear was of her finding out that I am a lesbian — to be honest I didn't even know the word — I just knew that I liked my friend Gaby, and that was it.

The first time, I was scared shitless after. We come down from heaven, of course, and boom, reality hits. It's like, what did I just do? I couldn't believe I did all those things. One, with a person, and two, with a *woman*. I didn't speak to her for weeks, and when I did, there wasn't anything to say. It was just bed.

At thirteen I knew what I was doing sexually. But emotionally, I was in love with my best friend. She's three years older than me, sixteen at the time. She was a god, as far as I was concerned, a goddess, damn right. Couldn't do anything wrong in my eyes. When everything blew up in our faces, and she rejected me as severely as she did, I almost went crazy. I was so devoted to her, I just couldn't understand the rejection.

Friendships

It took me a long time to come to terms with the fact that I was a lesbian, and when I did ... I always do things rashly. I take a long time to make up my mind but when I do, I do it with tremendous force — sometimes without thinking. I create very heavy consequences. The few women that I did let into my heart, or near it, were scarce. Friends, platonic friends, whatever, were far and few between. I didn't trust women. It was always very confusing for me because I was in love with most anybody walking in a skirt. My great fear was them finding out about me, then I rushed the gun by telling them, and they did one of two things. They either stayed friends with me and said it didn't bother them. Or they left, which almost never happened. Bad for me, because I always fell in love with them. But I didn't really trust women for a long time.

Out with the sun

At first I was a coward. My mother was going away for several years. On her departure, we were having a very nice conversation, and suddenly she just asked me, "Darling, are you gay?" — at the breakfast table. I undoubtedly dropped a few dishes, but I couldn't answer. I just simply couldn't answer. I was scared shitless. But my mother and I have such a close relationship that I did reply. She's my pal, and my mother. That's why she was the biggest and only hurdle, really. Anyone else, I just didn't care about their reactions. As long as my mother was okay with it, I couldn't care shit.

I'm not ashamed of it. I used to be. Before, it was easier being called a dyke or all the other names that we are called than it was being called a lesbian because that's a big word, a big statement. But a great group I was in brought me to the realization that a lesbian is exactly what I am and will always be. Why be ashamed of what I am?

Now, I don't think anybody could come out more than me, except the sun. I am totally comfortable being lesbian. I have regrets about how I handle some relationships, about a lot of things to do with relationships. I suppose it was a learning process. I went wild for a couple of years there. I think I was going for the world record in trying to sleep with women.

Wanting change in the community

I want our legal rights to change. Once we start there, there is nothing in the world that can stop us. Other than that, I'd like the hypocrisy to change, the back-stabbing that goes on. Nobody's together, but you know the force that we could be. It's every man for himself out there. There is no community spirit at all.

There is definitely not a sense of community. With one stipulation — within each clique. Do we band together and do all the soap and jelly stuff? No way. It's just basically friends stick with friends. The only time I see women who are not friends is in a party or at a function or something, like a play. Women don't support each other. I tell you how bad it is. You tell a woman that you need support in bed and you usually get support. You tell a woman that you need support in personal life, money, job, just being a friend, and you'll hardly find one around you.

Life in the life

They have some really butch women in Trinidad. They wear pants better than men sometimes. A lot of women in the country think they are more butch than the butchest of the men. But most of the women are not really butch. The ones who party every weekend are really working women, normal working women. You couldn't tell one from the next, actually. And I say normal in a very proverbial sense, because as far as I'm concerned all lesbians are normal. But, to the outside world, they appear normal.

If I was to judge everyone by their dress code, I think everybody's butch. Very casual dress. I've seen the most casual person dressing extremely butch. They get you confused sometimes. When you think you have quite a man on your hands, you have quite a woman. Take me for instance. I like low hair cuts, and I like not much jewellery. Jeans, stuff like that, goes with how I was. I was a tomboy, strictly a tomboy. As far as the relationship goes — my favourite topic, the bed — I like giving up the control. I like having women control me in bed.

Sex, that's all we discuss. You have a basic conversation with acquaintances. They come up to you and ask how you are and stuff, and then they go, "So, who ya sleepin' wit'?" That's it. And as Trinidadians, we can talk some stinkness. Once you comfortable with the person, sex is the main topic. How, where, when, who. And the harsher the better, the more explicit the better. But it's according to who you limin' with, because the gay society in Trinidad has a lot of class distinctions. No matter how much you try to disprove it, we do. You have uppity-up, and then you have the middle class, and then you have, as we like to say, the canal holes, I think that's how they put it. And those are the really rough, tough, scruff of the bunch. I've known people from all three. They have different ways of speaking about it, but they all speak about it.

AIDS

Everybody's concerned about AIDS, but they don't change their lifestyles. Everything is being changed on the surface but not really in people's hearts. They go from partner to partner to partner. Every time something doesn't work, they go to the next one. And they say, "Oh, I'm gonna change, I'm gonna change." But they really never do.

There's more concern among the heterosexual women than among the gays. Gay women are more concerned with their male friends having it. Or who is going to have it next. I don't think they feeling that they might be at some sort of risk. Not many lesbians are very educated about the fact that we can get it. We have to be careful. I don't think there's ever been an incident of AIDS among us, but it's gonna come.

The information is there, it's just we don't take an interest in finding out about it. It's not really publicized as much, they really focused on the gay men. We gettin' more information from away than locally. If you want to be educated, you go educate yourself, nobody's going to do it for you. I discuss it with my friends, but it's not an open discussion.

A NEW WOMAN IN MY LIFE

Suddenly a host of things happened in my life. Priorities are different. The only thing that's important in my life right now is my daughter. That's it. She'll be three weeks old in two days. I'm very into motherhood, I have a new woman in my life. All the things that I thought about how lesbians can't have children, can't enjoy the pleasures of becoming mothers, have been totally disproven I'm glad to say, by me. It's a wonderful experience being a woman, isn't it? I keep saying to myself that one joy of being a woman is bringing a child into the world. Second is loving a woman. It's a wonderful experience having a child. Wonderful. And I don't regret it at all.

A year ago I don't think anybody would have been able to tell me that I would have a child now. That's one of the greatest things that ever happen to me. I was really amazed at the reaction of lesbians to the fact that I was pregnant, a pregnant lesbian. I think they felt betrayed, 'cause I slept with a man. As if there's any other way to get pregnant. Other than the new technology, but I don't think that's down here as yet. When that gets down here you will see a really, really big band of them lined up for it. I think sleeping with a man to have a baby is not on the agenda of most lesbians. But they can all kiss my ass because I have one wonderful nine-pound baby girl.

When I Have a Girl
Rhonda Sue

I grew up in a family of three children, with a fourth born later. There is an eleven year difference between the third and fourth children. It wasn't easy growin' up. I was raised by my mother. My father leave for America many years ago. I know him only by picture. We lived in hope that we would go to America someday, but that hope vanished some years ago. My father, he keep changin' address all the time. We were raised by going to work to help our mother in holiday seasons. I went to work at five, six, seven years old. Carried bread, picked limes, weeded, and carried bananas. We lived at Castle Comfort and went to a large estate to work. We also lived in Giraudel and Roseau.

Sometimes I went to school in the afternoon, sometimes I didn't go at all. I left school in standard five. When I left school, I was twelve going on thirteen. After I left school I worked odd jobs here and there.

A Particular Friend

I had a lot of friends, but I always seemed to like one particular friend. I was always in love with a particular friend. I wouldn't tell her I loved her, I was too shy to say it. From eleven years old, that started happenin' to me. Always girls older than me, not girls in my particular group. It was secret. I used to write love letters to them and keep them. I couldn't tell them, couldn't face them. Some of them embarrassed me by letting me know how they felt. I felt I didn't want to know.

Girls liking girls was very common, but there was pressure from friends who suspected something like that. (Men, especially, would say I'm lesbian.) So, I'd keep away from some girls. There was a particular girl I never kept away from because I was in love with her. Many years after, I call one of the women I was in love with and tell her how I felt then. She just tell me she was never like that. I said, "Don't tell me you wasn't like that."

It goes way back

I come from a family of women like me. My mother was a lesbian, two of her sisters, aunts, cousins. My mother told me in conversation one day that she almost raped a girl. I couldn't imagine anything like that, never. I have a friend who comes from a family of lesbians too: her mother, her grandmother, her aunts.

Lesbianism runs in a family. I met a lot of friends like me, a lot of lesbians, and their parents, or some aunt of theirs. It runs in the family. Way back you must have a grandmother or grand aunt or some sister like that.

Fall in love with me

Many girls approach me the wrong way. I don't like people telling me, "Well, let's go and do this and do that." I want you to fall in love with me. I fall in love with you, something happens. But if you tell me, "Let's go and do this," you too forward. It's rude and out of place. Because of that attitude I didn't get along with a lot of other girls.

I started going out at fourteen. We lived at Giraudel. I was alone and my mother was in town. There was a girl who liked me a lot, but I liked her mother, who had six children and was forty-two. The girl was getting close to me. I didn't know what I was feeling. I didn't know what it was. One day, my mother wasn't there. She went to meet my sister in town. It was nighttime. I didn't want to be alone. When my mother didn't come back, I asked the girl to sleep at my house. I had to approach her grandmother for permission for her to sleep over at my house.

That was my first physical experience. The girl seduced me. I didn't want it to happen. I thought she was too young. I was fourteen. She was twelve. I was bigger, her mother's height. I thought she was too small, too short. Anyway, that night she kept calling me. She trouble me, trouble me, the whole night. I never slept.

I kept sayin', "But what?"

Around first light — I didn't have a watch — six-thirty or so in the morning, I finally agreed. And while I was with her, she asked me to stop. Of course, she was a virgin. I didn't want to stop. While I was there with her, her grandmother came callin' her, callin' her. I was so frightened. We never discussed that night. I stopped talking to her, to her grandmother, to everybody. I was embarrassed. I didn't ever want that to happen again. I don't want a virgin, I hate virgins. I like women older than me, with experience.

In those days, I wasn't wearing pants, I wore dresses. Girls still approached me. I don't know why. And I did not know if they were lesbians, maybe they were. I remember a girl who just held my hand and said, "Let's go and do this and let's go and do that."

I'd say, "You're too rough."

She call me hypocrite.

I said, "I'm not a hypocrite, you're too rough." That was just an excuse really, but she was too rough.

I remember a friend asked me, you know, show her. You know. And I said, "Show you what? Show you what?" I said, "I don't know nothing, show you what?" Then she told me, show her my vagina. And I said, "I cannot do that, show me yours first." And she did show me. When she show me, I didn't show her nothing. One day I climb for mango, and I didn't remember about that at all, and I caught the girl watchin' under my dress.

I was in love with another girl who I used to write little letters. She'd embrace me and sometimes she'd kinda turn me on. I'd tell her that. Sometimes her boyfriend would meet me and ask me to kiss her for him. I'd tell her he said that but I wouldn't do it. She'd say she didn't like my ways, because I didn't do it. Sometimes I'd go to her room and she'd ask me to comb her hair. I'd tell her, "You know, something is happening to me I don't like."

She'd say, "Oh, comb my hair," and say she liked the way I was handling her, those kinda things. She was twenty-one. I was fourteen, and all these things were happening to me.

I didn't want to be out. People suspected. Whenever I had a friend, people said we were zami. I knew what it meant. I always knew what it meant. I did not like the word. My mother didn't want me to have boyfriends nor girlfriends, so I felt safe with a girl.

Later, I read the word lesbian, that's how I knew about it. And I didn't care. But that zami business, I didn't like that. At that time, not many people knew what lesbian was. But the majority of people knew what zami was. You're makin' zami that means you're going with a woman instead of a man. It was not a pleasant thing to be called.

Not with him

My mother had a bad habit of sending me out nights to take messages. I don't know why. Whenever I went out, people were watchin' for me. Like I'm a fish and they have bait on a hook. I felt vulnerable. Somebody always wanted to come back home with me. I got in a lot of trouble, because I'd tell them I'd come back and I'd never come back. Then I got sexually involved with a guy called Randy. I was fourteen or fifteen. It happened once. I didn't want to do it again. I told him that I didn't like it. He asked me to masturbate myself and it was even worse. (That's when I started masturbating.) He asked me not for my own pleasure, but so I would be more open.

My mother used to beat me. At thirteen, I ran away and I had to sleep out in the kitchen when I came back. One night, I can't remember what I did, but I wouldn't go inside for fear that my mother would beat me. So, she locked me out. The houses were far apart. I started feeling afraid. I rapped on the door, I kept knocking, but she never opened the door. I had no choice but to stand on the side of the road. This man came from his garden, and he ask me what happened. I was cryin'. He could not believe my mother would lock me out. He rap on the door, but she didn't open. He said he cannot let me sleep outside alone. He was in his seventies. My mother didn't know where I slept. She went up and down, trying to find out where I slept. Then she found out I slept by that man, she started pressuring me. It's wasn't my fault — it was hers.

Because of her, I got involved with that guy. Not the same night. He told me anything I need, ask him. And that's what I used to do. At first, sex wasn't the thing. I never want to have sex with him. The first time he had sex with me, I kinda closed my legs, because I didn't want him inside me. That's how it was for most of the time we live together, many years. He would allow my girlfriends. I was with women and I was involved with him. Once or twice it happened that his penis entered me. I didn't like that. He promised me a lot of things, but I always told him I didn't love him.

My girlfriend came to know about him. I didn't tell her anything. I couldn't face her and tell her that. Though the man and I weren't involved, I was sleepin' at the man home. She had the idea I was sleepin' with him. When the scandal come out — that I was sleeping at the man's home — she took it hard. I stopped talking to her, broke up with her.

He didn't care that I preferred women. He gave me a house, land, a car, but I still had a woman. He didn't care. I washed for him, ironed his clothes. He started wearing different clothes. People would say he looked young because he have a young girl. I guess I made him like me a lot, but my family, they didn't want that.

While I was with him, I had three different girls. And he allowed me to bring them to his home, when he was not there. I was with the man thirteen years. When I think of that, I hate it. I always wanted children, but not with him.

I want the earth to open

I was seventeen or eighteen. There was a woman, she was thirty, thirty-one. She had a boyfriend and wanted to leave him. She knew he didn't love her. And well, she's more lesbian than anything else. Nights, I'd come to her home and she tell me show her, show her. But that's the wrong way to push a person, you know. She gave me sweets from her mouth. Then she was telling me that her boyfriend made her suck him once. I never heard of that before. All of a sudden I wanted to go home. I didn't want to see her again. I wanted her to stop talking, but I couldn't say, "I am going." I wanted the earth to open for me to go inside, I'm so embarrassed. I never heard of that before. I never heard about 69, and puttin' penis in your mouth. I want to ask her to go but I cannot say. So she ask me what I feelin'? Am I feel embarrassed? She told me, "You want to take sweets from my mouth again?"

I told her, "No way." I left that day. I stayed away a few days, but I still had some feelings for her, so I came back.

She asked me to stay with her. I would wait until she fell asleep before I go to bed. In the morning I got up early, early and I took off. Anyway, when you're young, you're stupid.

Everybody know

I really wanted a relationship with one particular woman, not with so many people. I never wanted it like that. But these things happen. Women like me, I don't know why, I was never part of the group that have parties and go as far as swingin'. They have orgies, a group of them. I am too shy, too myself. When I have a girl, it's like I'm married. So I don't take part in those kinda things. It would hurt me to see somebody else with my girl. Not my kinda thing. It kinda die out a little now.

There was a time when I believed I would never have children. I'm a lesbian. I always wanted my children. In my head I'd think, I'll meet somebody. I would not marry because it's not fair. It would ruin his chance of meetin' somebody he loves, and mine too. I just wanted to have my children and raise them with a woman. That's what I wanted to do. I thought that was possible.

There are woman who live like that here. Everybody knows. There's a woman, she raised her grandchildren, but she was always like that. She raised her children with another woman. The other woman have several children, but she left some with her parents. She had one child with her. They raised two boys together, and a granddaughter. Everybody knows, they live openly. I know two other couples like that.

I wanted something like that. It wasn't possible because I was always in a situation where I couldn't find a job to be independent. So I always had to rely on a man. That's what really set me back. I relied on that man not because I loved him, but because I couldn't find a job at the time.

We do it underneath

There are a lot of lesbians in Dominica, but they're very, very shy. They don't want you to know. They do it underneath, instead of doing it plain. But they are lesbians. It's just that they think of what people would say before they think of themselves. I had a friend who became a Christian. I would tell her I am a lesbian, and she'd say she's a Christian, so she's not in the life.

Some women are too scared to go public. I know a girl right now, she's livin' with her man, but she's a lesbian. When she met me she tol' me if I didn't have this girlfriend, she would leave her boyfriend and live with me. But I didn't love her enough for that, and I didn't want to get involved with her. She's a lesbian. She doesn't love men. She jus' doesn't like the way people talk about lesbianism, that's all. But she's a lesbian.

That's what I'd like, to be free of what people have to say, to live my life the way I want to and not because people want me to be with a man. I'd rather be with a woman, spend years of my life with a woman.

I had relations with men when I didn't have a job. Now that I have a job, I don't get involved with men any more. Whenever I had to go to a man, I had to think of a woman I was in love with to excite me. That's what I have to do.

Being a lesbian is not against the law, but they would want you to have it more underneath. You cannot talk about it openly, like sayin', "Oh, I'm a lesbian." You cannot talk that way. One of the reasons I couldn't go to work at the Grotto — a place that helps homeless people — because they heard I'm a lesbian and they didn't want me up there. They didn't have a reason, so they used that as an issue. Really, people don't like that.

This woman called me a hypocrite. She's a church-going person. Every time she's naked she ask me to come to her room and do something. I don't know what she trying, but that's not a person I'd go for. A lot of women in society are like that, undercover.

People talk about women, but they don't talk so much now. They kind of gettin' use to that. The Catholics and them come out with somethin' on the radio allowing women to take communion even if they are gay. Some people think it's a problem to cope with that, but other people think, that's a person's life.

There are no physical threats to lesbians here. A few guys on the corner would say, "Oh, a lesbian." But they gettin' used to that. The majority of men today don't want to work, so they go out with guys. People kind of accept it. One of the reasons they don't press the issue so much is they know it's there in their own homes.

Sometimes I ask my son if anybody ever tease him telling him his mother's a lesbian, she hangs out with white women, or with women, whatever. Nobody ever tell my children anything. I always ask my kids how they feel about it. I always tell them how I feel about a man, and how I feel about a woman. And that I go for what I want.

Women havin' a baby together, I don't think we have that here. That is a thing I might not like myself, you know. Do things the way it supposed to be. I don't think it's right, though I thought of it myself once, women coming together to have a baby.

Just actin'

Women discuss sex. Women discuss women. And men talk about lesbian sex. I met a lot of men who like the idea of discussing that. A guy once told me if I'm a lesbian, he likes it even more. Maybe he figures I'm going to bring women to him. If I was a man, I wouldn't want my woman to be a lesbian, because I know she doesn't love me, she's just actin'.

Lesbians here go with men and women, so you cannot know. I don't like that although I used to do it. I think it's not honest, that two-way thing, not fair. Either you love a man or you love a woman. That's why I try hard, you know, to find myself a job and stop that, because I was doin' it too.

Lesbians go out to night clubs and straight clubs. They can meet lesbians. They know by the conversations. They tell you what they are behind the backs of the men. Women suspect about you. A butch woman doesn't usually approach women, other women approach us, tell you they like to see you. I remember a few girls tell me, if I be in dresses they would go with me. But I'm too obvious, I'm makin' the public know exactly what going on. Passin' by the convent, some of them would call me. I guess they do that to men too.

They have their way of meeting each other, femmes. A lesbian who is with a man, she will be able to make out another lesbian very fast in a night club. They might observe, say, the way a woman dance with a man. There are a lot of women like that.

Women approach other women. They bold. I remember, one day I saw this woman, a femme, and I liked her. I just smiled. That was all I did. Well, at that time I had small children. I couldn't take it serious. She was wearing khaki pants and high heels. I saw her, I smiled. I was going up to the hospital with my child who was sick, and she smiled in return. On my way back, I passed toward the older bridge, I met that same woman, and she called me. And I said to myself that's the same woman I smiled at.

On the whole now, here, we been takin' the man's role economically. Men kinda step aside, like they don't take responsibility so serious, kinda idle. Some men feel you can't go against a woman, wanting freedom for herself, and wanting better for herself. They look at it from that perspective.

The men sit back and don't care about the gay men. People know who the gay men are. They used to do wickedness to them. But you know, they right there in high society. Most of them leave their wives for other men. Homosexuality is there, among the people that pass the laws. It affect them most, because more of the people in high society are gay than the boys on the side of the street. The boys on the side of the street know.

They kinda give people their freedom to live their life. Those that hide it, get away with it. Those that publish it, they just tease them a little and get used to them.

Two Happy People in the World

Carol Thames

I was born in Jamaica and lived there until the age of ten. I arrived in Canada just before my eleventh birthday. My mother left Jamaica when I was six or seven years old. My father was supposed to be responsible for my care and upbringing. He stayed around for three to six months. Then I was left to be taken care of by a woman who lived in the yard, who was my childcare person twenty-four hours a day.

Growing up in Jamaica was fun. There was a lot of freedom to roam, to run, to explore. You were not pent up in apartment buildings, in houses, because of the weather, the structure, lack of community support. You knew everybody in your neighbourhood and they knew who you were. Life was not in your home, it was outside. To shell the peas, women would go outside and sit and talk with each other. To do the laundry was a communal effort, the taking care of the children or disciplining them was a communal effort. Whether or not you had blood ties, you never had a sense of loneliness. There was always an extended family. It was good and needed

    My mother came to Canada as a visitor. When she got to Toronto International Airport, the customs officer asked her if she was coming to work and did she have a visa. She lied and said yes, I am here to work. She lived and worked underground for about two years. A man she met took her and another woman to the immigration office and said to them both, "You can use my name and my address as a contact." He didn't want anything from them in return, and my mother said they never saw him again. This man did both women a favour, to help them become legal immigrants. My mother worked as a domestic servant. It was a lot easier then for Black women to get jobs as domestics because they needed Caribbean women in the labour force. She also went to school at the same time. This was the mid- to late sixties.

My father was a mason. He left Kingston one day to go to the country area to find work — and never came back. That was the last time I saw my father, I was seven years old. I don't know if he is alive or dead. I don't know where he is, and I wouldn't know where to start looking for him. He was the man my mother had a relationship with for a period of time. They made a choice not to get married and out of that relationship I was born. My mother tells the story that they met an American reverend who was doing missionary work in Jamaica. He encouraged them to get married, but because of the culture, marriage was not a priority in their lives. So they never married. Separation was a lot easier and it became easier for them to lose track of each other. He started another family with another woman when my mother came to Canada. I have a younger brother who is about five years younger than me. The last time I saw him he was a babe in arms. Who's to say how many children my father has fathered? I have siblings whom I don't know and will never know. I have another brother, through my mother who I know but we don't have a close relationship. We are eight years apart, and there is a lot of anxiety and anger about our relationship and our history together.

A WOMAN-BASED CULTURE

Growing up in Jamaica, I heard stories about lesbians. They didn't use the word lesbian, they used the word sodomite. That's the word I heard to describe lesbians and lesbianism. Stories about women who dressed like men and lived what society would consider heterosexual life. What lesbians in Canada would consider "practising patriarchal behaviour." That's the way their relationships could survive. One woman would take on a male identity by wearing male clothing. She would also band her breasts. In Canadian lesbian society she would be considered a butch, and the other woman would be considered a femme. That's the way women survived, especially when you lived in small communities or when you lived in Kingston. Jamaica can be a very homophobic society. And it's sad because a lot of women end up raising their children without male partner support. It is not a patriarchal society but a matriarchy. Women raise the children, make decisions in response to their family. You have a father, but he takes on the role of a sperm donor. He is not really there.

I heard the stories when the women were talking. I was really quiet as a child. Because the motto is, "Children should be seen but not heard." I always ended up under a chair or table somewhere, sitting and listening to the story. I thought I had never seen any of the women they were talking about — lesbian/sodomite. But, looking back at my childhood, who's to say those women weren't talking about themselves. Many of the women did not have male partners. They lived in houses as two friends living together. Sharing expenses, raising their kids together. In Kingston, many of the houses are set up as tenements. A property housed seven families, all headed by women. Women in the yard, working, cultivating and taking care of their children. Looking at my culture, I wonder. I know many people would not validate this, but what I'm saying is my culture, in an unspoken way, is a lesbian-based culture or a woman-based culture. The priority is not so much around male partners but around your children, having children, raising them, carrying on the generation.

The intimacy is shared. More of an emotional compassion, touching, caressing, hugging, supporting each other — rather than based on sex. This creates a stronger foundation for their relationships. When you lose a friend, you don't just lose a sexual partner, you lose your lifeline. I watch women develop friendships. But friendships were also broken over simple things, because the investments were a lot higher and a lot greater.

In Kingston, just before I came to Canada, there was a woman who owned a bar at the end of the yard that I lived in. There was a tailor shop on one side, the bar on the other side. I was curious about the bar. I would sneak in through the back door, just to see what the big deal was. The place smelled of smoke and beer. Inside didn't smell so great. But the music drew me. I wanted to hear the music, I wanted to see the people.

One day, the woman who owned the bar chased me out and was arguing with me. I was arguing back with her, and she said to me, "Little girl, there are two things that hurt on a woman, her eyes and her pussy." And she said, "Don't fuck." I got the message. But there was a sense of respect, that I had the gall to argue back. That was a lesson learned. Her name was Shirley. She had a husband, he was there, but he was not really there. She wore pants and she ran the bar. There was a sense of strength about her. In North America, people would say she was a closet dyke, but in Jamaica that's a tough woman. A strong woman. In North American culture, women's strength is linked to lesbianism, to sexuality. In Jamaica, her strength is linked to her male energy. That was not looked on as a negative thing.

Like a Prison

Just before I left Jamaica, I was starting to explore women sexuality. One Sunday afternoon my cousin Dawn and I, we experiment with each other. We were tasting each other's vaginas. She said, "It's kind of salty."

I did not focus on what it tasted like. It was something I wanted to check out, to do and to explore. I look back on all the little details of my childhood. As kids you didn't think that this is something society views as bad. Needless to say, less than six months later, I was on my way to Canada.

I came to Canada and it felt like a prison. Late November and it was cold. I walked into an apartment building, which I had never lived in before. A new country, and the majority of the people was of a different colour and race. I did not see a lot of people who looked like me. I lived on the twentieth floor, up in the sky. I went on the balcony once. It felt like the building was moving. I didn't like that feeling. I never made it out onto the balcony again because I thought I was going to fall.

By January I started school. A whole different ball game. I spoke differently from the other children. I looked different from ninety percent of the children. I was made fun of, called names like chocolate face and jungle bunny or told, "Nigger, go back to where you came from." All those things. I don't know where the anger towards me was coming from. I would go home and talk to my mom. She would try to explain in her own way what was going on. Her response to the issue was to say, "You call them names back. You call them vanilla face."

That was the only way she knew how to deal with it. My mother had no theoretical analysis. Her response was if they call you names, you call them names back. If they hit you, hit them back. I got validation to fight back, not just to take it lying down. I fought in school, around the issue of racism. Other girls — white girls — felt like they had the right to bully me, to oppress me, to take my stuff away from me. I fought back. I got in a lot of trouble from the school system for fighting back. I really realised how racist this society is the day that I stood up to the school bully. All the other kids, white and Black, were afraid of the bully, this skinny white girl. Everybody was afraid of her but I had the audacity to fight with her over my belongings and not just hand them over to her. The teacher could not take it. It was brought to our teacher's attention and he wanted me to apologise to this girl who was trying to take my skipping rope away from me. I said, "Not sorry," so the "not" was under my breath but the "sorry" came out. In my heart of hearts I was not sorry for kicking her butt. I had to stay and clean up as punishment, sweep and mop the classroom floor, erase the board and do anything else that was needed. I arrived home late, and I didn't pick up my little brother from the babysitter. My mom was irate. I had to sit and explain to her what had happened. This is one of the good things I remember in my mother's relationship with me. She went to the school and stood up for me. She said, "No way, no way. If there is a problem with my child then you come and talk to me. My kid is not supposed to be here after school sweeping and mopping floors." Overall I was a good kid in school.

After grade six I went to junior high. That was a wonderful year. I met so many children of colour, and so many immigrant children. A pack of us travelled together. We were Blacks from the Caribbean, Asians, and Black Canadians. We share a common oppression, based on the colour of our skin, and the fact we are immigrants. There were girls I hung out with who were from Yugoslavia, they were Gypsies. There was all that cultural and racial difference among us. We walked to school and home together. We would gang up on boys and beat them up together. We smoked together. And we shared a common oppression.

My best friend was Charlene, a thirteenth generation Black Canadian. Her mom and dad were from Nova Scotia. I met Charlene when I first came to Canada. My family lived on Emmette Avenue in the apartment buildings. Charlene and I moved from grade six to grade seven together. In junior high I had my first crush on this girl. I thought she was so beautiful, her beautiful Black skin. I loved her sense of fashion. She wore this very long grey coat in the wintertime, and when she moved in her coat I thought that she was so cool. I mean she looked hot. I loved her so much. Her name was Kim, and one of the favourite games we played was hide-and-go-seek. We would play in the underground garage in the dark. And somehow, I always seemed to be hiding where Kim was. It was my infatuation, my need to be in her company. If I was growing up now, I would be more conscious and aware of what I was really feeling. But in 1973, I was not aware of what was happening.

All of a sudden when I went to high school, and I was the odd ball, there was lots of pressure to fit in. I wore polyester pants. That was a no no. My mother would not buy me blue jeans. She bought me corduroys and platform shoes, but no jeans. I remember my first platforms, blue and white. A major part of it was that my mother was struggling; she could not afford to buy me fashion clothes, like blue jeans. We moved to Malton, a suburb, in the seventies. This was a new housing development we were in, before sidewalks and lawns were put down. It was just houses and planks to walk across the mud into your brand spanking new home.

Malton was a new community being developed. Malton was predominantly white, what society calls "ethnically white." Lots of Italians, and along come Black people. The older houses had the British, who were living there first. As a result, a lot of racism was directed toward the Black homeowners.

Along comes another school bully that you have to do an initiation with, prove how tough you are. Pushing you in the hallway, "See you at three o'clock." So I say, "Okay, but I got to pick up my baby bother first." My first day of the big initiation fight. So I went and picked up my brother from school. I told him to sit here on the sidewalk, and watch my books. I said to her, "I showed up, I'm here to fight."

"Oh no, Carol. It's late now I've got to go."

I was so angry back then. My own trauma was taking place in my home. Home was not a safe environment for me as a young woman. On the whole, society was not a safe place either. I needed something to release my anger. "Let's go, let's roll." I was so angry, because nobody wanted to stop my pain.

By any means necessary

Boys came when I was fifteen. My mother didn't like the idea of me dating boys. I was not allowed to go out with boys. Every weekend I got my hair pressed. I was not consciously interested in boys because I wanted to go to school. I wanted to finish my education. I wanted to see that dream come true. Then the pressure came around having a boyfriend. I would hear questions like, "How come you don't have a boyfriend?" The pressure came from my friends. My mother was not big on the idea of me having a boyfriend. I remember going to my first party, just being there, and sort of sitting in a corner observing people and what they were doing. I was watching the interaction, watching people dancing and just not knowing how to fit in or if I belonged there in the heterosexual world. I was fifteen. This boy, he was nineteen, he was all over me at this party. It was yuk. I told him it was gross, "Stop it." I was the "new meat," the new victim, and, you know, I was not a bad-looking young woman. My mother had done my hair and I was wearing my short dress and my platform shoes. Feeling quite smart about myself.

I had to be home by eleven o'clock. The boy I met at the party volunteered to drive me home. At the door to my house he was trying to kiss me. I said, "No!" All I remember is his lips coming at me. I rang the door bell. His lips all over my face was not what I wanted. I just wanted to meet other young people like myself. I made a stupid mistake by telling my mother.

She blew up, told me I would not be allowed to go out. The doors were closed on parties. And while the doors were closed on the outside world, the trauma — the sexual abuse — was still taking place in my home.

I left home just before my fifteen birthday. I ran away. I ran away with the same guy — the lips — because I needed an out and he was my out. I ended up in downtown Toronto, a runaway for a few weeks and then I went back home. My return lasted a few weeks, then I left again. I got picked up by the police, one thing led to another, and I became a ward of the Children's Aid Society. I insisted that I did not want to return to my home and ended up in the Children's Aid for a year and a half. By the time I was sixteen, I demanded to be disawarded. Looking back on it, if I had a good enough worker, a worker that had cared about me, I could have stayed a ward of the Children's Aid until I was twenty-one. Then my struggle would not have been so hard as it was. I would have been able to establish myself sooner, rather than later. On the other hand, my struggles have enabled me to learn a lot. Some things I would change and some I would want to remain the same.

At sixteen, on your own in downtown Toronto, you survive. You survive by any means necessary. I didn't want to be adopted out into a white family because of the racism when I first moved to Canada. A lot of foster kids were used as servants, abused physically, sexually, emotionally. There was no safety network. For about a year and a half I lived out of a suitcase. To this day I don't own a suitcase. I never unpacked. Every home I went to, I'd open my white suitcase and take out what I needed for the time. Everything was well organized. I knew I would not be around for very long.

From the age of fifteen, for five to seven years of my life I practised bisexuality. I really went from being non-sexual, to experimenting, to bisexuality. I was never strictly heterosexual. Living on the streets, I hung out with gay men, pimps, prostitutes, drug pushers, thieves, hustlers — just everybody. My sexual satisfaction came from having sex with other women, because I fucked so many men — in order to survive — they were the last people I wanted to go to for sexual pleasure. So it was, "Yes, I like having sex with women. It's fun. It's nice." I had support networks of women who enjoyed hot and heavy sex. It was good to get seconds, so you go back for more. If not, you would just back off. These were young, hot, sexy Black women.

We all hung out at Soul Palace. Soul Palace was on Yonge Street, just north of Dundas. That's where I met these women. Also at the La Cockador which was directly across the street. Places like Mrs. Knight's and These Eyes. I remember when Katrina's was a club for bisexuals, lesbians and gays. Katrina's became a gay and lesbian only club. Before it became Katrina's, it was the Forge Hotel, which was a strip joint. Around the corner in the back alley on St. Nicholas there was David's, a gay and lesbian club. In the seventies, whether you were straight or bisexual, lesbian or gay, you could go to any club in the city. A lot of prostitutes, pimps and drug pushers would all end out at David's. It was one of the only clubs open beyond one a.m. At David's, you could sit and smoke your weed. No one would bother you. The great thing about David's was you could connect with other women for sexual pleasure.

A FREER TIME

The seventies was freer around sex, experimentation. We were the generation that came out at the tail end of the sixties, the sexual experimentation generation. There was the freedom, the love child, communal living, feminism, and being who you are. And growing up in the seventies, we were self-centred and egotistical, with our "Fuck you" attitude. It was always about "Me and my satisfaction, and taking care of my needs." And that is why it was a freer time.

The economy was better. Canada felt a lot freer then, although racism existed, access to resources was a lot easier. We would rent hotel rooms and there would be six of us sleeping in a bed together. There was a pack of about six women who ran together and we had one man who hung out with us. Looking back, I think he might have been gay. We all went to the gay and lesbian clubs together, and we all practised bisexuality. We went to the club, had sex, slept together. We took care of each other. Bisexuality was never an issue, it was something we just did. It was not a thing that you felt bad about. It just happened.

The first time I slept with a woman, all I did was foreplay, because she was shy about it. The next time I had the opportunity I was more assertive. After our sexual encounter, she came downtown to the Soul Palace before me, and told everyone. Everyone was teasing me. I remember looking at her and thinking, I will never sleep with you again. She was trying to remove herself, to say, "It's Carol, she is the one who likes sleeping with women. Carol is really the sodomite." I thought, if you feel that way, you are cut off. Sex never happened between her and me again.

In our pack we had Asian and white women, especially Asian from Jamaica — as in Chinese — because there was a common culture, a language that we shared as Jamaicans. But we never crossed into the white community — "the Canadian white community" — because there was still the sense of "us" and "them." We hung out in the Black gay male community. I hung with a lot of Black gay men in the seventies. But not with true blue lesbians. I already had a women's community. In the seventies, the lesbian community was a lot more insular, a lot more political. You had to be a true blue "Feminist Lesbian." Someone who was sleeping with both men and women would not be accepted into the community. They were looking for "real dykes," or should I say, "real lesbians," whatever they are.

We were the party crowd, not the intellectual types. If somebody said, "Here's a pill," you asked if it is an upper or a downer, and then you popped it. We lived in night clubs. We lived for the moment, and sex also part of living for the moment. I remember when David's closed down. It was a sad day. I started going to Katrina's. The man who owned David's moved and opened nother club called The Studio. I never went there. I walked by, but never entered. It felt different.

Life was changing. We were starting to break off, staring to see life differently. People were leaving Toronto and being deported. The eighties started, and more people were being deported. My circle of friends started to change. I started to hang out with an older woman, my relationships started to get more intense. I carried on a relationship with this woman for five years. I remember the day she broke my bubble, my heart. She moved a man in. That was confusing to me, I was only nineteen years old. I asked, "What about us? What about our relationship?" She just broke my bubble, told me there was no relationship, there was no "us." Within a week I moved out.

Lesbian Identified

I went back to high school full-time. In high school I started to meet women whom society considered "real lesbians." Women who did not sleep with men but only slept with women. That sort of left me going, oh there is also this option available to me. In high school I hung out with three other dykes. Through these women I became politically involved and gained a greater political analysis.

I remember going to the first "Take Back the Night" demonstration after Barbara Schlifer was murdered. I kept on meeting other lesbians, as I became more politically involved. There was a transformation happening. I was becoming more vocal. My socializing scene was changing. I was spending more and more time with women only.

I was still in high school and the goal was getting through school and doing my work. My lunch hour was spent looking for who had drugs, weed or hash. I was living on my own, downtown. The Fly by Night Dyke Bar was around the corner right next to Stage 212. I remember going to the Fly By Night one night to have a drink, sitting there and thinking, "This is it. I am where I want to be and this is where I should be."

I spent a lot of time after school talking politics over a jug of wine with three other lesbians. I was getting to know women, spending a lot more time with women who identified as lesbian. My attraction for women was growing stronger each day.

Just who we are

I started to lose track of the friends I hung out with in the seventies. My needs were changing, my wants were different. I met women in high school who were more politically active. I became fascinated. I met a lot of other lesbians, mostly white women. I knew very few lesbians of colour. In school I hung out with three lesbians, one Black woman and two white women. I tried to keep in touch but we drifted apart. I spent my time making sure that I stayed connected to the other Black woman. Then I realised there was a whole community and culture that I could connect with, be a part of, and express who I am. But there was also hesitation. I didn't want to be rejected.

Coming into the lesbian community, I felt like, if you were not white, you were not accepted. You didn't have a place. When I first started to date this woman, we would go to places like Together's. We would be the only Black women there. Or other Black women would be there with white partners, but they wouldn't talk to you as another Black woman. The bar is not the place to meet other woman unless you are trendy, attractive, young, white, and have money. Money is a super plus plus plus. A lot of dykes are poor. There is only a small percentage who get their needs met in the bar. And they are there to get lucky — "Don't call me, I'll call you if I need you" — they are not in there to develop a relationship. There is no sense of commitment or connection. In the lesbian community, connections can be momentary.

One night, my partner and I were in the bar when another Black woman and her lover came bouncing in. We went, "Whoa baby!" Then a wave of Black women started coming to the bar and we were no longer alone. We stopped going to the bar, as often, and we became locked into ourselves. We had friends, and a lot of our friends were straight. Without a sense of community, you can get locked into a pattern of being by yourselves as a couple. We started to reach out to some women, but there is still that sense of nervousness, because we had been able to survive without the support of the lesbian community. I didn't feel "safe." I didn't feel welcome in the lesbian community. I felt a questioning of who I am from women in the community. If I go into a bar in a dress, high heels and make-up, there is an assumption I am heterosexual, bisexual or a fag hag. If a white woman goes in the bar in a dress or make-up, she is called a "lipstick lesbian." There is a mistrust of lesbians of colour by our "white sisters." If I wear my pants, my dyke finery, then it is okay. Black dykes have to go overboard to prove that we are true dykes, true lesbians.

White lesbians and white gay men only need us when they feel their rights are being violated by society, then all of a sudden they feel as oppressed as us, we become a rainbow family. It is over when they no longer feel as oppressed as gays and lesbians of colour.

When I started to live with my present partner, I told my mother within the first month. That's just who I am. She wanted to know if she was white. I told her no. Then she said, "You were not born that way."

I said, "Mom, I have been sleeping with women since I was about sixteen years old." Her face went blank. "It's not like I am experimenting or going through a phase. I am at the end of my phase."

It took her a long time to understand. She was respectful in her own way, because I would not tolerate any homophobia. Things finally settled with my mother after the girls were born. Then she said, "It does not matter who you love, as long as you are happy, and it's your happiness that is my primary concern."

And so she is resigned to the fact of who her daughter is. The girls are her grandchildren. Lesbianism does not prevent a woman from having kids. To her, my life is now complete. I remember talking with one of the day care teachers and she wanted to know if the girls have always lived together. I said, "My children were born in my present relationship. My partner and I have been together for twelve years."

And she said, "Oh my God, you guys have been together longer than many heterosexual marriages." She confirmed for me what most heterosexuals think about lesbians and gays, that we are freaks and degenerate, that there is no sense of commitment, only hot sex. And when there is no longer hot sex, they move on. Having children, "Well then, they are not freaks, not degenerates. There is a continuity in their lives."

In the eighties, my partner and I used to go to a booze can just listen to reggae music. Reggae music was not played in the community. We would sit, have our beer, smoke a little weed. Nobody bothered us. Neither of us got gay-bashed, or endured homophobia. I remember my partner saying that the man who owned the house where she stayed once said to her, "If one is homosexual, it's okay as long as one is righteous." In other words, as long as you are a good person, that's all that matters. It was good to see the non-homophobic side of my community, the Black community. Most homophobia against me has been from other women of colour. People don't want you to be proud of who you are, don't want you to talk of who you are, don't want you to advertise or talk about societal abuse. This is how and where homophobia is bred from. I have been very fortunate that I have never been gay-bashed. I have been pretty open about whom I am. Because it's important to me.

Black lesbian community

There is a Black lesbian community. Some Black lesbians don't practice bisexuality. A lot of Black women are dykes and identify as dykes. Some Black women came out because they realized that heterosexual relationships and men are not what they need, like many white women. Some Black women practise bisexuality before they realize that lesbianism and loving women is their total being, like many white women. And many Black women are still bisexual, like many white women. So I have a problem when white women try to say that bisexuality is practised predominately by Black women. That is taking away our voice — Black women's voices — in the lesbian movement. White women try to say that Black women don't know what we are talking about because we are not "true dykes."

There is no true place within the lesbian community where Black women can say, "This is my community, I hear my music in the background, I see Black women with other Black women, there is a sense of comfort with each other." Because that does not exist, we tend to socialize in our own small circle. We don't go out to the bars as often. We tend to go to dances where we know who the dj is for that event. We need to see our womanhood as lesbians reflected more within the lesbian community and movement.

We don't go to bars because they are part of the white women's domain. You feel like a piece of meat. White women are there to get their "women of colour experience." For the most part, you are not acknowledged. White women you worked with, they pretend they don't know you. They need to take responsibility for their behaviour in the lesbian community and in the lesbian culture. Because they have set up the rules and the dynamic. And a lot of Black women have also taken on this kind of behaviour. I like to embarrass Black women for that kind of behaviour. Let's not pretend that that we don't know each other.

A lot of dykes out there in the Black lesbian community have made themselves the voice and the authority of the Black lesbian community. I want to let them to know they cannot speak for all of us as Black lesbians. If you are different, you are not acceptable to these self-appointed leaders. I need a my voice to be heard. I would like to see a bar, a club that is owned and operated by a woman of colour. As Black lesbians, if we begin to own and control our political socialization, we would have far more control over out existence. There has never been a bar or a club, a place where I can walk in on a Thursday night and hear our music, laugh, drink and see so-and-so. And you won't feel uncomfortable being there, you're not treated like a freak, or sex object. Don't dictate who I should be, or how I should dress. Just let me be, because the more of us that are around, the merrier. The more women of colour who come out, the stronger our community. Don't try to fit us all into one uniform. We won't all fit into a single mold.

Solve the political, free the sexual

As Black women we have taken on white women's definition of what a lesbian is supposed to be, rather than being able to express ourselves the way we feel, whether that be butch femme, femme femme, butch butch, women loving women, etc. Whatever is, we should have the room and the voice to be who we are. We are different racially and culturally. We are raised differently, and that is important to reflect within the lesbian community.

I would like to see the sexual not be the political. I don't want it to be all the same. Until gays and lesbians within this country get total recognition, as family, as couples, and recognition of our legal rights, then the sexual will be the political.

A lot of Black women are getting flack from other Black women in the community for being S/M dykes. How dare they censor two consenting adults? It's not about what you want me to do. As long as we are happy, then there are two happier people in the world.

Man-Royals and Sodomites:

Some Thoughts on the Invisibility of Afro-Caribbean Lesbians

Makeda Silvera

This is an excerpt from the influential and much-published article of the same title originally published in the mid-1980s. Makeda Silvera's biography can be found at the back of the book in the Author Biographies section.

I heard "sodomite" whispered a lot during my primary school years, and tales of women secretly having sex, joining at the genitals, and being taken to the hospital to be "cut" apart were told in the school yard. Invariably, one of the women would die. Every five to ten years the same story would surface. At times, it would even be published in the newspapers. Such stories always generated much talking and speculation from "Bwoy dem kinda naasti sah!" to some wise old woman saying "But dis caan happen, after two shutpan caan join" — meaning identical objects cannot go into the other. The act of loving someone of the same sex was sinful, abnormal — something to hide. Even today, it isn't unusual or uncommon to be asked, "So how do two 'omen do it? . . . what unoo use for a penis? . . . who is the man and who is the 'oman?" It's inconceivable that women can have intimate relationships that are whole, that are not lacking because of the absence of a man. It's assumed that women in such relationships must be imitating men.

The word "sodomite" derives from the Old Testament. Its common use to describe lesbians (or any strong independent woman) is peculiar to Jamaica — a culture historically and strongly grounded in the Bible. Although Christian values have dominated the world, their effect in slave colonies is particular. Our foreparents gained access to literacy through the Bible when they were being indoctrinated by missionaries. It provided powerful and ancient stories of strength, endurance, hope, which reflected their own fight against oppression. This book has been so powerful that it continues to bind our lives with its racism and misogyny. Thus, the importance the Bible plays in Afro-Caribbean culture must be recognised in order to understand the historical and political context for the invisibility of lesbians. The wrath of God "rained down burning sulphur on Sodom and Gomorrah" (Genesis 19:23). How could a Caribbean woman claim the name?

When, thousands of miles away and fifteen years after my school days, my grandmother was confronted with my love for a woman, her reaction was determined by her Christian faith and by this dread word sodomite — its meaning, its implication, its history.

And when, Bible in hand, my grandmother responded to my love by sitting me down, at the age of twenty-seven, to quote Genesis, it was within the context of this tradition, this politic. When she pointed out that "this was a white people ting," or "a ting only people with mixed blood was involved in" (to explain or include my love with a woman of mixed blood), it was a strong denial of many ordinary Black working-class women she knew.

It was finally through my conversations with my grandmother, my mother and my mother's friend, five years later, that I began to realise the scope of this denial which was intended to dissuade and protect me. She knew too well that any woman who took a woman lover was attempting to walk on fire — entering a "no man's land." I began to see how commonplace the act of loving women really was, particularly in working-class communities. I realised, too, just how heavily shame and silence weighed down this act.

A CONVERSATION WITH A FRIEND OF MY MOTHER

Well, when I was growing up we didn't hear much 'bout woman and woman. They weren't "suspect." There was much more talk about "batty man businesses" when I was a teenager in the 1950s.

I remember one story about a man who was "suspect" and that every night when he was coming home, a group of guys use to lay wait him and stone him so viciously that he had to run for his life. Dem time, he was safe only in the day. Now with women, nobody really suspected. I grew up in the country and I grew up seeing women holding hands, hugging-up, sleeping together in one bed and there was no question. Some of this was based purely on emotional friendship, but I also knew of cases where the women were dealing but no one really suspected. Close people around knew, but not everyone knew. It wasn't a thing that you would put out and broadcast. It would be something just between the two people.

Also one important thing is that the women who were involved carried on with life just the same, no big political statements were made. These women still went to church, still got baptised, still went on pilgrimage, and I am thinking about one particular woman name Aunt Vie, a very strong woman, strong-willed and everything, they use to call her "man-royal" behind her back, but no one ever dare to meddle with her.

Things are different now in Jamaica. Now all you have to do is not respond to a man's call to you and dem call you sodomite or lesbian. I guess it was different back then forty years ago because it was harder for anybody to really conceive of two woman sleeping and being sexual. But I do remember when you were "suspect," people would talk about you. You were definitely classed as "different," "not normal," a bit of a "crazy." But women never really got stoned like the men.

What I remember is that if you were a single woman alone or two single women living together and a few people suspected this ... and when I say a few people I mean like a few guys, sometimes other crimes were committed against the women. Some very violent, some very subtle. Battery was common, especially in Kingston. A group of men would suspect a woman or have it out for her because she was a "sodomite" or because she act "man-royal" and so the men would organise and gang rape whichever woman was "suspect." Sometimes it was reported in the newspapers, other times it wasn't — but when you live in a little community, you don't need a newspaper to tell what's going on. You know by word of mouth and those stories were frequent. Sometimes you also knew the men who did the battery.

Other subtle forms of this was "scorning" the women. Meaning that you didn't eat anything from them, especially a cooked meal. It was almost as if those accused of being "man-royal" or "sodomite" could contaminate.

A CONVERSATION WITH MY GRANDMOTHER

I am only telling you this so that you can understand that this is not a profession to be proud of and to get involved in. Everybody should be curious and I know you born with that, ever since you growing up as a child and I can't fight against that, because that is how everybody get to know what's in the world. I am only telling you this because when you were a teenager, you always say you want to experience everything and then you make your mind on your own. You didn't like people telling you what was wrong and right. That always use to scare me.

Experience is good, yes. But it have to be balanced, you have to know when you have too much experience in one area. I am telling you this because I think you have enough experience in this to decide now to go back to the normal way. You have two children. Do you want them to grow up knowing this is the life you have taken? But this is for you to decide....

Yes, there was a lot of women involved with women in Jamaica. I knew a lot of them when I was growing up in the country in the 1920s. I didn't really associate with them. Mind you, I was not rude to them. My mother wouldn't stand for any rudeness from any of her children to adults.

I remember a woman we use to call Miss Bibi. She lived next to us — her husband was a fisherman, I think he drowned before I was born. She had a little wooden house that back onto the sea, the same as our house. She was quiet, always reading. That I remember about her because she use to go to the little public library at least four days out of the week. And she could talk. Anything you want to know, just ask Miss Bibi and she could tell you. She was mulatto woman, but poor. Anytime I had any school work that I didn't understand, I use to ask her. The one thing I remember though, we wasn't allowed in her house by my mother, so I use to talk to her outside, but she didn't seem to mind that. Some people use to think she was mad because she spent so much time alone. But I didn't think that because anything she help me with, I got a good mark on it in school.

She was colourful in her own way, but quiet, always alone, except when her friend come and visit her once a year for two weeks. Them times I didn't see Miss Bibi much because my mother told me I couldn't go and visit her. Sometimes I would see her in the market exchanging and bartering fresh fish for vegetables and fruits. I use to see her friend too. She was a jet Black woman, always had her hair tied in bright coloured cloth and she always had on big gold earrings. People use to say she lived on the other side of the island with her husband and children and she came to Port Maria once a year to visit Miss Bibi.

My mother and father were great storytellers and I learnt that from them, but is from Miss Bibi that I think I learnt to love reading so much as a child. It wasn't until I move to Kingston that I notice other women like Miss Bibi...

Let me tell you about Jones. Do you remember her? Well she was the woman who lived the next yard over from us. She is the one who really turn me against people like that and why I fear so much for you to be involved with this thing. She was very loud. Very show-off. Always dressed in pants and man-shirt that she borrowed from her husband. Sometimes she use to invite me over to her house, but I didn't go. She always had her hair in a bob hair cut, always barefoot and tending to her garden and her fruit trees. She tried to get me involved in that kind of life, but I said no. At the time I remember I needed some money and she lent me, later she told me I didn't have to pay her back, but to come over to her house and see the thing she had that was sweeter than what any man could offer me. I told her no, and eventually paid her back the money.

We still continued to talk. It was hard not to like Jonesie — that's what everybody called her. She was open and easy to talk to. But still there was a fear in me about her. To me it seem like she was in a dead-end with nowhere to go. I don't want that for you.

I left my grandmother's house that day feeling anger and sadness for Miss Jones — maybe for myself, who knows. I was feeling boxed in. I had said nothing. I'd only listened quietly.

In bed that night, I thought about Miss Jones. I cried for her (for me) silently. I remembered her, a mannish looking Indian woman, with flashy gold teeth, a Craven A cigarette always between them. She was always nice to me as a child. She had the sweetest, juiciest Julie, Bombay and East Indian mangoes on the street. She always gave me mangoes over the fence. I remember the dogs in her yard and the sign on her gate. "Beware of bad dogs." I never went into her house, though I was always curious.

I vaguely remember her pants and shirts, though I never thought anything of them until my grandmother pointed them out. Neither did I recall that dreaded word being used to describe her, although everyone on the street knew about her.

A CONVERSATION WITH MY MOTHER

Yes, I remember Miss Jones. She smoke a lot, drank a lot. In fact, she was an alcoholic. When I was in my teens she use to come over to our house — always on the verandah. I can't remember her sitting down — seems she was always standing up, smoking, drinking and reminiscing. She constantly talked about the past, about her life. And it was always women: young women she knew when she was a young woman, the fun they had together and how good she could make love to a woman. She would say to whoever was listening on the verandah, "Dem girls I use to have sex with was shapely. You shoulda know me when I was younger, pretty and shapely just like the 'oman dem I use to have as my 'oman."

People use to tease her on the street, but not about being a lesbian or calling her sodomite. People use to tease her when she was drunk, because she would leave the rumshop and stagger down the avenue to her house.

I remember the women she use to carry home, usually in the daytime. A lot of women from downtown, higglers and fishwomen. She use to boast about knowing all kinds of women from Coronation market and her familiarity with them. She had a husband who lived with her and that served her as her greatest protection against other men taking steps with her. Not that anybody could easily take advantage of Miss Jones, she could stand up for herself. But having a husband did help. He was a very quiet, insular man. He didn't talk to anyone on the street. He had no friends so it wasn't easy for anyone to come up to him and gossip about his wife.

No one could go to her house without being invited, but I wouldn't say she was a private person. She was a loner. She went to the rumshops alone, she drank alone, she staggered home alone. The only time I ever saw her with somebody were the times when she went off to the Coronation market or some other place downtown to find a woman and bring her home. The only times I remember her engaging in conversation with anybody was when she came over on the verandah to talk about her women and what they did in bed. That was all she let out about herself. There was nothing about how she was feeling, whether she was sad or depressed, lonely, happy. Nothing. She seemed to cover up all of that with her loudness and her vulgarness and her constant threat — which was all it was — to beat up anybody who troubled her or teased her when she was coming home from the rumshop.

Now Cherry Rose — do you remember her? She was a good friend of Aunt Marie and of Mama's. She was also a sodomite. She was loud too, but different from Miss Jones. She was much more outgoing. She was a barmaid and had lots of friends — both men and women. She also had the kind of personality that attracted people — very vivacious, always laughing, talking and touching. She didn't have any children, but Gem did.

Do you remember Miss Gem? Well, she had children and she was also a barmaid. She also had lots of friends. She also had a man friend name Mickey, but that didn't matter because some women had their men and still had women they carried on with. The men usually didn't know what was going on, and seeing as these men just come and go and usually on their own time, they weren't around every day and night.

Miss Pearl was another one that was in that kind of thing. She was a dressmaker, she use to sew really good. Where Gem was a bit plump, Pearl was slim but with big breasts and a big bottom. They were both pretty women.

I don't remember hearing that word sodomite a lot about them. It was whispered sometimes behind their backs, but never in front of them. And they were so alive and talkative that people were always around them.

The one woman I almost forgot was Miss Opal, a very quiet woman. She use to be friends with Miss Olive and was always out of her bar sitting down. I can't remember much about her except she didn't drink like Miss Jones and she wasn't vulgar. She was soft spoken, a half-Chinese woman. Her mother was born in Hong Kong and her father was a Black man. She could really bake. She use to supply shops with cakes and other pastries. So there were many of those kind of women around. But it wasn't broadcast.

I remembered them. Not as lesbians or sodomites or man-royals, but as women that I liked. Women whom I admired. Strong women, some colourful, some quiet. I loved Cherry Rose's style. I loved her loudness, the way she challenged men in arguments, the bold way she laughed in their faces, the jingle of her gold bracelets. Her colourful and stylish way of dressing. She was full of wit; words came alive in her mouth.

Miss Gem: I remember her big double iron bed. That was where Paula and Lorraine (her daughters, my own age) and I spent a whole week together when we had chicken pox. My grandmother took me there to stay for the company. It was fun. Miss Gem lived right above her bar and so at any time we could look through the window and onto the piazza and street which was bursting with energy and life. She was a very warm woman, patient and caring. Every day she would make soup for us and tell us stories. Later on in the evening she would bring us Kola champagne.

Miss Pearl sewed dresses for me. She hardly ever used her tape measure — she could just take one look at you and make you a dress fit for a queen. What is she doing now, I asked myself? And Miss Opal, with her calm and quiet, where is she — still baking?

What stories could these lesbians have told us? I, an Afro-Caribbean woman living in Canada, come with this baggage — their silenced stories. My grandmother and mother know the truth, but silence still surrounds us. The truth remains a secret to the rest of the family and friends, and I must decide whether to continue to sew this cloth of denial or break free, creating and becoming the artist that I am, bringing alive the voices and images of Cherry Rose, Miss Gem, Miss Jones, Opal, Pearl and others ...

CATCHIN' MY TAIL
Tinkerbell

I was born in Trinidad in 1967. Family background is very straight. One parent is of Portuguese descent and one is of East Indian. My mother is a hairdresser, my father is a health inspector, but he's retired now. I have one brother who is two years younger than me, and he's a prison officer.

My family is difficult because my mother is very Indian, believes in the way she was brought up in her culture. My father is not like that, but he's very quiet. His silence doesn't do anything for me. He doesn't voice his opinion at all. Whether I am right or wrong, whether my mother is right or wrong, he just has nothing to say. He says to me, whatever I choose to do with my life, if I'm happy, and the police doesn't come in front his house to collect me for anything, then fine, I can do what I want. But my mother is a problem where my lesbian rights is concerned. My mother, she always compare us with her family. And somehow we are never good enough, she wants us to be like her nieces and nephews, well-educated.

Coming out there was the usual reaction from family and relatives. They're totally against it. They call you names behind your back. They don't have the guts to tell you in front of your face. 'Cause if they'd do, they have a good scare, maybe I'd knock them down or something. It wasn't nice. It doesn't bother me so much anymore.

I USED TO KISS THE GIRLS

All the other girls used to do the same things I do, except I used to kiss them, they never kissed me. I kiss them under the cherry trees. They always like to play dolly, all of them play with dolls and tea sets, and I never did. I always liked playing with the boys. Now I do weight-lifting and cycling. Everybody used to call me tomboy.

In my early teens in Form One, I had a big crush on this girl who sat next to me. I used to write her little love letters and ting. Askin' her to be my girlfriend and sayin' how much I loved her. But it was not a sexual thing. I was attracted to her, but I never thought about being sexually involved. I just feel I like her so much. She had a talk with me one day and she said, "We can't be girlfriends because it doesn't happen that way. We can be very good friends, but we can't be girlfriends."

And I said, "Ok, fine." And we turned out to be best friends. That was my first crush on a woman. At that age, twelve going on thirteen, I did not know, I never heard of the word lesbian. All I knew is that I was attracted to women. Sometimes it was uncomfortable, uncomfortable. If I kept it to myself I was fine, I could fantasize, and there was no problem.

Passionate kissin'

The first time it was a married woman with children. This was passionate kissin'. Passionate kissin'. I met her at a party at my uncle's place. She came on to me and I was real scared. I wanted the experience, but I was scared because we were at a family home and she was drunk. Not so drunk, but she came on to me. I wanted it, I didn't want it. I was a bit embarrassed because she was doin' things openly to me. And people were lookin'. She was like calypso playin' and she come on winin' and that kind of thing. I was nineteen going on twenty. My parents weren't around, I think they'd left earlier or they didn't come. And I wanted this experience so bad. I thought that I would split with her. "You have a car?" I asked.

She said, "Yes."

I said "Well, meet me outside in ten minutes."

We went into her car and drove down the street and started kissin' each other and thing. After a few hours I found out she was married. We kissed for a long time. Then I told her, "Look, I better go before they miss me and they'll know."

I met at her home, New Year's Eve. She was drinkin'. We never went all the way. We just kissed. I didn't want it actually, because she was married, with a husband and two children. I wanted to meet somebody who I could be with all the time. But I really *wanted* somebody. I didn't want somebody who would take me for a ride.

The same thing to tell each other

My friend Natalie and I were very close at this time. She is a good friend to me. I have a few best friends, actually. We both had something to tell each other. I didn't know what she had to tell me, and she didn't know what I had to tell her. So, one evening we bought some vodka, we told each other. Laughin', laughin' because we couldn't believe that we had the same thing to tell each other. She was out before me, going out within the gay circles. And I wasn't. I was scared. She started to invite me to parties. We've been very good friends. Actually, she's my only trustworthy gay friend. All my other trustworthy friends are straight.

Out is doing what you do

Women are very, very closeted and I don't think they're going to come out right now. The men are much more open and don't give a shit. But most of the women are closeted.

At work I didn't have problem, the woman who hired me supports gay rights. She writes articles trying to make readers understand gay people. She wrote a few articles in *The Guardian*. I know that she is for us, she comes to the shows and stuff.

Most of the time I am comfortable as a lesbian, sometimes it depends on the person. I wouldn't tell the church group I am in that I am gay. I would tell it to my counsellor. Out is doing what you do, is me and my girlfriend standing on the street like any straight couple would. Being able to sit there and kiss her in public. That's being out.

My girlfriend and I went to the botanical garden and we were just sitting there talking. When we were, walking out, somebody shouted, "Lesbians!"

So I turn around and I bowed, "I am proud to be a lesbian." My girlfriend was starting to walk fast and I said, "No, don't walk away so quick, he's only a bum."

She said, "You don't know if it some madman, he can come over and beat us up or something." Though there have been no incidents of lesbians being attacked, men are attacked. Couples get hassled and names called. But the men they get all kinda thing.

I ain't diggin in no car engine

They do have butch and femme in Trinidad. And femme and femme, butch and butch. It's always been easy with me, doesn't matter who is what. My partner and I, we share each other equal, you know. She insist that she pays for everything because she is much higher worker, has a higher salary. But when I have the money, I want to pay for us. She insist that I don't spend my money because I don't make as much as her.

From the circle, I get feedback that I'm butch. I call myself butch because of the feedback. I don't give a damn. And they say my partner is femme. She's into sports, into hockey, she's a goal-keeper. She don't wear the skirts on the field, she wear pants. She's into carpentry, masonry, fixin' cars. I am not. I am into the kitchen — cookin', cleanin', washin'. I am femme in that way, and she's butch in that sense. I look butch to girls in the community, but I not interested in diggin' in no car engine. That not my thing. If you want me to make a perfect meal for you, I can do that.

Being a lesbian in Trinidad

At times it's frustratin'. Before, it was much more frustratin', but now it's beginnin' to look different. Before, I was going through all this hurt and I just wanted to hurt somebody back. But I've gotten over it. It's like I'm startin' afresh. And tings are going much better, although I'm not employed. I'm happy with who I'm seeing now.

Things could be better at home at my parents, if I didn't have to hide. I don't like the hiding. I don't really pretend anymore, they know. But they just have these hopes that, "Oh gosh, she's going to change, maybe she'll get a man." I've been telling them that there's no way. Telling my mother, "I'm not going to do any of those things to please you any more." My father definitely knows because he said, "At least adopt a child." No. It's a great responsibility, and I don't really like responsibility. I mean, I do the simple little things, but I think having a child is something precious. You should really, really take care of it. I would get involved with a woman with children. I'd give it my best shot.

If I stayed in Trinidad, financially, I'd be catchin' my tail. Where my personal life is concerned, I'd be happy. But you must have both. I would want to take care of my friend and if I don't have any cash, I can't do that. I need both.

We get information, a lot of us who are into what is happenin' abroad. Like my friend Roger, he told me about the singer Melissa Etheridge. He said he always suspected, even before she came out. He's into what is happenin' out there. He go into the bookstores and second-hand bookshops, buy old magazines and stuff. There's a bookshop at the Express Building, they have lesbian novels and stuff. The price is ridiculous, so people don't buy them. They stand up and browse through them. Only a few people who can afford, they buy it, but it's too, too expensive. The booksellers know they're the only people who have that stuff. That's why the price is sky high.

Laws against homosexuality

Ever since the Queen ruled, there's been the law against homosexuality. There hasn't been any case prosecuted. It was only for men, but they recently made it for men *and women*. We didn't like it but again, we can' do anything about it 'cause it's such a small percentage of us. There aren't any cases where people were actually arrested. You get police comin' to bust your parties. Not in homes. There are a few pubs that rent their place out to us for parties because they make money off us, you know, so they don't mind. They don't arrest you, they just stop the party.

Trustin' each other

I'd like to see all the gay people in our community trustin' with each other and comin' together as one. I know we would never get our total freedom back. That is a long way, oh a long way. I can't see myself being totally free here, maybe end of the century or somethin'.

I would like us to be able to have our bars, a gay bar at least. A space. It's illegal for us to have anything at all, any sort of meetings or anything like that. I want us to be able to at least have that and be able to open bars. But if we do those things, if we open bars, it's obvious that the public is going to kick up against us and I'm sure people are going to attack us.

We are in cliques. If one clique bounces off another clique and you see a new face, someone you haven't met before, you go close to that clique. If you know somebody in that clique, you asked to be introduced to that person. You inquire if they're seeing anybody and that sort of thing. You have to know somebody. This is Port of Spain.

Community is gay parties, theatre, and Pelican Inn. And that's about it. Those who lime with each other like the cliques. They don't socialize outside, they have friends who lime at home. And if you know anybody who you should track, you invite them to come and you feel them out from there.

My support is my one and only trustworthy lesbian friend, Natalie, the person I am involved with now. My other lovers would not do that for me, no. I don't think lesbians support each other. It depends on the situation. Maybe if a policeman was to beat up on a woman because she was a lesbian, you get support. But that doesn't happen now.

Everybody knows when there's a break-up. Some get support and some don't. This couple broke up because they had third person and one decided, "I'm going to go with this third person and forget about you." They had a nasty fight and all kinda shit, and it made newspapers. It was on *The Punch* or *The Bomb*, one of those scandal papers. Everybody buy those. Cause a scandal.

I heard people say "Yes, they have threesomes," and I said, "Naaah." 'Cause I used to go across there and play cards. I said, "No man, you lyin', that's just gossip." And then the scandal broke.

We should learn to respect each other's relationships. Try and respect couples, not try to break them up — which happens a lot. If I like somebody who is going out with somebody else, I keep it to myself. I don't let them know at all. What I do not like for myself, I do not like for others. If I don't want somebody to come and break up my relationship with somebody else, I am not going to do it to you.

Where respect and love is involved, I am religious. But having to live your life to please the Bible, to suit the Bible — no. Homosexuality is not accepted at all, but I've been talkin' to a few people in my church group. They do not condemn, you know. They don't condemn me or tell me, "Don't do it." They just sort of give encouragement to continue to serve God the best way you know how. The main thing is that they don't want you to pull away from God and become a "heathen."

There aren't any rules in the community. You do your own thing. It's mixed: Black, white and Chinese. At the same time, everybody has cliques. At certain parties, you'll get a certain group of lesbians. And that group of lesbians would not go to a certain other party. More of the whites would be goin' to Gold's party, while more of the Blacks going to the parties at Cocoa House. You get a different crowd, depending on who having the party.

This year we have had cabaret shows and stuff for a week. The group organize it and mos' of the tings was free. Everytime you come to the meeting you give a donation. Some of the events were held at an actor's place. Some of the events were held at the Space Theatre. The cabaret show was very good. It was not advertised for the public, but you could bring along your straight friends who accept you. The same three men bring out plays every so often. Lots of plays runnin' right through the year. There have been a few gay plays and there have been a lot of write-ups about it, negative. But nobody paid attention to what they had to say and stuff, where theatre is concerned it's different, is accepted.

Young lesbians

It's difficult being a lesbian in Trinidad and Tobago. It's difficult for young lesbians, comin' out. For the ones who've already been out and have the experience, it's difficult to a point but not as difficult as somebody who's now comin' out. We don't have anywhere to go and socialize. Look at Valentine's Day. You know how much I long to take my lover to a restaurant, where we can sit together, have dinner hold hands and kiss each other? It's supposed to be *the* romantic day. I can't even look at her all moony and groony, can't melt into her.

I don't know what to tell a young gay person. Depends on your financial situation. If you are dependent, I would tell you to try not to let your parents know. I would tell straight friends of mine who had a lesbian daughter not to fight her. They wouldn't, because I've had discussions about that with them.

When I and a few others who came out, we were sceptical, always hidin'. We still do, but more so then. Paranoid kinda thing. A young girl comin' out now, well, she would have to have another friend who is gay. If it's a gay man friend that she has, he'd probably introduce her to other women. That's the only way. But if she doesn't have any friends, she'd have to figure it out herself. The ones who are comin' out now, I think they kinda happy that they're out. I don't know any of them personally, but from what I've seen, it's no big deal to them. They 'ave no problem with it.

FREE TO TOUCH
Daphne

I was born in Dominica (which is not the Dominican Republic). It's a little island in the Caribbean, in the Windward islands. I'm the first of three children. My mother was a single woman. She raised all three of us on her own. My childhood was a good one, a happy childhood. I grew up poor, by North American standards, but I was not aware of really needing anything. I had what I needed — I was adequately clothed and fed three meals a day, although my mother really had a hard time, supporting three children on her own. But she managed to give us what we needed.

IN THE YARD

I remember growing up in what we call a yard. Basically, the yard is a communal space, or it can be private. Everything happened in the yard. That's where I got my sense of community. I grew up surrounded by women, everyone around me grew up in the same kind of family, a female-run household. There were hardly any men around, as in fathers, permanent lovers or husbands and the men who were around were temporary. It was not unusual to find a woman with five kids and five different fathers. They did not plan it that way. It was common for women to have sexual relationships with men out of which they got pregnant, and the men moved on. That's the way it was. For the most part, the man never came back into the woman's life after their one and only sexual encounter, in which she got pregnant. Sometimes he'd financially support the child, sometimes he didn't. Some women prostituted themselves to feed children they already had, and ended up with another mouth to feed. Birth control was unattainable and abortion out of the question for most women.

I've had a lot of time to think back about growing up and the people who were important in my life. Truthfully, they were all women. I've tried to think what that's meant in terms of being a lesbian. Not to say growing up in an all-female environment have anything to do with who I am sleeping with today. But what it does mean is that I have very little experience or skills dealing with men. On an emotional level or in a sexual relationship, I don't know them. Sometimes I don't think it is natural being in an exclusive sexual relationship with a man. I have a brother, but it's a different kind of relationship. My brother is just my brother. I love him. It's a different bond. Other than that I have always had a very difficult time with men, as lovers or husbands.

I got involved with my first lover, my first male lover, when I was fifteen. He was about nineteen. I remember the day he approached me. Back then, the way you got involved with a guy, if you were a "decent" girl, would be to have him go to your mother or your parents, and ask for permission to see you. I remember when he approached me and told me he liked me. I said, "You have to go and see my mother and get her permission." He did, and we went together for three years. Everyone knew us as a couple. I think there was some expectation that we would get married, but I knew I would never marry him.

SHE WAS CRAZY ABOUT ME

The first woman I was involved with I actually met before this guy. I was close to fourteen and she was nineteen. It was not a sexual relationship. She was a very butch woman. I didn't know the term butch until many years later. She was crazy about me. I liked her, but at the same time I didn't like her. I was really young. We fought a lot. I was really mean to her. I was mean to her because — I don't think it had to do with the fact that she was a lesbian — we clashed a lot. She is a woman who does not have a lot of confidence in herself and it irritated me.

When I was fifteen I went to Monserrat. During my stay there she wrote me love letters, telling me how much she loved me. She spoiled me rotten. Anything I wanted, she would buy for me. She gave me gifts. I had a hair set, a brush, a comb and a mirror which she ordered from overseas for me. She also gave me a nice soap dish with the soap in it. She'd buy me sweets and other snacks, things that were a luxury to me. The mirror and the comb broke, but when I came to Canada at twenty, I still had the brush.

I had the brush 'til I was in my thirties when it broke. I was disappointed. It represented love and affection to me, reminded me of someone totally doting on me and spoiling me. It was nice to be spoiled.

We hung out together a lot. She went everywhere with me. She was my shadow. She was also very shy and didn't have many friends. I kind of brought her out. I helped my mother sell candy, peanuts, gums and other treats. My mother sold those things to supplement her income. I sat by the roadside with the tray after school and on weekends. In the afternoons, during the week, around five or six o'clock, I took the tray down to her workplace. After work she went by the cinema with the tray. My friend always went with me. On Sunday afternoons, I'd go by the cinema during matinée time to sell. When the movie began we walked around town selling peanuts. We'd go to the botanical gardens. There were less customers, but we could play and neck. We necked a lot back then. We necked and kissed, we did everything but have sex.

For some reason, her mother and my mother became arch enemies. They couldn't stand each other, and my mother hated me to be friends with this woman. She couldn't stand it. She had several reasons for not wanting us to be friends. She claimed this woman was bad company for me. She said my friend lived a double life. What my mother was saying was my friend slept with women and she slept with men, but I did not know that. I did not want to believe it. I fought my mother for that friendship.

My mother claims that my friend slept with men for money. I had no reason not to believe my mother. On the other hand, she was not working and I felt what she did was her business. The island I come from is really small. There is not a hell of a lot to do, in terms of earning an income. My friend was also very, very butch. At home we call women like her malnom (anti-man). It's derogatory, not a nice term, but for some reason men liked her, so she could have her pick. My mother tried everything to try to stop me from being friends with her, but I've always been stubborn. If I was going to end my friendship with her, it was going to be when I was ready, not because my mother didn't want me to be friends with her.

When I was sixteen, we fell out, it was very complicated. By then I got involved with my first boyfriend. My friend and I stopped talking to each other because of pressure from my mother. Also I was getting more aware of peoples' gossip, she was too butch. She was jealous. My friend got involved with another woman. I was very surprised when they got involved because the woman had a long-time, steady boyfriend. So, I got involved with my first boyfriend. I didn't speak to her again for sixteen years.

I thought about her a lot over the years, especially after I heard she had children. I thought about our relationship. I tried to figure out where my lesbianism began, thought about incidents when we were together. Where were the signs? I wanted to know what happened to her, even though we were not speaking to each other. I'd gone home twice and had not seen her. I didn't know what it would be like to talk to her again. In 1992, I thought, what the hell, I'm in my thirties. I don't even remember why we fell out. I was a child then. It's ridiculous. I need to see her and speak to her.

I went looking for her. I ran ino a guy who hung around with us a lot. He spied on us. He liked her. I think he wanted to catch us in bed. I asked him about her. He told me " If she sees you, she will eat you up." It was quite a reunion. I went to look for her, very clear about who I am and what I wanted from the meeting. I was much more mature and in control. A lot more sophisticated after living in North America and coming out as a lesbian on this side of the world. My whole intention was just to be friends with her. We were women now. I was not a young girl anymore. I had children, she had children and I wanted to start up a friendship with her. However, she claimed to be still in love with me. It was very trying and messy. I felt myself going between liking her and hating her again. I slept with her, because I hadn't when I was a young girl. Once, just to satisfy my curiosity. It became very complicated that little visit home in 1992.

Boys

I got involved with my first boyfriend, we were together for three years. I left him, I got married right after to a Black Canadian. The day I turned twenty, he claimed to have fallen instantly in love with me. I was a pretty teenager. I had my hair in curls, he thought they were dreadlocks. He was visiting the island and was coming back to Canada. He said he didn't want to leave without me. He proposed marriage to me a couple days after we met, and after talking to my really close friend at the time — we were accused of being zamis, and were not — I said yes. I told her I met this guy that he liked me, wants to marry me and take me up to Canada. What did she think?

She said, "Go on girl. Don't be stupid. Marry him."

I said, "But you know, I don't love him."

She said, "So you will get to love him."

I told my mother he had proposed. My mother, being the practical person and opportunistic, said, "Well, bring him over let me talk to him."

She met him, talked to him and asked him his intentions. She had to give permission for us to get married, because at the time I was too young, legally. My mother said her reason for agreeing was to give me the opportunity to come to Canada and to better myself. So I married him and we came up to Canada. We stayed together for three years. I hated being a wife, hated having his name. The first thing I did when we broke up was change my name back to my birth name.

I remember telling my husband once that I was really interested in sleeping with a woman. He was cool that way. Nothing came of the conversation. I remember having urges to sleep with women and always suppressing them because I felt it was a perversion, some kind of perverted fantasy. It was not possible in my mind. I didn't know there was such a thing as lesbianism. I didn't know the word lesbian or what it meant. I didn't know where to find lesbians. I didn't know women actually loved each other, lived together, actually had sex together, even though I had my teen experience, there was no context for it back then. I just had these fantasies of wanting to go to bed with a woman. In my wildest fantasy I'd go to a female prostitute, then I'd be disgusted with myself.

At the same time I befriended a girlfriend of a friend of his. I really liked her. I remember we were really close. I wondered about her and this other woman. She came over to my apartment, and we went out a lot. I was new to the country, so she was my friend. Sometimes when I showered, she would want to put lotion on my skin. A couple of times she tried to get me to touch her breast, but none of it sent clues to my head. Years later, when I ran into my ex-husband and told him I was living with a woman and that I was a lesbian, he said he wondered if this girl and I used to make out.

What a Fall

I came out as a lesbian when I was thirty-two. I met my lover and really fell for her. It was so natural to me. She was out, seducing women was nothing to her. It was the first time I was with a woman who was openly lesbian and openly showed her sexual interest in women. There was no shame or guilt, no apology. I knew of her through an ex-lover of hers who went to school with me. Through her ex-lover, I knew everything about her. When I ended up working with her I was really interested in her. That woke me up, that she was a lesbian. I was interested in how she lived, what she did and who she did it with. She was also very beautiful, sexy, gorgeous, to me.

I was straight and involved with my children's father at the time. I didn't think she'd be interested in me, but we got together. It was the most beautiful experience. For the first time in my life, I had fallen in love. Man, what a fall. I walked around with my eyes glazed for two years. Then the glaze started to come off a bit. Those rose-coloured glasses started to clear. Then I was faced with our relationship and the work began. It was hard work, lots of trial. Things happened which hurt us both. But we wanted the relationship and truly cared for each other, which made love beautiful.

I came out into her community. Through her I got to meet other lesbians and found myself in the cushion of lesbianism and a lesbian "community." It was mostly a white lesbian community. I never really felt one hundred percent comfortable in that circle. But the women were really nice, friendly and supportive. When I got involved with my lover, was the first time I found myself having to be so interactive with white people. Up until then, they were people — coming to this part of the world — I had to work with. I was in their country, so to speak. For the first time, I had to look at them up close. Before her basically, when I left work and went home, I left them behind. When I got involved with her, it was different. They were now becoming my community, my friends. I had some good times with those women. They are still my friends today though I only see them at social events. Through her and them, I learned more about lesbianism. I learned to like and appreciate women. If anybody really loves women, it's that woman, though I don't agree with her always sexualizing women. She taught me everything. She made it easy for me to come out as a lesbian. She woke up the lesbian in me — she will never sleep again.

I didn't come out with the trauma of most women. That feeling, "Oh, whoa, what will the community say?" or concerns about being ostracised from a community, because I was never really a part of the Caribbean community over here anyway. I lived separate from them although I had a few friends. I met more Black women as I attended more lesbian social events. I was fortunate to befriend women who were visible, out there. Radical, political, out lesbians. I admired them and their way of being helped me shape my lesbian personality.

Live, love and protect

I've always had a problem with the idea of being part of a lesbian community. I've worked on trying to figure out what that means for me. I would say there is not *a* community out there, but several. Community is not only about people who have some characteristic in common, but people who have a common goal, an objective, who support and like each other, nurture each other, protect each other. A community lets you live, love and retain your foundation. Among Black gays and lesbians in Toronto it is lacking. I'm not a part of the white lesbian community, I can never be.

Among Black lesbians there are groups and cliques of friends who are very tight with each other. For some people that means a lot and it gives them a sense of being part of something. In that respect I think we can build our own. But, people are scared, especially when we have other battles to fight, and we have given much to build the white gay and lesbian community.

I only think about "the community" because for other people it's such an issue. As far as I'm concerned, I left my community behind when I left Dominica and came here. Basically, I see myself as one of those wandering spirits. I don't have any roots here and I don't belong to any particular community. I have a lot of friends, people who are almost like my family. If it was not for them, Toronto would really be a scary place for me. I have managed to make my home here. In two years time, I will have spent half my life here, and the other half in Dominica. I really value my friends and my friendships, but I am not part of the lesbian community as I think a community should be defined.

Coming into myself

As far as coming out, my coming out experience was very positive. I have not had any negative experiences. In 1992, I got into a quarrel with my brother. He is the only person who reacted negatively to my coming out as a dyke. All in all, I have not experienced any violence, name-calling or shunning. I choose who I want to come out to. At the same time I am certainly not closeted. I am not ashamed about being a lesbian. It would be very sad if I had never come out as a lesbian.

In 1992 my friend told me she couldn't imagine me not being with a woman. I felt very happy to hear her say that. She made me feel I had come into myself. When I told other people that I was out as a dyke, they said they knew, they suspected. I found that really interesting since I hadn't known that about myself. I wondered, what it was about me that made them know?

My mother found out I was a lesbian because I dumped my children's father for my female lover. He thought he would create problems, or make me feel bad, when he phoned my mother and my sister long distance and told them. My mother said, "You are not a lesbian, are you?" We were walking on the beach in Boston, Beverly farms, when she said that to me. I didn't answer her and she said, "By you not answering me I know it's true."

My mother didn't make a fuss about it, though she was not happy. She didn't talk about it. She's had her moments of struggling with it, but she knows who I am. She knows I can be very stubborn. She never confronted me with it and it was never an issue. She said, "You made your choice and if you are happy, nothing I can say will make a difference anyway."

Then she met my girlfriend and really liked her. My mother has this attitude, as long as whoever her children are involved with are good to them, she's happy. As long as her children are not being ill-treated, she's happy. She saw I was not being ill-treated by my lover, that she really loved me and my children, that she really took care of us and was genuinely there with me. She was beautiful and that helped a lot. My mother has one of the first pictures we took together. I think that made a big difference to her. My mother won't go and march at Gay Pride Day or anything like that, but she accepted that I was living with a woman. If my mother had not accepted my lesbianism it would not have mattered to me. That is not my problem, it's her problem, though I would have been saddened. It would have been too bad but that's all it would have been.

Rumours about us

Growing up I didn't hear too much about lesbianism. I heard "zami." My friend was the one who told me what the word meant, because I was hearing rumours about us. She told me it meant women who slept with each other. When I was a young girl in school (thirteen, fourteen, fifteen) a lot of my friends fooled around with each other. It was something girls did. The sister of my best friend at the time necked and kissed with her best girl friend, and they both had boyfriends. Surprisingly, the rumours and innuendos come from men. I think they got a thrill out of it.

I knew of a group of women who slept with each other. These women had men and children. People knew what they were doing but no one threatened them. Maybe I was too young to pick up on people's reaction but I don't remember hearing or seeing anything bad.

I heard of women having small dicks, that sort of thing. Of course it was not true, but rumours spread like wildfire where I come from. Sleeping with women was something women did and I really don't have a lot of memory of that being an issue. It was unspoken, hidden and secretive, but at the same time you can't really hide anything there. So I didn't have a sense of lesbianism as a complete exclusive lifestyle. Years later, after coming out and going back home, women who live there and in Canada told me there are a lot of lesbians there. I've met a few, but I think they are hard to find if you don't know who they are.

I remember as a girl being very attracted to women's bodies. I felt embarrassed about it. I felt the urge to openly admire women was very perverted, something I didn't understand at the time. I wanted to look admiringly, openly, but somewhere I got the message that it was not acceptable. So I grew up not being a 100% aware of lesbianism as encompassing those desires. I was not 100% in tune with my own lesbianism. But, when I discovered it, believe me there was no turning back. What a relief to be able to look! I have never regretted it. I am enjoying myself. Living as a lesbian has been the happiest time of my life. I really enjoy being a lesbian, getting to know other lesbians out there, getting to know other Black lesbians, being friends with them, and being able to share my story with them.

How liberating

I love going to the bar. I go to the bar to dance, to be in the space, around women, to see women cruising women, women hugging and kissing women, women dancing, close and tight with each other. I know there is this unspoken rule that you are going to the bar to be picked up or to pick up someone. Even though there are times when I hope somebody would approach me, that has never been my experience. I have never been approached or sent a drink. I like going because I like dancing. I love going to lesbian dances. What I enjoy the most is being in a group of women just talking, hanging out, and joking with each other. I like the freedom of being able to express my liking for women. To me, that's what being a lesbian is all about. Being free to touch women, free to flirt with them, free to look at their bodies, fantasize about them and not have to suppress the fantasy. To be able to let my imagination go wild and not feel bad about it is the greatest freedom and pleasure. God, how liberating. That has been the positive thing about being a lesbian for me. I have really enjoyed coming out, and being out as a lesbian. I hope it's the same for most women, a good experience.

THEY CALLED LESBIANS ANTI-WOMAN
Mae

I was born in St. Kitts, second of seven (six girls and one boy). My mom went to England when I was about seven or eight. She left my oldest sister and myself in the charge of my grandmother, and she took the others. After my mother left, it wasn't any different because she hadn't been there all the time, from the very beginning. She went to Curaçao to work and had most of the kids there. So most of us weren't together at the same time. I stayed in St. Kitts 'til I was twenty-three.

IN ME I LIKED IT

I was brought up in the church, very religious. We weren't out much. In those days, they believed if you had a girl you had to keep her locked away. The only place I went to was school and church. We had friends, but they were from church. We did not "hang out." My grandmother thought two of us was enough. It didn't bother us none, we knew no better. The church gave us everything. You don't have sex before you get married, you don't have boyfriends. I stuck to those rules until I was twenty.

I didn't feel different from anybody else, even now I don't. When I was eighteen or nineteen, this woman took an interest in me. I met her at the hairdresser. I can't remember how it began, but she started coming to see me and taking me for drives. Nothing happened. Then somebody told my grandmother that she was a lesbian. My grandmother did not want to see her around me. They called lesbians "anti-woman." But, as far as I was concerned, she was a person. She was not doing anything. She was older than me. I liked her. She walked masculine, that was all. She looked feminine. Back home we don't wear pants to work. She wore pants after work, but not during work. She would pick me up in the evening, and we would sit and talk. And neck. In me, I liked it. But after, I realised it wasn't something I should be doing.

This older cousin used to come in the evening to watch TV. When she showed up to watch TV, I'd take off. My grandmother did not say anything, she was in the house. She did not see the woman. I saw that woman 'til I was twenty.

I met this guy who came to church, and we started going out. My woman friend and the guy had a fight over me. No sex happened between her and me, or him and me, because you are not supposed to do that, according to the church. I figured, why not see both? Then, I guess, I started seeing another woman as well. She was a nurse. So, I'm seeing three of them. I used to be a teacher. The school I taught at, you had to pass the nurses' quarters to get to the school. I met this girl at the nurses' quarters. She knew the other woman. She made the pass. I don't make passes at people. One evening the nurse and I were walking along the road (the nurses' quarters close at ten). I have the keys to the quarters. Up comes the first woman, grabs me and takes the keys away. I am saying, "Give the girl the keys, because when ten o'clock comes she can't get in."

She said she will give me the keys on the condition that I stay with her. So I stayed, and she gave her the keys. But time for me to go home, she won't let me go. My grandmother would lock me out. This guy that I know, who use to room with my boyfriend, came by and talked to her, asked her to let me go home. She won't. He went and got my boyfriend. He came and they had this squabble. She threatened to take him to court. Now, this have me really upset. If this thing end up in court — I'm a teacher — it's real scandalous. Anyway, she didn't do anything, but he told me not to ever speak to her again.

The thing then was to be married, me and the guy. A year later he left and came here. News travel real fast. He left, like Saturday morning, and by evening she was around looking for me. So we got back together. I was still seeing the nurse, and a lot of other people, too, discreetly. Most of them were nurses. They were not of marrying age. People did not know what was going on. We were just single young women getting a career.

I only knew four men that were obviously gay. Everybody knew, people spoke to them. Nobody paid too much attention them. I knew women who were real butch. People just accepted them. Just like her. Everybody accepted her as being that way. It's just that, as a young person, if you hung around with her, they automatically assumed. If you care about your reputation then you don't hang around with her, but by that time I had begun to not care what people think that much. I knew we were not having sex. I did not know about sex.

There was this one girl that taught at the same school where I taught. We were very good friends. Her boyfriend and my boyfriend left together. So we hung out. One evening, I ended up at her house. She lived at her mother. We were talking, and she started kissing me. I got really upset, because no one had kissed me like that before. I took off and did not talk to her for a while. But she was really serious about the whole thing. She started telling me she loved me, she wants me to break up with the guy. She was going to break up her engagement. I did not talk to her for a while, but she did not stop.

We had a short thing but we did not break up with our boyfriends. She used to come and sleep over. There was no penetration, she would just mount me and so on. And then the original woman started coming around again, because my boyfriend had gone. We had physical contact then. It was scary because she had another woman. We were at her house and who knows when her woman would have shown up. We could not go to my house, I was still at my grandmother's. That's how it was 'til I left.

COME, GET MARRIED, GET MY PAPER

I came to Canada at twenty-three, to meet my boyfriend. Somebody who saw me and this woman together told him, so he told me not to come. But then he changed his mind.

Originally, I did not tell anybody I was coming to get married. I told them I was coming to visit my sister who was in Montreal. But my grandmother started telling people, so it would have been embarrassing if I did not leave. I had told myself I would come, get married, get my paper and then leave him. I would leave him because he told me not to come in the first place.

When I eventually left, it was not vindictiveness. I stayed three and an half years. I could have been happy if he did not raise his hands. It might've lasted if he did not hit me, because during those three and a half years, I didn't think about women. Once I left him, I knew I was not going back. It takes me a while to make a move but once I do, there is no return.

I left my husband in April and got an apartment in June. Just before I got the apartment, I met his woman, a white woman who gave me her number and asked me to call, just like that. It turned out she was a lesbian, and I started seeing her. It was not a relationship, it was mainly physical. She wanted me to move in with her but I did not. I did not know how to explain it to my sister. Somehow I find the other people they are not like us, they don't care. I would try to make it not so obvious, but they don't care. It was an issue of discretion.

I went there every day. She was a lot older, too. She had a friend who kept trying to get me to go to the bar. One evening, just the two of us were together and she invited me to the bar, so I went. It was easier to go to the bar with a younger person. We ended up back at her place. Another evening, I went with her and she got really drunk, embarrassing me. I looked over and there was a woman staring at me and I thought, this is not me. The bartender came over and asked me what I was drinking, this woman wanted to buy me a drink. He pointed her out to me. I called her over and we talked. We managed to get my friend to the back of the car and dropped her home.

I picked up with the other one, who was from Montreal. She came here and was living with this Black girl who was seeing someone. We became good friends. Her lover used to treat her badly. She was married at the time and seeing this woman. One evening, I go to her place and the woman was there and she turned out to look really fine. Shuks, she looked really fine. She asked me for a drive home. We got to talk and I told her I have this rich white woman. She said to me, "I can take you out sometime?"

I said, "Sure," and I saw her a couple of times after that. Then all of a sudden she start calling me. We would talk for a long time. She was not as bad as I thought she was. She got married and we continued to see each other. I had keys to their house. People seem to think he knew. But I don't think so. I used to sleep in their house. It did not bother me that she was sleeping with him and with me. It did not bother me. I think she was bisexual. I consider myself exclusively lesbian. Anyway, I would not get involve with another bisexual again, but I was in love. We stayed together for seven years, then she died.

The bar seemed strange in that they had a space where they could hug and kiss and don't care. I don't think they acted different towards me as a Black woman. For me, the bar scene has changed. It is a place to go sometimes, not to go and pick up anybody there. Not Black women, they don't go to the bars. I go to the bar to meet my friends. People are more cautious about picking up people. Now I don't go to pick up people. The bar scene is really young. I am not interested in them. Someone told me once, when you have these young women they don't know what they want — I believe it. I met this young woman once. About three days into the relationship she told me she wants a kid. I don't want children.

Too old to hide

I am what I am but I don't think the world have to know. I am fine the way I am. For me it is not important to be a part of the community. For those who are political, issues like same sex spousal is worth addressing, but mostly it is white. In the political arena there is an exclusion anyway. I think they consider us immigrants.

Anything two people do when they are having sex is fine. For me, as long as I like it, that's fine. I am generally attracted to feminine women. I am not attracted to the butches. I like the lipstick, make-up, the works.

I am out to my family. My mother knows about me. I told my sisters and they told her, she told my aunt. They did not say anything to me. The thing that upset me is that my sister told my mom without talking to me. I decided to tell them because just recently this one sister came from England. She got a job. So, she is here and I figure I am too old to hide. If she is going to be around I don't want to hide.

I am out at work. Most of my friends are lesbians. I don't have straight friends. We have nothing in common. What am I going to talk to them about? I lived with a straight couple, they almost drove me crazy. She was always talking about her man and I could not talk to her about my problems, so I don't want to hear. To be a part of the hetero Caribbean community is tough. I have never been to social functions that the St Kittians have. That's one of the reasons I will never go back home to live. I can't live my life in privacy there. It's too small.

I Was Born the Day I Came Out

Angela Richards

I was born in 1960, in Kingston, Jamaica. I lived three years in Kingston, then my mother sent me to the country — Portland Long Road. Because my mother had to go to work in the city and look for a better, more stable life, I lived with my grandmother. There were seven of us living with my grandmother, plus four cousins. We lived in a two-bedroom house in the country. I am from a working class — or you could say poor — background. I guess it's all the same thing. Most of my life was spent in the country.

Looking Back

I did a lot of work, I can laugh about it now. I went two miles to go to school and to fetch water. Now it all sounds like fun, but, when I hear people say, "Let's go work on a farm," I think, aha aha I don't want to do that anymore, thank you. Working on a farm might sound very romantic and it probably is, but when you have no choice...

When I went to school in Jamaica, my school years were the best of my life. I was bright, very popular with both girls and boys, but mostly with the boys. I was tall and skinny and played a lot of sports. Very outgoing. I played roulette. I ran. They were good years.

Looking back, most of the women I knew were really strong women raising their children and other people's children. In Jamaica, if the mothers could not afford to keep their children, other family members would help care for them. I grew up with a strong sense of what it's like to be a woman. It was not only one woman doing it. Most women were doing it, so no one woman seem to stick out in my mind as being different. It is a small town and the women did every thing. Most of them were on their own. The guys, if they did not take off, were in the city working, or overseas working and sending money back.

There was this one woman, though, who was a cook. I can never recall seeing her with a man. She was pretty butch. She never got married, never had a man stick around. She did not need them, they did their deed and were off. You heard the word "sodomite" used sometimes, usually it was used if a guy called out to a girl and she dissed him. The guy would say, "Go 'way you dirty sodomite." Not because he had proof, but to make her feel bad. When I was in school we girls touched each other and played "feel up." Seemed natural then. There was no sense of guilt.

Culture shock

I was thirteen when I came to Canada to meet my mother. Talk about culture shock! I had not seen my mother in years. I started going to school here. Oh God, that was one of the worst times of my life. They put me a year back, because of my accent. They thought I was slow. Every time I opened my mouth the kids laughed, so I would not speak unless they asked me a question to which I could answer "yes" or "no." I tried not to speak. I lost my voice. All through high school, unless I was asked a "yes" or "no" question, I would not say anything. So there I am, outgoing smart and everything — and I regress. I start failing. I knew if I was home I would have done better. I was an excellent speller, I was good in math. I came here and it's like I was stupid because I couldn't keep up.

Also, the way you dress — my mother worked as a housekeeper, there were a lot of us — so we did not get the most beautiful clothes. That didn't help. There you are talking so-called funny, looking funny. No wonder my grades and self-confidence went down.

I never had problem with my identity. That is the good thing about being from a working-class family. You know you're Black, and you can't deny it. If you are from a middle-class family, you can get away with certain things, but when you are poor they tell you, "You're Black." A lot of people I know now are rediscovering their blackness. I did not have to do that. It's always been there. The thing I was a little uneasy about was my accent.

All through high school, I never dated a white man, never wanted to. During high school, I was very lonely. My mother is a good woman, she works hard. But when you have two, three jobs, you can't come home and kiss your kids. You don't have time to talk to them and to find out what is going on with them. You just want to come home and rest. So, there I was, not feeling good about myself, and of course guys are coming around, saying I look fine. And of course they want me to sleep with them, so I had a lot of boyfriends in high school. That is the only way I felt love.

I WANTED TO SLEEP WITH HER

The first time I realize that I really like a woman was when I went to Humber College. I was attracted to this woman in my class. I always knew when I went with guys that something was missing. I knew because even when they were making love to me I did not feel anything. But I did it anyway. God, sometimes when I think of the number of men I have slept with, I want to scream. About the waste, and not feeling anything.

I always admired women. The way they look, their brains. But, I did not see it in the context of sex. When I go to a movie the woman would be the one I am looking at. But I did not connect, I did not have anybody to help me make the connection. The school I went to was mostly Black, and all I was thinking of was survival. Sleeping with women was the furthest thing from my mind.

I admired this woman. I wished I was like her, smart like her. I was nineteen, at Humber College, when I realised I was not admiring the way this woman looked. I wanted to sleep with her. She was a Black woman. She was very straight, but something about her... Like most of us, I was raised in a very religious home. Believed in God and so on. So now, there is a lot of confusion and hating myself, thinking I am a bad person for thinking those things. Plus I was failing school. Later I learned I am dyslexic, but all those things were happening and I had no one to talk to.

Anyway, I would make sure I sat beside her and asked if she can help me with my work. We tried to be friends, we were polite acquaintances. We did not get the chance to develop anything more. I was failing, and my home life was not great.

I was sharing a room with my sister. One day she said something to me, something stupid. I don't know what it was, but I snap. Next thing I know my hand was round her neck. My mother came and said, "Angela, what's going on? Tell me, what's going on? This is not like you, tell me now."

But I did not say anything, I just shook and shook.

So she said, "You think you are a woman, just pack your things and get out."

Of course, I am out on my arse. I phoned my other sister and told her I needed to stay at her place for a while. I stayed with her for a while, but she was married. One day I woke up and her husband was standing over me with a hard-on. He told me he found me attractive, so then I knew it was time to move. From there I started moving all over the place.

Now I quit school because I can't afford to go to school anymore. After a while I decide this lesbian thing is not for me. I started going back to men. Started dating them like crazy, around and around. Started working in a factory because I had to pay my rent. After a while the feeling for women started to come back, because you can't suppress it for long. I was dreaming. I had this one boyfriend for two year. I had this magazine under my bed that I had to look at first, before I could let him touch me, every time he made love to me. So I would masturbate before he came over. I would have an image of a woman in my head and I would be ready. He was a good guy, he was kind, but I knew I could not do it anymore. And it was not fair to him either.

Call 923-Gays

When I was twenty-two, I was looking through the paper, and it said, "If you think you are gay, call 923-GAYS." I called them and they gave me the 519 Community Centre's Monday night group. That was Friday. I tell you, the days from Friday to Monday were the longest. I went on the Monday. The group met at seven o'clock. I got there at five or five-thirty. I was so anxious I walked around, back and forth. Then I decide to go in.

It was one of the scariest things I have ever done. The group was 99% white, with one or two Black women, and we did not want to see each other. We were afraid we would run into each other on the street, that sort of thing. A white woman came up to me, she was very nice. I needed that because I was unsure. She talked to me. I was wearing a skirt and heels and playing with my bag, looking so nervous. She said, "It's okay, everybody is nervous the first time." She kind of took me under her wing. There was nothing sexual because I really did not need anything sexual. Mark you, I would have had sex with her, just for the fact that she was so good to me, but it was very good that she didn't make any advances. That is not what I needed. I needed a friend.

The first woman I slept with was a white woman. I met her through that group. It was good enough for me to say, "Yes, yes, yes. This is what I want." It was a woman, and at the time I wanted a woman so bad I did not think about the fact that she wasn't my type. I was starving. If you have not eaten in four days or so, give you anything and you will eat it. I was shy and she was good, because I told her it was my first time and she did most of the work. If I had to do most of the work, I would have freaked out. It was a one-time thing. The next day she said, "Angela, I am sorry I crossed the boundary. All I want is friendship."

I was pretty pissed off, she should have told me this before. You know how it is when you just come out, you are so naive you will believe anything. I was hurt for a while, because I was starving and looking for love all these years.

I went to the group for about a year or so then I heard about LOC: Lesbians Of Colour. That is when I met lesbians of colour and I realised this is where I wanted to be. I will always be grateful to the 519 Community Centre. If it was not for them I would not have known where else to go. They were the stepping-stone to women in the Black community.

When I went to LOC I suffered another culture shock. There were these women, they were brilliant, smart and sexy. I wanted them all. I had crushes on almost everybody. But with that came disappointment, because I felt stupid again. Being around them was like, "Let me find my dictionary..." So, there was a sadness with that experience, too. I clearly did not fit in there either.

I did not understand what was going on. I did not stick around too long, because I did not feel smart enough, did not know what was going on, wasn't political enough. I think I made one friend. That's changing.

I'm slowly coming out, I came out to my mother, to my best friend, and to one of my sisters. When you choose to come out there can be sadness also. I felt as if I was living a double life, things are never going to be the same again. My family and friends took it well, but the sense of family I wanted to have was not there. I wanted to be able to talk to someone when I was coming out, especially my younger — we were very close. We lost that, we could not talk. I felt resentful. I would go for months without calling them because I felt, "I can't be myself, so why bother?"

COMMUNITY

I am going to different events so I can be aware of what is going on. I go to events in the community, different speeches. I am reading up on different books, like Alice Walker and all those Black writers that I had never heard about before. I came out, so I can at least know what is going on and fit into the community. I feel that is a prerequisite for being in the community, which is kind of sad. I think I am a very political person. People might say not, but I don't think you have to be a writer or whatever to be political. I mean I admire those women who are, I think they do a lot. But I think there are also other people who can make up the community. And I just wish they could be more respectful and open, not as condescending and not just use us for volunteer work. Respect us. If I say to you I work in a factory, I want you to give me the same respect as if I write a book. I did not find that was there. I went to a lot of events, and it is not just me. I have talked to a lot of women who don't go to so-called political or women events. That is one of the reasons they stay away. They might think you selling out, but that is not it. You go where you get respect.

There is a community, but there are strings attached to that community. You have to follow the rules, believe in the same politics, listen to the same music. Don't question. If I see a woman doing something wrong, I can't say, "Listen I think what you are doing to that person is wrong." It doesn't mean I don't like you anymore. I love you, but as a friend, as a Black woman, what you are doing to another Black woman is wrong. I think for me I couldn't be a part of that.

Friends make up my community. I have friends I've had for ten years, since I came out. Ninety percent of my friends are lesbians. I have a couple of Black male gay friends, and I am trying to find more. I have straight friends who know, because I can't have friendship with somebody who don't know. I don't want to limit myself to Black lesbian feminists. I need different things from different people.

The bar is important to me because I love dancing. I think if I had money growing up I would have studied to be a dancer, dancing is one of my passions. When I dance, I feel good. Dancing gives me the sense that I am good at something. When I am on the dance floor I feel free, I feel good and loved. I block everybody else out. I needed the bar to dance. I enjoy myself, but when I open my eyes, I see it is all white, the music is still not my music. I compromise, dance to music which, back home, I would not move my foot to.

I don't enjoy being looked at and women thinking, "I would not mind sleeping with her," (and that is all they want) so I never went to the bar looking for a relationship. I went there to fulfill the need to be with other lesbians. I get the look, I get a phone number, I get the feeling of being attractive. I understand why some people like to strip or whatever. It is the only time you get any love or any appreciation. There is nothing wrong with wanting to get appreciation for the way you look. Sometimes I feel guilty for feeling that way, especially when I first came out. I would think to myself, I should just enjoy.

When I go to certain dances, I censor myself, especially when I dance to reggae music. I get the sense that people think, "Why is she going on so?" I think people think it is a lower-class thing to dance in a certain way. Maybe it is just me being over-sensitive, but sometimes I sense that when I get on a dance floor and want to get on bad that people wonder why I get on so.

Coming out, I don't think I will ever experience that excitement, that challenge, again. I will not ever experience those same emotions again. It's like I was reborn that day. I was born the day I came out. It's been good. There is a lot of negative in our community but there is a lot of good. I want to thank all the women, especially the Black women, who paved the way for me to *be*, who were out there, who are visible, who put a name to the personal experience of being a dyke. Yes, with respect and love.

GROWING UP A LESBIAN IN ST. LUCIA

Pulcheria Theresa Willie

I was born on the tiny island of St. Lucia in the West Indies in 1966. My family of five sisters and three brothers was raised by a single parent, with the help of my grandma. I live on Long Island in the U.S., with my wife Donna and daughter Trina.

Growing up on St. Lucia in the seventies and eighties, "lesbian" was an alien word. I knew I was different, but I couldn't understand why. In my early teens, I yearned to speak to someone who could tell me why I was feeling the way I did. There were no words in my vocabulary to express the way that I felt. I only knew that I didn't feel comfortable around men. At first, I thought it was because there was never a father figure around, and though I had three brothers, I never felt that closeness to them. This made me crazy. I felt alienated and wondered if I was suffering from a chemical deficiency. All my girlfriends were attracted to and only spoke of boys. "Yuk," I hated that.

AN ALL GIRLS' SCHOOL

When I turned thirteen, I was transferred to an all girls' secretarial school. I was happy because I knew that my only contact with men, would be with my brothers. As time went by, I was chosen to spend the weekends at the school to improve on my typing skills. This meant that I would be around the principal a lot more, which was great, for I had a crush on her. Whenever she spoke to me, there was a tinkling in my inside. It was weird, I had never felt this way around anyone before.

With my inquiring mind, though still shy, I was determined to learn more about her. I asked around, and learnt that she was not married, but lived instead with her lover, another woman. I was flabbergasted. There I was, still unsure of the word used to describe women who loved women, but I felt relief. There was someone else like me in St. Lucia and she was my principal. I believed then that I was normal. Also, the way I felt about her was not imaginary, but I knew nothing would come of it.

During the remainin' four years at the school, I matured into a wonderful young lady. I was still trying to find myself, but had gained much reassurance from my principal that I was normal as any of the other girls at the school. I shared a special bond with both my principal and her lover. This mainly came about because I had a keen interest in learning and accomplishing my goals without letting peer pressure control me. And also because we all shared something — loving other women. It was from them that I learnt the word "lesbian." I was a lesbian, and was very proud.

I wanted to learn more about this lifestyle, and was also eager to meet with other lesbians, but all was so quiet. I couldn't understand the reason. There I was, filled with so many questions but no answers. I started on a long journey of disappointment, love and hurt.

I WOULD NOT LIVE MY LIFE TO PLEASE ANYONE

This quiet lifestyle haunted me until I was eighteen years old when I had my first encounter with a real lesbian, a woman who was open about her sexuality. It was Christmas of 1984. I'll call her Kay. She was a radio broadcaster then, and as rumours had it, the biggest queer in St. Lucia, and very popular. I had written to her and anticipated a dead end, so when I received a letter from her, I was taken aback. Because I was not familiar with any gay clubs, or even hangouts, I was unsure of our first date, which she arranged. I was taken to this cosy little restaurant called Virgo, near the beach. The name was as neat as the place. I learnt that it was owned and operated by a gay couple. They were very handsome and had such a great sense of humour that before long, my nervousness had disappeared, I relaxed and enjoyed my date.

Kay was 22 years my senior, and was in the process of ending a relationship that she had been in for about six years. I didn't really care about that, for the only thing I was interested in was forming a friendship. Our conversation was lively, as we were able to speak about everything. She was taken by my intelligence and I felt really proud. Our conversation was centred on one topic especially — why gays and lesbians lived such quiet lifestyles. I was given the explanation which went like, "Our society was a God-fearing people, and in their eyes, lesbians and gays were considered evil." I didn't understand it then, but vowed that I would not live my life to please anyone. I also promised myself to be open as to whom I was, a wonderful person who just happens to love women. This seem to have made quite an impression on her, and I knew then that we would be friends for a long time. Our date ended happily, we both made promised to keep in touch.

I felt on top of the world. I had met this wonderful woman, and she was a lesbian. It was difficult for us to see each other because of our work schedules, but we spoke to each other on the phone every day, and wrote letters whenever we thought of each other. Our friendship was beginning to develop into something more, which my mom didn't like.

She was against the relationship. She had formed her own conception of this person whom she had never met, except for the rumours she heard. Up to this day, I never really know how my mom knew of my sexual orientation. She told me things like, "Kay is much older than you, and would lead you astray. She is just the kind of woman who uses young girls for her own gain, and ends up throwing them aside when she has had enough." She also brought up the Bible thing. Like, "You were brought up a Christian, and know what the Bible says about women like that. The only place they will end up is hell." Yes, I was brought up a Christian, and yes I had read the Bible, but never once had I seen anywhere that God will hate me for loving another human being. I asked my mom what the difference was between loving a woman and loving a man. She couldn't answer. So like any teenager, I rebelled. This caused much friction between my mom and myself, so I decided to get my own apartment. She made a big deal about it by crying and begging me not to leave her home — which was heart-breaking — but I had to do what I felt was best for me. It was a big move, and it was sad. But I believe if that had not happened, my mom and I may have not had this wonderful relationship today.

As my relationship with Kay progressed, we were spending all our time together, and it became difficult just being friends. My first kiss came unexpectedly. We were having dinner at my house, when my fork fell to the floor. I bent over to get it, and when I raised my head, Kay kissed me. It was an intense kiss, which took my breathe away. I had never been kissed in such a way before, and I trembled. It was great. This would be the night that I would never forget. It was my first sexual experience ever, and I was scared. I did not know what to do, so I just laid there. Kay sensed that something was wrong, and thought I did not want to make love to her. She felt foolish, and I had to assure her that it had nothing to do with her, but because this was my first time, I was scared. She told me to relax and everything will come naturally. I did, and everything happened at once, this sensational feeling came over me, which was so overwhelming, it was like my heart stopped beating. It felt very, very good. It was a perfect night and Kay made me feel like a real woman. "I am a lesbian for sure now," I said to myself.

I thought I was in love with Kay after that night. Everything was so wonderful. She took such good care of me then, she showered me with love (so-called), gifts, and plenty of attention. It all felt normal for about fourteen months, until I found myself suffocating. It was like I was in this hole, and every time someone passes, they would throw in some dirt. I wanted to scream, but I couldn't. What was happening to me? I couldn't understand. "I have to put my life in perspective," I said to myself that night. I took a pen and paper and started writing what was going on in my life, and what I would do to fix it.

I realized that I no longer had any friends, except for my co-workers. I never went anywhere without Kay. The only persons calling me were my sisters, and everything I was used to doing, I no longer did. My co-workers teased me constantly about how Kay brought me to work, called to see with whom and where I was having lunch, and was there fifteen minutes early every day to pick me up. She would even send someone to get me if she was working late. I took all this for love. How stupid I had become! I had become a puppet on a string, just doing all what Kay wanted me to do. I no longer had dreams of my own. It was sad. I decided to speak to Kay about it that very night.

Making my feelings known to Kay, I expected some kind of compromise, but what I got from her was total denial. It was like I was making up everything. She didn't understand why I wanted a life different from what we had. She believed that I was seeing someone else. This was heart-breaking, and I cried. I couldn't believe that she would think that way, and I did not like it, so I made myself be heard. I said to her, "I am my own person, with my own dreams which I would like to fulfill. I do not want to live in your shadow but I would like you to be by my side to help me grow into the woman I would like to become. I want your support, not your handouts. And if you are not willing to do that, please let me go." It was then that I saw a side of Kay which frightened me.

She said these words with so much rage, "If you think you are going to leave me for someone else, you had better think long and hard about it. For you may never live to have a normal life." I was astonished, but held my own. I asked her to leave and never come back. She did, and I didn't hear from hear her until the following morning.

She tried apologizing and asked me to forgive her, but I had already made up my mind and ended the relationship. It was a sad move, but I knew it was for the best. I was twenty years old by then, I had matured both physically and mentally. I knew what I wanted out of life and was going after it. I had made other lesbian and gay friends, and hung out with them once in awhile. During that time, I tried pursuing other relationships, but nothing came of them. Most of the women I met were either too young or didn't know what they wanted from life. Because there were no outlets for lesbians, finding the perfect woman was a drag. The few I did know stuck to themselves, and it was boring.

All this changed about nine months later when I entered a pharmacy. I saw this amazing and most beautiful woman. I wanted to know who she was, so I made up this fake stomach pain and wanted the pharmacist to help me out. Wasn't I taken aback when she was introduced to me. I was speechless for about a minute or so when she spoke. She told me her name and she was ready to help if she could. There was this gentleness in her voice, to soothe any pain. I told her the same story of the (fake) stomach pains, and she did help. Little did I know that this would be the beginning of a wonderful relationship. I became her instant customer, and passed by every day just to see her face.

I wanted to know everything about her, so I wrote her a letter telling how beautiful I thought she was, and I would like to become her friend. She did reply, and this made my future look a lot brighter. We had our first formal date a week later. It was wonderful, but discouraging. I learnt of her age, which was 15 years my senior, this was all right with me, but when I learnt of the woman living with her, I was disappointed. Here I had finally met the woman of my dreams, intelligent, hard-working and beautiful. She possessed a great sense of humour, and cared for everyone. She had someone else, and I couldn't stand it. I was scared but pursued her anyway.

We continued seeing each other, and I was able to learn more about the other woman. She told me she had been with her for almost ten years, and right now, they were like sisters, rather than lovers. I didn't buy into this, but I was so in love with this woman that nothing else mattered. Everyone noticed the changed in my attitude, which was glowing. They didn't give me much encouragement. They all thought I was invading a relationship of a lifetime, and would eventually be hurt. I couldn't fathom this possibility. When I looked at this woman, I saw perfection.

Our relationship became very serious. This woman was my dream, my life, my love. She made me smile when I felt sad, she turned my grey skies to sunshine. She guided me in pursuing my goals. She allowed me to be my own person, and accepted me as the person I was with my flaws. She showered me with me with love so unconditionally that most time I would pinch myself to see if I was just dreaming. I loved her too, so very much, and I wanted her in my life forever. And for a while, I thought she would be.

My first sexual encounter with her happened about six months into our relationship. It was heavenly. It was like magic. Time stood still for those two glorious hours, which seemed like an eternity. I felt loved from my head to my toes. Our hearts, minds, bodies and souls became one that night. I have cherished this magical moment ever since.

We spent every spare moment together after that. Our minds were so in tune with each other that I would be at home longing for her voice and the phone would ring, and it was her. I would dream that she is standing by my bed, and when I open my eyes, she would be there. My life was happy. I felt fulfilled. I never dreamt of the day when we wouldn't be together. We had a wonderful and fulfilling relationship for three years, without a clue that something was wrong. When she broke up with me, my life ended.

I was in a state of total panic. I couldn't understand anything except that I was hurting — really, really hurting. There wasn't a soul in the world who could help me. I alienated myself from my family and friends. The only thing I did normally was work, and I still wonder how I managed that. I was in a trance, I couldn't sleep or eat. I did not have the will to go on. Nobody really knew what was wrong because I hid myself. My mom came to visit one day and I hid in the bathroom at work, I couldn't let her see my hurt. I did not want her to know how right she had been, and I was indeed paying for my sins. She did not get to see me that day, or for a very long time after that. I always found an excuse to prevent her from coming by. Those were the saddest times in my life. It was like a bad dream that would soon go away, but it never did. What did I do wrong? Is being a lesbian a bad thing? Was this the hell my mom had said I would end up in? I did not know, and there was no one to tell me. I was lost.

Fulfilling my Dreams

I had to find some peace in my life, to fill the void of my true love. I did not want another relationship, not for a long time at least. So the next best thing was to fulfill one of my dreams. I opened up my own pre-school. I had been saving up for this for such a long time and had been promised help from my dream lover. She wasn't around anymore, but it felt right. The new venture took a lot of my spare time, so there was little time to feel hurt. I was consumed, determined to have my first student on the first day of school the following year. It was January 1990. I welcomed my first little one, and the world around felt brighter. My grief was overcome by joy. My life was changed for the better.

The little ones made my days worth looking forward to, and my nights, I filled with plans for tomorrow. The hurt never left me, but at least I felt alive again. I had many lesbian and gay friends as well as straight, but felt lonely. I longed for someone else in my life, but no one measured up to my last love. I remained single for the next three years.

Change and Emigration

Things have changed considerably in St. Lucia over the years. Lesbians are more open about their sexuality, especially the young ones. Still, society believes that lesbians are going through a phase, and will get over it in time. They still think that if the right man comes along, we will go to him. I think St. Lucians are still in the homophobic state because of lack of education.

My life has changed too. I was still so very unhappy, in spite of all what I had accomplished. There was still this hole in my heart, and I longed for some change. I decided leaving home would do me some good, if not mentally at least physiologically. I came to the United States of America, the land where "freedom reigns." It wasn't easy at the beginning, and I felt lost in a world filled with chaos. I longed to meet another lesbian. Well, this changed when I found a newspaper and browsed through the personal ads. It was wonderful. I thought it would be nice to meet a woman of a different culture and background. I did meet that person, and we have been together ever since. It has been four years, and we are now married.

Coming to the U.S. has been an experience in itself. I have grown and have broadened my horizons in many aspects of my life. I have gone to places which were just a dream. I have also met many other lesbians and gays, gone to functions, clubs, the Parade, etc. I still realize that homophobic people are found everywhere. With everything America has to offer, they are still far behind in accepting a lifestyle where love rules.

My dream now is to help educate my fellow St. Lucians. I know we are a people full of love and tolerance. Through education, younger lesbians and gay youth may find some kind of solace.

THE REAL EROTICA
Gerri

I was born in Antigua, which is divided into a lot of parishes. I was born in the parish of Saint John. Then I moved to a rural district, Barnes Hill, about five minutes away from the airport. I grew up with my parents. I am the second of seven kids (three girls and four boys).

MY MOTHER IS THE BACKBONE

My mother is the backbone of the family. Actually, in my family, all the women are the backbone of their families. We have one uncle around and I really have a bond with him.

I went to school in Barnes Hill. I grew up in a family house, basically with my grandmother. My mother left us in the early sixties, when my last brother was about ten months old. She had to run, leave my father because he was abusive, lashing out at my mom for petty things. As a young girl, I growing up seeing that kind of abuse. He was not physically abusive to his kids, it was more or less my mom. She went to the Virgin Islands for a number of years. I think they smuggled her out of the country because she stabbed him. She had to defend herself. My grandmother sent her away.

My grandmother took us over for a number of years. My mom came back in the late sixties and took care of us. She built her house on an uncle's property and then she took us over. My father is still alive. I don't have a relationship with my father but I do my daughterly duty.

Going to school in the Caribbean

I had a good schooling. I went through the public school system in Antigua, which was a strong system in those days. But there were a number of prejudices. Antiguans are very proud people. Not only are they prejudiced against their own people, but also against other countries. Going to school, if you are within a certain bracket, if you are Mrs. So-and-so's daughter or son, then they look at you as a pillar of the community. My mother had a lot of status until she separated from my father. When she left him, the public school started to single me out. From then, I grew up with this attitude against the people who are in charge. Because I've seen students who can excel in school kept back and students who did not have the potential at all put forward. I was caught up in that system, because I was a child — not delinquent — who did not stand for nonsense. In those days you could not speak back to your teacher. I guess I did not care. I had the basic education, I was sent to a primary school, I was not forced into the public school. It turned out okay.

Going to school in the Caribbean, you had to be polished. My uniform was the longest in the class. I was a skinny child growing up, very slender. For some reason, I never liked to expose my skin at all. My legs have to be covered. Anywhere else can be exposed, but I don't like to show my legs. I was so thin in those days, they used to mock me and call me names like "Bones." After a while, as a child hearing those things, you become very self-conscious. In a sense it's a blessing that they ridiculed me, because I learned to appreciate a lot of things in life. I learned to be strong and independent.

That won't be me

I was always in a gang of girls. A bunch of us clustered together in parties, and we would go on a drunken binge on a Saturday. We would be on the school ground, laying on each other and playing. I knew then that I was "kinky" because of how I felt about this girl. At the same time I tried to develop a relationship with the opposite sex. It was always a bother. I never showed much interest in the male counterparts. I don't identify with them. Even at a young age, having sex with men was always, like, get you sweetness then get up and go about your business — on my part. Going in the company of females feels so much better. That behaviour was not acceptable. It wasn't. Growing up in the West Indies, it was terrible. Even though you hear stories about Mrs. So-and-so, or the lady live up the hill she . . . they used to call it man-woman.

My grandmother had a lot of livestock and what we called a plantation. She grew her own crops. There was lots of food and milk. I didn't see myself in a feminine role. I grew up as a tomboy. As a young child I was never groomed in the feminine fashion. I did everything a boy could do and better. It created a problem. I use to get a lot of spanking for it, especially when I stayed out late at night in the street playing ball or cricket. Or I was gone some place to play marbles, climb trees or take the donkey for a ride. Come back and get my arse whipped. I was never at home. Which is not acceptable for a girl.

I looked at it as a learning experience. I have seen what is happening, how men exploit the women in my village, how the women tend to use their bodies in a sort of economic reason. Like, "If I sleep with you tonight I will get twenty dollars to buy sugar for my kids." And I'd go to bed at night and I'd think, that won't be me. If a guy gets a girl pregnant, he'd deny the child, deny everything. Then the girl go find herself involve with another guy and pregnant again. Next thing you know, she find herself with six kids, six different fathers. And I said that couldn't happen to me.

I had a mother who was a champion, built like a boxer. A very strong and powerful mother. Also, a powerful, strong and independent grandmother. My grandmother was very religious. She taught us a lot: what is important in life, values, how to respect other people. Basically, she taught us everything she knew in her way, in those days. At the same time, it was, "Do this and do that." You had to sit there and learn to wash and cook and clean. I grew up very domesticated, in a sense that is a "plus." I was the oldest at home, so I had to look after my other brother and sisters. As a child, I had a lot of responsibilities.

You yearning for that tender touch

There were older women in my village that I heard used to have an attraction to my grandmother. There was one lady who was very masculine and very domineering. There was stories that she used to screw my grandmother, but it was never proven. The men in the village used to curse this woman, saying nasty things about her. As I grew older and did some research, I really understand what they were talking about. The disapproval came from the men. They are the ones who would take issue and carry it around the village.

In 4-H Club we used to go to St. Kitts. There use to be these women from St. Kitts. I remember as young girls, we used to peek through the door and see these women making love and kissing. I remember this woman Mavis, making love to a member of my gang. She was really making it, naked in that room. I remember peeking through and I started to get a headache. That was the first time I felt so darn good.

My mother worked in the airport. She brought a book home, it was basically a lesbian novel. I don't remember what it's called but I remember reading this darn thing, and all I felt was my private parts being aroused. I felt so horny that day, I just laid in bed and screwed myself. Every time I take up that book and read a chapter I would get all hot and juicy. Then I went out and got laid. But I got laid on my terms. I used to lay on the guys and screw them. I never let anyone lay on top of me. Then, when I have my bang bang bang, I just thank you. They would say, "Where you going? Where you going? I am not finished."

I would say, "But I am, and I am gone." I used to exploit the boys in my village, just call them and screw.

Being a lesbian was not about sex. It was after I reach my teenage years I understand how to be loved, how to feel love. Basically, no male ever showed me. I guess if I was romanced in such a way that made me feel good from a male, probably I would. But being seduced by a female was one of the most joyous occasions of my life. The female was able to explore every angle of your body and bring out the real erotica in you. Whereas the men, all they do is squeeze your breast, stick their finger in your pussy, get an erection and ride you to kingdom come. When they are finished, you are still laying down hot and dry. Then when you say you are ready, they are snoring. You have to lay beside them and masturbate yourself 'til you have that joy. At the same time, inside, you yearn for something more. You yearning for that tender touch. Something soft spoken in your ears. Someone to tell you how beautiful you are, and how good you are. But if you try to tell a male a certain part excite you, or you like it this way, they look at you as a whore. Whereas you just trying to tell them you know your body, that this is what you like and the way you would like it done.

When I got to my twenties the women I befriended were always older than me. The woman who seduced me was an older woman. At home, the partitions are not high, they go three quarters of the way. I remember lying in the bed with this woman naked and all you can see in the ceiling is you on the bed, and her father and mother in the other room. When I looked up, I said, "Is that me?"

And she said, "Oh my God, I think they've seen us."

I said to myself "I have to get out of here."

I met her through her sister. She was a woman who was also attracted to other women and obviously it was not her first experience. The night she fondled me, I almost jumped through the window. But she grabbed me back and asked me if I was going to go through the window.

I answered, "Why not?"

Playing with my other girlfriends in a group we do these things to one another but there was no actual sex involved. It was just fondling. But this woman put the charm on me. That burst everything wide open, that night.

At first I felt very awkward. I felt awkward because it was somebody twenty or thirty years older. She could have been my mother. I was a young girl and here was this older woman putting the hurt — I call it the hurt — on me. Aroused a feeling in me that was dormant for so long. I could not really explain it at all.

I knew it was not possible to carry on a relationship with a female. Growing up in my country, you would be singled out. Whatever feeling you had towards same sex, it would suddenly die. It would also burn you up inside, to know that you cannot express your love. At the same time, you don't know if your advances to that person would be received, and in what manner. It could ruin a friendship. Therefore, you do not press your luck or else your name might be around the village, bringing shame and disgrace on your parents. In those days, one had to be very careful.

With men it was acceptable, men are allowed to practice their sexuality or homosexuality openingly. You knew who they were. They worked, no one beat them up, and they were so-called respectable men, too. There were men singing in the choir in church, they were a pillar of the community. When they passed, they would say, "Anti-man," but that was that. But when they found out a woman have an attraction for another woman, it was different. I have a cousin that lived in another village that is also masculine and there are rumours going around that she is also a lesbian. The names they call her is awful. The way she is received she has no other choice but to go straight. To take people's mind off her, she even went and had a child.

I KNEW DEEP DOWN INSIDE

I came out in Canada at about twenty-four. I was living with a friend and I had a relationship with another friend. Soon after I came I was reading a paper and I saw this want-ad section. I remember asking a woman that I worked for what all these ads were about. She said I must be careful because they are kinky people. I said, "Kinky," and laughed.

I started answering ads in the paper and met people. Some I liked, others I did not really like. I did not really practice a lot, because I was doing a live-in job and did not really have privacy until I went on my own.

I knew deep down inside that I was a lesbian. It wasn't scary. It was more scary having to deal with that feeling at home than abroad. In a sense, no one know who you are, you are able to explore more. You have all the time you need to get to know who you are. I went about trying to find out who I am and what this thing is all about.

I basically met West Indians through the ads, I tend not to get involve with whites. I see myself as a private person and they are more liberal than I was. And I don't know how discreet they would be, especially since I was looking after kids. With the need for discretion in the way I conduct myself in a country I don't know nothing about, and without many friends, I always felt the West Indian would be more discreet than the average black or white Canadian. The people I met were very discreet. I would single them out. Usually professional West Indians, single women who were desperately seeking a female counterpart. Inside they are suffering, struggling with this feeling that they can't express openly. There is a large population of West Indian women in this country, who are lesbian and who are highly professional but are basically hiding because of the job or status they hold. Or they might be married or their family don't accept this type of behaviour.

The meetings were mostly indoors, in the home. We would have dinner and talk about growing up. Or go to places of interest, to the theatre. One woman would pay my cab fare to commute back and forth, to keep her company. She was a very popular woman, a chartered accountant. Such nice-looking West Indian women just sitting at home, dying inside because they cannot have a relationship with anyone, or they are afraid of who they will get themselves involved with. It's a shame.

Society thinks being a lesbian is a dysfunction. We have different genetic make-up. I think mine is half and half, and the dominant side is male. We are born with "x" amount of hormones inside of us and we cannot do anything about it. We can't pump lots of female hormone in our body so we can remain feminine. We can't pump more male so that we can be more masculine, so I have an imbalance which I wouldn't change. This is how I feel and I wouldn't change at all. There are times when the male side dominate the female side of me. If I was to say in the long term I would go back in a relationship with a man, it would be a domineering kind of relationship. I cannot see myself as a woman who wash, cook and clean for a man. At my age, if I don't know what I want, then I won't know. I made up my mind years ago, this is what I am and I am quite comfortable with the way I am.

I think my mother knows. I didn't tell her. My younger sister knows, so do an aunt and a cousin. I did not tell my brother. I've learned from friends that if you volunteer information to your family, it can create a problem. My mother tend to drop a line here and there. But she love me for who I am, I don't think I will lose that love. I have an open dialogue with her but I just don't discuss my life with her. There are times when she say I should get married, I should get this and that. And I say, "You were married to my father and he gave you seven kids and beat the shit out of you — and where are you today? Do you have him? No. Look how hard you have to work. If this is the life that I want, I am entitled to live it. And if you see me as less of a daughter, then that's you. If you accept me for who I am, I will be the best daughter you can ever hope for."

My sister is cool. She knows everything. I introduce my partner to almost every member of my family and they receive her very well. They probably take it as a friendship — except my sister and aunt. One year, my aunt educated my mother as to what lesbianism is all about. My mom said, we are nasty. That is her reaction, and that's it. I don't think my mother knows she is the one that is making her daughter cry.

A PRIVATE PERSON

I applaud the gay community for fighting. I don't see myself as an advocate, but if there is any community work, if there is a function, I will support it. Maybe because I am a private person, I don't want to see my picture or my face on camera. According to my friends I'm seen as a straight person. I don't really care if they know I am a lesbian — in my life, what I do is my business. And I never like the idea of flaunting my sexual behaviour or preference to the rest of the world. I see West Indians and Canadians as being ignorant as to your genetic make-up or predisposition. It is quite possible that not everyone can grow up to be heterosexual or live within the norms of society. If you don't live within the norms then you are considered to be dysfunctional or maladapted.

I have never experienced homophobia or been ridiculed about my preference because I manage to keep my life private. I separate my private from my social life in the work-place. I have a number of people who work with me and I am their boss. I have to be careful with what I do, because being gay or lesbian can have its drawbacks, and the majority of my staff are female. I have to be very careful in what I say, my body language, even touching, so that I am not ridiculed or accused of something. The way I conduct myself at work is in a professional manner.

Coming out is the most positive thing because I am relax. I should say it is a stress-free relationship. You encounter the same amount of arguments, as you do in straight relationships, but the arguments are softer, do not have the same tone. I would not say there is no abuse in lesbian relationships. But because women speak more and express themselves more than men do, we are able to rectify an argument.

I like my relationship. God knows, I have had a number of relationships. I am known around the city. I thought I was conducting myself in a discreet manner until I met an older woman from Barbados and introduced her to one of my toys. It's a lesbian sexual toy that I use to "play it safe" when I meet someone for the first time. I did not know that it left such a good impression. My name was all over. I have a bad name now — the fucker — as in good lover. I am ashamed. I thought I do it privately.

I like the mystery of my life. It's more intriguing. It leaves lots of people guessing. I like it and will cherish it for the rest of my life. I am who I am. I am quite happy and comfortable with my life and who I am. There are lots of lesbians who have up-and-down relationships, and it's a shame, not only as a lesbian but as a female. If you can't bear out a relationship with someone, then it all defeats the purpose. There are women who go from one relationship to the next — in search of what? I don't like that at all. If society see us as a group within a group who are stable, I think they will accept us. But if they see us as jumping partner to partner to partner, we are not showing any example. How can they give us the green light, when we are not stable? I'd rather stay with the person I am with. Whatever rough seas we have to sail, I think we can sail it together. We don't live together and maybe that's a plus. We have separate families and, so as not to cause a rift between the families, we have two apartments. But we share finances and other things together. If my family is here I can vacate my place and stay with her.

Fuck society

I don't think there will ever be a situation where lesbians will congregate in Antigua because it is a male-dominated country. A lesbian in Antigua have to be in the upper-scale income bracket. It more or less have to be women who control the finances, women who control the economics of the country. I don't go home to look for love or flirt, I go to visit family and friends. It's a small country, everybody knows everyone.

I think it is wrong for women who are lesbians to force themselves into relationships. I have seen women who marry and have kids, and after they have the children, they don't want to have anything to do with the men at all. Growing up in the West Indies, I've seen women who sleep in one room, the man sleep in the other, and they have all those kids. There is no love. I couldn't do that. If you know you don't love, don't do it because society say you must have two-point-whatever kids, a house and all those other things. I say fuck society. Whatever society dishes out for you is basically crap. You have to know what you want and what your life is all about, and do it.

MY ENTIRE BEING
Camile

I was born in Jamaica. I had a child at eighteen, and left for Canada at twenty. That was in the sixties. I worked in Canada for a number of years before returning to Jamaica to go to university. Then I came back to Canada and went to graduate school.

LIVING IN THE CARIBBEAN

I think a lot of Caribbean people live a bisexual lifestyle. If I was asked to identify myself, that is what I would identify as. If I had to put a label, I would put the label bisexual, mainly because I feel I would still sleep with men. I don't do it because I am in a relationship. But I am unlike my lover who says, "No I will not." We are at different stages on that.

I find Caribbean folks — men and women — live a bisexual life, even though they would prefer to be with their own sex, because of the pressures of the society. Who wants to be isolated, especially in the Caribbean? So you would have this main life, which is with your opposite sex partner and your children, and then you would have this other life. I don't think it is easy to live an entirely gay life in the Caribbean. Especially if you are not wealthy. Because I think you are really isolated.

I think in some ways there is another approach for me. Because of the whole economic status of women and their dependence on men I think that women in the Caribbean are indoctrinated to be competitive about the men. Even if the man is a piece of shit, you see all these women who are quite skilled, quite capable, fighting over this piece of garbage. Because you are less of a woman if you don't have a man. I think we are so trained to compete with each other over God knows what, that sometimes it is hard for the woman to have relationships. Whether they are heterosexual or lesbian, it is hard to overcome that training. And, even when they are lesbians, I find behaviour coming from that competitive place. To meet and relax and be together is very difficult. That's my observation.

I QUESTION THE NEED FOR ROLES

I don't want a man. I want a woman, but that woman does not have to be femme. I just want a woman, whoever she is. I question the need for roles. If you want to be femme it is because you choose to be. To have to play the role is questionable for me. I can see the beauty in playing the role, but to carry a particular role is not something that would interest me. What I find interesting, just observing, fewer Black women do the roles than white women, who clearly do the roles. I find that interesting. There are a few Black women that I see try to be butch. I don't know if they are butch or if they are playing at that, or if they are physically large or physically who they are. I have not seen any butches who have attracted me. I have seen a few who scare me. It is a certain kind of power that I find emanating that possibly might attract me, but I am not sure it would allow me to be myself. There are two particular white women I have seen, huge and tall, and I feel a certain amount of violence in them. They scare me. All butches are not like that, but those are the ones I think of when I think of butch. When I think of others, I think that's just the way that person is. And then I have to think, they do have a butch look.

Men who were particularly macho did not interest me at all. I usually wanted men who were a partner, period. Somebody to negotiate and do things with. My lover says that's because I am a butch. The first few times she said it, I was offended. I truly was. Then she said, "Why are you offended?"

"It connects certain kind of aggression and stuff I don't want to identify with." And then, I thought if I do see myself as a competent person, why is that not the image that I have? Why do I have this negative image?

Once my lover and I decided to go out and she got all dolled up. She had lipstick on and stuff, and I had slacks and my boots on. When we got home, she said, "Are you aware that you took control the entire night?"

I said, "I did?"

She said, "Yes."

I said, "What did you do?"

She said, "I just played the femme. I was fine."

On a day-to-day basis, it is not what I live with. I found I was comfortable with it that day. It is not a role I want to play because I have a connotation of the butch being one who does things and not receive. I don't want to be in that position, either way. I want to be able to give and receive. And so that for me is where I have an image of the roles, which is maybe the heterosexual image of the roles. I don't see myself fitting that. I want to be loved and loving. I want to be vulnerable and taken care of. Anything which connote me as the strong one and denies me of the other piece, I reject.

AS TIGHT AS TRUE COMMUNITY

It was interesting coming out into the lesbian community. I knew so many people within the community as a heterosexual, because of other stuff I had done over the years. In that sense, I did not seem to have the same struggle entering it. I have been with the Black Coalition for AIDS Prevention (BlackCAP) for a number of years, and know a number of people there. There were people there who had wondered about me, over a number of years, whether I was lesbian or not. Coming out into the community was easy for me.

What I find, though, is not having a place to go looking for older folks to talk to, that was difficult. Another thing I keep seeing is a lot of political activity, but I don't know if I see as much caring for each other as I would like. I see younger women, I am not sure I see people caring for them. I am not sure I see people making themselves available just to help them. I am not sure I see the connections as tight as I would expect if it's a really true community, I am not sure what I mean, but I know I don't see it.

I remember coming here in the sixties, when there was a smaller community. There was a lot more care just for each other than I see now. Politics sometimes seem to get in the way. There is a pressure to be politically correct instead of allowing you to be. When you are nurturing a person, they are not going to have all the values you have.

One of the things that was really good was Sistah's Cafe, a place where people meet. I don't know how much informal gathering there are in people's homes, just so long as there are safe spaces where you can call somebody and talk to them. We all need to work and we need our space for our families. When I saw this young woman with a young lady, every time I saw them together, I would ask how they were doing, how was the relationship going. She said, "You are the only person who consistently asks how we are doing, as if you are recognising and acknowledging we are trying something."

That took me by surprise because they are so political and so active. I just took it for granted that people would have been paying attention to them and trying to acknowledge them as a couple.

Struggle and Respect

Part of sex is the private, the struggle my partner and I have from time to time. I would say, as long as it is your business I don't care what you do, but you cannot put my business out there. And she will say, "What difference does it make?"

One day I was at a party. My lover and another woman was going at each other. The other woman was saying, "How many women have you slept with?" My lover was naming off the women. And I was furious. I walked away.

She said, "What is wrong?"
I said, "I am sorry, I find this conversation difficult and inappropriate."
And she is saying, "What difference does it make?"
I said, "It is your business. It is private."
And she is saying, "What is private about it?"
I said, "I don't know, it is just private."

For me, even as a heterosexual, there were very few people I would talk to about sex. I talk openly about sex, but to talk about who I had sex with is a different thing.

In the beginning, I had a lot of trouble with the concept of a dildo because it was a male organ. And I thought, I am not sleeping with a man. I see it as a male organ. I have moved slightly to just seeing it as a toy. My partner is quite open to talking about things as toys, and stuff. If there is a continuum, she is about a third ahead of me at all times, in terms of openess to ideas. I keep saying to her, "You are three steps ahead of me, dragging me along the way."

And she keep saying, "That is okay, I will wait around that."

I think that is coming from always having lived a heterosexual life. Not yet quite open to some ideas. At this point, I am locked into monogamy. I have had too many non-monogamous relationships with men. Non-monogamy is too linked into not being appreciated, not being valued. I don't know if I will move from that position. But for now, I need to be secure. Non-monogamy makes me feel insecure.

My partner and I came at non-monogamy very differently. I wasn't sure I knew what I wanted out of the relationship and where it was going. We talked about it. I knew where she stood, and I knew she would screw anything. I keep telling her I'd moved, saying, "It's okay, I don't expect anything until we are in a relationship. Your options are open. Mine are open."

I said all of those things and meant it. Then, she went off on holidays. I got all these wonderful letters from her. I was really looking forward to her being back, really excited that she came back. We spent the night, and then she told me about the friend she had when she was away. And I just about nearly died. I freaked out. Yet a week before I was spouting off at the mouth that it is perfectly okay.

I never thought I would have that reaction. I have had several men all my life and they have always had several women. I slept with a married man for twenty years, it was totally different. This person I told about my lover, and that was fine which is unusual for a Caribbean man, but he was an unusual Caribbean man. All along, very supportive, comes to the house, is fine. But he did ask me, "One of the things that attracted us is that, even when we were younger, we would always sleep with other people and come back together and talk about it. That was fine. We have had this relationship for many years, we have always talked about it. Suddenly you are having this relationship and you said we can be friends but we can't sleep together, why?"

Sex with me was sex. I have to like the man, but I can have a good round of sex and then I want you to go. I had never felt connected. Right now, with my partner, sex is just not sex. It's physical in a number of ways. It is very emotional. It is my entire being. I am connected, more than just the physical, and so the notion of having that attachment to somebody else...

My lover will argue you can just have sex and I will say, "I am sorry. I haven't gotten there yet."

She said, "For now we will both agree because I will try and meet your needs at this point."

I said, "I am hoping I will move from this place but right now, I am too vulnerable. I cannot handle it."

We keep coming back to it from time to time. I was away in Halifax away on a meeting and I said, "You know, I was thinking about this while I was away, where I am on that. I am making some movement but I am not quite there yet." I appreciate the fact that she has given me the time and seem to respect the fact that I need the time to do that.

I see some women who behave in a non-monogamous way as predators. I think they behave exactly as men behave and yet we accept it because they are women. I have said that is unacceptable. If a man walked in and behaved like that — walked in looked at a woman like that and touched her like that — we would be all over him. But there isn't a lot of dialogue.

Room for individuality and privacy

Part of the silence for me, is if (God forbid) me and my partner broke up, I would be loathe to have another relationship in the community. It is too small. And people seem to know people's business too much. It's too public, there is no room for individuality and privacy within that. My partner is the kind of person whom that kind of stuff does not bother, and that is okay. They know you but they don't know me. They know nothing about me and I want it to stay that way.

There is this tendency to want to go back and say you always were lesbian but you denied it. I think that may be true but I don't think that is true for everybody. It's possible to move from various stages of sexuality at different times and to have the ability to open up or respond. Sometimes it takes the right person.

Coming out it was pretty positive for me. At this point, I am not fully out. I am hoping slowly I will move there. Age makes a difference. So does knowing I can support myself and knowing a lot of people. But I can see where some of the horror stories existed for some people.

LOOKING FOR EQUALITY
Alex

I was born in Trinidad, Port of Spain General Hospital in 1954. My father is a production manager at one of the clothing factories, and my mother is a bank officer. I have a half-brother and three sisters (two are half-sisters). My early life was very traumatic. My parents had separated by the time I was six, and we were back and forth between my parents as well as my paternal grandmother. It was very, very difficult.

I WAS NOT AWARE OF BEING DIFFERENT

My grandmother believed that men ruled the roost. Because of the divorce, my mother wanted her daughters to be strong and not to allow themselves to fall into that sort of role. Compared to other girls I became strong from a very early age. I lived what some consider a tomboy life, but it was more that I can get anything I want once I put my mind to it. And I will.

Coming from a broken home, I never had very many friends. I never allowed people to get close to me. I kept a lot to myself, got into my homework and sports as ways of letting go. I guess you could say I was different, but I didn't know I was different from a lesbian focus.

In primary school, which is between the ages of five to eleven, I went to all-girl schools. I had one close friend. I was in secondary school for seven years. I had probably three close friends, that was it. Most of my friendships were with women, but I did have guys that I would hang out with, say, from around the street I lived on.

One afternoon when I was thirteen or fourteen, this boy started to hurl abuses and wanted to hit me, because I didn't pay him any attention. I launched a stone at him because he started throwing things. I hit him. The next day my uncle found writing in chalk on our wall surrounding the house. I gathered it said that I was a lesbian, but I never saw it and they never told me exactly what it was. Because I paid him no attention. I think the families had to work it out.

OUR OWN WAY OF LIVING

To be honest, I did not know that I was a lesbian. It never crossed my mind. I had no thoughts about it. It was the early seventies, and we were more interested in our Black Power movement here. We had the militant side, people concentrated on that. Politically, it was a very traumatic period, a period of growth for our country.

When I was eighteen going on nineteen and had left school, I fell in love. I was in school with her in my last year, and it was only in the last few months before I left that we became friends. That friendship developed into an affair. I fell in love without even realizing that I was in love. It was not something that I had planned, it happened. And I was also her first, so we sort of plodded through a gorge, coming up with our adjectives and our own way of living. At the time, I did not know anybody who that was gay. It was hard.

I thought that sexual experience was the most wonderful experience. I been out with men before, because it was the thing that you were supposed to be doing. And I realized I was doing it because it was expected of me, not because I wanted to. But when I fell in love, I wanted her. I wanted to lead her to sex. And when we finished I actually did cry. Not out of badness, or "What am I now?" I was so happy, tears came.

Fear was not part of it until my mother found out, and until I had to deal with the rumours flying about me. It affected our lives after that. When that first relationship was over, because of all the outside influences, then I had to deal with, "Am I? Am I not? What is this? How am I going to have kids?" I still hadn't met any gay person at that point in time. That is when I started going through the searching period, how I was going to deal with this.

It's not like my mother found out from anybody else. She actually walked into my room, a thing she never did, and caught me. My friend was over me. We were lying in bed, fully clothed, talking. She put two and two together and came up with the answer. She kicked me out of home and called up my friend's mother. There was a scene, you know, "You are not my daughter." She didn't know what she would do with me, telling me to get out of her life, that sort of thing. It was difficult. Community didn't bother me, because I had already grown up with behaviour that said nobody's going to hand it to you in life. You're gonna make enemies. And during those times we had the Black Power movement and racism issues.

I OWE IT TO MY FRIENDS TO BE OUT

I am extremely comfortable as a lesbian. It is who I am and what I am. I am so comfortable, I am out to 'most everybody that I know. Recently I told my father. We never had a relationship, but I came out to him because of an article in the newspaper in which I felt he could recognize me. My mother already knew, and my sister knew because my mother told her when she found out.

I think I owe it my friends, not to keep that part of me hidden. If I do, we wouldn't have a friendship, we would have an acquaintance. That means as soon as I get close to someone, or they start sharing intimate things with me that are extremely important to them, then I think they need to know. In Trinidad, if you are seen often in company of a lesbian or a gay man, whether you are straight, gay or otherwise, whether or not you know, have proof or don't — you are illegal.

In the country, people are attempt to be closer and accept this type of bonding as normal. When you in the city there are a lot more people. You don't have that kind of closeness. It tend to stand out.

I have no fear of losing my job because my organization is unionized. I am also on the executive of my union, and have been a shop steward for many years. We have an agreement and certain guidelines. To fire me, they have to find something for which to fire me. This country may not have any laws as far as gay discrimination goes. But if I get fired and I take it to the union, and if the organization's case against me is not justified, I am going to win a big law suit. It would set such a precedent that I don't think my organization — being a workers' organization — would want something like that.

I would like to see a lot more people out. I would like to see a lot more people happy with themselves. But that will not come until the fear that we have — and it's a justified fear in this country — is alleviated, until the laws are changed. We need laws where people can feel free enough, comfortable enough to come out. The only way it can change is if we gays and lesbians speak out ourselves and show — at least to the people that we come in contact with — that we are "normal." And I use the term "normal" in inverted commas. That we can and do hold jobs, pay taxes and add to the GNP of this country. We fit into every facet of life. We're lawyers, doctors, artists, actors, actresses. If we came out, and people saw that, they would know that we deserve respect. They would begin to accept us a bit more instead of thinking that we are predators who prey on young ones, that we are sick, and purely sexual, and that sort of thing. All those things would change. We also need to get Parliament and the Senate to pass laws.

A ROCKY COMMUNITY

On the whole, I do not think lesbians and gays in Trinidad have a sense of community. We just set up an organization this year and it is rocky because of lack of community, lack of togetherness. The lesbians don't even come out to parties. If you go to a party where there are a hundred and fifty people, there will be twenty lesbians, sometimes even fewer. They tend to have their little parties at home and they will invite their close friends. So you can't really say that there's a community. Lesbians tend to stay at home and build relationships that last a lot longer than gay relationships. They think they do not need to go out to parties and bars. You can't go to a meeting, because there's no other lesbians who will go. The sense of community is really lacking.

Friends invite friends over, to meet somebody else's hubby. That has been joke between myself and some of my friends. That there are two circles and we interchange partners, that's all. If a lesbian is throwing a party — and we have two lesbians who throw parties in Trinidad pretty regularly — you see a lot more lesbians than at other parties. So, there is support in that sense.

But within the larger gay community itself, there is a lot of what I would call bitchin'. Bitchin' among lesbians. Because they are intimate circles, if I'm upset with my lover, I talk to friends who are her friends too, and they get a perception of what the relationship might be. And because they need to support their friends, it's hard to tell them honestly what your lover did or said. You tend to get a lot of hearsay, a lot of misconceptions about persons. And then you get: "The reputation that you have does not match who I perceive you to be right now. I mean I've heard so much about you." A lot of bitchin'.

A Comfortable Lesbian

In all my relationships, what I am looking for is equality. During the period the relationship last — and I always get into a relationship hoping that it last forever — the roles change. I would have to rely on her and she would have to rely on me. But most of the time you could say I'm butch. I don't usually feel butch with regard to how I dress, but with regard to the manner in which I carry myself inside. We change. I'm supportive, then she is supportive. I have seen this where there are roles. There are some people who are much more comfortable being the aggressive type. There are some people who are very, very comfortable dressing or looking butch. They might dress with shirt and tie, but always be in the house cleaning and cooking. These women are prepared to be the homemakers. There are roles, but far as the woman goes here, the role-playing is not as visible as it is with the gay men. I am just judging by those I have met, personally or through friends. Generally speaking, I may not be correct for the lesbians of Trinidad and Tobago.

Sex is discussed. It's part of our lives. Because it's mostly as I say, your close friends, the talk eventually does tend to get around to sex, some way or the other. But lesbians here do not think that AIDS can be transmitted from woman to woman. I have been reading some magazines lately, some lesbian magazines, and they are actually saying there is proof of transmission.

I actually do like the term lesbian. Do not refer to me as a bull dyke. Or as a dyke. Or as some people like to say, a rubber. That really upsets me. A lesbian, I think, is connected to Lesbos, an island that has seen many women who are truly strong and they dealt with life without needing a shoulder to rely on. When they copulated with men, you know, it was only to continue their race. I think that I'm a very strong, proud woman. I'm a comfortable lesbian.

My Own Blackness
Aakilah Ashanti Ade

I was born in Barbados. I have an older brother. My parents left Barbados when I was about three. They moved to the Bahamas, because of politics. The Bahamian government, which was British, was importing talent. They would not use the local people. My father is one of those talents. I stayed in the Bahamas from age three to age fifteen.

Most of the time in the Bahamas, my mother was trying to keep us separate from what she called the local people, trying to make us different from them, even though they were Black and we were Black. I think she was never happy being Black. My father, who happens to be bi-racial, is more comfortable being Black than she is. She hated it to the point where she straightened my hair, and, even, told me we would have to straighten my nose. I was supposed to marry a Jewish lawyer or doctor, because Jews have money. For my dad, whatever you want is fine.

An open marriage

I found out later that my parents had an open marriage. My mom could party on her own. She had some gay male friends and thought that was wonderful. If my dad did not want to go out with her, she went out with these guys and they brought her home. As I got older I realised my parents also swung. They did not hide it, it just was not brought up. Mind you, I was searching through their stuff and I found photographs. They had a lot of white friends from Florida who would come down on their yachts and have these swinging parties. Everybody would be naked. When I first saw that I was upset. But eventually I realize, well, this is great, means they are open-minded. At an early age, I bathed with my mom or my dad or my brother. My mom walked around naked most of the time. Sexuality was never an issue.

In the Bahamas, you are a foreigner as long as you were not born there. My mom raised me and my brother to be Canadian. We spent all of our summers in Canada. There were no patios, no ethnic foods. We were Canadian and that was that. We went to a private British school which had predominantly white kids. We were the first Black kids to be enrolled. Deep down I knew there was something wrong with the picture. When I did see Black kids playing, I wanted to be a part of that. The music, of course, was different. They were more free. I isolated myself. I did not have any friends.

I knew I was lesbian in grade school. My parents, with their openess, had both *Playboy* and *Playgirl* magazines. Early morning on a Saturday or Sunday, I would jump into their bed. My mom would be reading *Playgirl* and my dad would be reading *Playboy*. I would read with them. I would turn to her and read stuff which was boring, turn to him and see women doing things to each other. That was exciting. I used to pick up the *Playboys* and read them with my dad. He never said anything.

Eventually, I started thinking, okay, I know my mom wants me to marry a white person but I want to make it a white *woman*. In my fantasies it was a white woman. I had this doll my mom bought me that was the same size as me. I used to practice on this thing. It was a Black doll, which was really neat. She bought us toys that reflected our heritage, but would not let us participate in it — really strange. The few Black friends that I did have had to be an exceptional, middle-class, pale-skinned, etc. If I got too close to my female friends, she interfered. I think my mom suspected there was something different about me. I never dated. The only crush I ever had was on David Cassidy, no big deal.

My mom had a lot of friends who came down from Germany and Canada and spent time with us. One of her friends said to her, "You better watch your daughter. I think she is a lesbian."

Well, that night my mom locked my door, "Be careful now. We don't know what she is up to." She thought her friend was after me. This woman liked men. What the friend saw in me really scared my mom. I had to lock my door for this woman's entire stay. I even began to think she was going to come after me.

In Toronto, my brother had a girlfriend who had a twin. They were white. I would get close with her twin, get to a certain point, still labelled "friendly." I kind of knew where that line was. Then I would get really frustrated, and treat her badly. She did not understand. She thought we were one big family. You know how straight people think, life is beautiful. I still did not get close to a lot of women. I did not have any female friends at the time, except my brother's girlfriend's sister. I spent a lot of time with little boys, playing street hockey and basketball. My family wondered, what is wrong with her? Why isn't she hanging out with kids her own age?

They started sending me to church, insisting that I wear skirts and nylons — which I resented. There is no freedom in that. I did that for a few months and I told them, if you want me to go to church I will have to wear pants. I am more comfortable that way. Eventually, they kind of let it go for a while. But they kept pushing that femininity issue. Then I cut all my hair off. That was freedom from this perming process that hurt me so much. My mom would perm my hair, put it in curlers so that it would flow a bit. I am talking about pain. Those thick plastic curlers and she would be combing my hair, saying, "This is your beauty. I never had long hair, you must have long hair." She even put me in ballet school because she wanted to be a ballerina and her father did not let her do it.

Thinking I am a lesbian

I went to college in Canada and did nursing. I went into nursing because my aunt told me, "If you want to escape your parents, go into nursing. In two years you are out. You are free." My mom wanted me to be a lawyer or a doctor and I was obsessed with her and with pleasing her. I was a foreign student in high school, so my parents paid double school fees. Every time I needed money, I would just say, "Mom and Dad, I need money." I hated that. I have lots of relatives here and I lived with an aunt. But my parents supported me financially.

I began to withdraw from society and family because I knew I needed to break loose but I did not know how. I did not know where to go and who to talk to. I read a lot of Gertrude Stein, Radcliffe Hall. I went to the library. I hated the words lesbian and dyke, degrading words, but I did my research under those words. I started skipping a lot of school to do this. I ended up in the counsellor's office for skipping school. My aunt had to come down and explain I was in culture shock, but I was thinking inside, *I am lesbian, I am lesbian*. That is what the problem is. Gertrude Stein and Radcliffe Hall were my role models. I thought they were aggressive women, and I can just be who ever I am. I started reading other stories. There was this story about emergence, a woman who went through a sex change. She was a nun and became a man. I thought that was interesting. Then my aunt, who was supposedly open-minded, found the book and started having discussions with me about "Are you not happy with who you are? Do you have a problem with your femininity?" Which made me resent her and resent the word lesbian. I know I did not want to be a man but I wanted to find out everything about this whole gender issue.

The aunt I was staying with insisted I go into residence. She felt I would eventually meet people my own age and hang out with them. When she went to university, she was in residence and it was a wonderful experience, as she tells it. She was the only Black kid and she made her claim to the seat she was going to sit in. No one would push her around. I had to be strong and carry on the tradition of breaking barriers. So I went to college and went into residence. There were all women on my floor, but I was still withdrawn. I did meet a woman of Italian descent. In my mind, white was beautiful. But, I don't want it too white, darken it a bit to Italian; I had all these stereotypes. I latched on to this Italian woman immediately, based on the stereotypes in my mind. We became very good friends. She happened to be very affectionate. I introduced her to my cousin and we would go to his place and sleep.

So I decided I would take her over this one time and make my move. We went to my cousin's place. We went to bed. I tried to kiss her and she started to freak out; shaking and crying in the bed, I am thinking, oh my God what is going on here. I thought she knew. I calmed her down, tried again and again she freaked out. I was afraid of damaging her mentally, that's what started to scare me. We slept apart.

There are other lesbians and gays in my family. My cousin and his brother are both gay. In the morning my cousin thought we were having sex. He was all happy for me, 'til I told him what happened. So she and I are going home in the morning, walking through a downtown mall, barely speaking to each other. I told her, "I can't be a friend of yours, because I like you more than that. We can't be friends at all, if you cannot give me what I want."

Now, I knew I was power-tripping on her, that was part of the problem. She was more upset and pleaded with me. But I said, "No," and sent her off. She discussed it with a few of her friends in residence. They all knew somehow that I was lesbian and they told her go for it. So she came back and wanted to be friends again. I said, "If you want to be friends you have to do a, b and c." She went for it. That's how badly she wanted my friendship. I knew that. I kind of used that against her.

I NEVER SAW MYSELF AS IN

I had fantasized about women before and actually came to orgasm over it, so I never understood what coming out meant. I never saw myself as "in." For me, coming out was being able to say the word lesbian without throwing up. I think actually I used the word gay more than anything else. It signified happiness to me, while lesbian, through those stories I had read — especially Radcliffe Hall — meant depression and destined to be alone. That is why I didn't use the word lesbian. I had no politics at that time either.

So, this woman, the Italian, she slept in my room a lot. I had a heterosexual roommate from the north who had never been in a big city. She cried every night for her boyfriend. We had a deal. Her boyfriend would come down once in a while, I'd let her have the room. And I could have my partner whenever. Eventually we decided to get a room together.

Things went from good to bad. I knew she was not lesbian, she was not even bisexual. She was a heterosexual woman, doing what I told her to do. I knew it wouldn't last but I was having fun. Unfortunately she developed cancer, in her arm. She had to get a lump removed. By this time, her mother had found out about us. I slept in her house one time. Her mother walked in during the night, apparently we were hugging. Her mother never confronted me, but she kept telling her daughter, "God is going to get you for that."

The first time I made love to her, it was a little bit awkward. I thought the clitoris was going to be right there where the book said it was. Although I know where mine is. I did not realise they were all different sizes. I dug around for a while and she was just so scared she just went along with whatever I came up with. I felt powerless with my parents: this was a real power trip for me. I know this now. Back then, I didn't.

By the fourth or fifth week we had it down to a science. I became abusive. She was at my beck and call. Whenever I wanted her, she had to be there physically. Since I was not getting much out of it physically, I was going a little beyond the norm to seek my satisfaction. Then we started getting into violence. She would fight with me. I would hit her. We would have sex. At that time, it suited me fine.

LESBIAN BAR

My straight friends came to me with their research about a lesbian bar. I hung out with them, went to straight bars, I even danced with a white man.

They found out about a lesbian bar. A small place. I can't even think of anything that small. We went. I was so scared. They are brave, they are straight. I am shitting bricks. We danced all night. I did not look at anyone. I thought they would be looking at me and they would want me, all those awful sterotypes.

The bar was mainly white women. There were a couple of Black women but they scared me. I kept my head down until my friends found a place where we could stand, and then I just talked to them. When I did look around, there was nothing there that attracted me. Up to this day I still don't know what that fear really was. My friends took me twice and then they pushed me to go on my own after that. I went once on my own. It was not as scary as the first time. I started taking my cousin. I was afraid of the environment, but I wanted to be around women. I knew there was a potential of meeting someone and I figured I would hold out for the best.

My own Blackness

When I saw a Black woman in the club scene, my first instinct was to turn away and pretend she did not exist. I don't think I thought beyond that moment. My cousin introduced me to one Black woman who worked with him, but my walls went up immediately. I said, "Hi," and turned away, pretended she did not exist. When I ran into her in the club scene, I barely acknowledged her. I don't even know if I ever said hello to her. She just disappeared for me.

My next partner was more Black-identified than I was. She was a white woman, her kids were Black. She used to live in New York, in Harlem. All her friends, men and women, were Black. I did not have to explain anything. The first time I slept over, after my shower, she said, "Oh, the lotion is on the table." That really impressed me. Because I did not have to ask for it. She knew everything. It was like living in a Black environment, without having to deal with my own Blackness.

We broken up after I joined a Lesbian of Colour group. My partner had said, "Why don't you go see what they are about?" She encouraged me to go. I went to some meetings, sweaty and scared. I did not give much input. At this time, I was feeling real good about these women and it was nice, but I started having problems when they would talk about white people, because my partner was white. The group helped me to see that I was in an emotionally unhealthy relationship and I was able to move on.

I met my first woman of colour, I guess I was maturing a bit. She was Portuguese and Black from Guyana. I was attracted to her straight off, then

I started thinking about colour and stuff like that. At first I thought she was South Asian and I thought, okay, fine, I would like to be with someone of colour. Black is still too threatening to me, this is at least half way in between so that is okay. I met her at a bar. My cousin, who is an alcoholic, would drag me out quite a lot because he needed to drink. I really did not like the men's clubs so I would take him to the women's. The night I met her, I was going with my cousin and his partner to a party. I stopped in at Chez Moi to meet a friend of mine, this artsy fartsy white guy. Then I saw her and I thought, who is this woman, she is very interesting. I danced with her and gave her my number and then I had to leave.

One thing led to another. She had kids and that was wonderful. The first time I saw our reflection together, I thought this is neat, we are both brown. This is what I needed. It was the first time I was really happy with a partner. I wanted it to work. I was determined to make this work. Sex was great, the kids were wonderful. Of course, the first two years is always wonderful. There was also a lot of men still in her life. One hit me once. I had to go to court to get a peace bond against him. The dad of the younger kid was coming into the house and smoking pot like he still owned the place. I had to put an end to that. She had a lot of friends, she was very friendly. And I was more rigid.

A lot of things had to change. I wanted a family. We had to do a lot of family things and look after the kids. We moved up a bit, changed location. We got a house together, her family wanted us to get a house. She was quite open. One daughter was three at the time, and I would put her to bed to bond with her. Sometimes she would say, "You know, Jack and Jill went up the hill to get a pail of water."

I would say, "Yeah."

Then she would say, "But Jack and Jill, that's a boy and a girl, that makes sense. But you are a girl and a girl."

I would say, "Well, what they don't tell you in Jack and Jill is, sometimes it could be Jill and Jill." And for about a week, she would keep saying this nursery rhyme every time I tucked her into bed. She was trying to understand. I was first female lover in her mom's life.

We decided I would move in, as a trial for a year, to see if we could make it together, before she moved out of where she was. The kids adapted very well. They just wanted security. Then it got very bizarre: they started walking in on us during sex. The first time they were freaked out. After that, they would hear us making noise and just turn the TV up. They could not care less. They were adjusted. At one point they would tell the teachers, "My mother is a lesbian," and the teachers would say, "Don't you say that, but they would say, "She is, she is." Then they would come home and be quite upset that these teachers would not allow them to say it.

I involved myself one hundred percent because these were the kids I wanted. I even called my mom. "Okay, I got the mixed kids for you. Can I send them down for summer?"

She said, "No." She was still not talking to me.

The relationship soured after a while. At one point I was going to stick it out because I wanted the kids. I wanted to be their legal guardian. I wanted so many things, but it wasn't given to me. I still am in contact with the oldest child. Her boyfriend is the son of my previous lover. It is all in the family.

The nice thing is, I am still their mother, they come and they see me. I am just really happy that I still have these kids. They tell me things that I did wrong but they also tell me the good things. The girls get along with my present partner and call her mom. So it worked out okay. But the one I missed the most is the younger sister. I raised her from age three to about nine, and we had a really good relationship. When I left, she did not understand. The night I was leaving she snuck a picture of herself in my bag so I would not forget her. That just about broke my heart. After that, I never really had any contact with her again. That was the most important thing that happened to me in that whole time.

Black friends have helped me

I did date a Black woman. She had five kids. She was okay at first. I invited her out a few times. Then I started smelling alcohol. I thought, okay, fine, let it be. But one time I went to a party at a friend's house and we went to pick her up. She was turning out the lights, and I heard her fall down the stairs. We got to the party and there was something different about her. I couldn't figure it out. She was coming out of the basement at the party and she fell up the stairs. I thought, there's something really wrong here. We are sitting around talking and she starts yakking, not making any sense. I realised this woman was drunk. I was turned off immediately. I was in shock. She was a drunk, making an ass of herself. All my friends were looking at me as if to say, you are with her? I drove her home that night and that was it. I never called her again.

This is an awful thing to say, and I know it is not politically correct, but the reason I spoke to her in the first place was to prove to myself that I wasn't racist. I felt I had to be with a woman of African descent. It did not work, not because she was African, but because of the alcohol. After that, I thought I still want to be with a woman of colour, so I dated a South Asian woman for a while. Once when she came back from the gym, she complained there was a bunch of big Black men there taking up space. That bothered me. She would say things referring to other Black women like, "Oh I glad you don't keep your hair like her. That looks nasty."

Some of my Black friends have helped me to see my shit and to identify it in other people. I went through Zami. I was so badly behaved back then that they would have to ask me to leave meetings. There was a lot of education in there. My previous committed relationship put me in a lot of Black spaces. She was Black-identified of Portuguese and Black descent. Her identity was so strong that it developed in me. I was beginning to feel really proud. The kids needed that education as well. We were all being educated together. And because of her need and desire to be in Black spaces I ended up in more Black spaces and began to be really comfortable with them, enjoy them and want them. You live in your experiences. I am glad I was with her. I would not have progressed to where I am today if I had not been with her.

Affirmations and community

When I started to become aware of what community meant, my first reaction was, "That's your community. I don't want to be part of any community."

I was seeing — this is my prejudice coming out — a lot of dreadlocks, a lot of so-called natural living. What I called "ghettoization." I did not like it. I would be at someone's house in a group, and they would be talking about, "We are Caribbean women or West Indian." What West Indian meant to them, you know, catching water and carrying it home or eating certain foods. I rejected that immediately. It was not my experience. I felt you had to have that experience in order to be part of that community. I resented that. I would go to someone's house and they would be cooking ackee and salt fish. I had never had that and I would say, "Where is the regular food?" I was really rude. What I saw as community, I did not want to be a part of. I was very disrespectful. I felt justified because I felt they were not accepting me as I am — as I was. Fortunately, one gay man addressed those issues with me. We had really good talks and I became very comfortable. I have to give him credit; a lot of other people were not that tolerant. I used the negative stuff to justify why I was not a part of the community. That was my shield.

I was beginning to absorb the politics. I am much older now and I try to live it. I definitely make demands at work as a lesbian and a Black woman and as a woman. I am out at work. My co-workers would talk about their wonderful weekends with their husbands and boyfriends and I talk about mine, too. My lovers have always came to my work place.

I was a board member of Black Coalition for AIDS Prevention (BlackCAP) for a while. This allowed me to get more involved with community stuff and meet a lot more Black women. My current partner and I got married at the United Church. We both wore black with white shirts and pants, but the role-playing is now only in the bedroom.

What I have resolved is that I am going to be with who I am attracted to. That happened in the period between the South Asian partner and my current partner. I decided, screw everything my mother put into my head, screw what I think is right and wrong, and the politics of the Black community. If I see someone, and I like them, white, brown, green or black, if I want them, I am going to be with them. I made some affirmations. It does not matter who I end up with. I want them to be good for me. They don't have to be pretty. I don't want a perfect person. I want someone who will help me to grow.

Growing and changing

I am comfortable with the word lesbian. The word dyke, I am still having problems with. I don't mind when other people use it, it's no big deal, but to refer to myself as a dyke is still difficult. I do not enjoy white lesbians. I really have problems with them. Alcohol is their way of socializing; it has never been mine. They don't seem to understand where I'm coming from. I am going from communicating with white lesbians to not being able to communicate with them at all. I don't feel bad about it. I look for Black women. I feel all this energy I had not experienced before. It is about us connecting.

ALL MY FRIENDS WERE GAY
Clarise

I was born in 1967, in Toronto. My father is Trinidadian, my mother is Trinidadian Indian. My mother was a housewife. I have three younger brothers. We moved a lot in Canada because my father chose to work freelance. I was twelve when we came to Trinidad. We've lived here in about three different places here, all south.

I was not particularly aware of being different growing up. In a way, because I was a non-Canadian in Canada and then I was a non-Trinidadian in Trinidad. But as far as gender identity, not really. I liked dolls and played with dolls. I suppose I was very contemptuous of girls for quite a while. By the time I left Canada at twelve, I was contemptuous of the entire human race. When we came to Trinidad I went to an all-girls school and had no interaction with boys until I was sixth form when we had a sixth-form club. I had to wear skirts to school, at home I wore jeans.

In Canada I don't think the concept of homosexuality crossed my mind. In Trinidad, as far as lesbianism is concerned, in school, at least, it was kind of a joke. But it was still something that didn't really exist, except theoretically. Around eleven or twelve I understood what homosexuality really meant. But, in general I was always a supporter of liberal ideals, and so gay existence was defensible from fairly early.

I wasn't interested in anyone, relationship-wise. I always liked boys better as friends. For a year I went to a mixed school, a senior comprehensive where all my friends were boys, except for one friend from my old school who had come along. Especially there, in a country school, girls were pretty silly and useless, country girls mostly. I repeated A-levels and then I took a year off before I went to university.

As far as friends go

About the same time, I started to have gay friends and move in gay male circles. I was, if anything, more strongly defensive of homosexuality. After school finished a few of us would go out together. A very good friend of mine from school and his friend started to lime. I always sort of assumed he was gay, too, but he claims not to be. After sixth form, bit by bit, I sort of realized that they were gay men, almost entirely.

For the most part, I didn't have many female friends, straight friends. I still don't have a lot. One woman was my best friend all through school and then my roommate in university. I never actually told her as such, but I think it was fairly obvious, I think from the company I kept. I still don't know if she really knows or not, she went away afterwards. We're still really close when we meet but because we were sharing an apartment then, I wasn't comfortable telling her. I think she would have been fine with it, but I didn't want to ruin something that was friendly and comfortable. I liked her as a friend, a lot. But I was not attracted to her. I have a few straight female friends now, comfortable friendships really.

As far as friends go, I probably feel most comfortable with gay men. I don't speak to anyone about personal things and problems and things like that. The closest friend, as far as someone to talk to, is gay. He's away now, and even him, I never used to talk to that much.

In and out

In 1989, I had my first sexual and emotional experience with another woman. There was an afternoon's worth of slight confusion and turmoil, one afternoon where I was just wondering. After that it was okay. It did happen to be the afternoon of a major exam. It wasn't exactly confusing, it was just a lot of thoughts going through your head. And it was a very bad moment for having to accept that you are gay.

I was a little bit uncomfortable about meeting other gay women, also at the same time interested. But I mean up to now, most of my gay friends are male, not that many females. I don't have many lesbian friends, but to me there doesn't seem to be very many femmes. I suppose there are. I don't go in for a role at all, but I prefer boyish women.

As far as I can tell, there is not much of a lesbian community, but I don't move in that circle very much. They seem to be more fragmented than the gays, different little pockets and groups. Maybe because the relationships tend to be longer lasting among women than men, they don't circulate as much. They would be more likely to have little gatherings at home than to go to a party, to be limin' home by people. When I have been to informal gatherings, it's just to lime, as far as I can gather.

I am reasonably comfortable with my sexuality at this point. Out? I'm not involved with anyone, I haven't been involved with anyone for quite a while. Therefore, it rarely becomes an issue. You don't go around telling everybody. If people ask, I would like to think I would have the courage and the integrity to say yes. I very openly say that I really don't want anything to do with boyfriends, I have no wish to get married or have children.

I'm not exactly out to my family. I've never told anybody openly, but I've never hidden anything either. Both brothers probably know. I get along reasonably well with them. With one of them, I get along fairly well and fight fairly well too. The other, one I used to get along with very well but he's sort of very distant to everybody these days. He's going through one of these phases. He's in university. My little brother definitely knows. They are both well-trained liberals. I raised them both as liberals. Actually, I think they are both comfortable enough with it. My mother should accept it, she should know. I mean I go crazy over my Melissa Etheridge and k.d. lang records. And she knows that I am very much into the rights and gay things. She also knows that I have a lot of gay friends. She's met quite a few of them. I have never discussed it with him, my father. It's not relevant at all. They are together, but I wouldn't discuss it with him. For the most part we don't really have much in the way of conversation. We can get along alright sometimes, we don't have much in common for conversation or anything.

Of my colleagues, one of them at least socialized a lot in gay circles. And another is a bit of a closet case. We have talked about homosexuality a few times, and he claims to have a problem with gays and be against them. But he says he has nothing against lesbians. He makes that point. The rest, I don't know.

COHESIVE FOR ONCE

The change I would like to see is to the fact that homosexuality and lesbianism is both illegal. And the general prejudice, the general level of ignorance. You can't stop people from being prejudiced one way or another. You can change the level of ignorance.

In the gay and lesbian community, it would be very nice if we could be cohesive just for once. As a member of Lambda, I know about the lack of cohesiveness and the use of things that came from the meeting as gossip on the street afterward. What I liked about Lambda, even though there was no actual support, in the meeting it felt like there was support and it felt really nice. Even though you know they are going to go out and gossip about you on the street the next day, it felt really good. It felt like there was a community group. I heard there is no meeting now. I really liked the meetings. For quite a while I tried to go regularly. I really liked the atmosphere there, and the way you left it feeling.

A Legitimate Choice
Debbie Douglas

I was born in Grenada, I'm from this little village called Paradise. I lived in Grenada until I was twelve, then I came here. My mother left before. I was left my grandparents. On my mother's side I am one grandchild out of one hundred and ten. My mother is the last of twelve children, and of her children I am the oldest. And the favourite grandchild, I like to think.

By the time I joined them, — my mother and her new husband — I had a brother who was one. We are eleven years apart. I guess the same situations come up for other families who immigrated. When the children have grown up without their parents and join them later, it's difficult to re-establish a parent-child relationship. We are coming from the Caribbean, so we have a very different way of being. Many people who immigrate, when we leave our culture, we think our culture stops, becomes stagnant from the moment we leave. Caribbean parents certainly hold this belief and can't understand why the children they left back home are not more like them when they were children.

I grew up within a very fundamentalist Christian family, fourth generation. I was socialized as a girl child, and the expectations were: going to university and finding male doctor to marry.

Because I am very dark, colourism was certainly very present in my life. I think my earliest memories are of being teased, being thrown in the drain and told to grin so they can see me. I got called "darkie" from a young age. I was told, "Thank God your nose is not too broad and you have long hair, so at least it takes away from some of the Blackness." So, I had all of those things.

Zami

From the earliest time I can remember, I have always fooled around with my little girl cousins. I think I have always known about zami, which is what we called sex between women. But I think we called all sex "zami" for a while. When we got older, we started to know that zami is actually sex between two women. But I think I have always had a sense that women had sex together. It certainly was not anything that I went through or in my own head to make me feel it was somehow wrong. Despite my Christian upbringing, I didn't have a sense of sin. As children, you keep those kinds of games away from adults. I don't ever remember hearing an adult talk about zami, although in Grenada, the older people in my family always spoke patois — a French dialect. As children, we did not understand. That's how patois was used. To keep certain information from the children. That is also why patois is now dead in Grenada; it was never passed on to us.

I did have some sense of who the women were in the community who — now that I have the language for it — were the butchy women, the women who were independent, took care of their families and never had any men around. They had children mind you, but never had any men around and did things on their own.

My earliest memory of the woman who probably had the biggest influence on me was the first woman I saw riding a motorcycle in Grenada. I must have been three when I saw her, and she stayed in my head. Her name was Merle. As I got older, I realised everyone called her Crazy Merle. And people would talk about, "Yes, Merle wears men underwear. She wears pants and rides a bike. She is mannish, as opposed to womanish." There was a sense of disapproval, but if she was passing on her bike, she would stop by my grandparent's house, for instance, to say hello and would be welcomed. From the way people spoke about her, I sensed that it was not approved that she was so independent and acting like a man, did all these manly things. But she really impressed me. It's funny, one night about two years ago, she came into my head, just when I was dropping off to sleep. The next morning I woke up, phoned my mother and said, "Do you know what happened to Merle?"

She was very shocked that I remembered this woman. Because I think it clicked something for her about my lesbianism and my memory. For the longest while, I fantasized that this Merle I remembered was Merle Collins, a Grenadian writer who lives in England. But I checked it and unfortunately it is not the same Merle.

Merle didn't have children, she didn't have men in her life. She had a motorcycle and she wore short khaki pants like the men. I heard some of my older cousins say she wore men underpants. She was the first woman I saw with her hair short like a man's. She really impressed me as a child. I have always had a sense in myself that was an opposite of what was expected of me as a girl child. From the time I was five or six, when people would ask me what I wanted to be when I grow up, I always said I wanted to smoke, drink and be able to go wild and party — which, at the time in Grenada, was a very manly thing. And for my strict Seventh Day Adventist family, a blasphemy.

I remember my lover, Gabriella, and I were home — in Grenada — in 1989. I thought we were both acting very straight, not letting people know what was happening. My cousin Paul, who was sitting in the other room, said, "You guys held hands all over the place. Called each other 'honey.' Everybody noticed."

What was interesting, when we were there, was that whenever a guy would check us out, try and pick us up, my male cousin would say, "No they not into that you know, they rub." I thought it was funny that my family was outing me all over the place without really talking about outing me.

There is a lack of acknowledgement of the importance of the relationship. So for instance I don't think anybody really say, "You lesbians, you should be killed." But people who do know I am in a relationship certainly don't respect that relationship — in terms of feeling that I am free to be picked up, that all I need is a good fuck or that I really don't know my mind. They say it's because I went to university that my head is screwed up. That is what happen when you go in foreign places, hang out with white people and act as if you learned. "The learned," as my grandmother would say.

Feminism euphemism

I think there are lesbian and gay people everywhere — regardless of the environment, of how welcoming or hostile it is. I keep hearing about a lesbian community in Grenada. I keep hearing about women who are active in government and identify as feminist. I hear that feminism in the Caribbean is often a euphemism for lesbianism, which is interesting. My mother certainly don't think that there is a difference. If you say, "I am a feminist," she hears "lesbian." And I think that's how it works. Women know they can't say, "I am a lesbian;" one of the ways they make contact with other women is to use the term "feminism." At least there is some sort of political ideology, some space where issues of sexuality can come up in the future.

But, I certainly saw close relationships between women, not named.

Now, whether or not those women are sexual, I don't know. I don't think it needs to be necessarily sexual to have a lesbian relationship. There isn't an active, out lesbian or gay male community in Grenada at this point, as far as I know. Although in 1996, a conference of Caribbean Gays and Lesbians was held in Curaçao and a Pan-Caribbean Lesbian and Gay movement was formed.

Fooling around with girls

I had my first Canadian experience at twelve. I had a wonderful friend. She still lives here in Toronto, but she is very straight. She was my little friend who I seduced. We were twelve. I didn't have names for what I wanted to do. I thought she was cute, and when you are twelve you have raging hormones. My friends wanted to fool around with boys. I wanted to fool around with girls. I never questioned that. In my own head, I did not feel there was a distinction between the two. I certainly knew I couldn't talk about fooling around with girls, but for me, I didn't feel there was a problem. I thought everybody wanted to, you just didn't talk about it.

She came over one night. I felt her up and stuff. She must have liked it because the next night there she was asking to sleep over. This went on for about a year. Now, she knows that I am a lesbian and I often wonder what she thinks about that time. But we have never had the chance to talk. The last time I saw her was about eight years ago when she said hello very briefly, didn't even want to be introduced to my partner and hurried away. She certainly did not want to be seen speaking to a lesbian.

At fifteen I came out as bisexual to my cousin. I had not done anything. I used the word bisexual because I had just discovered the term, and realised what it meant and felt, yeah, I like my girlfriends and my boyfriends. Plus, at fifteen you are trying to be cool and hip and older. So saying you are bisexual is a way to shock more than anything else. I told that to my favourite cousin at the time and she jumped five feet away. We were sharing a bed that summer, she slept on the floor all that time. It never came up again. I completely forgot about it until a couple of years later, my best girlfriend kept telling me that she was seeing all these lesbians all over the place. I kept saying, "How do you know?"

She would say, "Don't you see so-and-so is together?"

One day we ended up in bed and tried it. I took her virginity. We don't talk about it. She is straight. She has thought about it.

I really controlled the losing of my virginity heterosexually. I phoned the guy up, asked him to come over, seduced him and that was the end of that. It was a bet. I think you are still socialized to think you have to be heterosexual. So girls, girlfriends and women are always seen as something on the side. When I thought of losing my virginity, I thought of heterosexually losing my virginity. Which is interesting: why didn't I think of losing it to a woman? Maybe, I would not have thought I lost my virginity if it was with a woman. Even if there was penetration. I was a young teenager when I lost my virginity, that probably had a lot to do with it. My virginity was not something that I cherished.

Fooling myself

I got pregnant as a teenager, had a child, moved in with a man who was a dear, married him and came out eight months after my marriage. In my marriage, I came out as bisexual and was actively bisexual in my relationship. I think he thought it was kinky, hip and progressive. I think it goes back to heterosexism. Because I don't think he ever felt that he would be threatened by any of the women. He didn't think that any of the women could do for me what he could do. I don't think he saw lesbian relationships as valid and legitimate relationships. He was just thinking kinky, he had a wife who slept with women, and maybe he could get into a threesome every once in a while.

When I decided, in fact, that I was not bisexual, that I was a lesbian and couldn't continue within the relationship — then the whole thing changed. (My family didn't know until I left the marriage.) When I decided that I was really a lesbian and couldn't continue pretending to be this heterosexual woman with a husband and one child and started to come out, we had this huge talk. He said, "Okay, I understand. Give me a year until I finish school."

Stupid me, I stayed. He is my best friend. Yeah, right. What I got was a busted eye, all my blood vessels busted. Because after a few months I was not sleeping with him. I was taking my girlfriend to all the gay bars in the city. I was sleeping with every girlfriend of mine, and being very open about it. Because I was young, naive and stupid. And this woman I happened to be seeing at the time, I fell madly in love with. And felt I had to leave the relationship. Mind you, once I decided I had to come out, she quickly ran and got married. Which — now I can laugh about it — was very painful. She couldn't understand why I wanted to leave my marriage and come out as a lesbian, when I was just doing what I wanted to do anyways within my marriage.

I just felt I was being dishonest. I was truly a lesbian and had been fooling myself for all those years, and didn't have the language, didn't even know that being with a woman was a legitimate choice. And that I could set up a home with my child and my woman.

I found out about the bars through the *Body Politic*, a gay community newspaper around at the time. I remember, in my first year of university, that was the first magazine I picked up. From then I was a regular reader, and so I found the bars. At the time, I was also working at the Toronto Board of Education so I met film director Richard Fung and his partner Tim McCaskell, as well as Tony Sousa who was my mentor — a group of gay men. I became accustomed to and knowledgeable of the gay community. In fact, my ex-husband and I used to have dinner with Tim and Richard all the time. We had gay friends.

After my ex-husband beat me up and tried to rape me, I phoned Richard the next day. He told me, "Oh, I have a group of lesbian friends who are actually looking for a roommate. If you are sure you want to leave, then I will fix it up." And he did. That's how I met Makeda Silvera and Stephanie Martin, co-founders of Sister Vision Press. And I moved into their house in 1984.

A week after I left my husband, I phoned up my mother and told her I was a lesbian. Of course, it is the same way she responded when I told her I was pregnant.

"You think this is something to joke about? What kind of nastiness you talking about?"

For the longest time she said I was in a phase. Mine and Gabriella's twelfth anniversary is coming up, and it is only now my mother is starting to think, maybe she is a lesbian.

COMMUNITIES

First of all, we — my family of origin — belong to a very strong Black Christian community. That was diverse and spread out over Toronto. And we have always lived within the Black community. By the time I came out as a lesbian, I knew lots of people. When I came out, everybody knew. My ex-husband had made sure he told everybody in the community where we worked. He and I were both working and active there. It was an attempt to humiliate me. It was also an attempt to humiliate the woman I was involved with. She actually lost that job and had to move on, quit before she could be fired because he had told everybody that I left him for her. And she had a new husband, which I thought was funny in the long run.

When I was growing up in the '70s, Rastafarianism was very active and was a saviour for many of us in terms of Black cultural identity. So, I had lots of friends who were Rastas. Everybody knew in that community. And it was interesting, because I certainly needed to go through and see which friendships I needed to work on across sexuality and which friendships I was willing to let go. It's amazing my real friends are still my friends. I still have my friends from when I was a teenager, but I lost a lot of the people who were in my life. I think that was an exchange. I don't think I went from losing the Black heterosexual community to not having a Black community. What was different about me is that I went from the Black heterosexual community right into active Black lesbian and Black Caribbean Lesbian/Gay communities.

It did not help that there was a lot of talk that went around saying that, because I was a lesbian, there were all these other Rasta women who were lesbian. I got blamed for other people's sexuality. There are certainly times now when I don't come out in Black spaces, where I feel there is a certain environment, people are saying things like, "If my child was gay, I would shoot him." I don't think that is the time for me to come out and educate them. And it's unfortunate, because I don't go to the parties I used to go to before I came out. My feminism has a lot to do with that as well.

My introduction to any sort of white community was through coming out as a lesbian. I always remember, the first time I went to a dance where there was white people, where there is such a thing as bar closing time. I had never known such a thing. When I was heterosexual, you went out to dance. You didn't go out to drink. It was a very different concept of why you went out.

At my first lesbian dance I was amazed, just amazed at the sheer energy. I was amazed that there were so many white women out in the world, that there were so many lesbians in the world. Then all these women took off their tops, and I think it was the first time where I saw women not being self-conscious around body image and stuff.

Of course, I cracked up. I will always remember that night. When I went home I said, "Did you see those white women take their clothes off?" And only one Black woman. I wanted to go over and say, "Sister, put your shirt on." It didn't help that I knew her as a sixteen-year-old, so this was her in another life. I thought, I know that woman, she is taking off her clothes. That is how I got introduced to the white gay and lesbian community.

Lesbians of Colour

When I came out, Lesbians of Colour (LOC) was being organized. LOC certainly provided a political space. I came out at a time when the community had lots of energy. There was excitement, newness. There was a woman whose house had been stoned by previous friends in the Black straight community. They accused her of being a traitor to the race because of the profile she had in the community at the time. For a time, she was the only one getting the brunt all of that homophobia from our community.

When I came out in the early eighties, there was a real sense of organizing. LOC had come about, so there is also organizing along racial lines. I think, at the time, the established lesbian and gay community was not meeting the needs of gays and lesbians of colour. There is a sense that you had to come out as soon as you are a lesbian or gay and you recognized it in yourself. You had to come out publicly. Not understanding that for people of colour, once you come out, that may lead to isolation from your cultural community. And often times, your cultural community is the only community where you get support — unlike white gays and lesbians, who live in a white culture. They were not leaving one community and going to another, which is a devastating loss.

We had our own issues that we had to address as lesbians. I don't think we felt at the time (or now) we could take up a separatist agenda. Because there is a real need for us to work with men. And not only Black gay men but Black heterosexual men too.

A lot of political issues of class, race and identity came up — which was empowering. It gave us a sense of being political subjects and seeing our selves as valid, as important and having our own issues. We were able to lead our own movement, in terms of gay and lesbian liberation. Right around the time that LOC was dying — for many reasons, many of them just political differences — a group of us got together and had a discussion about the need for a gay and lesbian Black and Caribbean group. Zami was born.

At that time, there were four of us, two men and two women, willing to put our faces out. Myself, Symadel Coke, Douglas Stewart and Derek Gloudon. And so the *Body Politic* did a cover of us, the new Black group in the city, dealing with racism within the gay community, and homophobia/heterosexism in the Black and Caribbean communities.

LIKE GOING TO A WHITE CLUB

The bar scene was very white. I have never been picked up in a bar in Toronto. I knew Black women should not go to the bars alone if they expected to be picked up. I think the other Black people in the clubs were also very reserved in terms of approaching another Black person, for a number of reasons. For Black gay men approaching a Black woman, she could be anybody, could be your sister's best friend. After all, you are closeted. The last thing you want is for your sister's best friend to tell your sister, "I saw your brother at the gay bar."

There is also a sense of colourism. Given my dark skin, I don't think I was one of the first women that people saw or thought was cute. I was not "pick-up material." I always felt I needed to go to the bar reinforced. It's interesting, eleven, twelve years later, I still feel as if I have to go with a group when I go to the bar.

I was hoping to find other lesbians. I was hoping to find women, which in my head, meant Black women because I didn't have that connection with white women. I did not have a white community, I lived in the Black community. I guess I went looking for other Black women who were lesbians. I saw Black women. Whether or not they were lesbians...? Probably not. Those women I saw in the bars in the early eighties are certainly not around now, maybe for different reasons.

What I have found over the years, is that women who you find at the bars are not women you find at political meetings. Anyway, I just didn't feel a sense of welcoming. When I did see Black lesbian couples together in the bar, it certainly lifted my spirits. Made me know I was not the only one. It truly was not a white thing. Black women were not just lesbians who had husbands to go along with it. There were women who were out and dancing with each other. And for me, it was not that I did not have female lovers while I was married, but it was that whole sense of public affirmation. Of being able to go out with a female partner and treat her like a lover, the way I could go out with my husband — and have our affection accepted.

EXCITING DEVELOPMENTS

One of the things that is exciting is the new developments discussed in the Black press around gay and lesbian issues. In Toronto, *Metro Word* and *Pride* magazine are attempting to correct many of the wrongs that had been done in terms of complete silence from our community papers around issues that affect us as Black gays and lesbians. But there is still a long way to go.

In 1984, the four of us who were the first four members of Zami took an ad to *Contrast* magazine, a Black community newspaper and *Share*'s biggest competitor at the time. The receptionist took the ad, went on the phone and said to us, "Okay, I will place it." But what he did on the phone was to call everybody in the office saying, "Black lesbians and gays are here." As we were walking away up the street, we turned around and found that everybody in the *Contrast* office was staring at us through the door. The four of us held hands with our partners and waved. And of course, the ad was never printed. When we wrote letters about that, the letters were not printed. It was interesting. *Share* magazine said they would print it as long as we paid for it. But then, as now, they listed community organizations and groups for free.

Five years ago, they were singing a completely different tune. Now you rarely find any coverage of gay and lesbian issues in *Share*. Yet *Pride*, which first started out with this very homophobic editorial stance, is shifting slightly. The more progressive people you bring in to work on your magazine the more you see that reflected.

THE MOUNTAIN ALL AROUND & YOUR CARIB IN YOUR HAND
Verlia Stephens

I was born in Ottawa. At the age of four I went to Trinidad where I lived until I was twenty, then I returned to Canada. In Trinidad, we lived in Arema, which was a small town. It ain't small no more. I was brought up an Anglican, then became a Catholic. I went to church at least three times a week. I was in the choir and the youth group. I was the perfect church girl. My grandparents were well-known, my grandfather was the principal of a boys' school. Everyone knew me, so I couldn't do anything wrong anytime. Everyone knew I was Laura's grandchild.

SHE LESBIAN

My first experience meeting somebody who was like me, somebody who we call a lesbian today — because I didn't know what to call she before — I was about seven or eight. She taught in the boys' school where my grandfather was principal. She was like a man, you know. She dated boys and was always wearing jeans, shirts and shades. Her voice deep. Actually, over the years she started growing a beard. She was really tough and ting. I used to admire her. My grandmother said someting was wrong with her. People talked about her, but they accepted her. This is who she was, and she had no problem in Arema at all.

I always looked out for her. Every evening she would come and talk to me. I would hear her out. When I was about fourteen, she disappeared, I don't know where she went. But the whole of Arema knew her, all of Arema knows everybody. If she was walking with the boys from school, she would have some woman walking with her, yet she always seemed alone. Everybody liked her. Looking back today, I would say, she lesbian. I always remember her.

I grew up in a middle-class home, and my parents and grandparents tried to shield us from things. I did find out some things, but homosexuality, in terms of women, never came up except for that woman. Not up to today. The men, yes. They would dress in drag and ting. They leave them alone, everybody knows them. If you had money, you gave them.

When I grew up, there was no violence against the men. They are just there. When I was in my teens, more drag queens were on the scene. They killed this guy and that was kind of strange, it was glorified in the papers. That is the only killing I can remember. We were getting more American and British stuff on television. I think it was influenced. In the seventies it became gays, faggots, because now we had the two channels on television and we started to get more negative media about homosexual men. But even today, I can say in honesty, I could live there with my lover. There are people at home who know I am a lesbian, because they are too. A few of my very good friends who I grew up with know.

"Gosh, I'm no lesbian"

In Trinidad I couldn't come out. Everybody called me weird. I knew I was weird. I never ever wanted boyfriends. I always had a best girlfriend, and if she happen to get another friend to lime — hangout — with, I would be totally crushed. I had a friend named June, we were inseparable. She was a little butch-looking thing. We were always together, we were in love. When I moved up here she stayed there and I grew. But, there was no way I could think about this as a relationship, I did not have whatever it took to know that, or to make that move. I never went out with a guy in Trinidad. When I came up here to Toronto, I came out.

I came from Trinidad to Ottawa to go to Carleton University. After four or five years in Ottawa, I started going to the women's bookstore and to the women's union. I did not talk to anyone when I visited these places. I was only interested in the books on lesbian stuff. I wanted to join the women's union. However, the first ting I heard from people is that a bunch of lesbians hung out there. By this time I was not going out with any of the men on campus. Instead, I had this tight ting with this woman. In my opinion, we were lovers, we just didn't sleep with each other, okay. People called us lesbians. It was, "Oh, gosh. I'm no lesbian," but still I continued to be tight with her. I would go out with her on dates.

That woman was the first Black woman I met in Ottawa. We were seeing each other for five or six years. I practically lived with her. We would have parties. She wouldn't touch me. Mind you, I knew when I came out, it was difficult for her, but she has to deal with it. It is very hard when she sees me. We talk about me being out. I've tried to talk to her about her lesbianism, but she doesn't want to look at herself. So many of us are like that. Towards the end, we had a break-up over some woman.

In Ottawa, I worked as the president of the International Student Centre (ISC). Because the Centre was located next to the women's union, I could observe a lot of things. People talked about these lesbians who were in the women's union. One day, I sneaked into the place. I wanted this book edited by Barbara Smith. I took it, and stupid me, left it in the ISC office. When people asked who was reading about this lesbian stuff, I said I had a paper to write. Shortly after, I dropped out of university. I never finished.

I couldn't take it anymore. I did not want to be in that school anymore. Everything was planned for me by my mother. And I was sick of it. I did not want to be in school, the courses sucked. I was so weird. I didn't want any men. It was really ridiculous. When I slept with men, there was nothing. I felt strange. And when I read those books, I got really turned on.

One Tuesday I said, "I am going to Toronto." Wednesday, I am in Toronto. Dixon Hall Community Centre had a job opening. Thursday, I went to the job interview. Friday, I got the job. Monday, I was working. Two months later I am working at a women's shelter, and that's it! The whole collective is lesbian. I just broke loose.

Breaking loose

Leaving Ottawa was the most empowering thing I had ever done. As soon as I got to Toronto, I did my hair in dreadlocks. I always wanted to, but I was under heavy manners from my family. The women at the shelter were good. I asked them who were the Black lesbians. At the time, one was around. She was the one I was coming out with, she showed me around. When I went to the club, women told me I was pretty. Girl, I was coming from "ugly and fat." I was just "ugly and fat." I am still dealing with that today. I hated my body. I hated my breasts. When I was fifteen, I wanted to save money to have an operation on my breasts.

I came out at the women's bar called The Rose. Those little white girls would be looking at me — I was not interested — but it was like "Whoa!"

People say they don't like The Rose because the women dress like straight women, make-up and the hair, but that was just perfect for me. There were these women, Black women in particular, who I could have known — straight — and they are there. And they are hugging and touching each other. Oh my God. The deejay was a First Nations woman. She came and asked me to dance, the first woman I ever danced with. Luther Vandross was singing, I really love Luther. The song was a slow dance, it was, oh my God! Now, this feels right! This feels right!

I went to the Women's Common, but that was not the place for me. But, I went to The Rose by myself all the time. It was the first time I could go to a club all by myself. One thing though, there had to be Black women there for me to stay. I did not talk to them, they didn't want to talk to me, and that was fine, but they had to be there. With the white women, it was their space. I have to say, coming out as a lesbian, one ting that have been destroyed for me is good dance music. I have yet to be in a lesbian club where I can be satisfied with the music. It is disgusting. The music is clearly for the white women in the club.

I did not get too many coming-ons from white women, even if I wanted them. As a Black woman, you never go to the bar with the assumption that you are going to be picked up. That never enters my mind. White women say, "Oh let me go see if I can pick up a woman tonight." My reaction is, "Oh, really." I could never see myself actually going to pick up or to be picked up. But I like the bar.

In Ottawa I was very political, the straight Black woman stuff, that is how people there knew me. While I was working at the shelter I got a phone call from this girl who went to Carlton University. She wanted to visit Toronto and asked if she could stay with me. I went out with her one weekend and everybody in Ottawa found out about me. Some people said, oh, they knew. Others said they could not believe it, because I was so man-crazy. I had to challenge one guy about that. The whole Black community in Ottawa knew. There were a few people who didn't want anything to do with me but I didn't care. I wanted to leave and so that didn't bother me at all. I was too happy. I made my own space in Toronto.

With my family, I came out about a year after. When I left Trinidad, I had to get away from my mother. It was rough. Since I came out we are getting along great, but before, it was rough. I did not talk to her for a long time, over a year. Then I wrote her a letter and told her I was a lesbian, and I told my sister. That was before my sister got married and found the Lord. At the time, she said she sees me as being really settled and happy. My mother is fine. She tells me, "That is who you are, I cannot understand it but it's fine." She is cool. She goes to all kinds of those lesbian tings. She has books and stuff.

But my sister, she did a big turnover as soon as she found the Lord. Suddenly I was going to hell, and she prays for my soul everyday. I had to tell her if that's where the lesbians are — in hell — I want to go. So don't bother praying. My brother knows but he doesn't care.

The thing is, when my father left, I was sixteen. I grew up with my mother. I am thirty, and up to now my mother has no man. She always have these good friends, women friends. There is always some conflict about jealousy, the same like I had in Ottawa. With my mother the energy is so strong, but she would never do it. So she is going to be alone. I don't like that, no dates, no lovers, nothing for years. Just these very good girlfriends, very nice girlfriends, who get vex if she is going out with one too long.

Nothing sweeter than that

After I came to Toronto, I did not go back to Trinidad for four or five years. Before that, I went home at least twice a year. I finally went home. I already knew who I should hook up to. My mother is in theatre, she is a big actress back home. I asked her about certain people. She would answer that she does not ask people about their business. On this visit to Trinidad, for about two weeks, I was straight. I went out with men who I knew and flirted with them a little, it felt nice because I was home. But it only lasted for about two weeks.

One day I went to a play about AIDS. After the play, I went to the pub. I went up to the guy behind the bar and said to him "I am in the life, I want to know what is happening." In Trinidad, if you don't tell them you are "in the life" they won't let you in, that is how they keep away arse holes. It's a way to identify yourself. Then everybody looks out for you.

In this pub, men and women were there. The guys were really campy. It's a theatre crowd, so I took a chance. I started talking to people. They told me about a party. I met a woman, so cute. There was an audition for a play, I went to audition for the ting. After the audition, I saw these women. They were so butch. I knew one of the women knew my mom, so I said, "Hi." I said, "I just went for this ting and I don't have nowhere to go, where all you going? I could come and lime?" I have never done this ting before in my life.

They said, "Sure, come lime with us. We going to the pub." When I got into the car, the woman who is my mother's friend is there, she is a lesbian, real closeted. They are talking about me, and this Caribfesta that was going on. The closeted one is saying how this white man want to get her.

So I thought, oh, well, I guess she is not. I started talking to the other woman, who is her cousin. We are carrying on our conversation, then the one who has been talking about men wanting her says to me, "You don't want to talk to me? I am a lesbian, too."

I reply, "Well the way you have been carrying on about what kind of man you like, you lose me."

She took me to my first gay party in Trinidad. The party was in the hills facing the mountains. The music was great, there were drag queens and dykes, this was the first time she had ever been to a gay party. She knows people who are gay but she never came out. She was going through a hard time, because she outed herself.

When I saw those Trinidadian dykes and gay men, I was overwhelmed. It was amazing. Oh boy, I was in command at that time. I was in the hills, the sea was just over there. When the women are making their noises, it is Triny sound. I had to sleep with a woman that night. It was only one night, and it felt good. For three months, besides those first two weeks of playing straight, I went only to gay parties every weekend, Friday, Saturday, Sunday. Sometimes there would be two parties in one night and I wouldn't know which one to go too. I partied out for three months.

The men are more out. It is hard to reach the women. There was this lesbian couple who have been together for years, everybody knows about them, they took us out to the river and the beach. We made fish soup on the beach, fried fish and ting. We took off our clothes, sat in this little basin in the river. A group of lesbians down from Toronto. We had beer and rum and did lesbian tings. I really enjoyed myself. Girl, do you know what it's like to go to a beach party with only gay people and the warm Trinidadian breeze, mountains all around and your Carib beer in your hand? Nothing sweeter than that.

Changing with that strength

When I found the white anarchist at the women's shelter, that was a rough time, let me tell you. Sam Anakode was speaking at a local theatre. The women were going and then to this straight club after. I followed them. All the Black women were there. I met them all.

I wanted to join this very political Black women's organization, but they told me the collective was closed. They said I could be a friend of the organization. To be in, you had to go through this interview. I was totally taken aback by that. Then I found out what being "a friend" meant. It meant running up and down, putting posters everywhere. That bugged me. But I also felt, this is my community, I want to meet Black women. I got what I needed. I needed to feel like I was not alone. I needed to feel that excitement and sexiness. I wanted to feel all of that.

It was working for a while. For the first time, I got some support because, forget about self-esteem, I had none. I felt I could ask and I would get something back, which was good. So I am getting stronger and stronger, and feeling it. I am getting out there and working where I want to work. Then things started changing with that strength.

Suddenly I felt I did not have to be taken care of anymore. The Black lesbians I got to know were the political ones, the feminist ones. What they were saying was rhetoric. I learned so much from these women. I am trying my best to live it. But these women weren't living it. When you are talking about Black women, you are supposed to be talking about all of us. Not take that knowledge and keep it all by your clique. I am not bitter, life goes on.

Let's say I am just coming up from Trinidad and I am coming out. I want to meet women. I want to talk. I want to learn. I am a feminist also. Where do I get support? I am not talking about a physical space. You get into this clique thing. The stuff we say we don't want, we turn around and do it to ourselves. It really depresses me sometimes. I have stuff to deal with. I have to deal with HIV personally in my life and I don't have anywhere to go where I feel safe, to get my sisters to listen. To be able to tell them, "I am really freaking out today. What's going to happen?"

We don't have a community, we have cliques. You have the bar clique, and the Black women who go to the bars will tell you, "I don't want to talk to the feminists, they intimidate me." There is no way of feeling safe in coming into that space. Feminists have so much knowledge and we keep it. We talk about our stuff, but not in the language that all of us can know. It is supposed to be feminist, grassroots, but it was at the expense of everybody.

Now I am getting to know Black lesbians who are not political. The way I plan to live my life right now, I am creating my community in my personal space. I wish I had my community to go to. I want a space for Caribbean lesbians where we can talk about home. Some of us don't get to go home.

Stories

Horace's Marriage Proposal
Lesley Chin Douglass

Horace wanted to marry Auntie Moe. But she didn't intend to marry him. Auntie Moe was pushing for thirty, and you could hear Granny Green more and more regular, sucking her teeth and grumbling low under her breath, "Monica, chile, you shaming me. People will start to talk. You ain't ugly. Why you can't find a husband?" The truth was that many men would come courting Auntie Moe. She didn't care for any of them. They would eventually give up and find some other girl to moon over and give flowers and chocolates to. Auntie Moe would eat their chocolates, but she threw their flowers into the dustbin, or gave them to me to make prints with.

Horace was not like other men. Horace adored Auntie Moe. He said so, desperately, when he thought they were alone in the front gallery, with the light off, only a faint glow coming through the curtains from inside the house. He was a big, tall strapping man, very black, with crisp, curling hair. When he talked, his voice boomed. But in the gallery with Auntie Moe, he seemed more like a little boy, pleading and sulking when he didn't get what he wanted. It was enough to make you want to laugh out, though Auntie Moe didn't see the humour in it. Horace vexed her.

"She will marry him," said my cousin Natalie. "Wait and you will see." Natalie and me used to hang out by Boodoosingh's shop with her boy friends until it got dark and Mr. Boodoosingh chased us home to our supper.

"Auntie Moe will marry Horace," said Natalie with a knowing expression. She sucked slowly on her mango seed. "That is the way it always is. When they fight, it mean they in love." Natalie is a little bit younger than me. She wears tight American jeans and walks with a jiggle in her bottom. She wears rouge on her cheeks and lips, and drenches herself in some terrible musk perfume guaranteed to attract men by the dozen; it said so right on the bottle when she bought it. Beside her, I feel skinny and ugly, in my baggy shirt and dungarees.

"Why you don't try and look more like a girl?" Mummie would say. "Look at Natalie. You-all are the same age. Why you can't dress up a little bit, child?"

But Auntie Moe would suck her teeth loudly and say, "Leave the girl alone, she don't want to look like no whore."

The truth of the matter is, Natalie liked the attention the boys gave her. She laughed and flirted with them in a way she never did with me. She flirted the most with Vidal Ramdass.

"That man Horace is a fool," said Vidal, tossing his candy wrapper onto the road outside of Boodoosingh's. "If he marry your aunt, is trouble for him. Ain't nothing worse than a fickle, nagging woman."

"How you would know?" I asked loudly.

"I know, I know," said Vidal, standing close to Natalie. "Like aunt, like niece. Fickleness run in families."

Natalie pushed him away from her. "I hate you, Vidal," she said. But her eyes said something else.

"I will go home and kill myself," threatened Vidal, making a long puppy face.

Natalie tried not to smile. "See if I care, fool."

Vidal ambled off down the road, his hands in his pockets. "Goodbye for the last time," he called sorrowfully.

"I don't like Vidal," I said. Natalie and I started to walk home. Natalie looked at me with surprise.

"Ai-ai! And why not?"

"He conceited and stuck-up."

"He have class is all," said Natalie. "He is more of a man than all the form two boys put together."

"I ain't see what you like about him. He is one stuck-up coolie." I was starting to feel like Horace, whining and pouting. I didn't like it one bit, but I didn't know how to stop from feeling that way.

"Vidal want me to be his steady girl," said Natalie. "I going to ask Mummie if he could come with us to Tocco."

"If he going, then I staying home."

Natalie sucked her teeth loudly. "Stay home, nuh. I don't care as long as Vidal will come. Vidal say he want to marry me."

"Vidal is just a stupid, fresh-up little boy," I said.

We had reached Natalie's place. It was already dark, just past seven o'clock. "See you in school," said Natalie, shutting the gate between us. "And don't go fretting yourself about Vidal." Quickly she ran up the steps, opened the door and disappeared inside.

"Where you gone liming, child?" I could hear Auntie Mart in the kitchen above the rattle and clatter of supper dishes in the sink. "Everybody done eat already. You better stop with this lateness, you hear me?" Auntie Mart liked to fret, and she always claimed Natalie gave her plenty of opportunity to keep on fretting.

I went to visit Auntie Moe. Auntie Moe still lived in her mother's house, which was just as well, everybody said, because Granny Green was getting feeble-minded and needed somebody to take care of her. The back of Granny Green's house is easy for me to see from my bedroom window. And a little further up the hill, on the west side, is Natalie's place. Everybody lives close together, which is sometimes good and sometimes bad, depending on what kind of gossip is circulating. Once Auntie Moe and Auntie Mart didn't speak to each other for a month. Another time, when I was small, Mummie and Auntie Moe caught Uncle Harry red-handed cheating on Auntie Mart in Auntie Mart's own house. Auntie Mart was in Barbados. It was a little fair-skinned girl from Uncle Harry's office, Mummie said. When Auntie Mart found out, she left Uncle Harry. But afterwards, they made up again.

It is a five minute walk from Natalie's to Granny Green's place. Horace was sitting in the gallery when I arrived there. "Auntie Moe ain't come yet?" I asked him.

"Is half-seven," said Horace wearily. "She tell me six-o'clock."

I sat on the bannister near to him. "She will come," I said, and tried to sound reassuring.

"Your mother vex because you late for dinner. A little while ago, I hear her calling you from all-you house. You just like your Auntie Moe, always keeping people waiting. Where you been, pipsqueak?"

"With Natalie." I studied him. He was very handsome, so smartly dressed in his white and blue pinstripe shirt and serge trousers. I felt sorry for him. He sat in the wicker chair with his elbows resting on his knees and his big, black hands dangling down, and stared at the floor with dejected eyes.

"Well, girl," he said, rising. "I think I been blanked again. I better take myself home now. Say hello to your Aunt for me."

"I will tell Auntie Moe she is a no-good," I called as he ambled down to the gate.

Horace turned and waved. Then he was gone up the road, only his white pinstripe shirt showing in the darkness. I didn't go home. The smell of Granny Green's chicken pelau wafted out into the gallery, making my belly growl for its supper. But I sat and waited for Auntie Moe. I could hear Granny Green inside, her voice gravelly and quarrelsome. "Where the devil that Monica gone? Have that poor boy Horace sitting up in that gallery so."

There was nobody to answer her, so she answered herself. "Eight o'clock and she can't come home yet. Stchups. That Monica ain't have no kind of behaviour, nuh. None at all. Who would think is I raise she?"

Sitting on the bannister, I leaned up against the gallery post. It was hot. I thought about Horace and Auntie Moe and how bad she was always treating him. Then I thought about Natalie and Vidal and me. I thought about Tocco. It would be the five of us, as well as Auntie Mart and Uncle Harry, for the weekend. Auntie Moe said her friend Veronica was coming. Thank God for that, I thought, because I liked Veronica, and she could keep me company while Auntie Mart and Uncle Harry ran things, Moe and Horace fought, and Natalie and Vidal went off to be alone together. I thought about Natalie. She didn't care if I stayed home. She only had eyes for Vidal Ramdass. I hated Vidal and I hated Natalie; I suddenly hated Auntie Moe too for the way she treated Horace. I jumped down from the bannister and stamped down the steps and out through the gate.

"That you, Monica?" called Granny Green from inside. But I didn't bother to answer her; I just slammed the gate shut and started for home, trying hard not to think of Tocco.

Veronica was tall and pretty, and all the men liked to sweet-talk her, but she didn't pay them any mind. Veronica laughed a lot, and everybody liked her and she liked everybody. When I was small, she used to live up on the hill right next to Granny Green's house, that is how Moe and she got to be friends. But when her parents moved to Arima, she could only come on weekends. I liked Veronica almost as much as I liked Auntie Moe.

There are only three bedrooms in the house in Tocco, so after Uncle Harry and Auntie Mart chose their room, all the girls had to sleep separate from the boys. That meant Horace and Vidal, and Auntie Moe, Veronica, Natalie and me. It was the only time I could see Natalie without seeing Vidal. I wanted to share the bed with her, but she jumped in beside Auntie Moe. That left Veronica and me, which after a little while, I didn't mind because Veronica was prettier than Natalie anyhow, and just as nice to sleep near to, maybe even nicer.

The light was out, we were in darkness. It was just starting to quiet, only the sea rustling, and crickets chirping in the bush. I could smell the musty wood of the beach house, and the moth-ball scent of the sheets and pillows, and I could just see the slip of a new moon low in the sky outside the window. I could feel the warm from Veronica's body next to mine, and with everything so perfect, I started to smile inside. Natalie had to spoil it.

"I wonder what the boys doing now?" she said.

"Forget about the boys," said Auntie Moe. "You will have plenty of time to spend with them in the morning."

"I missing Vidal," said Natalie.

"You spend the whole damn day with him," I said loudly. "What you want to see him again for?"

Squinting, I could just see Natalie sitting up in the darkness. "You don't know nothing, girl," she said.

"You don't like to be with us?" asked Veronica, playing surprised.

"Being with Vidal is much nicer. I like to be with him."

"I sick of the damn name Vidal," I said.

"Shut up," whispered Natalie. "He will hear you."

"Good."

"You-all, stop that bickering," called Auntie Mart from her bedroom.

"You see?" hissed Natalie. "If Mummie hear, that mean Vidal hear too."

"Good, I done say already."

In the morning when I woke, Natalie was gone from beside Auntie Moe. I could hear Horace coughing as he rattled breakfast plates in the kitchen, so I slipped into my clothes and went out to help him.

"You see Natalie?" I asked.

"Yep. She down on the beach with Vidal."

I sucked my teeth.

"What happen? You jealous?"

"No."

"You want a fella too?"

"No!"

"You just ain't reach the right age yet," said Horace, winking. "Wait a little while, you will see. You will be running behind fellas just like Natalie."

"Not me," I shook my head hard, but from his smile, I could tell Horace didn't believe me.

"We having scramble egg and bacon today," said Horace. "Later me and Vidal going fishing. Tomorrow, it will be fry bake and king fish!"

"Good," I said. "I can have Auntie Moe's share. Auntie Moe don't like fish."

"Auntie Moe don't like plenty things," said Horace, more like he was talking to himself than to me. "Your Auntie is a fussy woman. Hard to please."

"She spoiled because she is the youngest of her three sisters," I said.

"That so?"

"Yep. The youngest always spoiled." I felt pretty wise talking to Horace, and grown up, almost like I was older than him. "Auntie Moe is easy to handle. You just have to spoil her."

Horace's face brightened.

"— But not too much. Don't let her know you spoiling her. You have to do it kind of sly, so she don't notice."

"Your Auntie Moe does notice everything."

We laughed. Horace fried the bacon while I scrambled the eggs up together. The aroma brought out Moe and Veronica, still in their night clothes.

"You better make plenty," said Auntie Moe. "People real hungry."

"Yes ma'am," said Horace, standing at attention.

I laughed at him.

"See what I tell you," he said, when they went to dress. "Just like a platoon sergeant."

We served out the breakfast in enamel plates and the four of us sat down together.

"Where everybody?" asked Veronica.

"Harry and Mart still sleeping," said Horace. "And Lord know where Vidal and Natalie gone."

"Better keep an eye on those two," said Veronica. She chuckled and winked at Horace and me.

"What you say you and me go for a walk later?" said Horace, looking at Auntie Moe.

"Sure, we could all go."

"I mean, just — Not just you and me?"

"I said, we can all go."

It got quiet, with only the sound of knives and forks clashing.

"Me and this girl got things to do," said Veronica at last, putting her arm around me. "You-all go and enjoy yourselves."

"What things?" I asked.

But Auntie Moe was glaring at Veronica, and Veronica was glaring at Auntie Moe, and Horace was glaring out the kitchen window.

"Don't bother," said Horace, getting up suddenly. "I like to walk by myself, too." He didn't bother to put his dishes in the sink; he just walked out the door and went downstairs, his footsteps falling loud and angry all the way to the beach below.

"I was only trying to make things easy," said Veronica.

"Well, don't," snapped Auntie Moe.

"He care about you."

Auntie Moe sucked her teeth loudly.

"You insult and hurt him all the time."

"I don't care. I wish he would leave me alone."

I got up and went down to find Horace. He was sitting alone at the bottom of the steps, staring at the sun rising above the ocean, and slowly sifting sand through his fingers.

"She don't mean to be so nasty," I said, sitting down beside him. "Is just so she is."

"She nasty whether she mean to be or not."

"She like you."

"The same way cat like dog."

"Natalie say that is always how women act when they in love."

Horace shook his head slowly. "She don't love me," he said. "She don't love me at all." He looked at me, smiling, but there was no smile in his eyes. "I think I got to take loss, girl." Then he got up and walked off down the beach, alone.

Natalie and Vidal were standing far out on the wooden jetty. They weren't noticing anybody, too absorbed in their own private talk. They stood close together, laughing and talking, and they had their arms draped across each other. I could hear Auntie Moe and Veronica arguing upstairs, and trying hard to keep their voices down; but every now and then they would get louder than they wanted to be. I didn't want to sit there on the steps trying not to look at Vidal and Natalie, and trying not to hear Veronica and Auntie Moe. So I got up feeling kind of vexed, and trudged the two miles up the main road just to get a Solo sweet drink from the soda shop.

Horace didn't come back until dark. And when he came, he smelled of brandy and stale cigarettes, his foot heavy on the wooden steps and his face ornery.

"Ai, Horace," I said. "Uncle Harry and Vidal catch fish. Auntie make king-fish soup." I was glad to see him. "Horace, sit down, and I will get a dish for you."

"Where Moe?" asked Horace. He didn't look glad to see anybody.

"She and Veronica done gone to bed."

"Is only eight o'clock."

"They was tired, they say."

Horace laughed, but his face was hard. "Tired. Tired. All-you blind or what? All-you can't see what going on between them two girls? Them two is lesbians."

Uncle Harry sucked his teeth loud. "You had too much to drink, boy." He didn't even bother to look up from the table where he was sitting in his undershirt and khaki shorts, with his playing cards. Vidal sniggered from the lumpy couch where he and Natalie were reading the funnies section of the newspaper together.

"Oh, gosh, Horace," said Auntie Mart. "I know you and Moe fighting, and I know you vex with her, but that is going too far."

Horace stood in the middle of the room alone, his big nostrils flaring. "I serious," he said, and his voice was loud in the night silence. "What you think they does be doing, always up on each other so, alone, alone all the time? What you think they doing now?"

"Oh, Geeeeed!" screeched Natalie.

Auntie Mart scowled at Natalie and me. "You girls and Vidal, go outside."

"Mummie," wailed Natalie. "It dark!" But Natalie didn't really care about that. What she really wanted was to stay and listen to the conversation going on inside.

"Go outside," Auntie Mart said. "Now."

When Auntie Mart says "Now" in a certain tone of voice, you always do whatever it is she is telling you to do, if you have any sense in your head, and know what is best for yourself. So we all obeyed, Vidal leading the way, clambering down the rickety wooden steps like a bull-elephant.

"It pitch-dark," Natalie whined. "I frighten!"

"Don't frighten," said Vidal, in his deepest voice. "You have *me*!" And Natalie started to squeal and dance up because Vidal was tickling her. "Lesbians, lesbians, lesbians," squeaked Vidal, high and girlish-like.

Natalie hissed, "Shut up, fool!" and flopped down in the sand beside Vidal and me, in the little sliver of light falling from the window above us. After a while she sat up and looked at us, her face serious.

"You think it true?" she asked.

Vidal whispered, "Be quiet, I want to hear what going on."

"You can't hear anything, dotish," said Natalie. "They talking quiet."

All of us strained our ears in the darkness.

"So," asked Natalie again. "You think it true?"

"Maybe," said Vidal. "Who would ever think it, eh? Auntie Moe a zami woman."

"Auntie Moe is no zami," I said.

"How you would know?" asked Vidal. "When you think of it, your Auntie Moe ain't the most feminine thing. She like to wear them zami-boots and dungarees. Come to think of it, kind of like you." And he inspected me with a comical, purse-lip, old-lady-prude-looking-over-the-rim-of-her-glasses expression. "Zamis does stick together, you know."

"Oh gosh," said Natalie. "Vidal, leave the girl alone, nuh."

Something fell on the floor and broke upstairs. Natalie grabbed Vidal and I grabbed Natalie. Footfalls thudded hard across the floor above us. Somebody was shouting "Moe! Moe! Get up and come out here." It was Horace's voice.

"Horace, catch yourself!" Auntie Mart was warning.

Natalie was beside herself with excitement. "Oh Jesus, we missing all the action!" she moaned.

It was quiet. We tried not to breathe, in case we might miss anything. All I could hear was my own heart beating, the sea grumbling, and crickets chirping loud enough to drown out everything.

Then, I could hear Auntie Moe's voice. "Yes. Yes," said Auntie Moe.

Vidal and Natalie and I looked at each other. Wide-eyed. "Yes, what?" whispered Natalie.

"Yes, it true," Auntie Moe was saying loudly.

"Moe, be quiet," somebody else was shouting, who sounded like Veronica. "Don't say anything."

But Moe was saying many things, and so was Horace, and Auntie Mart started wailing, "Oh Gawd, Oh Gawd, Harry, bring the Limacol," and Vidal, Natalie and I rushed up the wooden steps because we all knew that nobody would notice us in the midst of all the commotion that was happening.

"Ting turn ole mass," and "Shame and scandal in the family," Vidal was singing under his breath as the doorway filled up with the three of us.

Horace's face was ugly with brandy and anger. I had never seen him look that way. I looked at Vidal. He was watching and grinning eagerly.

"That is what we are," said Auntie Moe. "Lesbians. I sick of hiding the truth. Sick of it."

Auntie Mart had collapsed on the couch, and lay there with her legs sprawled, fanning herself with the newspaper.

Veronica was sitting at the kitchen table, far apart from Auntie Moe. Uncle Harry had one hand in his pocket and the other one in his hair. Horace and Auntie Moe were standing and facing each other.

"I care about Veronica," said Auntie Moe. "She is the only one I care about."

"Oh Gawd!" Auntie Mart screeched, and tossed away the newspaper. She made the sign of the cross over herself a few times well.

"Shut up your mouth, Monica," said Uncle Harry. "You say enough for one night already."

"She doesn't know what she's saying." Veronica was glaring at Auntie Moe.

"I know exactly what I am saying," said Auntie Moe. "And I going to keep saying it. Veronica care for me and I care for Veronica."

"Girl, that kind of careless talk around the place will get you a beating or worse," Uncle Harry said to Auntie Moe. "The family will never live down the shame."

"Father Beddoes," said Auntie Mart. "We will have to take her to Father Beddoes. Either that or a psychiatrist."

"I ain't going to Father Beddoes or no psychiatrist," Auntie Moe was shouting. "Nothing wrong with me, you hear?"

"You see?" pronounced Auntie Mart. "She crazy."

Auntie Moe shoved past Vidal, Natalie and me, her footsteps thudding on the steps as she stormed down them. Veronica cried out "Moe!" and thudded down after her. I craned my neck over the stairwell, my eyes straining, but the darkness consumed them and their voices together.

Horace stood confused in the centre of the room, rubbing the back of his neck with his hand, his unfocused eyes gazing stupidly about him. "I love her," he was saying over and over again. "I still love her."

"You would still marry her?" asked Uncle Harry, looking at Horace.

"Yes. Yes."

"Well, then. We will announce the marriage as soon as we go back home. Moe will get over this thing, whatever sickness is ailing her, wait and see. Marriage will help her."

"Yes," said Horace. He looked over to the doorway where Vidal, Natalie and I were standing, and for the first time, he smiled. It was a big, lopsided smile, and Horace was grinning right at me. "Guess what, pipsqueak?" he said. "Is married for your Auntie Moe and me."

That was the first time I ever saw morning rolling in over the black sea in a mist veil, its breath damp and brine-smelling. Morning came, and there was no Veronica or Auntie Moe. I was the only one waiting, sitting on the bottom step of the beach house, hugging myself against the night chill. Waiting. Upstairs, it became quiet, as people talked in soft voices. Then there were footsteps padding to bedrooms, and no voices at all. Somebody called out for me a few times. They sucked their teeth loudly. "She will come back," said Natalie. Auntie Mart muttered something. Then, there was only the quiet, and the sound of the crickets and the sea, and I sat, leaning up against the night, waiting and looking. I fell asleep a few times, but the cold woke me. I thought about Horace and Auntie Moe. I wasn't happy for Horace or Auntie Moe. Making Auntie Moe marry Horace was like forcing Natalie to marry me. Natalie loved Vidal. I felt miserable when I thought about the way Natalie looked at Vidal, but I knew it was true, she loved him.

People started to stir upstairs. Today was going-home day. Eat breakfast, pack up, drive back into town, up the hill in Saint Joseph where, at the gate, Granny Green would be waiting. Somebody came into the kitchen, and there was the sound of pots and pans rattling, and then the smell of coffee brewing, king fish frying and fry-bake making. My stomach grumbled. Auntie Mart called me from the kitchen, and I heard Uncle Harry, and Horace, and Natalie and Vidal talking in sleepy voices. Auntie Mart called me again. The sun began to rise out of the sea like a weak child. Waves draped themselves sighing across the sand, and slid out again. The beach stretched long and empty and white into the distance. But there was no sign of Veronica and Auntie Moe.

I sat and waited.

Limacoli is an alcohol and lime-based liquid essence applied to the face and brow for alleviating headaches, fever, fainting spells, etc.

MOMENTARY LAPSES

Jannett Bailey

Weak yellow rays from the forty-watt bulb washed over Joanna's hair and shoulders. Shoulders covered in goose pimples from the caresses of cool early morning air. She noticed the chill but refused to add more clothes to the full slip she'd slept in. It was an old black thing, so soft she barely felt it against her brown skin. The thin straps were pulled up and tied so most of her full breasts were hugged and covered by the lace top. From halfway down her midriff, the worn satiny material flowed to just above her knees. If Malcolm were here, he'd tell her to put on more clothes, but since he was not, to hell with what he wanted. Joanna picked up a comb from the dresser and brought it to her head.

She was used to the image in the mirror so there was no need to look at it. Not her face that was beginning to wrinkle. Just the hair that came down straight and thin to her shoulders. That she paid attention to as she raked the old black comb from scalp to hair end. She did this several times, combing the hair straight back from her high brown forehead. Then she parted the hair in the centre, front to middle. She was greying more. Joanna didn't grey like some people, going silver or white. No, her hair went from jet black to a rust-gold colour like old metal. The pale light picked up the rusty strands, now as plentiful as the black ones.

Oh, well. She supposed she was lucky. Her mother had been totally grey by the time she was forty. Joanna was forty-two. Malcolm had been dead for more than a year now and there was no one to notice the change over. Not that he would have cared one way or other about her greys or her woes. They'd been indifferent to each other for a long time before she'd used her fingertips to close his eyelids for the last time. She paused and looked at the wedding band she still wore. She supposed she should take it off. But then some jackass might see that as an invitation; think she had completed her mourning and would welcome his attention. Truth was, the mourning hadn't lasted beyond the first handful of dirt on the pine-wood coffin, but having no one on the other side of the bed meant she could spread out for the first time in her life. Joanna wasn't about to give that up.

She twisted the thin gold band around and around on her finger. It had been there since he put it on her twenty years before. She couldn't remember ever taking it off. Her finger was slimmer now than when she'd married and the ring had been loose for a long time. She held her hand up to the light and looked at the grooves on the band that had become more and more shallow with the years. Like her marriage. She smiled slightly.

Joanna smoothed back her hair with the palms of her hands then pulled the hair together in one scrawny bunch, holding it with her left hand. She wrapped the fingers of her right hand around the hanging rust-gold and black hair and pulled along the length until she reached the ends. A few strands came out in her hand. She looked at them, flicked her fingers so they dropped onto the dresser, and repeated the action until no hair came out.

Years ago it had been just a strand or two. Now she lost so much hair each time she combed it, she found no pleasure in the act. She had just started twisting the hair into its customary tight braid when a faint knock on her bedroom door made her fingers pause. She glanced at the clock ticking on the dresser. Five fifteen a.m.

"Come."

The doorknob turned and Lucille pushed her head into the room. Joanna smiled at the other woman. It was the same every time she saw Lucille. A soft bubble of happiness settled somewhere around her heart and stayed there, like a warm promise. They would go for months without seeing each other or communicating in any way, but the moment they came together, it was as though no time or space had passed between them. And Joanna always wondered why she allowed her friendship with Lucille to go neglected for such long stretches of time.

"Ah wake you?" Joanna asked. Lucille had slept in Sandra's room, next to hers. Sandra was Joanna's daughter. These days her room stayed empty while she was away at university or off somewhere visiting Lord-knows-who. It was something Joanna was still getting used to. The emptiness.

Lucille pushed the door wider and entered, her tall full body still in a thin shift she'd worn to bed. The material was a faded print, almost white next to her dark skin. Her big breasts were loose under the cloth and pushed against it, as if protesting their confinement.

"No. Me been up since four thirty. Me see your light when me pass go bathroom just now."

"Country girl," Joanna jeered. "No cows and pigs to feed in town, child. Go back to sleep."

Lucille yawned and sat on the edge of Joanna's bed. It squeaked and sagged under her weight. Her shift rode up to reveal an expanse of firm brown flesh. Lucille did nothing to cover the strong thighs that were exposed. She lapped the shift between them and rested an elbow on her knee. She cupped her chin in her hand and looked at Joanna. Her broad smile, showing a twisted front tooth, was familiar.

Joanna turned back to the mirror and combed her hair again. "You sleep well?" she asked.

"Yeah. Was strange to hear the cars and ting outside though. Me couldn't live so close to a main road and all. People have no manners. Like them nuh know other people inside and want sleep. Them always talk so loud when them pass people house at midnight?"

Joanna laughed. She had lived in this house so long she didn't notice those sounds anymore. Lucille had come to visit occasionally but never stayed the night. She was always in too much of a hurry to get back home — too much to do before the sun got hot — for her to spend the night in Montego Bay.

"When Sandra spend the week with you last year she come back and complain 'bout crickets and birds and croaking lizards and dogs and pigs and how them make noise all the time."

Lucille hissed her teeth affectionately. "Big girl like that, insist on locking the windows nights because she 'fraid bullfrog going jump through onto the bed. No matter you can't breathe in the heat. Me had was to sleep in the living room the whole time she there. When she going back to university?"

"Next week. And Ah hope she find her tail back here in time to pack her own clothes. Ah know she banking on me packing it for her, but she going be in for a surprise if she get back here from that friend o' hers the day before she due to leave." Joanna began plaiting her hair into a single braid.

"You must be proud o' her though, full scholarship and straight A's all last year. She get her brains from you, you know. Here, let me do that."

Before Joanna was quite aware of what Lucille intended, she felt her hair being taken from her surprised fingers. Lucille's hands, so much larger than hers, held her hair.

Shock, embarrassment, surged through her. Exactly why, Joanna was not quite sure. Lucille's fingers were gentle. Gentler than hers. Unexpectedly gentle for someone who used them for digging and planting and picking. They moved slowly through Joanna's hair as she unbraided it. They'd been friends for a long time. They'd hugged, shared a bed on rare occasions, swapped stories and tears, but she couldn't remember Lucille ever touching her like this. *This?* This what? There was nothing unusual about combing another woman's hair. She was being silly. Must be her own discomfort with the changes her body was going through, the aging taking place without her permission.

In the mirror, Joanna stared at the long brown fingers softly smoothing back her thin hair. Strong brown fingers you could trust. Fingers meant to hold onto. Joanna closed her eyes as the fingers began moving gently over her scalp. No one had touched her hair in so long. She washed it herself, creamed it herself every three months or so when the roots grew out, rolled it on curlers, and when it dried, combed out the curls and braided it. She'd watched the strands fall for years, at first with concern, then resignation and indifference. Well, maybe not indifference. She still hated to see what used to be one of her best features rolled up in a ball she kept in her dresser drawer.

You didn't throw away your hair. If birds got it and used it for nest, you could go crazy. If other people got a hold of it, no telling what they would use it for. No, you were never careless with the hair that fell from your head. When the ball got big enough she'd bury it some place. That was supposed to make your hair grow again, but she wasn't sure she believed that. Lately it sure hadn't been working for her.

"Where you keep the hair pins?" Lucille's voice pulled Joanna back into the room.

"Ah-Ah have a couple o' them somewhere here." Joanna's nervous fingers moved hastily over the dresser and located a small coconut shell container with knick-knacks. There were mismatched buttons, a few latch pins, hooks and eyes, and two hair pins.

"What you want hair pins for anyway? Just plait it and tuck it under."

"Uh-uh. You hair too weak. If you keep plait it like that all o' it going break off. When you come home this evening me will treat it for you with castor oil and fowl eggs. Give me the pins."

Joanna did as she was asked and watched Lucille gently fold the hair around itself, felt her even more gently pin it to the back of her head. A warm shiver coursed down her spine from somewhere near the base of her neck. Her ears were warm. Oh, Lord, what was happening to her?

Lucille stepped in closer to Joanna's back and reached around with her long brown fingers to brush a few wayward strands into the soft knot she'd created at the back of Joanna's head. Her touch was feather light, and all Joanna's senses concentrated with precision at the exact points where Lucille's fingertips connected with her body. When everything was to her satisfaction, Lucille stepped away. Joanna was immediately aware of cool air on her body, of goose pimples popping up all over her back. She hoped Lucille hadn't noticed.

This was silly. She shouldn't be embarrassed by Lucille doing her hair. They'd been friends for longer than she could remember, long before Sandra was born, and the child was now a woman of twenty. Thing was, the strange warmth and tingle did not quite feel like shame but something else she had no name for.

Lucille sat back down on the bed and Joanna watched her through the mirror, pretending to be examining her new hairstyle. She could feel her heart pounding, hear it like drums in her ears.

"What time you need to get to work?" Lucille's voice penetrated the beating drums.

"Uh, Ah not going in today. Ah decide to take the day off since you in town."

"And you call me country girl? You got nothing to do but you still get up before sun?"

Joanna mirrored Lucille's smile and turned around to face her. "Ah glad you decided to come spend a few days before you leave. You excited?"

"Sometimes me think anything better than digging yam all day then trying to persuade people to give you a fair price for you produce — but me no know. Me not sure if Kingston is where me want to be. And me definitely not sure if me want to be there with Charlie."

"What you mean? You and Charlie been together now, what, ten years?"

"Eight. But we never live together. Him spend the night when me want him to and other than that me go me ways as me please. This different."

"Yes. But you been complaining you need a change. And you can't make a living from that tired piece o' land no more, so what else you going do? That's why Charlie go town in the first place. To look life for the two o' you."

"Me know, me know. Ah the one that encourage him to go when him brother make him the offer. But me just don't know right now, Jo. Truth to tell, me was more excited 'bout coming see you than..."

Joanna came over and sat beside Lucille on the bed. "You just nervous, girl. Is a big move, yes. You packing up you whole life and making a change."

"Me forty years old, Jo."

"So what?"

"What the hell Ah doing moving in with man?"

"Charlie love you, girl. Him will take care o' you."

Lucille held out her big hands, palms up. The lines were deep and strongly marked. They're softer than they look, Joanna thought, and felt another shiver as if the hands were again touching her head.

"Me can take care o' meself. Me been taking care o' meself all me life. Me not like you."

Joanna's head snapped up. She stiffened. "What you mean, not like me?"

Lucille's hands opened and closed compulsively. "You always had a man in you life, Jo. You and Malcolm together since you sixteen. You don't know any other way but being with a man."

"What you saying, Lucille?" The glint in Joanna's voice caught Lucille's attention.

"Me mean ... Me mean say ... You know what me mean, Jo."

Joanna's eyes narrowed. She folded her arms below her breasts, pushing their softness up above the lace of the slip. Her skin was a lot fairer than the worn black lace. One nipple was almost poking through the worn cloth. Lucille blinked and met Joanna's eyes.

"Me just mean that it must be hard for you to be without Malcolm taking care o' you. But is not the same for me."

"Malcolm been dead fifteen months, Lucille. You see any other man skulking around me bed?"

"Maybe not." Her big hands opened and closed, opened and closed. "But don't tell me the insurance money don't come in handy."

Joanna was on her feet. Something like pain — sharp and searing; something like disappointment — bitter to the taste, was contracting her chest. "What exactly you saying, Lucille?"

"Me mean ..."

"You mean you don't think Ah could feed me own damn self without Malcolm to back me up!"

Lucille stood up too. "It ..."

"Well make me tell you something, Lucille Brown. Ah haven't touched a cent o' Malcolm dead-money. That's what Ah been using to keep Sandra at UWI. The scholarship she get only cover the tuition, it nuh take care of her board and books. You know how much that cost? You know how much it cost to make her stay in that Mary Seacole Hall place? And what one science book cost? It already eat up half o' what we get from them people."

Joanna stopped speaking and bit her lip hard. She didn't want to start crying like an idiot. What was there to cry for anyway? Just because Lucille thought she was weak and incompetent? She saw Lucille open her mouth to say something, but she didn't want to hear anything from her. Not yet.

"Ah get up every morning God send, put on me clothes and go to work, you hear me? Come weekend, Ah cash me cheque and pay me bills. It no different from when Malcolm alive. Except Ah don't have to fill him mouth as well."

Lucille stared at Joanna's tight lips, their fullness thinned out to a narrow line. "Me-Ah-me... But you always ..."

"Yes, Malcolm worked, him wasn't a lazy man, Ah will give him that. But every cent o' it went into him woman-dem pocket, not mine. This house — this roof that over me head — Ah had was to fight and push him to build or by the time him pass we would still have been in rent-house. Ah been working and paying me bills and taking care o' me child by meself since Ah don't know when. So you got no right, Lucille, no right whatsoever to look at me and call me dependent. Where the hell you get that notion from anyway? How the hell you could think that when we been friends for so long?"

"Ah sorry. Me sorry, Joanna." She touched Joanna's shoulder and it was stiff and resentful. "Me did just think that ... Is just that you never said anything. And Malcolm — Ah mean, you know how Malcolm was."

"That's right! Ah thought you know how it was. That all that come out o' him mouth was hot air and bad breath. Ah thought you was me friend, Lucille." Joanna turned her back to Lucille. She could feel tears burning behind her eyes, constricting her throat and tightening her stomach.

"Me can't read yuh mind, Jo. Good God, how me was supposed to know? How often me see you? Twice a year? Maybe three times if me get the chance to come up here. How I supposed to know?"

Lucille reached up again, with both hands this time, and rested them on Joanna's shoulders. Joanna tried to move away but Lucille held her easily and after a minute Joanna stopped protesting. She remained still, with Lucille's hands gentle on her shoulders. "Me sorry, girl. The last thing me mean to do is hurt you feelings. You know me care 'bout you."

Lucille felt a shudder beneath her hands and Joanna's muscles relaxed as she kneaded the flesh with her fingers. Joanna's skin was cool and soft, pliant to her touch. She concentrated on moving her fingers firmly into the cords of knotted muscles at the base of Joanna's neck, until she felt them give. Then she cupped the entire neck with her right hand and rubbed gently. Joanna moaned ... from deep inside her throat.

The sound startled Lucille, sent a weird reverberation through her body that settled in the lowest point of her groin. Settled and pulsed like a beating heart. *Jesus.* Her hand checked its motion, rested quietly against Joanna's neck as she frowned, trying to identify the emotion tossing around her insides like water in a corked bottle.

Joanna murmured softly, protesting, Lucille realized, the stillness of her hand. She started rubbing again and her left hand moved down Joanna's body. It slipped around the smaller woman's waist and encountered soft belly encased in the satin of Joanna's slip. Lucille spread her palm open over it and pressed. Joanna's belly muscles contracted and the sounds that came from her throat were unmistakable. Passion.

Passion? Lucille felt her entire body flood with heat. Her breath whooshed up through her throat and out her mouth. *Jesus Christ!* Joanna sagged against her and Lucille's hand tightened automatically, pulling her closer. *What me suppose to do now? What me suppose to...?* The words circled in her mind, chasing each other like panicked children. *What me suppose to do?*

But her hands knew. They knew the answer without waiting for the question. One moved up and cupped a full heavy breast through the soft old lace, found a nipple poking through and rolled it between thumb and forefinger. The other slid over the softness of Joanna's belly, pressed and felt a tremor that found an echo in herself. Joanna clutched Lucille's hand. Lucille brought Joanna's hand to her mouth and sucked.

"Oh Gahd..."

Lucille heard Joanna's voice through a fog. Her tongue moved over Joanna's thumb and pulled it into her mouth.

Joanna kept repeating, "Oh Gahd, ohGahdohGahdohGahd..."

And when Joanna turned into her arms Lucille did not hesitate. She pulled her closer and covered her mouth with hers — soft moist lips over softer moister lips. For a moment they both stood stock still, eyes wide open, hands halted in their quest of each other's body.

It was the time to pull back, to cough, stutter, apologize for a moment's insanity, or maybe pretend they had only been comforting each other. Pretend that the fervour behind the hot breath and pounding hearts was not what it was. Not carnal passion, not raw sexual craving aroused by the touch of an old friend. An old friend of the same sex! Dear God, who ever heard of something like this?

Lucille had seen dogs in heat indiscriminately mount each other, male dog jumping on the back of male dog, trying to bury its thing in a convenient hole. Young rams did the same thing. But females? She'd never seen that.

So what was she doing? She didn't even like sex. Not really. Charlie complained all the time that if he didn't initiate the act, nothing would happen, and most times nothing did on her part. She did what she'd done with the few men she'd been with, lie still and allow them to hump away until they got tired. Half the time it was painful, and a little embarrassing to listen to their grunts and groans. This thing with Charlie had lasted so long because on the occasions she gave in to his desire, he was gentle and demanded no more than she could give.

She'd survived the looks and whispers from people in her district all through her late teens and twenties when she neither sought nor kept a man, and didn't become bloated with pregnancy from her infrequent coupling. Survived the questions about her womanhood, her lack of desire to be matched and mated with one of the men who cast their roving eye in her direction. She wasn't bad looking, and besides, she was big and strong and hard working and submissive, as far as they could tell.

Her mother had encouraged her to ignore them all. To do only what made her comfortable. And when her mother had died and Charlie had been there for her, she made room for him in her life. They'd been lovers until six months ago when she'd helped him pack and seen him off at the crossroads on his way to Kingston. They had written back and forth during those six months. Practical letters informing each other of the other's progress. Letters signed, "Love Charlie," "Love Lucille," without thought of what that meant.

Now here she was holding a woman in her arms, her heart pounding, her hands sweating in anticipation of God knows what. Sweating and pounding so hard she could barely see straight in the early morning light. Nothing like this had ever happened to her before, nothing that left her knees so weak she was just about ready to collapse. So she clutched the woman squashed up against her and waited.

It must be menopause, Joanna thought. She'd read about that. Women did strange things when those hot flashes took over. They went insane for blinding periods of time and had to be forgiven those momentary lapses, on account of hormone imbalance. That must be it. Hormone imbalance, due to menopause.

True, this was her first experience with those hot flashes described in the book. And her period was still as regular as clockwork. But how else could she explain the need to go on holding Lucille, to do more than just hold her big hard body in her arms?

It wasn't the kind of hardness like Malcolm had had. Lucille was hard and pillowy soft at the same time. There were spaces inside Lucille that Joanna knew she could sink into, places that would hold her tight and swallow her up all at the same time. She could feel some of those places if she pressed in closer, instead of pulling away like she should.

But her breasts were squashed up against Lucille's, her nipples so hard and tight they were painful. Painfully in need of something from Lucille. And the throbbing in her groin made her want to press her knees together and scream, made her want to open her legs and tell Lucille to do something, anything that would stop her from exploding like a carbonated drink that had been shaken and shaken and shaken for too long before opening.

It had been forever since she'd felt like this. Not since she'd found out about Malcolm's other women and something inside her soul had shut down. After that sex had been good between them, when they had it, but not like when they'd first met. And gradually, even the lukewarm passion had grown cold. She'd assumed it was like that with everybody. Age took away desire in women, and men roamed the street. So why was this happening now? And with another woman!

Joanna felt Lucille's hand move along her back, down to her bottom, and squeeze. Her heart flipped up into her mouth and she almost choked. Her eyes flew open and met Lucille's dark questioning gaze. *What was she asking? What did she want to know?* Joanna moistened her lips with her tongue and saw Lucille's gaze refocus there. Joanna felt something gush in her crotch.

Oh Jesus, had her period started? She calculated quickly and realized, unless she had become irregular for the first time in twenty years, it wasn't possible.

Lucille squeezed again. Joanna thought she'd faint. Hot flashes. Got to be one of those hot flashes. That's why she was grinding her crotch into Lucille's. That's why Lucille was pulling her closer and she wasn't protesting, just groaning and mumbling and grinding and grinding. They were both going through menopause. This was their momentary lapse into insanity.

Lucille wondered for a moment why she was the one doing most of the fondling and touching. She'd always been passive in moments like this. Now here she was with hands that would not be still. They just wandered and wandered all over Joanna's body. And her mouth was doing the same thing, seeking all the available places on Joanna's face and neck that she could kiss, not sure how to approach the moist soft lips she wanted.

Joanna finally held her head still, placing her palms on either side of Lucille's head, holding her, so their lips could touch, their tongues meet.

From that point on, images became brilliant and disordered. A hand on a hip; tongue flickering over a brown nipple, then sucking; raspy uneven breath; the taste of mint someone had brushed with; an ear so soft against a twisted front tooth; fingers delving into moist pulsing places; and the sheets on the bed getting tangled and flung to the floor. And skin. All that soft brown skin everywhere, impossible not to touch it, suck on it, nibble and lick it.

When all the images finally converged, overlapped and erupted into radiant colours and sounds Joanna found herself strewn contentedly across Lucille's softly snoring body. Later on, she thought.

When she wakes up, Ah'll explain about menopause. About momentary lapses for which we shouldn't be blamed. We're just lucky, Joanna decided, that we got those hot flashes the same time.

from the Joanna Collection

OUT ON MAIN STREET
Shani Mootoo

1.

Janet and me? We does go Main Street to see pretty pretty sari and bangle, and to eat we belly full a burfi and gulub jamoon, but we doh go too often because, yuh see, is dem sweets self what does give people like we a presupposition for untameable hip and thigh.

Another reason we shy to frequent dere is dat we is watered down Indians - we ain't good grade A Indians. We skin brown, is true, but we doh even think 'bout India unless something happen over dere and it come on de news. Mih family remain Hindu ever since mih ancestors leave India behind, but nowadays dey doh believe in praying unless things real bad, because, as mih father always singing, like if is a mantra: "Do good and good will be bestowed unto you." So he is a veritable saint cause he always doing good by his women friends and dey chilren. I sure some a dem must be mih half sister and brother, oui!

Mostly, back home, we is kitchen Indians: some kind a Indian food every day, at least once a day, but we doh get cardamom and other fancy spice down dere so de food not spicy like Indian food I eat in restaurants up here. But it have one thing we doh make joke 'bout down dere: we like we meethai and sweetrice too much, and it remain overly authentic, like de day Naana and Naani step off de boat in Port of Spain harbour over a hundred and sixty years ago. Check out dese hips here nah, dey is pure sugar and condensed milk, pure sweetness!

But Janet family different. In de ole days when Canadian missionaries land in Trinidad dey used to make a bee-line straight for Indians from down

South. And Janet greatgrandparents is one a de first South families dat exchange over from Indian to Presbyterian. Dat was a long time ago.

When Janet born, she father, one Mr. John Mahase, insist on asking de Reverend MacDougal from Trace Settlement Church, a leftover from de Canadian Mission, to name de baby girl. De good Reverend choose de name Constance cause dat was his mother name. But de mother a de child, Mrs. Savitri Mahase, wanted to name de child sheself. Ever since Savitri was a lil girl she like de yellow hair, fair skin and pretty pretty clothes Janet and John used to wear in de primary school reader — since she lil she want to change she name from Savitri to Janet but she own father get vex and say how Savitri was his mother name and how she will insult his mother if she gone and change it. So Savitri get she own way once by marrying this fella name John, and she do a encore, by calling she daughter Janet, even doh husband John upset for days at she for insulting de good Reverend by throwing out de name a de Reverend mother.

So dat is how my girlfriend, a darkskin Indian girl with thick black hair (pretty fuh so!) get a name like Janet.

She come from a long line a Presbyterian school teacher, headmaster and headmistress. Savitri still teaching from de same Janet and John reader in a primary school in San Fernando, and John, getting more and more obtuse in his ole age, is headmaster more dan twenty years now in Princes Town Boys' Presbyterian High School. Everybody back home know dat family good good. Dat is why Janet leave in two twos. Soon as A Level finish she pack up and take off like a jet plane so she could live without people only shoo-shooing behind she back... "But A A! Yuh ain't hear de goods 'bout John Mahase daughter, gyul? How yuh mean yuh ain't hear? Is a big thing! Everybody talking 'bout she. Hear dis, nah! Yuh ever see she wear a dress? Yes! Doh look at mih so. Yuh reading mih right!"

Is only recentish I realize Mahase is a Hindu last name. In de ole days every Mahase in de country turn Presbyterian and now de name doh have no association with Hindu or Indian whatsoever. I used to think of it as a Presbyterian Church name until some days ago when we meet a Hindu fella fresh from India name Yogdesh Mahase who never even hear of Presbyterian.

De other day I ask Janet what she know 'bout Divali. She say, "It's the Hindu festival of lights, isn't it?" like a line straight out a dictionary. Yuh think she know anything 'bout how lord Rama get himself exile in a forest for fourteen years, and how when it come time for him to go back home his followers light up a pathway to help him make his way out, and dat is what Divali lights is all about? All Janet know is 'bout going for drive in de country to see light, and she could remember looking forward, around Divali time, to the lil brown paper-bag packages full a burfi and parasad that she father Hindu students used to bring for him.

One time in a Indian restaurant she ask for parasad for dessert. Well! Since den I never go back in dat restaurant, I embarrass fuh so!

I used to think I was a Hindu *par excellence* until I come up here and see real flesh and blood Indian from India. Up here, I learning 'bout all kind a custom and food and music and clothes dat we never see or hear 'bout in good ole Trinidad. Is de next best thing to going to India, in truth, oui! But Indian store clerk on Main Street doh have no patience with us, specially when we talking English to dem. Yuh ask dem a question in English and dey insist on giving de answer in Hindi or Punjabi or Urdu or Gujarati. How I suppose to know de difference even! And den dey look at yuh disdainful disdainful — like yuh disloyal, like yuh is a traitor.

But yuh know, it have one other reason I real reluctant to go Main Street. Yuh see, Janet pretty fuh so! And I doh like de way men does look at she, as if because she wearing jeans and T-shirt and high-heel shoe and make-up and have long hair loose and flying about like she is a walking-talking shampoo ad, dat she easy. And de women always looking at she beady eye, like she loose and going to thief dey man. Dat kind a thing always make me want to put mih arm round she waist like, she is my woman, take yuh eyes off she! and shock de false teeth right out dey mouth. And den is a whole other story when dey see me with mih crew cut and mih blue jeans tuck inside mih jim-boots. Walking next to Janet, who so femme dat she redundant, tend to make me look like a gender dey forget to classify. Before going Main Street I does parade in front de mirror practising a jiggly-wiggly kind a walk. But if I ain't walking like a strong-man monkey I doh exactly feel right and I always revert back to mih true colours. De men dem does look at me like if dey is exactly what I need a taste of to cure me good and proper. I could see dey eyes watching Janet and me, dey face growing dark as dey imagining all kind a situation and position. And de women dem embarrass fuh so to watch me in mih eye, like dey fraid I will jump up and try to kiss dem, or make pass at dem. Yuh know, sometimes I wonder if 1 ain't mad enough to do it just for a little bacchanal, nah!

Going for a outing with mih Janet on Main Street ain't easy! If only it wasn't for burfi and gulub jamoon! If only I had a learned how to cook dem kind a thing before I leave home and come up here to live!

2.

In large deep-orange Sanskrit-style letters, de sign on de saffron-colour awning above de door read "Kush Valley Sweets." Underneath in smaller red letters it had "Desserts Fit For The Gods." It was a corner building. The front and side was one big glass wall. Inside was big. Big like a gymnasium. Yuh could see in through de brown tint windows: dark brown plastic chair, and brown table, each one de length of a door, line up stiff and straight in row after row like if is a school room.

Before entering de restaurant I ask Janet to wait one minute outside with me while I rumfle up mih memory, pulling out all de sweet names I know from home, besides burfi and gulub jamoon: meethai, jilebi, sweetrice (but dey call dat kheer up here), and ladhoo. By now, of course, mih mouth watering fuh so! When I feel confident enough dat I wouldn't make a fool a mih Brown self by asking what dis one name? and what dat one name? we went in de restaurant. In two twos all de spice in de place take a flying leap in our direction and give us one big welcome hug up, tight fuh so! Since den dey take up permanent residence in de jacket I wear dat day!

Mostly it had women customers sitting at de tables, chatting and laughing, eating sweets and sipping masala tea. De only men in de place was de waiters, and all six waiters was men. I figure dat dey was brothers, not too hard to conclude, because all a dem had de same full round chin, round as if de chin stretch tight over a ping-pong ball, and dey had de same big roving eyes. I know better dan to think dey was mere waiters in de employ of a owner who chook up in a office in de back. I sure dat dat was dey own family business, dey stomach proudly preceeding dem and dey shoulders throw back in de confidence of dey ownership.

It ain't dat I paranoid, yuh understand, but from de moment we enter de fellas dem get over-animated, even armorously agitated. Janet again! All six pair a eyes land up on she, following she every move and body part. Dat in itself is something dat does madden me, oui! but also a kind a irrational envy have a tendency to manifest in me. It was like I didn't exist. Sometimes it could be a real problem going out with a good-looker, yes! While I ain't remotely interested in having a squeak of a flirtation with a man, it doh hurt a ego to have a man notice yuh once in a very long while. But with Janet at mih side, I doh have de chance of a penny shave-ice in de hot sun. I tuck mih elbows in as close to mih sides as I could so I wouldn't look like a strong man next to she, and over to de l-o-n-g glass case jam up with sweets I jiggle and wiggle in mih best imitation a some a dem gay fellas dat I see downtown Vancouver, de ones who more femme dan even Janet. I tell she not to pay de brothers no attention, because if any a dem flirt with she I could start a fight right dere and den. And I didn't feel to mess up mih crew cut in a fight.

De case had sweets in every nuance of colour in a rainbow. Sweets I never before see and doh know de names of. But dat was alright because I wasn't going to order dose ones anyway.

Since before we leave home Janet have she mind set on a nice thick syrupy curl a jilebi and a piece a plain burfi so I order dose for she and den I ask de waiter-fella, resplendent with thick thick bright-yellow gold chain and ID bracelet, for a stick a meethai for mihself. I stand up waiting by de glass case for it but de waiter/owner lean up on de back wall behind de counter watching me like he ain't hear me. So I say loud enough for him, and every body else in de room to hear, "I would like to have one piece a meethai please," and den he smile and lift up his hands, palms open-out motioning across de vast expanse a glass case, and he say, "Your choice! Whichever you want, Miss." But he still lean up against de back wall grinning. So I stick mih head out and up like a turtle and say louder, and slowly, "One piece a meethai dis one!" and I point sharp to de stick a flour mix with ghee, deep fry and den roll up in sugar. He say, "That is koorma, Miss. One piece only?"

Mih voice drop low all by itself. "Oh ho! Yes, one piece. Where I come from we does call dat meethai." And den I add, but only loud enough for Janet to hear, "And mih name ain't 'Miss.'" He open his palms out and indicate de entire panorama a sweets and he say, "These are all meethai, Miss. Meethai is Sweets. Where are you from?" I ignore his question and to show him I undaunted, I point to a round pink ball and say, "I'll have one a dese sugarcakes too please." He start grinning broad broad like if he half-pitying, half-laughing at dis Indian-in-skin-colour-only, and den he tell "That is called chum-chum, Miss." I snap back at him, "Yeh, well back home we does call dat sugarcake, Mr. Chum-chum."

At de table Janet say, "You know, Pud [Pud, short for Pudding; is dat she does call me when she feeling close to me, or sorry for me], it's true that we call that 'meethai' back home. Just like how we call 'siu mai' 'tim sam.' As if 'dim sum' is just one little piece a food. What did he call that sweet again?"

"Cultural bastards, Janet, cultural bastards. Dat is what we is. Yuh know, one time a fella from India who living up here call me a bastardized Indian because I didn't know Hindi. And now look at dis, nah! De thing is: all a we in Trinidad is cultural bastards, Janet, all a we. *Toutes bagailles!* Chinese people, Black people, White people. Syrian. Lebanese. I looking forward to de day I find out dat place inside me where I am nothing else but Trinidadian, whatever dat could turn out to be."

I take a bite a de chum-chum, de texture was like grind-up coconut but it had no coconut, not even a hint a coconut taste in it. De thing was juicy with sweet rose water oozing out a it. De rose water perfume enter mih nose and get trap in mih cranium. Ah drink two cup a masala tea and a lassi and still de rose water perfume was on mih tongue like if I had a overdosed on Butchart Gardens.

Suddenly de door a de restaurant spring open wide with a strong force and two big burly fellas stumble in, almost rolling over on to de ground. Dey get up, eyes red and slow and dey skin burning pink with booze. Dey straighten up so much to overcompensate for falling forward, dat dey find deyself leaning backward. Everybody stop talking and was watching dem. De guy in front put his hand up to his forehead and take a deep Walter Raleigh bow, bringing de hand down to his waist in a rolling circular movement. Out loud he greet everybody with 'Alarm o salay koom.' A part a me wanted to bust out laughing. Another part make mih jaw drop open in disbelief. De calm in de place get rumfle up. De two fellas dem, feeling chupid now because nobody reply to dey greeting, gone up to de counter to Chum-chum trying to make a little conversation with him. De same booze-pink alarm-o-salay-koom-fella say to Chum-chum, 'Hey, howaryah?"

Chum-Chum give a lil nod and de fella carry right on, "Are you Sikh?"

Chum-chum brothers converge near de counter, busying deyselves in de vicinity. Chum-chum look at his brothers kind a quizzical, and he touch his cheek and feel his forehead with de back a his palm. He say, "No, I think I am fine, thank you. But I am sorry if I look sick, Sir."

De burly fella confuse now, so he try again.

"Where are you from?"

Chum-chum say, "Fiji, Sir."

"Oh! Fiji, eh! Lotsa palm trees and beautiful women, eh! Is it true that you guys can have more than one wife?"

De exchange make mih blood rise up in a boiling froth. De restaurant suddenly get a gruff quietness 'bout it except for a woman I hear whispering angrily to another woman at de table behind us, "I hate this! I just hate it! I can't stand to see our men humiliated by them, right in front of us. He should refuse to serve them, he should throw them out. Who on earth do they think they are? The awful fools!" And de friend whisper back, "If he throws them out all of us will suffer in the long run."

I could discern de hair on de back a de neck a Chum-chum brothers standing up, annoyed, and at de same time de brothers look like dey was shrinking in stature. Chum-chum get serious, and he politely say, "What can I get for you?"

Pinko get de message and he point to a few items in de case and say, "One of each, to go please."

Holding de white take-out box in one hand he extend de other to Chum-chum and say, "How do you say 'Excuse me, I'm sorry' in Fiji?"

Chum-chum shake his head and say, "It's okay. Have a good day."

Pinko insist, "No, tell me please. I think I just behaved badly, and I want to apologize. How do you say 'I'm sorry' in Fiji?"

Chum-chum say, "Your apology is accepted. Everything is okay." And he discreetly turn away to serve a person who had just entered de restaurant. De fellas take de hint dat was broad like daylight, and back out de restaurant like two little mouse.

Everybody was feeling sorry for Chum-chum and Brothers. One a dem come up to de table across from us to take a order from a woman with a giraffe-long neck who say, "Brother, we mustn't accept how these people think they can treat us. You men really put up with too many insults and abuse over here. I really felt for you."

Another woman gone up to de counter to converse with Chum-chum in she language. She reach out and touch his hand, sympathy-like. Chum-chum hold the one hand in his two and make a verbose speech to her as she nod she head in agreement generously. To italicize her support, she buy a take-out box a two burfi, or rather, dat's what I think dey was.

De door a de restaurant open again, and a bevy of Indian-looking women saunter in, dress up to weaken a person's decorum. De Miss Universe pageant traipse across de room to a table. Chum-chum and Brothers start smoothing dey hair back, and pushing de front a dey shirts neatly into dey pants. One brother take out a pack a Dentyne from his shirt pocket and pop one in his mouth. One take out a comb from his back pocket and smooth down his hair. All a dem den converge on dat single table to take orders. Dey begin to behave like young pups in mating season. Only, de women dem wasn't impress by all this tra-la-la at all and ignore dem except to make dey order, straight to de point. Well, it look like Brothers' egos were having a rough day and dey start roving 'bout de room, dey egos and de crotch a dey pants leading far in front dem. One brother gone over to Giraffebai to see if she want anything more. He call she "dear" and put his hand on she back. Giraffebai straighten she back in surprise and reply in a not-too-friendly way. When he gone to write up de bill she see me looking at she and she say to me, "Whoever does he think he is! Calling me dear and touching me like that! Why do these men always think that they have permission to touch whatever and wherever they want! And you can't make a fuss about it in public, because it is exactly what those people out there want to hear about so that they can say how sexist and uncivilized our culture is."

I shake mih head in understanding and say, "Yeah. I know. Yuh right!"

De atmosphere in de room take a hairpin turn, and it was man aggressing on woman, woman warding off a herd a man who just had dey pride publicly cut up a couple a times in just a few minutes.

One brother walk over to Janet and me and he stand up facing me with his hands clasp in front a his crotch, like if he protecting it. Stiff stiff, looking at me, he say, "Will that be all?"

Mih crew cut start to tingle, so I put on mih femmest smile and say, "Yes, that's it, thank you. Just the bill please." De smartass turn to face Janet and he remove his hands from in front a his crotch and slip his thumbs inside his pants like a cowboy 'bout to do a square dance. He smile, looking down at her attentive fuh so, and he say, "Can I do anything for you?"

I didn't give Janet time fuh his intent to even register before I bulldoze in mih most un-femmest manner, "She have everything she need, man, thank you. The bill please." Yuh think he hear me? It was like I was talking to thin air. He remain smiling at Janet, but she, looking at me, not at him, say, "You heard her. The bill please."

Before he could even leave de table proper, I start mih tirade. "But A A! Yah see dat? Yuh could believe dat! De effing so-and-so! One minute yuh feel sorry fuh dem and next minute dey harassing de heck out a you. Janet, he crazy to mess with my woman, yes!" Janet get vex with me and say I overreacting, and is not fuh me to be vex, but fuh she to be vex. Is she he insult, and she could take good enough care a sheself.

I tell she I don't know why she don't cut off all dat long hair, and stop wearing lipstick and eyeliner. Well, who tell me to say dat! She get real vex and say dat nobody will tell she how to dress and how not to dress, not me and not any man. Well I could see de potential dat dis fight had coming, and when Janet get fighting vex, watch out! It hard to get a word in edgewise, yes! And she does bring up incidents from years back dat have no bearing on de current situation. So I draw back quick quick but she don't waste time; she was already off to a good start. It was best to leave right dere and den.

Just when I stand up to leave, de doors'dem open up and in walk Sandy and Lise, coming for dey weekly hit a Indian sweets. Well, with Sandy and Lise is a dead giveaway dat dey not dressing fuh any man, it have no place in dey life fuh man-vibes, and dat in fact dey have a blatant penchant fuh women. Soon as dey enter de room yuh could see de brothers and de couple men customers dat had come in minutes before stare dem down from head to Birkenstocks, dey eyes bulging with disgust. And de women in de room start shoo-shooing, and putting dey hand in front dey mouth to stop dey surprise, and false teeth, too, from falling out. Sandy and Lise spot us instantly and dey call out to us, shameless, loud and affectionate. Dey leap over to us, eager to hug up and kiss like if dey hadn't seen us for years, but it was really only since two nights aback when we went out to dey favourite Indian restaurant for dinner. I figure dat de display was a genuine happiness to be seen wit us in dat place. While we stand up dere chatting, Sandy insist on rubbing she hand up and down Janet back — wit friendly intent, mind you, and same time Lise have she arm round Sandy waist. Well, all cover get blown. If it was even remotely possible dat I wasn't noticeable before, now Janet and I were over-exposed. We could a easily suffer from hypothermia, specially since it suddenly get cold cold in dere. We say goodbye, not soon enough, and as we were leaving I turn to acknowledge Giraffebai, but instead a any recognition of our buddiness against de fresh brothers, I get a face dat look like it was in de presence of a very foul smell.

De good thing, doh, is dat Janet had become so incensed 'bout how we get scorned, dat she forgot I tell she to cut she hair and to ease up on de make-up, and so I get save from hearing 'bout how I too jealous, and how much I inhibit she, and how she would prefer if I would grow *my* hair, and wear lipstick and put on a dress sometimes. I so glad, oui! dat I didn't have to go through hearing how I too demanding a she, like de time, she say, I prevent she from seeing a ole boyfriend when he was in town for a couple hours *en route* to live in Australia with his new bride (because, she say, I was jealous dat ten years ago dey sleep together). Well, look at mih crosses, nah! Like if I really so possessive and jealous!

So tell me, what yuh think 'bout dis nah, girl?

Coquibacoa

Maria de los Rios

From the beginning, there was lust. Lust was, from the beginning, bigger than desire. The type of lust that does not recognize name, colours, boundaries, or limits. This endless lust floated aimlessly inside my Cenozoic depths. Sometimes, this lust escaped my rib cage and glided over the chocolate-looking surface of Sinamaica, the Caribbean lagoon at Coquibacoa. Othertimes, this erratic lust landed, flapped its wide wings, ruffled its dark brown feathers, broke the water mirror, and created myriad reflections. After wandering around minding its own business, this lust would stretch its wings and engage in flight again. Like a vagrant poem, lust would fly free across hues of intense light blue searching the Earth's topography with natural elegance. Deep within, this lust wanted to caress my companion's cinnamon skin, kiss her thick juicy lips, explore that enigmatic cavern guarded by a gate of moonstone.

Time after time, this lust would find a refuge inside my body. I paddled in fluent silence. The beauty of this everlasting scene rose up through the wooden oar, reached my hands, and rushed up and down my spine, like a forceful river rushing over rocky terrain. Under an effervescent spell, I continued, propelling the vessel forward. My thoughts, lost in wonder, adventured, imagined, and slowly plunged into her underground cave.

Her sacred name like an ancient myth dwelled in my underside. The idea of calling up her name flew in circles within; again and again. That precious word, unlike ordinary words, did not seem to know its way out. That mystic word throbbed behind my chest. Its plumage tickled my lungs, shortened my breath. reached my throat, caressed the inside of my mouth rim. My lips would close tight, and her name flew right back where it came from.

In the crossroads of my mind, she danced naked. Her lips smiled at me. Poetic lust traveled the blue roads of my blood. Abruptly, this lust with no name burned my loins and steamed my crotch with the fury of a tropical storm. It oozed through my pores, in the form of sweat. Droplets of lust slipped through my skin, dripped into the lagoon. There, my lust fought against the current of her delta, climbed her continental crust, overflowed her shore, licked her beach, traveled her dunes, examined her marshes, dived into her depths.

Crispy coconut palm leaves rattled. From the opposite end of the canoe, her features and outlines enticed. My body spoke eloquently without words. My eyes scanned the panorama crowded with moriche houses, in search of privacy.

Against the horizon, thin dark hair cascaded her shoulders and moved sensuously with the hot breeze. Her black Guajira eyes twinkled with the glitter of the water's surface. Suddenly, the entrance to a narrow creek appeared. I paddled stronger and faster in its direction. Like the baba who kidnaps her prey and hides behind the mangrove line to devour it, I kidnapped this woman and would attempt to devour her. She read my thoughts.

Her hands moved from the canoe's edge to her legs, slowly pulled up her raw cotton skirt. Her legs opened to expose her rain forest. The tip of her tongue left a wet trace on her dry lips. Her wide open eyes detailed my landscape, entered my dreamscape, invited me in. A bolt of fire traveled down my spine. The creek reached a live end, in this spot embraced by mangroves and sea grapes.

Under the ardent sun rays, I dropped the padlock, gave freedom to this lust pounding carnival rhythms within, approached her. Our lips touched, tasted, kissed, played, sucked. My tongue broke barriers, trespassed her moonstone gate, explored her inner velvet, traveled slow down her neck. My hands released her breasts from constraint, fondled, squeezed, teased. I savoured her contours, and journeyed to her underworld where I tasted her zesty faults and folds, immersed in her lowlands, dived into the cavern where her river was wild. And there, in frenzy, I absorbed her backwaters.

In Coquibacoa, portal where civilized Native nations had hearts bigger and more courageous than the crown, conquerors set foot centuries ago. Sinamaica, the magical lagoon with pockets of moriche houses, inspired in these foreign savages the big name of Venezuela, to them "little Venice." In this same place where European men gave birth to genocide and rape, I named my woman lust. There, in brown chocolate waters, where palm trees swing free in the mellow breeze, I reclaimed my tricultural roots, my mixed blood, my Mestiza passion, my womanhood, my Caribe Raza. This half Amazonian/half Caribbean heart big and courageous, birthed lesbian lust for the first time, in Coquibacoa.

Sinamaica is the Native name of the Venezuelan lagoon where Europeans arrived in the late 1400s.

Coquibacoa is the Native name of the region where the lagoon is located.

Moriche is a particular type of palm tree native to this region located on the northwest coast of Venezuela. For centuries, the moriche palm has been used by Native people to build their moriche houses, also known as *palafitos*. These houses are built on wood shafts inside the lagoon and appear to be floating on the water during rainy season. The roof is woven using the palm leaves. This type of housing existed at the time of European invasion. The illusion of a "little Venice" gave birth to the name Venezuela. Today, Native people continue building the same type of housing. Sinamaica is one of the most intriguing sites in the world where the old ways have prevailed almost intact and the new ways mimic the old.

Guajira is a woman member of the Guajiro.

Baba is a small species of alligator that finds habitat in this region.

This story, originally written in Spanish, was translated to English by the author.

As American As . . .
Tonia Grant

The telephone rang twice. Caryl hung the colourful record jacket *Day Dreams*, with the smiling face of Doris Day, on one of the many little brass nails that studded the red walls. It was the *perfect* way to store the records, and decorate what they now called the music room. She ran into the living room and scooped up the receiver on the third ring, "Hello."

"That you, Caryl?"

"Hello, Mother." Caryl sat on the wide window-sill which overlooked the backyard. It was a gray-yellow spring day.

"How are you?" asked Mrs. Glenn.

"Not bad."

"And Lori?"

Caryl swung both feet up onto the sill, settling into a comfortable L-shape in the window frame. "She's okay. She's ironing her uniform."

"I felt sure that one of you was sick." Her mother persisted. "Is the car broken down?"

"No, Mom," Caryl laughed. "All of us are okay, including the dog. Just slightly overworked."

"Are you eating properly?"

"Umhumm," Caryl was nodding her head for emphasis. Self-conscious, she looked across at the dirty back windows of the "Muni," as the Municipal Shelter for Men was called in the neighbourhood. No one looked back. She wondered why the client-inhabitants were not prevailed upon to clean the windows.

"You haven't even come to Brooklyn to pick up your mail," Milly Glenn complained.

"Anything important?" Caryl asked, realizing why the indigent men could not be pressed into service. By cleaning the windows, they would be working for the city, forfeiting their eligibility for municipal services.

"One from Macy's, one from Sears, and one from a lawyer on Court Street."

"Oh. Open the one from the lawyer, please."

Mrs. Glenn was surprised, "Open your letter?"

"Yes, Mother. Open that letter. The bills can wait."

Caryl gazed from the third floor window down at the well-tended green strip of land that separated the high walled, sunless backyard of 14 East from the rear of the Muni. What had seemed to be the dreary, windowless first floor of the Muni was actually a separate fifteen foot high stone wall, camouflaged by twisted, old, gray-brown boughs that clung, vine-like, to it. Curious, she stood up, opened the sash and leaned out; the high wall enclosed the beautifully manicured lawn.

"Caryl," Her mother's voice sounded metallic in the receiver, "Are you there?"

"Yes, Mother."

"What are you doing? You sound far away."

"Just looking out the back window."

"At the cemetery?"

"The — what?" Caryl took a step back from the window.

"The graveyard! Marblehill Cemetery. It runs for two blocks down there. Behind everything! I mean, everything down there was built up all around it. You know?"

Now I know, thought Caryl uneasily.

"Your father saw it when he went to check — see — what a run-down neighbourhood you girls moved into. He said, it's the only clean, cared-for place in your slum. It's Dutch, or something foreign like that, but with money, money, money to keep it up. In perpetuity," Milly paused. "Caryl," she said softly.

"Yes, Mother."

"Didn't you know?"

"No..."

"Aaiieeee —" The lamentation for her cub trilled through the telephone, "Knowing how you feel about the dead and duppies,* I was so surprised.... I guess I thought you had gotten over it working in the hospital, you know? What will you do Caryl?"

"Nothing," Caryl lit a cigarette. "What did the lawyer say, Mother?"

"Oh. He says your charter is approved. And he wants a hundred and forty-two dollars. What do you need a charter for?"

"It gives us the right to assemble," said Caryl.

"But that's silly, Pudding! You're spending a hundred and forty-two dollars for nothing. All Americans are guaranteed the right to assemble. It's in the constitution somewhere. I remember when I was studying for naturalization, that we —"

"I know," interrupted Caryl. "The charter proves the right. The reasons for assembly are spelled out."

"Do you have to pay the hundred and forty-two dollars because you're dealing with 'funny' people?"

"Not 'funny,' Mother. Why not say 'gay'?"

"Because the ones I've seen are funny! I haven't seen one of your funny friends that seem gay. Even the ones that were drinking or partying were not gay. Gay means happy, Pudding!"

"All right then, funny! Queer is the term though .... like nigger is, for Negro!"

"Caryl!" Milly was indignant. "You getting mad?"

"No, Mother." Caryl said wearily.

"'Cause I didn't make the rules, you know! God knows I don't know what I did to make you turn out this way!"

"Mother — "

"What?" snapped Mrs. Glenn.

"Don't tell Lori," Caryl whispered into the mouthpiece.

"About what?"

"You know — "

"No. Oh. About the cemetery?"

"Yes." Caryl's voice was normal again.

"She knows! She was right here when your father told me. Remember when she came to get the six hundred dollars I gave you?" Her mother began whispering, so Caryl knew her father was home.

"Loaned me, Mother. It's a loan."

"A loan is a loan when it's paid back," Milly's West Indian logic peaked. "Right now it's given to you. Don't quarrel. It is not nice."

"Okay, Mum. What did she say?"

Mrs. Glenn hesitated, then laughed into the phone. "She said not to tell you! Lori must think you're a dumb, superstitious nigger. And now, you say don't tell her, so you must think the same foolish things about her!" Too late, Milly realized that the intended derision had steered her bumptious tongue straight into the unmentionable condition; the unnatural mutual bond which had developed between her daughter and *that* white girl. "So you're opening the Studio next week," she said, changing the subject.

"If all goes well." Caryl suppressed her amusement.

"So, you won't be coming to Brooklyn. Too busy, right?"

"I have to, Mother. To get the charter."

"Lori coming?"

"Yep."

"All right, I'll cook cuckoo. Salt fish or liver?" Mrs. Glenn knew that Lori liked the Barbadian dish that was mainly a heavy cornmeal mush cooked with okras. The choice of fresh fish, salt fish, or meat provided the flavour of the lavish gravy served with it.

"Just a minute, I'll ask Lori." Caryl covered the mouthpiece with her hand. "Lore!" she shouted. "What do you want with our cuckoo — codfish or liver?"

From the kitchen, Lori answered, "Codfish, of course!"

"Salt fish, Mum," Caryl said. "Thursday okay?"

"I don't go to work, Pudding. Every day is okay. See you then. Bye."

"So long, Mum," Caryl hung up the telephone. She felt compelled to look at the grass-covered burial ground again. Lori's attempt to attempt to guard her peace of mind touched her tenderness and stirred a need.

Lori came out of the kitchen carrying the stiff-starched, ironed uniforms on wire hangers. "When are we going to Brooklyn?" she asked.

"Thursday." Caryl answered absently.

"You didn't ask me if I wanted to go."

"No, I didn't — did I?" Caryl turned away from the window, "Wither thou goest et cetera," she chirped, following Lori into the music room.

"Don't you know any other biblical quotation? I looked it up, and it's about a woman and her mother-in-law. Ruth and Naomi!" She hung her uniforms in the walk-in closet, which had been full of old remnants a few months ago.

"They just kept their gay tricks in the family, in those days." Caryl scanned the record collection on the wall.

"Is that blasphemy I hear?"

"If it is, don't tell my mother! Let's hear this," Caryl said, lifting the Jackie Gleason album, *Music for Lovers Only*, from its place on the red wall. She slid the record out of its jacket, handling only the edges, and put it on the turn-table.

"That's a strange selection for this afternoon, Caryl."

"I feel strange. Come feel my head." Caryl slumped into a wrought iron, black canvas sling chair. The nostalgic tones of *Alone Together* drifted from the blue, imitation leather speaker. Her head lolled from side to side, against the black canvas...slowly...to the tempo of the music. Lori put her hand lightly over Caryl's brow; the swaying forehead brushed the palm of her hand.

"I'm not sure what you expect me to feel," Lori said, after awhile. "You seem normal." She laughed, "I mean, no temperature."

Caryl opened her eyes. "Are you sure? Oh, you've just been ironing. I've been sitting in the window. That's why I feel cool to you."

Lori knelt in front of the sling chair. "I didn't say you were cool. Your head hurt?"

Caryl leaned forward from the waist, and put her head on Lori's shoulder. The refrain for *I Cover the Waterfront* was playing now. "No," she murmured, nuzzling the smoothness of Lori's neck.

Lori slipped her arms around the languid figure. "Caryl, you have to go to work — soon!"

"I'll cover your waterfront — " sang Caryl, bawdily.

Lori was surprised by the unexpected vulgarity, and stunned by the sudden tingling through her body. "Plebeian!" she pronounced pleasantly, tightening her arms to squeeze closer. Their clothed shoulders touch, they rocked to the music. Lori's tongue traced a circle along the near ear. "Urchin," she whispered.

They knew the physical imperative of letting bare breasts make contact, tender round conduits, soft siphons of frenetic energy, cooling controls of passion. The hand behind Caryl raised her sweatshirt, deft fingers unhooked her brassiere, and Caryl unbuttoned the three top buttons of the smock that Lori was wearing — still holding her close. They stood as one; with breasts and bellies united, they danced, basking in their intimacy.

For an instant the music stopped. They stepped apart. Eyes locked, they undressed, dropping their clothes on the floor. *Someday* floated from the portable player. Two lean bodies, so different in their sameness, pressed together. Tongues met; lips and teeth had no part in this greeting. Then a brown nipple hardened between full lips, firm flesh caressed by brown hands, until pink fingernails etched four gray-white tracks on dark skin. Lips met shoulders, necks, eyes. Mouths joined. Limbs tangled. A frantic hand cast about — found, and then held onto hair. A flower unfolded, blossomed in the warmth of a familiar gentle touch.

A marvelous creature evolved on the hard wood floor, cushioned by mystic clouds. An animal possessed of one spirit, two heads, twenty stroking and exploring fingers, and four legs. Its motions were rhythmic, fluid

— changing tempo — it writhed and twisted, now seeming to function in unison. At its centre alert passion buds demanded attention and received admiration from the whole organism — coaxing, promising, inviting, opening, opening, struggling to implode! Ten toes curled, uncurled; two legs stretched, momentarily rigid. One mouth gasped, from the other a muted series of sighs.... The two-faced creature looked at itself, closed its eyes, relinquished the sorceresses, and slept.

The hi-fi's continuous rendition of Jackie Gleason's melodies roused Lori. For a moment she hummed along, then she propped on her elbow and studied the composed face next to her. "Care," she whispered.

"Ummmm."

"I wish we could have a baby."

Drowsily, Caryl smiled. "We can't afford one."

"I mean it, Caryl."

"You'll have a baby someday, Lore."

"I know that — but I mean your baby!"

An afternoon breeze swept through the room, chilling Caryl. She sat up, "We can't have everything, honey."

"It's not fair. We'd make such a beautiful baby — "

"Honey, don't confuse making love with making babies." Caryl got up on her knees, "C'mon." She held out a hand to Lori.

Lori ignored the hand. "You're acting the way I bet a man would. After."

"What do you mean?" Caryl asked sharply.

"I mean about the baby."

"Gosh, Lori — we've got the whole thing planned!" Caryl began picking up their strewn clothes. "I'm learning everything I can about artificial insemination, at the hospital. When we can afford it, you can have a baby. Okay?"

Lori sat up, thoughtful. "Maybe we could both get pregnant at the same time. Go into seclusion together — "

"And have twin deliveries," Caryl broke in, "and pledge a spooky midwife not to let us know which one of us birthed which kid!"

"Well, not exactly," Lori stood up.

"Lori, since I was nine years old, I knew I didn't ever want to get pregnant." Caryl's tone changed from mild sarcasm to self-pity. "It's a balance. For myself. I'm scared of birth and death. I'm quite satisfied to have complete control over at least one of them!"

"You're sooooo romantic!" Lori snatched the small bunch of clothes from Caryl. "After!"

Caryl shook her head, "I'll never understand — myself." she said, indicating womankind.

"Good! That makes two of us!"

Caryl laughed. "Isn't that what I've been saying? Please adjust the shower, Lore, I don't want to be late for work."

"Isn't that what I've been saying?" Lori mimicked. "Did you light the hot water heater?"

"Yes, before my mother called. Your baby is the only one I'll ever need. I'll love it so much, it'll be a bonus. It'll be an extra bit of you."

Lori stopped in the doorway to the living room, "Suppose it's a boy, Caryl?"

"A baby is a baby is a baby, boy or girl!" Caryl went into the bedroom.

Duppy (dupi). 1774.(Afr.) Name among W. Indians for a ghost or spirit. (*The Oxford Universal Dictionary on Historical Principles*:1955)

Hablas Espanol?
Mary Vazquez

Carmen poured a fourth teaspoon of sugar into her coffee. Whenever she was mad — right now she was boiling — she took her coffee sickeningly sweet. Carmen stirred furiously, bangles jangling, and slammed her spoon on the kitchen table. "So I can't speak Spanish," she snapped at her lover, Millie. "What's the big deal? A lot of people go through life without speaking Spanish."

"True." Millie calmly stirred her coffee. "But," she leaned over the table and lowered her voice to a whisper, "A lot of people are not Puerto Rican, so it doesn't matter. You, Chica, are Puerto Rican, so it does matter. You," Millie leaned back and ran her fingers through her black curly hair, "you should know the language that you were born with."

"Millie Sanchez." Carmen glared back, dark eyes crackling and smoldering like a live volcano, "What the hell are you talking about? I wasn't born with a language. I said 'goo goo' like any other kid learning to talk. You know my parents spoke English and that's what I learned. Mommy, not 'que pasa' or anything else in Spanish. I'm telling you for the hundredth time, I was not born into the Spanish language and that's the way it is." Carmen took a big swallow of coffee and threw Millie a don't-you-dare-contradict-me look.

Millie shoved her chair back and stood up, smoothing her short black skirt. "Listen Carmen," she said, carrying her cup to the sink. "I think you could learn Spanish. You don't know Spanish and it sounds like you don't want to know. That's all I have to say." Millie walked to the kitchen door and opened it. She stood looking at Carmen for a minute. "I still love you,

Carmen. It don't matter to me, okay? I think it matters to you, so take a class or something. Listen, Chica, I'm going to take a bath. Why don't you come in when you're finished with your coffee?" Millie left the kitchen, quietly closing the door behind her.

Carmen hated when Millie stayed so calm while she felt like jumping out of her skin. Too much sugar she thought, rising and throwing her cup to clatter in the sink. Maybe she's right. Maybe I should take a class.

Millie had told her about a class beginning at the university, during their last heated discussion. Out of curiosity, Carmen had looked into it. She knew the class began in a week. Maybe it's time for me to finally be a Puerto Rican, she thought. I'll sign up tomorrow during lunch.

The next day at work, Carmen sat at the switchboard and listened to a caller trying to tell her in broken English that she needed to talk with someone who spoke Spanish. "You Spanish speak?" the caller asked.

"I should Spanish speak, lady but I don't," Carmen wanted to yell back. Instead, she offered to transfer the call to Millie, who did. Carmen transferred the call, and before she could change her mind punched the university's number. Over the phone she signed up for Beginning Spanish. By day's end, Carmen wasn't sure she had done the right thing. There were butterflies fluttering in her stomach and she hadn't even attended the class.

Tuesday had never arrived so fast. Carmen barely had time to run a comb through her hair before class. Why did I listen to Millie? she thought, sitting in the classroom scared half out of her wits. She looked around. She had taken a seat in the last row near the door, so she could make a break for it if she had to. The instructor, Mr. Torres, had just explained that for the next hour they would speak in Spanish. Carmen's stomach began to ache and her vision to blur. Get a grip on yourself, Carmen, she reproached herself. It's only a class and the door is right there. Carmen looked at the other students, who had all taken seats in the front row. They were already trying to speak Spanish to each other, laughing and carrying on. There were seven students besides herself. A young woman with red hair and skin covered with freckles, was teasing a tall skinny guy with stringy blond hair, calling him Carlos. He had pale blue eyes that pierced Carmen's existence in the back row.

"Hey, you hot tamale," he yelled to Carmen.

That's all I need, she thought to herself. Some jerk trying to pick me up in Spanish. I knew I should have worn my "Nobody knows I'm a lesbian" T-shirt. Carmen ignored him, but he persisted. "You look like the real thing," he said. "How about a private Spanish lesson later?"

Before she could respond, the teacher called the class to order and began talking in Spanish to the students. Carmen's stomach clenched, as if she had just eaten an entire jar of hot salsa. Should she tell Mr. Torres that she felt ill and had to leave the class? Should she just faint? She could ask to be excused but Mr. Torres might make her try to say it in Spanish. She might be so angry she'd cry. She wished she was invisible; she wished she could tell them all to go to hell in Spanish. Wouldn't that shock them!

Mr. Torres was going around the room, asking the students their names and God only knew what else. Carmen figured out the name part when that stupid blond guy faced the class and said something in Spanish that ended with Carlos. He doesn't look like a Carlos to me, Carmen thought. She had heard one of the students call him Carl earlier. What a creep. This is not working at all. My parents should have taught me Spanish, she thought. They said it was better if I learned English and became American. It will be easier, they said. We came to the States from Puerto Rico and had to learn to speak English, they said. It is not a good thing to be a Puerto Rican, they said. Don't learn the language, and stay out of the sun so your skin won't become so dark. Eat the American food. It is better for you, they said. Now look at me, Carmen thought. I'm paying a stranger to teach me to speak my own language. This is really fucked up.

Mr. Torres was talking to her. The class turned around to look at her. Sleazy Carl winked. Mr. Torres was speaking in tongues. Carmen jumped up and ran out the door, slamming it behind her. She could hear the other students laughing. This is just not funny, Carmen thought, humiliated. I'll tell Millie I'm just a crappy Puerto Rican who will never know Spanish. Millie will pat my head and say, "Oh you poor thing, but I still love you, Chica." Carmen sighed. She hurt inside her soul.

Carmen left the building with tears streaming down her face, scolding her dead parents. "You didn't make it easy," she hissed. "You made it worse."

Carmen walked slowly to her car, trying not to cry. Crying was giving her a stomach ache. Or were those hunger pains? She realized she had been too nervous about the class to eat all day. When in pain, she thought, have something good to eat. Carmen got into her old Toyota and slammed the door. I'll go to Yvonne's.

Yvonne's Caribbean Palace was Carmen and Millie's favourite restaurant. Yvonne, the owner of the Caribbean Palace, was as short as she was round, and seemed to Carmen the wisest and happiest woman that she knew. Yvonne had five kids ranging from seven to twenty-four. Her husband had taken off for parts unknown a few years back. Carmen and Millie had discussed that fact many times and had the feeling that Yvonne knew exactly where he was, but preferred he stay there. She didn't talk about him, and neither Carmen nor Millie asked. Yvonne was Puerto Rican. Carmen and Millie loved having little talks with her about the island. Yvonne always had an opinion about the politics of Puerto Rico. "Most Puerto Ricans are just plain crazy," she always said with a laugh. "Including me."

I'll give Millie a call when I get there, Carmen thought. She can come cry into my tostones with me. Carmen pulled out of the university driveway and headed to Yvonne's. She put her favourite Tito Puente tape into the tape player, and before Tito had a chance to finish a song, she swung off the road into the parking lot of Yvonne's restaurant. There were plenty of parking spaces at Yvonne's tonight. Tuesdays were usually a slow night. Carmen and Millie loved to go to Yvonne's when it was slow. Yvonne would pump up the salsa music so Carmen and Millie could dance. Sometimes Yvonne would even come out of the kitchen to join them. Of course, that was when Carmen wasn't feeling like shit.

She stepped out of her car, remembering not to slam the door. A 1986 Toyota could only take so much abuse. Being out of that classroom made Carmen feel a little better but now she would have to listen to Millie and sometimes Millie could be pretty damn unsympathetic. Carmen made her way to the pay phone outside the restaurant, dug some change out of her purse and dialed home. Millie answered on the first ring.

"Millie, get over to Yvonne's right now," Carmen said, trying not to sound desperate. Then she hung up without waiting for Millie to answer. Carmen opened the door to the restaurant and sat at her favourite table. "Hi Yvonne," she said as Yvonne came out of the kitchen.

"Hey Carmen, why you look glum? I will bring you a big plate of rice and beans, some Caribbean fajitas and some tostones. How does that sound? Then you can tell me what is the matter, okay?" Yvonne went back into the kitchen to prepare a small feast for Carmen, who once again, felt like crying. Just as she was about to let go with more tears, Millie walked in the door.

"Que pasa Chica?" she said, her tone much too cheerful for Carmen.

"Millie," Carmen looked up at her. "You have no idea what hell I've just been through. That Spanish class was embarrassing, humiliating and I still don't know a damn word of Spanish. What's the use?" she said in exasperation. "I'm just a failure."

"Listen Carmen," Millie answered. "I'm really sorry it didn't work out for you, but don't be so hard on yourself." Millie sat down, gently taking Carmen's hands, which were nervously tapping the table. "I have a great idea, you know? I've been thinking, why don't I teach you Spanish, okay?"

Carmen stopped tapping and looked at Millie. "You want to teach me

Spanish? You would do that for me, Millie? I thought you'd think I was hopeless because I left the class."

"Listen Chica," Millie said, still holding Carmen's hands, "Your heart is hurting you, and in all the time I've known you, this is the only time I've ever heard you this upset because you don't know your language. Maybe it's because of your new job at the switchboard, but whatever the reason, I want to help you. What do you say?"

Carmen's heart soared. "Millie, I love you and I accept your offer."

Millie sat back in her chair, fluffed out her hair and smiled. "Good," she said. "The first sentence I want you to learn is Vete al infierno." She said it slowly so Carmen would get it. Carmen repeated "Vete al infierno. What does that mean?" she asked.

"I'll tell you in a minute," Millie said. "First, I want you to say it loud, with some punch behind it. Like this: VETE AL INFIERNO."

"Okay, okay I got it. You don't have to shout at me," Carmen said, jumping in her chair. "How's this? VETE AL INFIERNO," Carmen screamed, louder than Millie.

"Hey Carmen," Yvonne said, coming out of the kitchen with a plate of food. She glanced around the restaurant, surprise on her face. "Hey Carmen," she repeated, setting the food down in front of her, "who are you telling to go to hell, me or Millie?"

Millie laughed and Carmen blushed. "That's what I just yelled at the top of my lungs? That's the first thing you taught me, go to hell?"

"The best teachers always begin with the swear words," Millie said. "What do you think Yvonne, am I right?"

"Oh yeah, Millie." She looked at Carmen, winked and said, "You will learn quickly, little one." Yvonne headed back into the kitchen still chuckling to herself.

"Okay, Carmen," Millie said. "Repeat it again and be mad, okay?"

Carmen thought of the class, of that stupid blond Carl, and said in a loud and clear voice, "VETE AL INFIERNO!"

Yvonne stuck her head out of the kitchen and gave her thumbs up. "Spoken like a true Puerto Rican."

BEST FRIENDS
Ayiah Jahan

Miranda ran home, Gayle's words echoing in her ears. Why had she said what she did to Gayle? Why couldn't she just have kept her mouth shut, like she always did? But she hadn't, and she had Gayle's voice in her ears, sneering, nasty, hostile.

"Dirty Lesbian!"

There were tears in her eyes as she reached home. She hoped her mother wasn't there, she just wanted to hide, escape to her room and torture herself about what Gayle had said and what she might do.

How could she face school on Monday? Prickles of fear went up her back. But Gayle would not tell, would she? Gayle was her best friend, at least she had been, Miranda thought miserably. She scrambled for her keys. As usual, they had fallen through the hole in her pocket. Miranda put the key in the door and, very quietly opened it. Miranda listened. Her mother was home, her coat and bag in their usual place in the hall for all to see. But where was she?

"Miranda, is that you?" her mother called.

Miranda quickly stepped in and roughly rubbed the tears from her eyes with the sleeve of her coat. Her mother was upstairs, there would be no escape that way. She dived down the hall and into the kitchen. She could not answer. She needed time to pull herself together, to put on the face of the dutiful, helpful daughter that her mother was proud of telling her church friends about.

In the kitchen she dumped her coat and bag on the table and poured herself a glass of water. She had nearly finished drinking it when her mother appeared.

"Miranda, didn't you hear me calling you?" Mrs. Matheson asked, a quizzical look on her face.

"Yes mum, but I wasn't feeling too good, so I came for a glass of water."

Mrs. Matheson looked at her youngest daughter and knew that she had been crying. Miranda's eyes were bright and red, the hand holding the glass had a tremble. She paused, not certain what to do. She had never been much good at giving her children emotional support. Her strength had been in keeping a roof over their heads, clothes on their backs and food in their bellies. It was something that, as a single mother struggling to bring up five children, she had felt a great deal of pride about. How she loved to take them to church, dressed in their Sunday best, each with their own collection money. The congregation never failed to be impressed by how she kept them so clean and polite, and all by herself, too. She had every right to be proud they would tell her, and she would feel her chest swell, and the feeling from singing, praising the Lord and being praised herself, would carry her through to the next weekend. Even now the memory touched her, though most of the children had long left home, leaving only Miranda and herself. That situation was fine until times like this. She focused on her daughter again, who seemed a little calmer. Mrs. Matheson was unsure what to say, she wished one of the older children were here. They'd know what to say.

"You alright, Miranda?" she asked, almost warily.

"Yes mum, I'm fine, just felt a little sick that's all, I think I'll go lie down."

Mrs. Matheson made no objection, relieved that she had not been called upon to deal with crying and emotion. Miranda was a good girl, Mrs. Matheson consoled herself. When she was ready, if she felt a need to, she would tell her mother what was the matter.

"Yes, you go lie down, dinner's ready whenever you are."

Miranda nodded and sidled out of the room, grateful that her mother was not one of those who always wanted to be in the know. Her friend Elisa had a mother like that, and whilst it sometimes sounded fun, it had its disadvantages too. A mother like that now would be a definite disadvantage as far as Miranda was concerned. How could you tell any mother that your best friend had called you a lesbian, and was probably at this very moment spreading it all around the school? Miranda entered her room as if arriving at an oasis. The curtains were closed, as always, but her room was at the back of the house so her mother let her get away with it. Mrs. Matheson had definitely mellowed out in her old age. Miranda's brothers and sisters were always spinning tales about how strict she used to be in the old days, and Mervyn, her eldest brother, had tales to tell of both their mother and father. Mervyn was the only one who remembered their father really well, remembered what he'd been like before he became sick and died. Miranda had no memory of him at all. She had still been a baby in the womb at the time, but she loved to hear tales of him. She wished Mervyn was here right now, telling his stories, like fairy tales. It would be better than listening to the voices circling round and round in her head.

Alone in her room, her mind once again started to chastise her. Why on earth had she said anything to Gayle? She flopped on her bed, closed her eyes and buried her head under a pillow. The whole distressing scene played in her mind like a bad movie. In glorious technicolour she saw Gayle and her boyfriend, Tom, a tall lanky youth, wearing clothes at least six sizes too big. But he could dress in a way that made you look at him. And he was eighteen and he was working, a rare combination in the young Black men that Miranda and Gayle knew. A world apart from the young Black men at the church that Miranda and Gayle attended, at least as far as Gayle was concerned. Miranda squeezed her head with her hands to get the voices and motion picture out and hold her head together. She had never been concerned about the boys at church and had excelled at her self-appointed role of keeping them from Gayle, around whom they swarmed like bees to the honey pot. She had enjoyed that role, it gave her chance to do something for Gayle and she couldn't think of anything that she enjoyed more than the feeling of protecting Gayle. Gayle was her best friend, confidante, advisor, spar, buddy, whatever, until, of course, Tom came along. Then everything changed, Gayle had not wanted her protection then. For the first time in their long friendship, Gayle wanted to be with someone else. The shock had been so great that on many levels Miranda did not comprehend it and would not accept it. Not even when she saw Gayle and Tom kissing could she accept that Gayle loved someone else, rather than, her.

Miranda had talked to Simone about it, the only one of Mrs. Matheson's daughters who came to visit regular. Simone had been around when Miranda first saw Gayle and Tom kiss each other. Miranda had been so enraged. She had never experienced that before. It burst out of her the first chance she and Simone had a moment to themselves. Simone had talked with her and though it had mostly been along the lines of "it's all part of growing up" and "you'll feel different when you meet a boy you like," Miranda had felt better. Simone, at least, had understood she was hurt and responded, something their mother had never really been able to do. What would Simone say now if she told her what she had said to Gayle? Miranda groaned, this was getting her nowhere.

The movie resumed, displaying all her jealousy and anger as Gayle got closer and closer to Tom. And further and further from Miranda, or so Miranda felt. Today, as far as Miranda was concerned, had been the last straw. They had been talking after school, like they used to, down by the old canal, behind the brick shed that nobody seemed to use except them. It was their own private hidey hole, where they had often gone before the days of Tom. When Gayle suggested going there after school Miranda's heart soared. Tom was losing his hold, Gayle was coming back to her one true friend, and she, Miranda Matheson, was more than pleased and grateful to have her back. They walked to the shed talking excitedly, Miranda felt all the old magic coming back, everything looked beautiful, even the dirty water in the canal had sparkle. What's more, Gayle had said that she had something really important to tell her. Miranda imagined that Gayle had finished with Tom and wanted her, Miranda to be the first to know. She stared in disbelief when Gayle had shared her secret with her. Shock had numbed her words, her face, her whole being. Gayle wanted to sleep with Tom.

"Why?" Miranda had finally blurted out.

"Why do you think?" Gayle had retorted. Miranda truly had no idea.

"I thought you didn't like him doing that heavy stuff," she said. Gayle just shrugged.

"That was then, this is now," she said.

"But you're not in love with him!"

"How do you know, I might be!"

"But you're not old enough."

"Miranda! You sound worse than my mother." Gayle had said, surprised at the passion with which Miranda spoke.

"Besides you don't have to be in love with somebody to do it you know. I just want to see what it feels like with someone who knows what they're doing, that's all." Gayle had sounded so casual and grown-up. This was no longer the little girl she had always protected. It was as Simone had said it would be, when you grow up you change. Gayle had changed. In a few short weeks she had gained a confidence that Miranda had never seen before.

"But Gayle, you said you didn't like it when he tried it."

"Yes, well, it's different now. I want to now, I want to know what it feels like to make love."

Then it happened. Miranda was looking into Gayle's eyes, sitting close, heads bent down whispering, almost cheek to cheek. Miranda was suddenly aware of Gayle's natural scent in her nostrils and the soft feel of Gayle's body. Gayle's words "making love" excited something in her she had never felt before. In that second she accepted that she didn't just love Gayle as her friend. She loved her as a lover, she wanted to love her as a lover would.

"You don't have to sleep with Tom," she had said, her voice deep with her emerging passion. "He'd never make you feel the way that I could."

Gayle's lips had been so temptingly near, before Miranda was aware of what she was doing her lips had brushed Gayle's. But Gayle's lips had been opening not to kiss her, instead she had screamed and started shouting.

"You're a lesbian, a nasty dirty lesbian." Gayle scrambled away from her, as if Miranda had suddenly become contaminated with a contagious disease. Miranda had been too stunned to respond. When she did, Gayle had already left their hiding place and was scrambling down the river bank.

"Gayle," Miranda called desperately, "Wait." She scrambled after her, but it had been no use. Gayle screamed whenever Miranda got close and, in the end, Miranda had let her run off down the tow path. It was only then that she realised fully what she had said. She stood stock still, put her hand on her mouth as if that could stop the words that had already come out, and looked around. There was nobody about, the nearest people would be the fishermen, who usually fished just around the bend. She moved fast in case any of them had heard Gayle's screams, and decided to investigate. She got home on instinct, totally blind to the outside world, filled instead with her own inner turmoil.

Questions bombarded her, each one filling her body with a new fear. What if Gayle told people that she had tried to kiss her? They'd definitely believe that she was a lesbian if Gayle told them that! What if her mother found out? Miranda cringed at the thought. She couldn't begin to imagine what her mother would do. Or her sisters, brothers and friends. What friends, she thought bitterly to herself. If Gayle said anything to anyone Miranda would lose the few friends she had. She had never really had time for anyone other than Gayle. Her whole life had collapsed and it was all her own fault. Why on earth had she said what she did?

There was a knock on the door.

"Miranda?" She jumped up with a start. Her mother rarely came to her room, she must have been calling her from downstairs.

"Yes Mum?"

"You alright, dear?"

"Yes Mum."

"Well, just let me know if you need anything."

"Yes, Mum." Then she was gone.

Miranda lay on her back. What was she going to do now? She could not go back to school, at least not Barrymore Secondary High. The gossip, the sneers, would be bad enough, but to know that Gayle hated her, thought she was a dirty lesbian was more than she could bear. It's not dirty to be a lesbian, Miranda thought to herself. She had always been fascinated by lesbianism, not that she knew much about it. She watched the gay programmes on channel four when she finally had a television of her own in her room. She had never thought much about it, she was simply interested to know what all the fuss was about. Gayle had even watched them with her, and afterwards they would have long discussion about men loving men and women loving women. Gayle had never used the words "dirty lesbian" before. What was dirty about lesbians? What was dirty about love? It was just like the discussions on television, the way the people had talked about coming out to their friends and the reactions. Miranda got up and went to the mirror. It had gotten dark. No wonder her mother had come up stairs. It was quite late and Miranda had not yet had her dinner. That would definitely cause her hard-working mother concern. Miranda had no intention of going downstairs. She was not hungry. Her stomach was tight and threatened to cave in on her at the very thought of food. She looked in the mirror instead. Her reflection showed her puffy eyes and swollen face.

"Lesbian," she said. She turned another way. "Lesbian, lesbian, lesbian." The more she said it the better she felt. "Lesbian, lesbian, lesbian." She stood squarely facing her reflection. "I am a lesbian," she said. The reflection smiled at her. She was smiling at herself.

When she finally went to bed, Miranda slept deeply, through sheer emotional exhaustion and didn't wake until well into midday. She lay on the bed feeling groggy, her eyes heavy and weighed down. It took a while for her to focus on the fact that she was awake. The house felt very still, maybe her mother had gone out shopping. She hoped so. Shopping with her mother was Miranda's least favourite pastime. Mrs. Matheson always behaved as if she was still having to count the pennies to make sure that all six of them got fed, even though now there were only two. Miranda preferred to shop for her mother by herself. It made things a lot quicker and meant she bought stuff she liked to eat. She wondered why her mother had not called her. She dragged herself off the bed and realised that she was still in her school clothes. The memory of the night before engulfed her. Quickly she pulled open her door and stepped onto the balcony, her haven from the night before held too many memories. The house was quiet and still as she liked it, especially this morning. Everything was so quiet, so peaceful. So normal, so ordinary.

"It didn't happen," she told herself, it was a nightmare, a dream. "It didn't happen, it didn't happen." She chanted it like a mantra. She walked down the stairs and into the living room. "It didn't happen," she said again, but this time the uncertainty echoed in her ear. She looked at the phone, could she ring Gayle and tell her about this dream, this nightmare? Her hand reached out, then she was crying, tears forced their way through eyes still tired from crying, a scream caught her throat. It made no difference. Chant or no chant, she had said what she had said. Gayle no longer wanted to be her friend. How long she cried she didn't know. But the fear of her mother coming home and finding her still in school clothes, howling on the sofa, forced Miranda upstairs.

Later, after washing and getting dressed, Miranda went to the kitchen. She made a cup of tea, more out of habit than out of any real intention to drink it. She watched it grow cold. She wondered again if she should ring Gayle, as if nothing had happened or maybe even apologise for what she had done. She wanted to ring but she didn't want Gayle screaming at her again. After all, she hadn't done anything wrong. Tom had tried to get his hands into Gayle's knickers and she had forgiven him. Now Gayle wanted to sleep with him. Everything was all wrong. Nothing made any sense. Miranda groaned, why couldn't it still be last week? At least then she and Gayle were still friends, even though she was totally miserable about being ignored. She wished that she could just make Tom disappear. If it hadn't been for him none of this would have happened anyway.

But then I wouldn't know I was a lesbian, Miranda thought. For some reason that thought gave her a warm glow inside. It was like they said on the television, it made you feel good inside. It was like knowing you were Black and being proud. It was the same kind of glow. Her eyes wandered in the direction of the phone. Maybe Gayle wouldn't even come to the phone. Beside what would she tell Gayle — that she hadn't meant what she said? That would be a lie. How could she deny what she had said when all she wanted to do was hold Gayle in her arms and kiss her? She shivered. Just thinking about Gayle like that brought her out in goosebumps. What on earth was she going to do? It was already Saturday afternoon. Day after tomorrow was school. She couldn't face going there, not knowing if Gayle was her friend. What if the teachers found out, what if anybody asked her if it were true, what would she say? She could say she wasn't, but that would be like saying she wasn't Black. Maybe she could say that she didn't know, after all she had not done anything with a woman. Nearly kissing Gayle didn't count. The moment of it captured her again, the memory of their closeness filled her being. How close they had been, how sweet Gayle's lips had tasted, even in that brief touch. Her eyes closed as she replayed that brief, brief moment. She couldn't hold it for long. The screams started and Gayle's lips became her shocked and angry face.

"Oh Gayle, I'm so sorry, I'm so sorry." The tears started again, like a force that would tear her apart. How would she survive this, how would she live another day?

By the time her mother returned Miranda had run and rerun the scene in her mind a million times and was none the wiser about what to do next. Her mother arrived loaded with shopping. Glad to have something else to think about Miranda went to her mother and helped put the shopping away. Mrs. Matheson chatted all the gossip that she had heard in town, which was another reason Miranda didn't like going shopping with her. Every two steps, it seemed, her mother would meet someone she knew and stop for a chat which took hours.

"I saw Gayle in town," she said. "I told her you were home and not feeling well. She was very concerned. She was with some boy. I suppose that one you told me about. He looks much too old for her. Doesn't look like he goes to church either, but he was polite. Maybe Gayle will come round later. That will cheer you up. She usually comes round on a Saturday doesn't she?"

At the mention of Gayle's name Miranda froze. Her mother had seen Gayle in town. With Tom. Gayle must have told him everything. Tom, of all people. Miranda felt sick at the core of her stomach. Gayle and Tom. She wondered if they had done it yet. Gayle had probably gone and done it in a hurry, just to spite Miranda. To get away from her. To get away from the possibility of ever being called a dirty lesbian, too. Miranda leaned her head against the fridge door. It cooled her brow. Her mother was still talking, about somebody else now. Miranda wished that she could just walk out but she couldn't move. Gayle and Tom, why did it hurt so?

The day dragged on. Miranda's feelings and thoughts tormented her, second by second, hour by hour. What was she going to do, leave home? Her thoughts took her this way and that. She stayed in her room. And her mother, worried that there might really be something wrong, rang Simone to say Miranda was acting strangely. Simone's pronouncement was that Miranda had probably just fallen in love with some boy but agreed to come around.

"After all," she said to Miranda, "What are big sisters for, if not to give a shoulder to cry on?" They sat on Miranda's bed in Miranda's room, like they had done so many times before. The only difference was that for once Miranda had nothing to say. Miranda listened to Simone talk about why she had come and how it had felt for her when she had first fallen for a boy, how painful it had been when she found out that he fancied someone else. Miranda hoped that if she looked like she was really listening, Simone might get carried away with her own tales and forget why she had come. It had happened before. It didn't happen this time.

"So, what's eating you?" Simone asked, putting a sisterly arm around Miranda, the way she would have liked someone to do for her when she was younger and going through her love growing pains.

"Who's stolen your heart?"

Gayle, Miranda wanted to say, except she didn't. Instead she said nothing. How could she tell her sister that she was a lesbian or thought she was, at the very least Gayle thought she was? Gayle, who was probably telling the whole city. Monday edged ever nearer.

"It's OK, you don't have to say anything, although sometimes it does help to talk, just to get it off your chest you know, sometimes just doing that makes you feel better."

Miranda wanted to talk, she knew she would feel better if she talked to somebody. It would be a relief to be able to say those words out loud and get them out of her system, out of her ears. Dirty Lesbian. Would Simone call her that if she knew? No, not Simone, but that didn't mean she would be any more accepting either.

"Look I've got to go, why don't we meet up in the morning and go to church together?" Simone suggested. It was the last thing Miranda wanted to do, unless it was for her own funeral. She kept forgetting that Simone was really into the church. Simone got up to go.

"I'll call for you around 8:30," she said.

"No, it's alright Simone. I don't want to go."

"Now come on Miranda. What are you going to do, stay here and mope. That's not like you. Get on with your life. Find someone else. Church is a perfect way to start, there are some very nice boys down there."

Miranda was not listening. How could she get on with her life with Gayle hating her and wanting to sleep with some juvenile because she wanted to know what sex was like? Simone could see Miranda was not taking any notice of her, so she said good night and went downstairs where Mrs. Matheson waited for her.

"What's wrong with Miranda?" Mrs. Matheson asked as Simone's foot touched the bottom stair.

"She hasn't told me anything," Simone replied. "We'll leave it for a couple of days and see what happens. I told her I'd come for her for church tomorrow morning."

Sunday morning dawned with the threat of Monday morning that much nearer. Miranda had been awake for hours. She had never really been asleep. She stared at the ceiling and dreamt of Gayle. A sharp knock at her door broke her reverie. It was her mother, waking her for church. Miranda crawled further under the covers, but she knew there was no escape. She had been bending the rules all weekend. She washed, dressed and went down to a cooked breakfast. Simone was already there, drinking coffee. Mrs. Matheson greeted Miranda with a beaming smile, which went down a few notches when she noticed the trousers. They made it through breakfast, Miranda forcing herself to eat. By the time they reached the front door Mrs. Matheson was nervous. She suggested that Miranda may prefer to wear a dress. Miranda looked at her with her mouth open, then went to comply. What difference does it make what I wear? She thought to herself. Nobody would care if they knew what I was. She pulled on the first dress to come out of her wardrobe, a long one with a full skirt. She went downstairs and they got in the car and went to church.

Mrs. Matheson was proud. Proud of her daughter owning a car, proud of Simone coming to take her to church, proud to be going with two of her daughters. Even through her sulky haze, Miranda could feel her mother's pride. It burst out like a daffodil in bloom when they entered the church. At least someone's happy, she thought to herself. I've helped to make someone happy, even though I feel like it's the end of the world for myself. Miranda pondered the strangeness of life. Simone and Miranda sat near the back of the church, Miranda tried to make herself look inconspicuous. Mrs. Matheson was doing the rounds. Miranda looked at the simple front of the church and saw Gayle. Miranda felt her face burn in shame. Gayle was looking right at her. Not blinking, not smiling. Just staring straight at her.

Miranda found herself slowly rising to her feet. She felt like a robot just learning to walk. Gayle's stare followed her. Miranda left her row and went up the aisle. She felt everyone was staring at her. At the same time, it was as if she was in a universe where there was only her and Gayle. She stopped in front of Gayle.

"Hi," she said. She had her fingers crossed behind her back.

"Hi," said Gayle. They stared at each other. Neither said a word. Somewhere inside Miranda, something changed. Gayle was no longer angry with her. She saw it in Gayle's eyes. They were clear and brown and deep and full of love as they had always been. The music changed and people started moving to their seats.

"I'll see you after," Miranda said before returning to her seat. Gayle nodded.

All the way through church Miranda sang as if her heart would burst, all the time Gayle kept looking round and they would giggle, like they did when they were children. Only this time it was different. Church couldn't end soon enough. Then it was time to go. Miranda dragged her heels until Gayle caught up with her, then they slipped out as fast as they could and ran around the back of the church to the Lovers' Bushes, so called because of the number of condoms that could be found there after a Saturday night. They stood, getting their breath back and giggling. Then gradually, they were quiet and a kind of awkwardness started to fill the space between them.

"Your mum said you were ill," said Gayle.

Miranda tried to appear nonchalant. She didn't know what to expect, but Gayle was her friend and it had said on the TV programmes that all true friends would accept.

"Well, I wasn't really ill, just sort of well, not very well." Did that sound stupid? Miranda felt nervous. There was another awkward pause.

"I was coming to see you yesterday but I had to go and see Tom."

Hatred mingled with relief as Miranda listened to Gayle. Tom! Why was Gayle mentioning him? Miranda kept her head. She wasn't in any position to make demands or have likes or dislikes.

"Yeah?" she said.

"Yeah," repeated Gayle. They stood awhile more. "Is it true then?" Gayle asked.

"What?"

"That you're a lesbian?"

Miranda eyed her. What was going on. She didn't know whether to say yes or no. Maybe Gayle was giving her the chance to deny yesterday. She would love to take her words back, just think not speak, to never have said them. But deny them?

"Why do you want to know?" Miranda asked.

"Because if it is, then I want to say that I'm sorry for the other day, I just freaked. I mean it was a bit much you know, me talking about Tom, you talking about me, it was you know, a bit scary."

The world left Miranda's feet at Gayle's words. "That's alright," she said. "I suppose it was a bit of a shock."

"Yeah, at the time, but when I thought about it, it wasn't really. I suppose I always kind of knew. I mean you were never into boys and you were always jealous if any of them came round me, and you were always watching them gay programmes."

Guilty as charged thought Miranda. "Yeah, I suppose it is kind of obvious now, I didn't know myself before Friday."

"Yeah?"

"Yeah."

"So what made you find out on Friday?" Gayle's voice was low and almost seductive, teasing.

Miranda hesitated. She didn't want to spoil things again, but as her sister liked to say, you can only say what you feel. Miranda took a deep breath. "Well, I suppose I finally realised that I was jealous of you and Tom." She felt relief at her words.

"There's nothing to be jealous about," said Gayle.

Miranda said nothing. Was Gayle making fun of her? Miranda was sure Simone was right, it was better to speak your feelings, but maybe it wasn't good to be honest all the time. Having just retrieved Gayle's friendship she didn't want to say anything that might frighten her off.

"No, there's nothing to be jealous of, we're best friends aren't we," she said in response. Gayle nodded. Everything was alright in the world. Why then, did Miranda's heart feel so heavy?

The Monday after the worst weekend Miranda had ever had started cloudy, threatening rain. It suited Miranda's mood exactly. Making up with Gayle had helped a lot, but it didn't change the fact that Gayle was going out with some dumb boy instead of her, Miranda. The phone rang. Miranda ran downstairs from the bathroom, toothbrush in mouth. Her mother had gone to her early morning cleaning job.

"Hello," said Miranda through the foam. It was Gayle, suggesting that she come round for Miranda before school. What about Tom, Miranda almost said, but settled for yes. She was excited. She ran upstairs to put on her school uniform. She wore her best skirt and a new shirt that her mother had put away for emergencies. She felt a buzz. Eat your heart out, Tom, she sang to herself. She was ready and waiting at the door when Gayle knocked. There was something different about her. Miranda was not sure what it was.

"What you done to your hair?" asked Miranda. Gayle suddenly looked a bit shy and self-conscious.

"Nothing much, just styled it different," she said.

"It looks nice."

"Thanks," Gayle looked away. "You looked nice yesterday," she said.

For some reason Miranda blushed. "You ready then?" she said, to change the subject. Gayle nodded. Miranda locked the front door and they walked down the street. They talked all the way down the road, on the bus and up the school path. The bell was ringing as they arrived. They talked all the way down the corridor, in the classroom and through assembly. They talked all the way through their lessons. Everyone told them off. They took no notice. Gayle didn't mention Tom once. Then it was the last lesson of the day, the last bell and they were out in the corridor. In the crush a blonde girl purposefully came up to them, Susan Smythe.

"Hey Gayle, is it true that you finished with Tom?"

"What's it to you?" asked Gayle, not to pleasantly.

"Nothing, just making sure I don't step on anyone's toes."

Gayle's eyes grew wide in disbelief. "Well, he wouldn't go out with you!" she shouted. "Bloody cheek," she said when the girl had gone.

Miranda was in shock. "You're not going out with Tom," she said, but Gayle was out in front of her now, flowing with the crowd, dealing with other comments which Susan's question had stirred. Miranda struggled to catch up. "You're not going out with Tom?" she repeated, pushing past some other girls eager for the gossip.

"No," said Gayle, looking flustered. Miranda took her arm and pulled her away from the little group that had gathered.

"Why not?" she asked.

Again Gayle looked shy, "I'll tell you by the canal."

They walked to the canal deep in their own thoughts. Miranda didn't say a word until they were settled in at their favourite spot. How things can change, thought Miranda. Not too long ago this place had been the scene of her ultimate despair, now she was back again, and this time Gayle was telling her that she was no longer with Tom.

"What happened?" asked Miranda.

"I finished with him."

"You finished with him." Miranda was incredulous, "but last time I spoke to you, you wanted to sleep with him."

"That was then, this is now," Gayle said laughing.

"When did you finish with him?"

"Saturday."

"Saturday! You never said."

"You never asked," said Gayle smugly. "I told you I had to go see him."

"But I thought..." Miranda stumbled over her words. Nothing was making sense. "Why'd you finish with him?" she asked.

"Because..."

"Because of what, did he try something on you?" Miranda felt her fists tighten.

"Yes, no, well, he did, but that's not the reason."

"You going to tell me or what?" Miranda asked with mounting frustration.

"Well, if you must know, it's because of what you said."

"What I said?"

"Yes."

"What did I say?" Miranda asked, totally at a loss.

"Well, nothing really," Gayle said irritatingly.

Miranda clenched her fists again. "Gayle, stop winding me up."

"OK, OK keep your hair on. If you must know, it's when you were saying about you know...."

"What?"

"Miranda!" It was Gayle's turn to get frustrated. "You know what I'm talking about."

Miranda looked at her and thought for a while. She had a feeling that she did know, but it couldn't be true, could it?

"You mean, what I was saying about me and you, instead of you and Tom."

Gayle nodded.

"You mean it?"

Gayle nodded.

"You look like one of those stupid dogs you see in the backs of cars when you do that," Miranda observed. Gayle laughed and gave Miranda a playful swipe. Miranda hit her back. They played around for a few minutes. Then they stopped and looked at each other.

"I ain't done it before you know," Miranda said.

"Neither have I," said Gayle.

"But you said you wanted to sleep with Tom because he had."

"I don't want to sleep with Tom," shouted Gayle.

"OK, quiet down, those fishermen will hear you."

When they spoke next it was in lowered tones, they shuffled closer to hear each other's whispers.

"What we going to do then?" asked Miranda, feeling that Gayle expected her to know something she didn't.

"Do what you were going to do on Friday."

Miranda looked at her with wide eyes. "Really?"

"Really." They looked at each other some more. "I'll kiss you," said Gayle, "because I've been kissed before and I know how to do it."

Miranda sat as still as a statue. Gayle looked round to see if anyone was watching and then she kissed Miranda squarely on the lips. Miranda did not move. Even after Gayle moved away Miranda sat with pursed lips.

"Miranda," laughed Gayle, shaking her, "Stop being such a complete fool."

"That was beautiful," whispered Miranda, "Do it again."

"Alright, but this time you have to kiss back." Miranda nodded. Gayle moved closer again. Their lips met, and the sky and ground expanded away from Miranda's feet. Her heart beat with a new exciting pulse. Her lips felt tingly sweet.

"I thought you said you never kissed nobody before."

"I haven't," said Miranda from a point of bliss.

"Well, you're a good kisser."

Miranda beamed. They talked and kissed for a long while. Darkness fell.

"God, my mum'll go spare," Miranda said when the lateness of the hour finally sunk in.

"Don't worry," Gayle said "It'll be alright if you say you were with me. Our mums will be pleased that we're not with any boys."

"Yeah, but I'm not sure they'd be wild about knowing what we were doing instead."

"It's OK, we don't have to tell them."

"Well," said Miranda "I'm going to tell my family someday."

"Why?" asked Gayle.

"Because it's better, it feels better to say who you are. You know I was real upset on Friday. I thought I'd lost my best friend — and look, today it's even better. Maybe none of this would have happened if I hadn't said anything."

"That's true. I could still be with Tom, but I like you better."

"So, when did you realise that?"

"When you got close to me like you were trying to kiss me, it really turned me on, more than being kissed by Tom ever did."

"But you called me a dirty lesbian. I was afraid you'd tell the whole school and everybody would be laughing and getting at me." Some of Miranda's hurt and pain spilled out.

Gayle looked ashamed. "I'm sorry Miranda, truly, I was just so afraid. Tom was always trying something on and I never felt anything, then you tried to kiss me and I got all these feelings inside me. I just didn't know what to do."

Miranda looked deep into her friend's dark brown eyes. There was something else she had to say. She took a deep breath. "You're a lesbian, too, Gayle."

Gayle's eyes filled with tears. "I know, I know. But I wanted to blame it all on you, but I couldn't." Gayle was crying. They held each other, Miranda felt her tears coming. They comforted each other. After they wiped away each other's tears, Miranda felt that she saw the world in a new light. She felt older. They went down to the path. It was misty dark. Lamps shone and reflected in the canal.

"I want to hold your hand," said Miranda.

"Why?"

"Tom used to."

"That was different," Gayle started to say, but didn't quite finish.

"Just while we're on the tow path," said Miranda. "Nobody will see."

"OK," said Gayle, holding out her hand. Miranda took it. Slowly, very slowly they walked down the path.

ON THE ROAD WITH MARCEL PROUST
Desoto Wong

Every word I write brings me closer to yet further in time from the Jamaica of my childhood, which I love. It brings me towards what I do not want to write about — the subsequent existence in Miami, which I hate.

Last night while falling asleep I had a sudden memory, and thought I would remember it in the morning. Stupidly, I did not get up, turn on the light, and write it down. Now, nine sleep-clogged hours later, I cannot recall that memory. I don't know what it was about, even vaguely. It has reburied itself in the slag heap of life, stored in the grey matter inside our skulls, under rigidly locked fontanelles. Maybe it will resurface in another fifteen, twenty years, triggered by an odour, a dream, an emotion, a need to discharge or restore its enormous load. Maybe it will never resurface again.

Every human has her own devices to bury or exhume remembrance. For Proust's character Marcel, it occurred fortuitously. When Marcel was having tea with his mother, he dipped a pastry, known as a madeleine, into his tea. With his spoon he sipped linden blossom tea-soaked morsels. Suddenly, he was inundated by the memory of having tea and madeleine sometime long before. Opened to him was the trail of things past.

But when I am nineteen and in France for the first time, I discover that the madeleine is a pastry that disappoints. It is a puffy, sweet, dumpy thing. The madeleine seems elegant because of Proust's prose, now enshrined, and its name. Madeleine could be an haute-bourgeoise, elegantly slim though not anorexic, we hope, long hair pulled back in a bun, or not, depending on her age. She has a silk scarf around her neck, some dull, discreet design, and as she passes you on the sidewalk she doesn't see you. The sky glows grey like an enormous pearl, and you don't care as you stroll past the booksellers lining the Seine, you bob against the current of tourists from all over the world. You dip this madeleine in tea, soften it, watch the crumbs swim in some sort of weak *tisane* that only a guy like Marcel could like; crumbs eddying like memory being sucked into the vortex of disappearance. Maybe someday the crumbs will be spotted in a waterspout over the Sargasso.

Madeleine doesn't do it for me. My "Open, sesame" will be earthy and greasy. Something from Jamaica, my Jamaica. Maybe slabs of braised pork and collops of yam steamed together in a complex mix of five-spice powder, Hoisin and oyster sauces. As the dish gleams from under a shining layer of fat, its aroma wafts sinuously to your nostrils and invokes your saliva. In back of the family grocery in downtown Kingston, we politely devoured it, then sat back and patted our gall bladders. Maybe my madeleine will be my mother's Sunday roast beef, well-done is how we like it, the black edges crunchy and sizzling with flavour. A chorus of potatoes, anointed in copious beef drippings, now garlicky and very salty. Perhaps, if I weren't such a strict vegetarian, it would work.

What about rice and peas? Pigeon peas diaspora'd in white rice with flecks of thyme, scent of coconut cream, and a Scotch Bonnet (a Jamaican pepper shaped like a tam). This single pepper sits on my father's plate, wrinkled and fuming, angry that it has bled just a hint of its nature into the rice. My father is the only one who can tolerate its searing flesh, a square millimetre of which is enough to set your palate aflame. Maybe my madeleine will be soft yellow ackee and fibrous saltfish, with floating tomatoes whose resistance has been cooked away so they burst into hot liquid in your mouth. With marbled, caramelized brown and yellow flesh, sweet deep-fried plantain lie on a plate heavy with oil. Smoky corn in its husk, bought from a man on a mountain road, who cooks his wares in a converted steel drum. The kernels are smothered by large crystals of salt and chunks of butter that seem to have materialized from the surrounding trees or from my imagination that coats everything with a rich sheen of nostalgia.

Past the man selling roasted corn, the narrow country road rolls on. Each time the asphalt disappears around a green, shadowy bend, drivers sound their horn so that oncoming vehicles will stay on their side and not bulldoze them off the mountainside, into the air, then down on a bed of scrambling tropical overgrowth celebrating the sun. Most fascinating are the buses that carry people from village to marketplace and back. Around the corner the behemoth sways, only its tires cling to the road as if magnetized. Boxes, bags, chickens in pens on the luggage rack above, all shift with each curve and threaten to fly off into the ferns, taking the leaning bus after them. On each turn, we rock as a body into each other and share one another's breath, sometimes casting an uneasy glance out the window at the river bed winding smooth boulders far below us. The driver has only the steering wheel as his anchor. He leans on the horn again, and we all hang on.

But then there's boiled white chicken flesh dipped in a simple concoction of mushroom soy sauce, chopped scallion, and a half inch of oil. A thick slice of white hard-dough bread slathered with margarine, or bearing yellow tiles of cheddar. Hard knobs of Jamaican chocolate that soften in boiling water while a dried cinnamon leaf dances crazily. To this is joined globs of sweet condensed milk, elixir of developing nations. Drops of oil surface. Cocoa butter, milk fat. As it goes down, the dark brown liquid coats your tongue, your throat, your memory. After such a feast, the driver miscalculates his payload. Farting diesel fumes, the overcrowded bus lurches over the edge, cleaves the clean country air, eases into the parabola of taking a dive. We brace ourselves and burp. What a way to go, mon.

By now, the reader may be wondering what is so important about that memory, or my memories. There is, in fact, nothing special about my memories. Just an assortment of tin trinkets and knackered knickknacks, dusty tarnished gimcracks and gewgaws with chipped, variegated paint, "Made in Japan" or "Made in China" somewhere on the bottom. Perhaps they will be worth more, as time goes on, because less baubles from that era will be left to look at, to demonstrate the distance from there to here. I think of the Musée Seita in Paris, with its collection of smoking paraphernalia. Quotidian objects now precious and carefully labeled. *Ivory opium pipe, ca. 1800s. Silver snuff box, 1840s.* There is the Musée des Lunettes et du Lorgnon, full of spectacles that gaze at the observer through a pane of glass. Perhaps no such shortage of memories will raise the value of my tchockas, my mementos of moments past. They are important only to me.

To make sure that the memories at hand don't recede into the morass of time, the slag head of life stored in the grey matter inside our skulls, I have amassed this pile of poor, disparate little fragments into a lopsided souvenir sculpture. This is all I have left. From this recollection of trifles packed into a structure that leans like the battle between inertia and a bus on the edge of a cliff careening, I offer you a house, a garden, a city, an island, an afternoon's walk. I offer you the Jamaica of a time that no longer exists, a Jamaica that turns up occasionally among the pig's tails and yam in pumpkin soup, a Jamaica that can be divined in the volumes of steam rising from callaloo, spotted like a waterspout in the distance, on the horizon, over the Sargasso.

Sister

Desoto Wong

One afternoon my mother and I drove to the convent. As the car went up the long driveway, a large field of uncut grass swayed in a wave as the wind skimmed across its tassels. Tall trees full of rustling leaves and shadows hunched over the convent, as if to cloak it. I eagerly scrutinized the colonial-style building, repainted white with black trim, as if its exterior might reveal something about the occupants within. Built by a plantation owner, the mansion had somehow fallen into the hands of the church. Sister Alethia came running out, adjusting her habit. As she crossed the veranda, a single lock of bright red hair sprang out of her habit and tumbled over her forehead. The Vatican had recently decided that nuns could expose some hair. The older nuns, such as the headmistress Sister George, still kept everything pushed underneath.

"I was just taking a nap," Sister Alethia explained her relative state of undress. I loved listening to her Scottish burr. It chose strange syllables to accentuate or to suppress. I was happy to know that they allowed her to sleep during the day if she wanted. White robes draped over her lankiness. I was used to teachers in layers of white clothing down to their ankles throughout the year, in both the cool and the hot seasons. I didn't know it then, but Sister Alethia was still a young woman.

My mother handed her a sweet-potato pudding, for all the nuns. Sister Alethia leaned into the '62 Chevy Nova, smiled, and said, "If you grow up to be like your mother, you'll be a wonderful, wonderful person."

I didn't say anything. I didn't want to be like my mother. I couldn't articulate what bothered me about it. Was it using hair spray every morning, baking cakes on birthdays, having children? Why was Sister Alethia, who led a life so different from my mother's, telling me not to be like herself, my beloved teacher?

As we were saying goodbye, a younger sister and the new priest came walking together from the darkness under the mango trees. The other priests were broad, grey, and a little frightening in their authority. This one's hair was still dark against his pale English face, and he was slim. He was pushing a bike, and he and the woman were smiling into each other's eyes.

"Some of the novices don't take their final vows," my mother said with a slight frown as we drove down the driveway to the traffic of Hope Road. I asked her what that meant. "They're still young," was all she let slip.

I often wondered about Sister Alethia. She was on a little island called Jamaica, far away from her home in Scotland. Did she miss her family, friends, town? Did she miss the sound of bagpipes, the sight of heather on the hills, the aroma and taste of haggis, delicious to her, and the opportunity to tease men in kilts about not wearing underwear? I hoped not. She was my very favourite teacher in all my short life, and I did not want her to dismiss class one day and step on a plane to Glasgow the next.

On weekends, I even wished it was Monday so I could go to school and see her again. While my parents thought I was in the garden, I rode all around suburban Kingston to pass the time. In the foothills of the Blue Mountains, homes gazed toward the distant harbour. Streets sloped up past tidy houses behind fences made of formidable concrete blocks enlivened by variegated paint. Ecstatically, grasshoppers jumped across sidewalks full of medicinal weeds. Shame-lady closed her fronds when caressed. Flowering bushes offered up their plenty, like starlets in their prime. Laundry flapped on backyard lines. From behind iron gates, dogs ran up to greet me. Occasionally a mongoose would dash across the street in the haze of the afternoon, shimmering road, mirage on tar. The streets were quiet and empty, hills rose up in the background, lush, huge, benevolent.

My bike would blur around gentle curves, the handlebars cresting in the green breeze as I crossed my arms nonchalantly over my chest. One Saturday I was trying to ride my bike by holding the left side of the handlebars with my right hand and the right side with my left hand. We came down a crushing tangle of red bicycle and skinny brown limbs. On elbows and kneecaps, graze marks were filling with blood. With no one else was there, my tears stopped of their own accord. The macadam road was so soft in the hot, still, lonely midday that I took a sharp stone and drew initials inside a heart. Then I crossed everything out.

When I went to school on Monday, Sister Alethia gave me a big hug.

"Ow," I protested. Her face softened as she saw the Band-Aids stuck generously on my body, covering my stigmata. She understood that my protest was not because I didn't want to be hugged by her.

"Oh my wee lamb," she murmured, holding me again, gently. Her white robes emitted a smell. Was it of an ascetic laundry soap, a bare wooden closet, or her particular body, with red hairs curling against an impossibly white skin in a Kingston school yard? I don't know, but if I came across that fragrance today, I would fall in love at once.

In a classroom lined with our drawings — experiments with colour we called patterns, the boys' military battles and girls' flowers, assignments such as a circus scene or a landscape — we obediently sat according to Sister's chart. Each pupil kept his or her textbooks and notebooks inside a desk. The wood desktop swung up to reveal the inside of the grey-painted oblong metal body. The design, at least, of the desks was old, since there was a hole in the wood in the top right corner where you could stick your quill into your bottle of ink safely placed inside the desk. There was also a groove along the top where we kept our pencils. On the first day of every new school year, teachers would make us sand down the year's worth of graffiti published on the wooden desktop. I liked to imagine that the deepest words, engraved with a compass point and stained with ink, were at least as old as me. Try as I might, I could not sand down *jackass*, BLOODY BORING! or *RAS*.

We all loved Sister Alethia's clear lessons and her idealism about our capacities and intentions. The whole class appreciated that she called on everyone, not just the smart ones. Even though she tried to distribute her attention evenly, I noticed that she would often give me the privilege of cleaning the blackboard erasers. Each week in Composition class, she gave us a subject to write about. We would fill a page or two with our unsure print in pencil. Once she had us describe a school friend without using names, and everyone had to guess who it was. Everyone laughed when the person described as bursting out of his shirt turned out to be Royce, a chubby brown boy. But it was not malicious; his friend Trenton had linked this characteristic to Royce's vigour and prowess at soccer. Several girls wrote about someone with sparkling eyes, always a smile on her lips. Of course, this was Sister Alethia. Another time we were to describe a day in our life as a humble penny that was passed from hand to hand. One week we wrote about the sunset, the orange, pink, and gold of the clouds, the sun sinking behind hills, going down in the glittering, shadowy sea, or disappearing into tin rooftops. Flowers opening and closing in the softening light. The stars that waited till the sun's departure to blink timidly. The calm we felt.

Sister Alethia was also preparing us for the cleansing rigors of our first confession and the mystery of our first holy communion. We had a special textbook for this. One day, Sister Alethia had us draw a picture of Communion. I drew and coloured a triangular bunch of purple grapes and a yellow sheaf of wheat with a green and red cross. Sister said it was beautiful.

Sister Alethia thought I was a good person, but I knew she was wrong. During previously announced or unscheduled power outages at night, my parents would ignite a gas lamp that hissed out a blue-white light. I would light a candle and walk to an empty room. As I passed, shadows trembled and stretched. I would sit on the tile floor in an empty room and watch the little triangle of flame dance on the wick. When the melted wax in the meniscus was about to overflow, I would pour the liquid wax on myself. The hot viscous residue of ancient plants would burn a hole of sensation in my skin, concentrate its flammable energy in a little pool the size of a coin. Eventually the wax would congeal. At first I did this on my hand, and when I flicked the wax off it was imprinted with a reverse finger- or palm-print, like me, the opposite of how good Sister Alethia thought I was. Later, the sensation dulled and I tried more sensitive parts of my body: my forearm, the sole of my foot, my stomach.

I wasn't original. I had read about people in medieval Lenten parades, carrying candles on their bent backs, walking with sharp stones in their shoes, whipping themselves. They wanted to go through fire and mortification of the flesh to purify their souls.

Inside our airy white church, the light glows ethereal blue, through blue-glass windows. Small bas-reliefs mounted on white beams depict the fourteen stations of the cross. People spit at Christ, soldiers gamble off his clothes, jeering crowds feed him vinegar, he falls twice — or is it three times? — under the weight of the crucifix. Holy water in round stone receptacles look like fat hands offering water and solace to Jesus after his forty days and forty nights in the desert. Statues of saints, gold gilt on purple or red velvet, lit candles glowing tremulously in the half daylight, freshly-cut flowers. An exercise in guilty, tempered, meticulously-channeled voluptuousness.

Behind the altar, the ceiling soars up, and there's a mural, a sort of line drawing in gold metal against hopeful green: Peter and Paul are gigantic, over fifty feet tall, their halos almost touching the roof. Both are slim, bearded, in robes. Stars glimmer around them. Peter holds the keys to the kingdom, three large stylized ones. And floating in upper-left heaven is the lamb. Only two steps above human level is the altar itself, resembling a coffin shrouded in white cloth or the operating table from which the

Frankenstein monster arose during a violent thunderstorm. At the most important part of the mass, *This is my body, this is my blood*, transformation takes place here. The priest will raise the chalice, the altar boy will ring a bell, we will all kneel, and then we will be able to partake of the body and blood of Christ. At seven, I believe in transcendence.

My parents were married in this church, my siblings and I were all baptized there, and I was old enough to remember my cousin Loulou's baptism, when she was a small wrinkled bundle. Every Sunday we got there just before the priest ascended up the centre aisle with the organ's emphasis, a crooked brass sceptre in his hand and two altar boys in his train. We would pray in an archaic English: "Our Father who art in Heaven, / Hallowed be Thy name." Some sitting in the pews around me still said their mass in Latin.

In preparation for Eucharist, we must offer Jesus a cleansed temple. The day of our first confession, the church was empty except for two classes of us, seven- and eight-year-olds now endowed with the ability to know right from wrong, life from sin. I was anxious. My classmates were happy, because they were innocent. I had a heavy burden to unload. And I did not know how to express this sin. Among the few adults ushering us to the back of the church was Sister Alethia, looking happy and radiant.

We all knelt in a line in the pews closest to the confessional, a curious tripartite box-like structure made of wood. It had three doors. The middle door was for the priest. He would sit inside and await the penitent. The doors on either side of him were for the sinners, who would open their door, kneel facing the priest's box and wait for him to open the little window in the wall, first on one side, then on the other. When the priest opened the wooden panel from inside his box, there would still be a heavy screen, so that the sinner would remain concealed from the all too human eyes of the priest. In theory, the priest does not know the identity of the sinner. The priest is obliged to keep to himself what he hears in the confessional for the rest of his life.

I was determined to state all my sins at my first confession. If I was to be worthy of Sister Alethia's teachings, I would confess the one failure I shamefully kept hidden away. I tried to suppress it, but it always came seeking me out. Again and again I grappled unsuccessfully with Satan's temptations. My mind had been obedient to me before. Math, grammar, art, I was usually able to pull something off. My eternal well-being now depended on me to speak — something I found already difficult — but about intensely personal matters. Now in the dark wooden cubicle, I wondered if I should go ahead with my plan. Kneeling on a very thin pad over hard wood, I could hear murmuring coming from the other side. The priest's voice was a low rumble, and a classmate's reedy whisper. I was relieved to note that however hard I strained my ears, I could not make out distinct words. There were shuffling noises, then a longish-seeming silence. Finally, I heard cloth shifting its attention to my side. The wood made resonant noises as the priest opened the small panel in front of me. Through the thick screen I tried to see which priest it was. I made out some grey hair on an otherwise dark bulk. He began by mumbling some prayers.

"Yes, my child," he prompted me. He whistled the *s*.

I hoped he would not be able to connect my frightened voice with the small Chinese girl in a short white veil, white dress and black patent leather shoes that surreptitiously squeaked together in time to the organ. I would accompany my mother to the ten o'clock Sunday mass. We would sit on the left side, near the back, the better to get out fast and before the hourly traffic jam in the parking lot. I didn't think he would recognize me; my mother was not one of the parishioners who waited after the service to say hello to the priest.

"Bless me, Father, for I have sinned. This is my first confession. These are my sins." This was just reading from a script.

"One time I did shoot a dog in the leg with my brother's BB gun." I was truly sorry about that.

"Another time, I stole two shillings from my sister's piggy bank," I rattled off. *Do unto others as you would have them do unto you.* I didn't want Julia stealing from *my* piggy bank.

Abruptly, I fell silent. Locked in a position of prayer, my palms scratched themselves nervously against the wooden ledge jutting into my chest. The priest cleared his throat several times. I thought I heard him drumming his fingers on his side of the box. The luminous square at his throat shifted as he urged, "Go on, my child. You know, it's a sin to hold anything back from God." *Tap, tap, tap.*

My heart stared over a wide gulf. A throat cleared, a collar bobbed. When he stopped tapping his fingers, I could hear the rush of my blood through the veins in my ear.

"What is it? You can't hide it from God."

But I thought of Sister Alethia and rushed on. "Father. I think I am..."

"Yes?" I seemed to see bushy eyebrows arching and white tufts bristling out of his ears, ear hairs that only old men from England have, sometimes transfixing pieces of dandruff. I couldn't breath, I had trouble breathing. I felt like my chest was in a vise. I forced air into my lungs.

"Father I think I am a homosexual," I exhaled in a rush. All of a sudden, I was aware of the sour smell inside the confessional, the odor of sweat, shame and repented pleasure.

"Why do you think that, my child?" the dark intoned.

I was stunned. Surely this holy grown-up knew more about it than me. I had only recently discovered the word in the *Oxford English Dictionary*. Was the priest asking me to reveal my fantasies to him, here in church? Most of them involved holding hands with Lola Eng. With long black hair, a perfect oval face, a slightly aquiline nose and dark brown eyes, she was the most beautiful girl in school. And Lola was great at rounders. In some of my daydreams, we were in our bathing suits at the foot of Dunns River Falls where patches of fresh water remained cool before mixing with the warm salt water. In others, we kissed, while the Newcastle morning fog and the aroma of bamboo and ferns swirled around us.

"Ahm...I have certain thoughts, Father," I finally managed.

"Ah. Well, it's simple. Try not to think those thoughts anymore. You will grow out of it and the Lord will forgive you, if you really try." He whispered more sibilant prayers to himself and sent me off with the light penance of two Hail Marys and one Our Father.

I knelt in front of the statue of Mary in polished white stone. The wooden pews smelled of furniture polish. A sweet breeze swept through all the open doors of the church. Outside an elderly poinciana tree nodded its branches. I resolved not to think those thoughts anymore.

At the end of the following year, Sister Alethia had to go back to Scotland as I had feared. I now had the dreaded Mrs. Cannon as my teacher. During the school assembly, because we loved Sister and would probably not see her again, most of the girls in my class cried through the hymn we sang in her honour. The girls and boys in Sister Alethia's present Prep One class openly burst into tears.

"Don't cry," she said, though she was touched.

In the afternoon, I rushed out of my last class, Mrs. Cannon be damned, and ran down the hallway to Sister Alethia's classroom. She was dismissing her last class. The children who looked much smaller than me made a big fuss about leaving. "Have a safe trip, Sister. We love you, Sister. We'll miss you, Sister." I waited at the doorway. After they had all left, I crept into the classroom. She was erasing the blackboard.

"Want me to clean the erasers for you, Sister?" She turned around at the sound of my voice.

"I was wondering when I'd see you, Desoto." She smiled. I ran into her arms and started sobbing. "I'll write, my wee lamb. We'll stay in touch." I looked up and saw tears in her eyes.

Two years later I prepared with the rest of my class for confirmation, but it was without the joy that had sprung forth for Sister Alethia. I chose Brigid as my confirmation name, after the Irish saint who led a band of seven virgins in her mountain hideaway, patron saint of blacksmiths and poets. The bishop, who had ninety other children to confirm, misheard me. I was confirmed as Bridget, after that old Swedish married woman who had eight children, including Saint Catherine of Sweden. So I felt nothing. No speaking in tongues, no little flame above my head, no dove flying through the breezy church. No Holy Spirit.

Even so, Sister Alethia kept her promise. We corresponded, at first regularly, then more and more sporadically. Enclosed in one of the last letters I received from her was a photograph. It's a black and white snapshot. Sister Alethia is standing by a fountain. Water is spewing out of a cherub's mouth. Her hand is resting on the shoulder of another, unnamed nun whose lips are parted, shyly. They look into each other's eyes and smile.

A Rejuvenation of Sorts
Vashti Persad

Here finally. Exhausted, sticky, sad and happy. After Bermuda, Antigua and a stop, Guadeloupe, Grenada, Barbados. I see the mountain range of Trinidad's north coast. How beautiful. How full, rich and hot. This is my home. This was my home. The colours are familiar. So are the houses, roads, cars, bush fires and the memories. Home? Familiar yet distant. Under me now, a land I come to openly — but I have to remind myself it's not always safe. I leave part of myself in Toronto when I come here. It's the "safe thing" to do. And yet I come here to rest and make my soul strong again.

    Right now I feel a kinship to the land I see beneath me. The memories of crossing this range on a Saturday morning to get to the best and roughest beach on the island. It was mine and I still defend its temper with mine. Maracus — brings thoughts of sitting on a car bonnet burning my young legs to get my picture taken by my Dad, the best photographer in my world; thoughts of finding a bush to wee-wee behind and then making sure the world was not looking at a six-year-old pee; thoughts of swimming in the sand because the water frightened me and then having my Dad pick me up and take me to what seemed like the middle of the sea just to be ducked under a wave; thoughts of bottles of rum, pots of rice and chicken and cars of relatives. Maracus, my childhood. The roads were steep, the cliffs were frightening and our little Hillman always won the challenge.

    Two days ago, I turned twenty-nine. Two days ago, I was touching a woman whom I never wanted to leave. One day ago, I hugged a woman whom I will always love.

Now I just had a seven-hour flight with a man next to me whom I did not know except for his rum breath and his elbow which kept nudging me and waking me up; and it wasn't even his assigned seat. Yes, I spent seven hours being possessive about a seat I did not pay for. In addition to having to put up with this intrusion, I was battling obsessive thoughts of a lover — or an ex-lover — or whatever she wants to call herself. Back and forth, like a pendulum. Walk away, forget it all, risk the pain, protect myself, give it all to her. It was driving me crazy.

Now we have landed.

I am here to calm myself, collect my thoughts, my emotion. I am here to strengthen my soul. I am at a crossroads, searching for calm.

Right at this moment, I can't wait to face the hot air as I walk off the plane. Thoughts of the beach, sweat and starry nights await me. Before I leave the plane I must say goodbye to those two beautiful women. Ooops, I thought I left that part of me in Toronto. Again I think, where is home?

It is a week since I have been in Trinidad. There is comfort in being one of the many.

I am at the beach.

I am here for three days with my aunt, one of my Mothers. I look at the waves coming to the shore. The tide is low. The sea is calm except for that one wave which crashes to the sand. I am that wave — coming to these shores only to leave again — collecting what there is to keep, leaving what is heavy on my soul.

Strangely, I come here to free myself of chains I build in Toronto. Sitting here I can create a peaceful detachment. The things and events and circumstances which brought me pain seem small and manageable. The pain of lost loves find a meaning. I find peace. I find a part of myself.

Ironically, finding peace has very little to do with my passion. My peaceful existence accepts my passions, but does not bring them to life. As I sit here and look at the sea and this one wave, I also picture one woman. I remember seduction. Just as the open sea pulls me deeper and deeper, and calls me to its depth, so I allowed myself to be called by a lover. The pull was magnetic. The force of this emotion was powerful. I look at the sea, and I dream of being surrounded, of being carried away, of giving in, of surrendering. Again, it is a search for home, for belonging. I am with the sea but my woman is not here.

Earlier this morning, after my eight a.m. swim, I attended a Hindu religious ceremony. I attend with respect but know that my knowledge of my heart takes me on a wider path. A little bit more, I find myself.

Reflecting now, I see myself being drawn into the life which my Trinidadian family respects. "Yes, I'll get married when the time is right," laughing when they all try to set me up with a young man.

Now sitting here watching the sea, I think to myself — where is the truth? How can I live my truth in this world? Yet finding peace has everything to do with finding truth.

This morning I was reading the BOMB, while the poojah was going on. It was a story about a man who found his wife in bed with another woman. The headline read, "The worst kind of horn: Donald is shocked: Darling, Is that you?" Though appalled at the appearance of the story in the paper, I smiled. The husband described the women as being like "snakes intertwined holding each other." I was disgusted. I hated the imagery and I hated the article, yet in my mind the thought of these two women together brought a warmth and excitement through my body.

Yes, I am a lesbian.

I am a lesbian.

This is part of my truth.

I can only reveal this on these pages, however.

The world I know in Trinidad, which only includes my relatives, is not a safe place for this. I realize my limitations. I hear from friends about another world here. When I come here though I only become a part of my family's world — a world which warms me, strengthens me and cares for me; but in which I also feel caged. I can challenge it and I do, but I choose not to push the boundaries all the way. Political and spiritual boundaries are one thing — the boundaries of passion are something else.

So, I make my choices out of a need for this world. I want it. When I come, I come to hold and be held by my grandmother, to show her I love her. I come to retrieve my history from the hearts of my people and the words and vibrations of the island. I cannot lose this. There is lots of me on this island. When I find myself trapped and tortured by the weak links of love, by the isolation, the anger, the blindness, I need to run back here to nurse my soul. I will leave here in one week, wanting to get back to Toronto where my silent parts can begin to speak. I will go back stronger, calmer, more patient and more at peace. I will carry the love of my home country, my grandmother, my aunts, my relatives and the Trinidadian people. I will return to Toronto, longing to connect with my friends who give me a different sense of belonging and empowerment. I will recapture what I left behind.

Tonight I am saying goodbye to this solitude as the sun sets slowly over the ocean. As I stare in amazement at the orange sky, I say to myself, my land, the beginning of my heartbeat. I feel proud to be of this land. I feel sad to leave it. Yet I am ready to go. It's strange. There is a pull to keep me here on this beach in seclusion, yet there is something calling me away.

It is a nice dilemma. A young man who lives here calls it magic.

He tells me to stay. His brother mentions marriage. Now I feel I am at that door. It opens widely every time I come to Trinidad, inviting me to come in. I see the tunnel it leads into. As my heart feels out the door, I realize how dangerous the desire to "fit in and be a part" can be. The pressure is extreme. And one more time I hear "It's lonely, you need a husband, you can't live alone, it's not safe." They all mean well. It seems over the years I have learned to accept this without much rebellion. At seventeen, at twenty-one and at twenty-four, I used to put up a fight, and I always threw the argument at them that I had to get an education and work a while. It always worked to keep the pressure off. Now these phrases are overused. I'm twenty-nine and almost past the "catching a boy" years of a girl's life. It's downhill from here. What will I do for the rest of my life if I do not take advantage now and "get a man."

I joke about this but a sadness comes into me. What about my truth? My love?

When I love a woman it's one of the most selfless and beautiful experiences I can have, and when I lose a woman's love, it's the worst pain I can feel. Yet I cannot share it with these people whom I love.

Last night, I slept with a woman I had spent a summer making love to when we were both seventeen years old. She touched me, played with my hair, caressed me. I returned the tenderness. Her husband and children lay sleeping in the "master bedroom." I was a guest for the night.

The memories were strong. We reminisced. It meant the same for us at seventeen — yet our love went in different directions. We are both twenty-nine and the passion of twelve years ago easily comes back. The love was here. Commitment elsewhere.

So what does this say to me? Three days before I leave the island and after one and a half weeks of reflecting on the silencing of my sexuality, I find a night which is familiar. She was desirable and I sensed a passion within her. A little part of my love was getting a voice. Only I understood and I followed it softly and gently. When we were not reminiscing she was telling me about her husband, children and in-laws.

It is now morning and I am laughing to myself. I feel like I have completed this circle. I enjoyed the night, lying in her arms, knowing that I would be moving on.

I am treasuring my last three days and nights. I am spending my time close to my grandmother and my aunt. I am sad. I cannot make my Ma understand that she is one of the strongest women I know. She feels inadequate, somehow a failure, because her four children, her four daughters all live alone. It does not matter if they have re-married or if they live with someone. To her they are alone, all living in their separate houses. I tell her that she should be proud because she has brought up her daughters to be independent and strong. "They are survivors, just like you, Ma," I tell her. I am surrounded by strong, wise women, not only on my Mother's side but also on my Father's side. No wonder I am who I am. If only my Ma could feel this good. She is growing weak. She is afraid to leave. We argue. I try to understand. I lose my understanding. I get angry. She cries. I hug her. She hugs me, and talks to me like a little child. We carry on. I rub her head. She offers me food. It is always obvious that the energies between us are strong and stems from love.

As I look at my Aunt, my Ma's eldest daughter, she looks at me. As I think of something to say, she says it. As I find myself questioning, she gives me the answers. We talk without talking. There is a peace I experience in her presence. She is also one of the reasons why I come here. A rejuvenation of sorts. I am learning to understand. Everything seems to have a cause. Everyone seems to have a reason. I feel in control of myself. I am broadening my vision and I am excited. These words don't quite say it.

It's hard to explain. I feel it. I am beginning to know it. *IT* being who I am. *Who I am* being my home. Home having little to do with geography.

Tomorrow I am leaving my Island. Tonight as I rub my Ma's head, shoulders and back, tears come easily. She was having a mild heart attack. I froze as I thought of losing her and I knew deep inside of me that I would carry her within me.

I stare out the back window of her house, mesmerized by the countless stars in the black sky and comforted by the warm night air, the breeze through the coconut trees and the smell of curry and rain.

I breathe in deeply to capture that energy within myself but realize that it is already inside of me.

BABY
Makeda Silvera

Asha woke up to find Baby close. Her nipple was sore from Baby's hunger of the night before. She was tired, her eyes red from too much crying. She eased Baby away, so as not to wake her. Asha left the bedroom and walked down the hall to the bathroom, avoiding a small stain on the carpet. Shit, one of the cats must have vomited last night.

Downstairs in the kitchen, she made herself a cup of coffee and curled up on the sofa with Mooney, the oldest cat. She had five. Mooney was almost seventeen years old.

She was a sucker for cats. A stray only had to come to the front door or the back yard a few times, with an unkept look, hungry eyes, and she would take it in. Friends teased her often.

"Girl, you should have been a vet, you have no business wasting your time as a school teacher, look at all dem hundreds of strays just waiting for a home. If we had money girl, we would done set you up on a farm." They would laugh, rolling their eyes at each other as if she were the strangest person they had ever met.

She got up from the couch, fed the cats and helped herself to another cup of coffee, this time adding ice. It was daybreak, but she could already feel the approaching heat. The cats circled her, some at her feet, others on the couch. When Asha got up they followed her to the half-open kitchen window.

"Dammit, why am I so absent-minded? I have to remember to close this damn window at night," she mumbled to herself as the cats dashed through. Asha paused and whispered a silent prayer: "Thank God, this isn't back home. They would have climbed in and stolen every goddam thing but the cats."

She needed to be active, take her mind off last night. Doing housework gave her time to think. She washed towels, sheets and a basket of Baby's clothing. By noon she had changed the cat litter, washed the pots and dishes from the night before, and swept and washed the kitchen floor, working up a bucket of sweat.

Asha felt worn, but still she craved the closeness of Baby. She wanted to lie next to her. To listen to her quiet breath and to feel Baby turn lips to breast.

She went back to bed and stripped to her panties; it was going to be a hot one. Oblivious to the heat and still half asleep, Baby reached for Asha's breast. Despite the soreness and the slight bruise, Asha gave in to her, and feeling a sudden warmth come over her body, she slowly drifted in and out of sleep, barely noticing Baby's pull.

It had been an early night. They'd had supper. Fed the cats. Settled upstairs in bed to watch television. A few sitcoms, a game show, a mystery.

Kneeling in front of Baby, Asha had gently undressed her and stroked her with her tongue.

"I would die for you," said one. Said the other, "I would kill for you."

Passion talk.

Love talk.

Woman talk.

It doesn't matter who said what.

With Baby so close, Asha felt grateful for the privacy Canada had given them. Sleepless, she stood in front of the window, looking out. The moon loomed high. The maple tree outside the window, with its full green protective canopy, made her ache for home. No paradise but full of life. She missed the loud dance hall music pushing itself through closed doors, the boisterous talk in the streets, the boys hanging out on the street corner, the sudden knock on the door from an unexpected friend. No maple trees, but fruit trees of every size and description: mango, coconut, orange, papaya, all luscious. Naseberry, guava, sweetsop, and sugar cane, she could almost taste it, juice so s...sweet. Oh, what joy, what pain, that sugar cane. Turning to molasses, turning to rum, turning to export, sweetening white tongues while black tongues taste ash.

Asha was pulled out of her thoughts by a sudden scream from Baby. Baby sat upright, a sour look on her face.

"What's the matter, Baby?" Asha asked, concerned.

"I had another bad dream. I can't take them anymore. It's the same one. Do you love me, Asha?"

"Baby, you know I do; why are you asking me this?"

"The dream, it comes every now and then, it's always the same. We are in a parade, dressed up in masks, costumes ... and then you disappear on me. I can't find you anywhere." Baby sulked.

"Baby, it's only a dream; you know I won't leave you. Not now, not ever."

Baby jumped up suddenly from the bed, chased the cats out of the room, cursing each one by name, and slammed the bedroom door.

Asha sat quietly, watching Baby.

"We have to talk, Asha. We have to talk about us. I can't go on like this."

Asha got up quietly and lit two candles to aid the moon's glow as it crept through the window. In the flicker of the candlelight, Baby's eyes sparked anger and determination.

"We have to talk, I tell you. SOMETHING is wrong with our relationship. That dream is about us." Baby's voice went higher. "Talk to me, talk to me!" she demanded. "We go nowhere together, excepting the Hotspot Restaurant, which don't count. We hardly have any friends. All we do is watch TV. It's like I'm invisible in your life..." She was now pacing the floor. She waited for a response, but Asha just sat, staring at no place in particular.

"This goddam TV. Aaah, I wish I were a violent person. You know what I'd do?" Baby paused, and with no reply from Asha, she went on. "I'd kick the shit out of it and throw it through this goddam window.

"Asha, we can't go on like this. I want out. Do you hear me? O-U-T. Out. Watch my mouth, I want to live like a normal person, not in a closet."

Asha's face was hidden behind a glass of water. "What do you mean, Baby?" she asked, just to fill the silence.

What Baby could not express in words she said by raking her hands over Asha's face. "Stop it," Asha commanded. "Let's talk, but don't pounce on me like some animal." Then, her voice soft, she asked, "Why are you turning on me, Baby? We were fine a few hours ago. Don't let the dream do this."

233

Baby replied in a voice as heavy and dark as the night outside, "These dreams mean something, Asha. They don't just come from no place. They're in my head and my head don't lie. You know what I mean. You do nothing but watch TV. When was the last time we went to the movies? Or to a women's bar? Or to a party at one of my friends' house? We've never even gone to a damn gay pride parade. Every time I ask you to go out, it's 'Oh Baby, there's a good program on TV tonight.' Or 'Oh Baby, you know I hate the bars.'"

It was Asha's turn to say something. "Baby, you know I don't like the bars, it's not a lie. I don't like the smoke. Have I ever stopped you from going?"

"Who wants to fucking go out alone? My lover is home watching TV and I'm out all alone. What about bingo? What was your excuse last month? Oh yeah, you didn't like gambling. Then the movie, a clean wholesome environment, with popcorn and a soft drink? 'Oh Baby, that will come on TV soon.' Christ, Asha. I'm only thirty-five years old. I'm not ready for the cobwebs to start growing on me."

She stopped there, waiting for Asha to say she'd try to change. Asha said nothing.

"Say something, dammit. Look, you don't even respond. Sometimes I just want to walk out of this house and never look back."

Asha was sitting up in bed, her eyes filling with tears. She tried to pull Baby close.

"Don't touch me, DON'T. If you can't talk to me, don't touch me. You think you can cry a few tears, and everything will be okay, don't you? I should be the one crying. My name is Baby, isn't it?" she goaded. "No, Asha, I can't cry, that's reserved for you. My well-cultured, well-classed high school teacher, and that elegant face all dipped in milk chocolate." Baby stopped now, her smile sharp.

"Isn't it interesting, every time we have a quarrel, you throw my class, my education and my colour in my face. Why is it only when we disagree that they become a cross?" Asha demanded, her face now bitter chocolate.

A look of satisfaction rushed over Baby's face. She'd cut deep.

"Well, I'm packing." Baby began pulling sweaters and jeans out of drawers. "I'm tired of this closet. You enjoy it with the cats."

"I know what I am," continued Baby. "I'm a lesbian. A zami. A sodomite. A black-skinned woman. I got no education or family behind my name. I'm just a woman getting by. Asha, I'm ready for war. And you? You're ready to protect the little you have. Your job. Well, for me it just isn't enough."

Asha bent over to touch Baby's hands.

"Baby, some of what you say is true, but it's unfair for you to throw class at me every time we fight. And tell me, Baby, do I run back to class for shelter? You are so critical of me. I can't please you, everything I do is wrong. Baby, please try to understand. I love my work. I am a good teacher, and the Black students need that model. They need to see us in positive roles. They need to see more than the pimps-prostitutes-junkies. You know if the school finds out I'm a lesbian, they'll find a reason to get rid of me. And don't even talk about the parents." She was desperately trying to elicit some response from Baby.

Baby had piled the sweaters and jeans on the floor and was grabbing more clothes out of the closet and throwing them into a suitcase. Asha grabbed her. "Baby, listen to me. Don't leave. We belong together. We've been together for three years. Why now, why break up now?"

"I can't take it any longer, Asha. I can't. We can't go on gay demos because someone from school might see you on TV. We can't do this, we can't do that. I'm tired. I don't want to live like this. I can't stop my life because some people hate Blacks. And I am bloody well not going to stop living my life because another group hates lesbians. No job will ever keep me in the closet."

"Baby, are you saying I should just quit my job? Just walk out in the name of being a Black lesbian?"

"For God's sake, Asha, don't be so fucking dramatic. Live your life how you want. Stay in your closet. Me, I need fresh air. And if I have to fight for the right to enjoy it, then I will."

"I'm not being dramatic, Baby. But what do you want me to do? Just go in tomorrow morning and say 'Hey principal, hey fellow teachers, hey students, look at me. I'm a lesbian, have been all my life, just thought I should let you know.' Is that what you want?"

"Asha, sometimes I don't know you. Honest to God. Who are you hiding from?" Her voice became softer. "Asha, I love you. I want you to start living. I want us to start living."

Baby was the first to hear the sound outside the bedroom door.

"It's only the cats, Baby," Asha reassured her. "They want to be in here with us, to feel everything is all right." In a softer tone she added, "Baby, they don't like it when we fight, when we get unhappy." Asha pulled her close to kiss her. Baby didn't pull back. They dropped to the pile of clothes on the floor.

The man standing outside the bedroom door had come into the house through the kitchen window. He was of average height. He had black curly hair, cut close to his scalp. The right side of his mouth pulled up in a nervous twitch. He wore a pair of navy blue cotton shorts and a plain white cotton T-shirt. He wore no mask. He had a white plastic bag in his hand.

He was no stranger, had lived next door in a rooming house for the past year, but was planning to go out West any day now. The women knew him, too. They didn't know his name, but he was a familiar face in the Hotspot, where they sometimes went to eat or have a beer. The Hotspot served as a hangout for locals. It carried a good Caribbean menu, Caribbean beers and rum. The Hotspot was always jammed — jobless neighbours dropped in on the way back from one more no-go interview. The ones with jobs came to cash a cheque, the hangers-on were there all day, waiting to strike it big in the lottery. The juke box never stopped playing. The back room housed gamblers and folks with items to sell.

Some of the regular customers paid little notice to the two women who always came together. Others talked about them. The man hung around the Hotspot after work and on weekends, drinking beer and looking for a way to get in on the conversations of the regulars.

"When I win di lottery, 1 going home to soak up some of dat sun, buy a nice house, car and find myself a good woman."

"My boss man is like a slave driver. I can't even take a leak without the supervisor coming to look for me."

"They lay me off after twenty-five years' service and tell me times rough."

"Bwoy, dem girls different. Dem need a good fuck. Can't understand how nice Black woman like dem get influence in dis lesbian business."

"Nastiness man, nastiness. Satan work."

He'd overheard the last comment many times. He'd watched the two women closely each time they came into the Hotspot. They had an independent streak about them. He didn't like it. They come to Canada and they adopt foreign ways, he thought to himself.

He stood silently outside their bedroom door now, fingering the shiny black gun he had removed from its plastic bag. It was a .38 calibre automatic he'd bought from a stranger at the Hotspot Restaurant. The seller was looking for cash, had to leave town in a hurry. The man had the money. "Why not?" he'd said. Tonight he was going to put a stop to all this nastiness. He'd try to help them, and if they didn't listen, then they'd have to face the consequences. God never intended them to be this way. God wanted man and woman together.

"Oh, Baby, I don't want you to leave me," whispered Asha.

"Love me forever, Baby. Don't stop."

"I won't. But Asha, save some of this for later. Don't let the well run dry," Baby teased.

He could hear it all through the closed door. The gun was getting warm and sticky in his hand. The front of his shorts jumped like a trapped crab.

"What do you want me to do, Asha?"

"Baby, you know what I like best." Without another word, she pushed Baby's head down.

The crab jumped higher. He switched the gun from hand to hand. He wanted to fire it through the door. He took the crab out of his pants to give it room. It was hard. He played with it, pulling and squeezing it.

Bitches, sluts, ungodly creatures. He intended to tie them up. Strap their legs against each other. Oh, he was going to teach them a lesson. Let them do those things to each other right before his eyes.

He was excited, the crab more restless, the gun hot in his hand.

Tie up them lezzies. Then fuck them. Let them feel what it's like to get fucked by a real man. He wished he had carried his knife so he could slit their throats, watch the red running down their tits.

The crab throbbed.

Bitches. Let the dirty bitches feel the real thing. He might even let one of them feel it in her mouth.

When he was finished with their bodies, he would rob them, take their money and jewellery. Use the silencer. Do a good clean job, then leave through the kitchen window. He'd already packed his few belongings. Leave early morning on the Greyhound bus. He was tired of his job as a security guard in the stinking rotten high-rise building in downtown Toronto anyway. He'd had enough of Toronto and its dirty filthy morals, its dirty filthy women, dirty filthy life. Things were different in Vancouver, he'd heard. Nice people, nice open land. Mountains and ocean. That's what he needed. A place like back home. A place big enough that he wouldn't have to see women like these, his own people, stooping to this.

Standing at the bedroom door, he was reminded of conversations he'd picked up on at the Hotspot.

"I would like to fuck dem girls. Give it to dem good in di ass."

"Ass, boy? I want to throw dem legs over di shoulder and pump everything in."

"Dem gal need to learn lessons. Man fi woman and woman fi man. None of this nastiness, none of this separation."

The cats had come upstairs. They sat staring at him. He couldn't stand the goddam creatures. Hated their fur and their tongues.

"Can't stand the bitches," he muttered, wanting to use the gun.

He could hear Asha and Baby clearly. Ignoring the cats as best as he could, he turned his mind to the crab. It couldn't wait. He jerked it back and forth, leaving a small puddle on the red carpet, only partly muffling the grunt that came from his mouth.

"Those damn cats," Baby muttered.

"Leave them alone, Baby. They're just playing. In fact, they're watching over us. They're our guard cats."

Asha and Baby had tumbled off the pile of clothes, wrapped around each other.

He stayed outside. The crab had gone to sleep and he was getting tired. They were so loud. Bitches. He'd give them a few more minutes. Wait for them to start up again, then he would kick down the door and watch them.

"Asha, this doesn't change anything, you know."

"What do you mean, Baby? What do you want me to do?"

"I love you, Asha, but this isn't the Middle Ages. For God's sake, get involved in a gay group for teachers, or something. I just can't live like this. I won't live like this. I'm tired, Asha."

He was getting impatient. Too much arguing. He wished he had kicked the door in earlier. He should have done it when the crab was awake. He'd never wake it now.

The gun went back into the plastic bag. He walked down the stairs and climbed out through the kitchen window.

Screen Memory
Michelle Cliff

The sound of a jumprope came around in her head, softly, steadily marking time. Steadily slapping ground packed hard by the feet of girls.

Franklin's in the White House. Jump/Slap. *Talking to the ladies.* Jump/Slap. *Eleanor's in the outhouse.* Jump/Slap. *Eating chocolate babies.* Jump/Slap.

Noises of a long drawn-out summer's evening years ago. But painted in such rich tones she could touch it.

A line of girls wait their turn. Gathered skirts, sleeveless blouses, shorts, bright, flowered — peach, pink, aquamarine. She spies a tomboy in a striped polo shirt and cuffed blue jeans.

A girl slides from the middle of the line. The woman recognizes her previous self. The girl is dressed in a pale blue starched pinafore, stiff and white in places, bleached and starched almost to death. She edges away from the other girls; the rope, their song, which jars her and makes her sad. And this is inside her head.

She senses there is more to come. She rests her spine against a wineglass elm. No one seems to notice her absence.

The rope keeps up its slapping, the voices speed their chanting. As the chant speeds up, so does the rope. The tomboy rushes in, challenging the others to trip her, burn her legs where she has rolled her jeans. Excitement is at a pitch. Franklin! Ladies! Eleanor! Babies! The tomboy's feet pound the ground. They are out for her. A voice sings out, above the others, and a word, strange and harsh to the observer's ears, sounds over the pound of feet, over the slap of rope. *Bulldagger! Bulldagger! Bulldagger!*

Bulldagger! The rope sings past the tomboy's ears. She feels its heat against her skin. She knows the word. Salt burns the corners of her eyes. The rope-turners dare, singing it closer and closer. Sting!

The girl in the pinafore hangs back. The girl in the pinafore who is bright-skinned, ladylike, whose veins are visible, as the ladies of the church have commented so many times, hangs back. The tomboy, who is darker, who could not pass the paper bag test, trips and stumbles out. Rubbing her leg where the rope has singed her. The word stops.

Where does she begin and the tomboy end?

Fireflies prepare to loft themselves. Mason jars with pricked lids are lined on the ground waiting to trap them. Boys swing their legs, scratched and bruised, from adventure or fury, from the first rung of a live oak tree. Oblivious to the girls, their singing — nemesis. The boys are swinging, talking, over the heads of the girls. Mostly of the War, their fathers, brothers, uncles, whoever represents them on air or land or sea.

The woman in the bed can barely make out their voices, though they speak inside her head.

Sudden lightning. A crack of thunder behind a hill. Wooden handles hit the dirt as the rope is dropped. Drops as big as an elephant's tears fall. The wind picks up the pace. Girls scatter to beat the band. Someone carefully coils the rope. Boys dare each other to stay in the tree.

The girl in the blue pinafore flies across the landscape. She flies into a window. To the feet of her grandmother.

Slow fade to black.

The woman in the bed wakes briefly, notes her pain, the dark outside. Her head is splitting.

She and her grandmother have settled in a small town at the end of the line. At the edge of town where there are no sidewalks and houses are made from plain board, appearing ancient, beaten into smoothness, the two grow dahlias and peonies and azaleas. A rambling rose, pruned mercilessly by the grandmother, refuses to be restrained, climbing across the railings of the porch, masking the iron of the drainpipe, threatening to rampage across the roof and escape in a cloud of pink — she is wild. As wild as the girl's mother, whom the girl cannot remember, and the grandmother cannot forget.

The grandmother declares that roses are 'too showy' and therefore she dislikes them. (As if dahlias and peonies and azaleas in their cultivated brightness are not.) But the stubborn vine is not for her to kill — nothing, no living thing, is, and that is the first lesson — only to train.

While the rose may evoke her daughter, there is something else. She does not tell her granddaughter about the thing embedded in her thigh, souvenir of being chased into a bank of roses. Surely the thing must have worked its way out by now — or she would have gotten gangrene, lost her leg clear up to the hip, but she swears she can feel it. A small sharp thorn living inside her muscle. All because of a band of fools to whom she was nothing but a thing to chase.

The grandmother's prized possession sits against the wall in the front room, souvenir of a happier time; when her husband was alive and her daughter held promise. An upright piano, decorated in gilt, chosen by the King of Bohemia and the Knights of the Rosy Cross, so says it. The grandmother rubs the mahogany and ebony with lemon oil, cleans the ivory with rubbing alcohol, scrubbing hard, then takes a chamois to the entire instrument, slower now, soothing it after each fierce cleaning.

The ebony and the ivory and the mahogany come from Africa — the birthplace of civilization. That is another of the grandmother's lessons. From the forests of the Congo and the elephants of the Great Rift Valley, where fossils are there for the taking and you have but to pull a bone from the great stack to find the first woman or the first man.

The girl, under the eye of the grandmother, practices the piano each afternoon. The sharp ear of the grandmother catches missed notes, passages played too fast, articulation, passion lost sliding across the keys. The grandmother speaks to her of passion, of the right kind. "Hastiness, carelessness will never lead you to any real feeling, or," she pauses, "any lasting accomplishment. You have to go deep inside yourself — to the best part." The black part, she thinks, for if anything can cloud your senses, it's that white blood. 'The best part,' she repeats to her granddaughter seated beside her on the piano bench, as she is atilt, favouring one hip.

The granddaughter, practicing the piano, remembers them leaving the last place, on the run, begging an old man and his son to transport the precious African thing — for to the grandmother the piano is African, civilized, the sum of its parts — on the back of a pick-up truck.

A flock of white ladies had descended on the grandmother, declaring she had no right to raise a white child and they would take the girl and place her with a 'decent' family. She explained that the girl was her granddaughter — sometimes it's like that. They did not hear. They took the girl by the hand, down the street, across the town, into the home of a man and a woman bereft of their only child by diphtheria. They led the girl into a pink room with roses rampant on the wall, a starched canopy hanging above the bed. They left her in the room and told her to remove her clothes, put on the robe they gave her, and take the bath they would draw for her. She did this.

Then, under cover of night, she let herself out the back door off the kitchen and made her way back, leaving the bed of a dead girl behind her. The sky pounded and the rain soaked her.

When the grandmother explained to the old man the circumstances of their leaving he agreed to help. To her granddaughter she said little except she hoped the piano would not be damaged in their flight.

There is a woman lying in a bed. She has flown through a storm to the feet of her grandmother, who is seated atilt at the upright, on a bench which holds browned sheets of music. The girl's hair is glistening from the wet but not a strand is out of place. It is braided with care, tied with grosgrain. Her mind's eye brings the ribbon into closer focus; its elegant dullness, no cheap satin shine.

Fifty cents a yard at the general store on Main Street. "And don't you go flinging it at me like that. I've lived too long for your rudeness. I don't think the good Lord put me on this earth to teach each generation of you politeness." The grandmother is ramrod straight, black straw hat shiny, white gloves bright, hair restrained by a black net. The thing in her thigh throbs, as it always does in such situations, as it did in front of the white ladies, as it did on the back of the old man's truck.

The granddaughter chafes under the silence, scrutiny of the boy who is being addressed, a smirk creasing his face. She looks to the ceiling where a fan stirs up dust. She looks to the bolts of cotton behind his head. To her reflection in the glass-fronted cabinet. To the sunlight blaring through the huge windows in front, fading everything in sight; except the grandmother, who seems to become blacker with every word. And this is good. And the girl is frightened.

She looks anywhere but at the boy. She has heard their "white nigger" hisses often enough, as if her skin, her hair signify only shame, a crime against nature.

The grandmother picks up the length of ribbon where it has fallen, holds the cloth against her spectacles, examining it, folding the ribbon inside her handkerchief.

The boy behind the counter is motionless, waiting for his father's money, waiting to wait on the other people watching him, as this old woman takes all the time in the world. Finally: "Thank you, kindly," she tells him, and counts fifty cents onto the marble surface, slowly, laying the copper in lines of ten; and the girl, in her imagination, desperate to be anywhere but here, sees lines of Cherokee in canoes skimming an icebound river, or walking to Oklahoma, stories her grandmother told her. "They'd stopped listening to their Beloved Woman. Don't get me started, child."

The transaction complete, they leave — leaving the boy, two dots of pink sparking each plump cheek, incongruous against his smirk.

The woman in the bed opens her eyes. It is still, dark. She looks to the window. A tall, pale girl flies in the window to the feet of her grandmother. Seated at the piano, she turns her head and the grandmother's spectacles catch the lightning.

"I want to stay here with you forever, Grandma."

"I won't be here forever. You will have to make your own way."

"Yes, ma'am."

"We are born alone and we die alone and in the meanwhile we have to learn to live alone."

"Yes, Grandma."

"Good."

They speak their set-piece like two shadow puppets against a white wall in a darkened room. They are shades, drawn behind the eye of a woman, full-grown, alive, in withdrawal.

"Did something happen tonight?"

"Nothing, Grandma; just the storm."

"That's what made you take flight?"

"Yes, ma'am."

"Are you sure?"

"Yes, ma'am."

She could not tell her about the song, nor the word they had thrown at the other girl, to which the song was nothing.

She could not tell her about the pink room, the women examining her in the bath, her heart pounding as she escaped in a dead girl's clothes. They had burned hers.

Two childish flights. In each the grace which was rain, the fury which was storm chased her, saved her.

In the morning the sky was clear.

"Grandma?"

"Yes?"

"If I pay for it, can we get a radio?"

"Isn't a piano, aren't books enough for you?"

Silence.

"Where would you get that kind of money?"

"Mrs. Baker has asked me to help her after school. She has a new baby."

"Do I know this Mrs. Baker?"

"She was a teacher at the school before we came here. She left to get married and have a baby."

"Oh." The grandmother paused. "Then she is a coloured woman?" As if she would even consider having her granddaughter toil for the other ilk.

"Yes. And she has a college education." Surely this detail would get the seal of approval, and with it the chance of the radio.

"What a fool."

"Grandma?"

"I say what a foolish woman. To go through all that — all that she must have done, and her people too — to get a college education and become a teacher and then to throw it all away to become another breeder. What a shame!"

With the last she was not expressing sympathy for a life changed by fate, or circumstances beyond an individual's control; she meant *disgrace*, of the Eve-covering-her-nakedness sort.

"Yes, Grandma." The girl could but assent.

The woman in the bed is watching as these shadows traverse the wall.

"Too many breeders, not enough readers. Yes — indeed.'

"She seems like a very nice woman."

"And what, may I ask, does that count for? When there are children who depended on her? Why didn't she consider her responsibilities to her students, eh? Running off like that." Watching the shadows engage and disengage.

"She didn't run off, Grandma."

No, Grandmother. Your daughter, my mother, ran off, or away. My mother who quit Spelman after one year because she didn't like the smell of her own hair burning — so you said. Am I to believe you? Went north and came back with me, and then ran off, away — again.

"You know what I mean. Selfish woman. Selfish and foolish. Lord have mercy, what a combination. The kind that do as they please and please no one but themselves."

The grandmother turned away to regard the dirt street and the stubborn rose.

The granddaughter didn't dare offer that a selfish and foolish woman would not make much of a teacher. Nor that Miss Elliston — whose pointer seemed an extension of her right index finger, and whose blue rayon skirt bore an equator of chalk dust — was a more than permanent replacement. The bitterness went far too deep for mitigation, or comfort.

"Grandma, if I work for her, may I get a radio?"

"Tell me, why do you want this infernal thing?"

"Teacher says it's educational." Escape. I want to know about the outside.

"Nonsense. Don't speak nonsense to me."

"No, ma'am."

"And just how much do you think this woman is willing to pay you?"

"I'm not sure."

"What does her husband do, anyway?"

"He's in the navy; overseas."

"Of course." Her tone was resigned.

"Grandma?"

"Serving them coffee, cooking their meals, washing their drawers. Just another servant in uniform, a house slave, for that is all the use the United States Navy has for the Negro man."

She followed the War religiously, *Crisis upon Crisis*.

"Why didn't he sign up at Tuskeegee, eh? Instead of being a Pullman porter on the high seas, or worse."

"I don't know," her granddaughter admitted quietly, she who was half-them.

"Yellow in more ways than one, that's why. Playing it safe, following a family tradition. Cooking and cleaning and yassuh, yassuh, yassuh. They are yellow, am I right?"

"Yes, ma'am."

"Well, those two deserve each other."

It was no use. No use at all to mention Dorie Miller — about whom the grandmother had taught the granddaughter — seizing the guns on the *Arizona* and blasting the enemy from the sky. No use at all. She who was part-them felt on trembling ground.

Suddenly —

"As long as you realize who, what these people are, then you may work for the woman. But only until you have enough money for that blasted radio. Maybe Madame Foolish-Selfish can lend you some books. Unless," her voice held an extraordinary coldness, "she's sold them to buy diapers."

"Yes, ma'am."

"You will listen to the radio only at certain times, and you must promise me to abide by my choice of those times, and to exercise discretion."

"I promise," the girl said.

Poor Mrs. Baker was in for one last volley. "Maybe as you watch the woman deteriorate, you will decide her life will not be yours. Your brain is too good, child. And can be damaged by the likes of her, the trash of the radio."

Not even when Mr. Baker's ship was sunk in the Pacific and he was lost did she relent.

"Far better to go down in flames than be sent to a watery grave. He died no hero's death, not he."

"Full fathom five, thy father lies;
Of his bones are coral made;
Those are pearls that were his eyes:"

The baby with the black pearl eyes was folded into her chest as she spoke to him.

"Nothing of him that doth fade,
But doth suffer a sea-change
Into something rich and strange."

She imagined a deep and enduring blackness. Salt stripping him to bone, coral grafting, encrusted with other sea-creatures. She thought suddenly it was the wrong ocean that had claimed him — his company was at the bottom of the other.

"Sea nymphs hourly ring his knell:
Ding-dong.
Hark! now I hear them — Ding-dong bell."

She heard nothing. The silence would be as deep and enduring as the blackness.

The girl didn't dare tell the grandmother that she held Mrs. Baker's hand when she got the news about her husband, brought her a glass of water, wiped her face. Lay beside her until she fell asleep. Gave the baby a sugar tit so his mother would not be waked.

The girl was learning about secrecy.

The girl tunes the radio in. Her head and the box are under a heavy crazy quilt, one of the last remnants of her mother; pieced like her mother's skin in the tent show where, as her grandmother said, "she exhibits herself." As a savage. A woman with wild hair. A freak.

That was a while ago; nothing has been heard from her since.

It is late. The grandmother is asleep on the back porch on a roll-away cot. Such is the heat she sleeps in the open air covered only by a thin muslin sheet.

The misery, heaviness of the quilt, smelling of her mother's handiwork, are more than compensated for by THE SHADOW. Who knows what evil lurks in the hearts of men?

The radio paid for, her visits to Mrs. Baker are meant to stop — that was the agreement. But she will not quit. Her visits to Mrs. Baker — like her hiding under her mother's covers with the radio late at night, terrified the hot tubes will catch the bed afire — are surreptitious, and fill her with a warmth she is sure is wrong. She loves this woman, who is soft, who drops the lace front of her camisole to feed her baby, who tunes in to the opera from New York on Saturday afternoons and explains each heated plot as she moves around the small neat house.

The girl sees the woman in her dreams.

On a hot afternoon in August Mrs. Baker took her to a swimming hole a mile or two out in the country, beyond the town. They wrapped the baby and set him by the side of the water, "Like the baby Moses," Mrs. Baker said. Birdsong was over them and the silver shadows of fish glanced off their legs.

"Come on, there's no one else around," Mrs. Baker told her, assuring her when she hesitated, "There's nothing to be ashamed of." And the girl slipped out of her clothes, folding them carefully on the grassy bank. Shamed nonetheless by her paleness.

Memory struck her like a water moccasin sliding through the muddy water. The women who would save her had her stand, turn around, open her legs — just to make sure.

She pulls herself up and comes to in her hospital bed. The piano in the corner of the room, the old lady, the girl, the jumprope, the white ladies, recede and fade from her sight. Now there is a stark white chest which holds bedclothes. In another corner a woman in a lace camisole, baby-blue ribbon threaded through the lace, smiles and waves and rises to the ceiling, where she slides into a crack in the plaster.

The woman in the bed reaches for the knob on the box beside her head and tunes it in; Ferrante and Teicher play the theme from *Exodus* on their twin pianos.

Her brain vibrates in a *contre coup*. She is in a brilliantly lit white room in Boston, Massachusetts. Outside is frozen solid. It is the dead of winter in the dead of night. She could use a drink.

What happened, happened quickly. The radio announced a contest. She told Mrs. Baker about it. Mrs. Baker convinced her to send her picture in to the contest: "Do you really want to spend the rest of your days here? Especially now that your grandmother's passed on?" Her heart stopped. Just like that.

The picture was taken by Miss Velma Jackson, Mrs. Baker's friend, who advertised herself as V. JACKSON, PORTRAIT PHOTOGRAPHY, U.S. ARMY RET. Miss Jackson came to town a few years after the War was over, set up shop, and rented a room in Mrs. Baker's small house. In her crisp khakis, with her deep brown skin, she contrasted well with the light-brown pasteled Mrs. Baker. She also loved the opera and together they sang the duet from *Norma*.

When she moved in talk began. "There must be something about that woman and uniforms," the grandmother said in one of her final judgments.

Miss Jackson, who preferred "Jack" to "Velma," performed a vital service to the community, like the hairdresser and the undertaker. Poor people took care to keep a record of themselves, their kin. They needed Jack and so the talk died down. Died down until another photographer came along — a traveling man who decided to settle down.

Jack's portrait of the girl, now a young woman, came out well. She stared back in her green-eyed, part-them glory against a plain white backdrop, no fussy ferns or winged armchairs. The picture was sent in to the contest, a wire returned, and she was summoned.

She took the plain name they offered her — eleven letters, to fit best on a marquee — and took off. A few papers were passed.

"Will you come with me?"

"No."

"Why not?"

"I can't."

"Why not?"

"Jack and I have made plans. She has some friends in Philadelphia. It will be easier for us there."

"And Elijah?"

"Oh, we'll take him along, of course. Good schools there. And one of her friends has a boy his age."

"I'm going to miss you."

"You'll be fine. We'll keep in touch. This town isn't the world, you know."

"No."

———————

Now there was nothing on the papers they sent — that is, no space for: *Race?*

Jack said: "And what do you propose to do? Say, hey, Mr. Producer, by the way, although I have half-moons on my finger nails, a-hem, a-hem?"

She was helped to her berth by a Pullman porter more green-eyed than she. In his silver-buttoned epauleted blue coat he reminded her of a medieval knight, on an iron horse, his chivalric code — RULES FOR PULLMAN PORTERS — stuck in his breast pocket. He serenaded her.

"De white gal ride in de parlor car.
De yaller gal try to do de same.
De black gal ride in de Jim Crow car.
But she get dar jes' de same."

He looked at her as he stowed her bag. "Remember that old song, Miss?"

"No."

Daughter of the Mother Lode. The reader might recall that one. It's on late night TV and also on video by now. She was the half-breed daughter of a Forty-Niner. At first, dirty and monosyllabic, then taken up by a kindly rancher's wife, only to be kidnapped by some crazy Apaches.

Polysyllabic and clean and calicoed when the Apaches seize her, dirty and monosyllabic and buck-skinned when she breaks away — and violated, dear Lord, violated out of her head, for which the rancher wreaks considerable havoc on the Apaches. You may remember that she is baptized, and goes on to teach school in town and becomes a sort of mother-confessor to the dancehall girls.

As she gains speed, she ascends to become one of "the more-stars-than-there-are-in-the-heavens, and her parts become lighter, brighter than before. Parts where "gay" and "grand" are staples of her dialogue. As in, "Isn't she gay!" "Isn't he grand!" She wears black velvet that droops at the neckline, a veiled pillbox, long white gloves.

She turns out the light next to the bed, shuts off the radio, looks out the window. Ice. Snow. Moon. The moon thin, with fat Venus beside it.

The door to the room suddenly whooshes open and a dark woman dressed in white approaches the bed.

"Mother?"

"Don't mind me, honey. I'm just here to clean up."

"Oh."

"I hope you feel better soon, honey. It takes time, you know."

"Yes."

The woman has dragged her mop and pail into the room and is now bent under the bed, so her voice is muffled beyond the whispers she speaks inconsiderate of the drying-out process.

"Can I ask you something?" This soft-spoken question comes to the actress from underneath.

"Sure."

"Would you sign a piece of paper for my daughter?"

"I'd be glad to."

If I can remember my name.

The woman has emerged from under the bed and is standing next to her, looking down at her — bedpan in her right hand, disinfectant in her left.

The actress finds a piece of paper on the bedside table, asks the girl's name, signs "with every good wish for your future."

"Thank you kindly."

She lies back. Behind her eyelids is a pond. Tables laden with food are in the background. In the scum of the pond are tadpoles, swimming spiders. Darning needles dart over the water's surface threatening to sew up the eyes of children.

A child is gulping pondwater.

Fried chicken, potato salad, coleslaw, pans of ice with pop bottles sweating from the cold against the heat.

The child has lost her footing.

A woman is turning the handle of an ice-cream bucket, a bushel basket of ripe peaches sits on the grass beside her. Three-legged races, sack races, races with an uncooked egg in a spoon, all the races known to man, form the landscape beyond the pond, the woman with the ice-cream bucket, the tables laden with food.

Finally — the child cries out.

People stop.

She is dragged from the water, filthy. She is pumped back to life. She throws up in the soft grass.

The woman wakes, the white of the pillow case is stained.

She pulls herself up in the bed.

The other children said she would turn green — from the scum, the pondwater, the baby frogs they told her she had swallowed. No one will love you when you are green and ugly.

She gets up, goes to the bathroom, gets a towel to put over the pillow case.

"Hello. Information?"

"This is Philadelphia Information."

"I would like the number of Velma Jackson, please."

"One moment please."

"I'll wait."

"The number is ..."

She hangs up. It's too late.

"She did run away from them, Mama. She came back to you.

I don't think you ever gave her credit for that."

"And look where she is now, Rebekah."

"She ran away from them, left a room with pink roses. Sorry, Mama, I know how you hate roses."

"Who is speaking, please?" The woman sits up again, looks around. Nothing.

What will become of her?

Let's see. This is February 1963.

She might find herself in Washington DC in August. A shrouded marcher in the heat, dark-glassed, high-heeled.

That is unlikely.

Go back? To what? This ain't *Pinky*.

Europe? A small place somewhere. Costa Brava or Paris — who cares?

251

Do cameos for Fellini; worse come to worse, get a part in a spaghetti western.

She does her time. Fills a suitcase with her dietary needs: Milky Ways, cartons of Winston's, golden tequila, boards a plane at Idlewild.

Below the plane is a storm, a burst behind a cloud, streak lightning splits the sky, she rests her head against the window; she finds the cold comforting.

AUTHOR BIOGRAPHIES

Jannett Bailey writes plays, poems and short stories. She considers herself a fusion of third and first world which hopefully allows for a point of view that is interesting and certainly needed. In Jamaica where she grew up there isn't even a word for "lesbian" in the dialect — which at least hints at how hidden we are there. She has an MFA in theatre, a BA in literature and politics, and teaches in New York City where she has lived for the past nine years.

Lesley Chin Douglass was born in Trinidad and emigrated to Canada as a child in 1966. Her writing has appeared in a number of anthologies, including *Intricate Countries: Women Poets from Earth to Sky*; *Countering the Myths: Lesbians Write About the Men in their Lives* and *Image Fiction*. She has also published articles in journals such as *Fuse* and *Melus*. Presently, she is completing a doctoral dissertation entitled *Dissin' the Power*, which examines metaphors of trial and the oppositional force of the Black priestess in the texts of African American women from 1774 to the present.

Michelle Cliff is the author of the books *Bodies of Water*, *No Telephone to Heaven*, *The Land of Look Behind*, *Abeng* and *Claiming an Identity They Taught Me To Despise*. She edited the collection *The Winner Names the Age* and was co-editor, with Adrienne Rich, of *Sinister Wisdom* in the 1980s.

Maria de los Rios (aka Maria L. Masque) born in Habana, Cuba, lived in Venezuela for eighteen years and currently lives in the wetlands of central Florida. Served as member of the advisory board of the Latina lesbian magazine, *Conmocion*. Published poetry fiction and non-fiction in *Conmocion*,

MamaRaga, and *Revista Mujeres*. Work in progress includes *Yellow Leaves*, to be published by Burning Bush Press, Santa Cruz, California.

Tonia Grant is a Barbadian-American writer, with a background in theatre. An alumni and writing major of Queens College at the City University of New York, she was the recipient of a merit scholarship at the Women's Writing Center at Cazenovia. Currently, Ms Grant is a director of Damas Gracias Writers & Artists Workspace, a retreat located in the northern Catskill Mountains, and is working on her epic novel *As American As...*

Ayiah Jahan: I live and work in London, visit Dominica regularly and enjoy learning and practising holistic ways of being and healing.

Shani Mootoo was born in Ireland and grew up in Trinidad. She is the author of the novel *Cereus Blooms at Night* and the short story collection *Out on Main Street*. Her poetry has been anthologized in *The Very Inside* and other writings in *The Skin on Our Tongue*, *Forbidden Subjects* and *Left Bank #6*. She has written and directed several videos including *English Lesson*, *The Wild Woman in the Woods* and *Her Sweetness Lingers*. Her visual art is exhibited internationally.

Vashti Persad is Soul, here on this physical plane to create in the forms of political activism, writings, photography, gardening and herself. Born in Trinidad, she has recently travelled through India to walk the land of her Great-Grand-Parents — an unforgettable journey of connection made with her lover of five and a half years, Vasu, the woman who challenges her most to unfold.

Makeda Silvera is the author of two collections of short fiction, *Remembering G and Other Stories* and *Her Head a Village*. She has edited and co-edited numerous anthologies including *Piece of My Heart*. She is the founding editor and co-publisher of Sister Vision Press and a former journalist.

Mary Vazquez was born in Bayamon, Puerto Rico. Her writing has been published in *Bless Me Father: Stories of Catholic Childhood* and *Queer View Mirror 2*, and her photographs have been published in *The Femme Mystique*.

Pulcheria Theresa Willie was born on the tiny island of St. Lucia in the West Indies on September 10, 1966. She and her family of four sisters, and three brothers was raised by a single parent, with the help of grandma. She has overcome many adversities in a country where the word "lesbian," was hardly mentioned, to be a woman who believes in herself and stands up for what she knows is right. Theresa works as a nursing assistant and lives on Long Island in the U.S. with her wife Donna and their daughter Trina.

Desoto Wong was born in Kingston, Jamaica. Her work has appeared in several journals and anthologies. She now lives in the Boston area and is working on a book-length manuscript about leaving Jamaica.

Photo by Michele Paulse

Rosamund Elwin is the co-author of two children's books, *Asha's Mums* and *The Moonlight Hide and Seek Club*. She is an anthologist who has worked on the anthologies *Dykewords, Getting Wet: Tales of Lesbian Seduction, Out Rage, Tangled Sheets,* and *Countering the Myths*. *Tongues on Fire* is her eighth book. Rosamund lives in Toronto with her two children.